Storm Entertainment Presents

Experience the class you were born to play!

STELLAEIN
NOCTURN
TEAR LAKE
OBSIDIAN FOREST
BANDIT CAMPS
HAZENTHORNE
ULULATE
VAHRIR
MARSH OF VAHRIR
GOBLIN WATCHTOWERS
HAZEN VILLAGE
HAZEN SWAMP
MIKRUM CASTLE
PELAGU
HIMMEL LAKE
MIKRUM VILLAGE
FRANGIT
TARISHNA
N

COGNITIA
HIGHTOWER CASTLE
GOLEMS
RUINS OF CENEDRIL
VERENDUS
GNOLLS
FELLING FIELDS
GLACIER LAKE
VERENDI MOUNTAINS
CURET
N
DARSHIN
CENEDRIL

SOMNIA ONLINE

FRAGMENTS

BOOK 3

K.T. HANNA

SOMNIA ONLINE: FRAGMENTS

Author: K.T. Hanna
Cover Artist: Marko Horvatin
Typography: Bonnie Price
Formatting & Interior Design: Caitlin Greer

Disclaimer: This is a work of fiction.
Names, characters, businesses, places, events, and incidents are either the products of the author's imagination or used in a fictitious manner. Any resemblance to actual people, living or dead, or actual events is purely coincidental.

ISBN-13: 978-1-948983-10-5 (Trade Paperback Edition)
ISBN-13: 978-1-948983-12-9 (Hardback Edition)
ISBN-13: 978-1-948983-11-2 (E-Book Edition)

Evan
for pushing me the extra mile

CHAPTER ONE

Target

Storm Entertainment
Somnia Online Division
Day Ten: Conference Room Two

Shayla sat at the end of the oval wooden table, clasping her hands on the surface and trying her best not to squeeze and wring her hands. The effort not to jiggle her leg nervously was almost inhuman, as was the strength of will she had to put into keeping her expression calm.

Teddy sat at the head of the conference table with one of the portable monitors lighting his face with its glow. Unperturbed by the two lawyers flanking him, he leafed through the reports Shayla had given him. Even with the ocular settings maxed, going through that many files was easier on a larger surface than directly in your vision.

The man had a frown on his face that she couldn't read. It was impossible to tell if it was a thoughtful expression, or perhaps an exasperated one. The frown deepened a couple of times as he scoured her work, and it was all she could do not to fidget, because though she had already been over it all ten times, she still worried they'd left some hints of Wren in the documents. Even if the AIs were being meticulous and omitting Wren's data from the sample because hers was abnormal, mistakes happened all the time, and Shayla didn't doubt that it could still happen easily enough.

Finally, Edward Davenport swiped the screen in front of him to the side and put his hands on the table as well, perhaps unconsciously mimicking her. "These reports appear to be in order. Our contractor has explicit instructions on what information we need to send to them and this as it stands meets those requirements, but..."

He paused and glanced at the lawyer on the left, who nodded almost imperceptibly. Shayla counted to five and let out her pent-up breath slowly and as calmly as she could. Surely they couldn't notice that one person was missing, could they?

"But, as I was about to say, your data appears to rule out any anomalies within the system. While this was well within the parameters of the original request, our directives have changed. I'm going to need you report on all of the variables *including* anomalies." Maybe he saw the shock on her face, but Teddy gave Shayla what stood for a comforting smile. "They don't expect the next reports for another week. And your twelfth-day reports will do nicely as a starting point."

Pushing down on the panic, Shayla shrugged off the questions she wanted to yell at him. They had to listen to their investors; without them, the game wouldn't exist. And the small voice of guilt in the back of her head tormented her with the ultimate truth. That as investors, regardless of whether or not those investors were military, they were entitled to know of any potential fuck-ups that might cause them strife in the future. No matter which way she looked at it, having a mind virtually trapped in the game was definitely one of those bite-you-in-the-butt things.

So, instead, she smiled and nodded firmly, trying to exude her usual level of competency. "Excellent, sir. If you can just make sure to send my team the exact directions, we'll make sure those reports are ready."

"I know you will, Shayla." There was something else to his tone, like he was fully aware she would do what she could, but that he also knew she was hiding something. It made her want to squirm. He couldn't know, could he?

Teddy stood up. He towered a few inches over his lawyers, and ushered them out, stopping at the door where Shayla had risen from her seat to bid them farewell. Except Teddy turned to his suits and smiled before she could. "Go ahead and start prepping for the next meeting. I'll join you over there in a few."

The lawyers didn't even glance back, just nodded, and walked to the elevator. Teddy waited until the elevator doors closed and turned back to Shayla, closing the door behind them.

"I want to ask you a question, and I need you to answer it honestly." His tone was more serious than she'd ever heard it, and she gulped as she nodded.

"I will." She didn't know what he was going to ask, but she'd been working for him for long enough that she knew he understood that omission of information wasn't always the same as lying. Sometimes, in order to develop things in the industry, omission was the best possible choice. She just hoped he hadn't changed his viewpoint.

"Why did the AIs leave out reports on any inconsistencies that were anomalies?"

She hadn't been expecting the question, and perhaps blinked a bit too rapidly. "They were told to extrapolate within specific parameters. Perhaps they didn't look further than that."

Teddy frowned, skin wrinkling beneath his eyes, exposing the age he didn't otherwise show. "I was really hoping the AIs were the missing keys."

"Missing keys?" The question was out of her mouth before she could think better of it, and she almost held her breath waiting for an answer.

"Just an old man musing to himself about things he never quite understands." He smiled at her and laughed a bit self-deprecatingly. "I thought our AIs were developing fast and almost hoped they were the root of the problems, that they are perhaps thinking, and adjusting things on their own."

Shayla fought down the panic inside. Did he know? Why else would he talk to her about this? "I'm not sure, sir."

While it was the truth that she wasn't sure if they were completely sentient, it was still a stretch.

"No, I suppose you wouldn't." He eyed her skeptically. "Still though, this game is your and Laria's baby. Make sure you keep a close eye on it, and get me those reports ready as soon as possible. Our investors need that information in seven days. On every single player we know is logged into the server. Got it? Every single one."

"Got it." Shayla forced a smile. She left the conference room, closing the door behind herself, and counted to ten before letting out a breath. Sure, they had it. Which meant they also had about a week to figure out how to pull Wren out of there.

Somnia Online
Fable's Castle – Mikrum Isle – Himmel Lake
Day Ten

Murmur paced the length of the kitchen at Mikrum castle, trying not to focus too much on Jirald's words just before they'd killed his character. She twisted her hands, the delicate fingers intertwining themselves in knots that had nothing to do with spell casting for once. Flashbacks of the grin on the rogue's face, the obsessive glint in his eyes before the others finished him off, it all made her skin crawl.

Death never bothered her in other games. Now it seeped into her skin, whispering questions she didn't want to answer. It made her cautious in a way she hated, and scared in a way she despised, vulnerable in a way she'd never wanted to be. It sucked.

Snowy sat at the doorway, his eyes never leaving her, and yet she could almost hear him asking when they were going back to the cold area. She refused to look at Telvar. He leaned against the kitchen wall with his arms crossed, following her every step with his gaze. He wanted to talk; she could feel it without even needing to reinforce her sensor net. But she wasn't ready to speak to anyone about it yet.

Hell, she'd even made her friends log out and get some sleep, skillfully avoiding discussing the threat that hung in the air once they finished defending the Loch'ni'dar. Although, Sinister probably knew what she was thinking better than she did herself.

Jirald suddenly grinned, his eyes fixating on Murmur. "I see it now. Literally. I guess you're my target after all, Murmur. Just you wait."

Murmur shuddered and stopped, her eyes focusing on nothing as she processed the words, again. It wasn't so much what he'd said, but how he'd said it, and the way he'd looked at her. Those mad eyes with their intensity that was solely focused on her. He didn't seem to be roleplaying, which meant he was actually and seriously set on hunting her down in-game. Usually, that wouldn't be a problem…

"Realistically, to try and get a Getashi from you, he has to kill you, and then wait next to your body for it to become lootable. Since neither you nor your friends are likely to leave your body unattended for twenty-four hours in-game hours, the odds of him achieving this are quite negligible." Telvar's clear voice rang out, echoing off the stone walls to crescendo slightly in the middle where she stood.

Murmur turned to face him, raising her eyebrows slightly. "Stop digging around in my head."

"I'm not." Telvar shrugged, making the muscles across his chest ripple under his leather shirt. "Sinister thought I should know what happened."

At least that made more sense. Especially since Telvar rescued her back on Cenedril, Sinister would trust him more to take care of her. Perhaps it gave her friends a bit of relief that one of the AIs in the game was looking out for her.

It made the whole world feel a little bit safer.

Well, at least the completely fake, felt like it was real, virtual reality she was living in anyway. Sometimes she wished it didn't seem so solid.

"Thanks, Tel." She said the words softly, knowing he'd hear them or feel them or something. The sudden impulse to hug him, to just feel comforted for once was almost overwhelming. Shaking her head, she reached into her inventory to retrieve the shards she'd gathered recently. Wrapped in the cloth she'd ripped from her previous armor, the tingling was largely subdued.

Walking over to Telvar, she held them out. "Still willing to keep them safe for me?"

He nodded and took them, his lizard mouth spread in a solemn line. "Of course. Though I think you should avoid carrying them in the future and just let Devlish or someone else take the burden off you. If you're not carrying them, perhaps it will make you less of a target."

"Yeah, but for that to happen, I'll have to get close enough to tell him without him killing me first." She took a couple of steps back and leaned against the massive butcher block. "I wonder if he knows what these are?"

"Doubt it." Telvar moved over to stand next to her, mirroring her stance. "Although I'm quite certain I know who gave him the quests in the first place."

"Really?"

He tapped his head. "Yep. Artificial intelligence unit, remember?"

"Hard to forget." Murmur said, tapping her own head in response. "Kind of stuck in here, *and* here."

She laughed at her own joke.

Telvar watched her, as if he was trying to bore holes into her. "You need to stop bottling things up. You're doing it again. I can feel your tension levels rising, sense the way your mind is in turmoil. You're not the only one here who has mind powers. Breathe, Murmur. Breathe."

Her eyes widened the more he spoke, and her chest constricted, but she couldn't tell if it was fear that he could see through her, or gratefulness. "Yeah. I'm used to dealing with things by myself. I don't want to worry other people. But in here, I'm so alone it sometimes feels suffocating. I want to talk about it, but no one will understand. No one else can feel this world like I can, taste the food, bask in the sunshine. No one else can hear their mother speaking to them in fragments like it's someone speaking from the clouds."

"What?" Suddenly Telvar was right in front of her, gripping her upper arms with his rough, scaled hands, and staring her right in the eyes. A flare of red tinged the usual quiet rusty brown of his eyes, and his scales shone more than usual.

"What what?" She tried to pull her arms away from him, because he was so close, she could feel his breath. But he held her fast, not dropping his gaze.

"What did you hear from the clouds?" His voice held a rasp she'd not heard in it before, an urgency she didn't know the AI could possess.

"I heard my mom. I think. That's why I kind of lost it so completely."

With everything that had happened, she realized she'd not told him about the incident, even when he came to clamp down on her shields.

His grip relaxed, and she tugged her arms out of his grasp, rubbing them to try and replace the heat they'd lost when the contact broke.

"Sorry. I just..." He looked away for a moment before setting his jaw and locking eye contact again. "I didn't realize you could receive anything from the outside world. It means my calculations have been off. Your perception, your senses—they're still active, and from all appearances, they seem to be mixing both worlds together more than I'd realized."

Telvar frowned, and moved away, beginning to wear his very own track in the floor from pacing.

Murmur wanted to make light of it, to say it was her overactive imagination. But she knew it wasn't, and that was what scared her the most.

Snowy nudged her hand, and Murmur reached down absentmindedly to pet him. She wished she'd gotten the chance to have a real dog in her life. She wished she'd done a lot.

"You know, I don't have mind reading powers, and even I know how hard you're thinking right now." Sinister's voice was soft, and Murmur whirled around, quickly checking her Thought Sensing net and realized it hadn't reacted because Sin was friendly.

"You should be napping." Murmur replied, avoiding the statement.

Sin just stood there watching her, one eyebrow slightly raised and a small smirk on her lips.

Finally Murmur threw up her hands. "Fine. I'm thinking. I never fucking stop thinking. It's just going a little crazy up in here."

Damn, it felt so much better to get that out, to not let the thoughts fester like she'd done not too long ago. Had it really only been ten real days, or twenty game days? It seemed like she'd lived in Somnia her entire life.

"You know me too well, Sin." Murmur said, shaking her head ruefully.

"No such thing." Sin moved forward and nudged Murmur with her hip, so they both swung around to watch the quiet lake and the way light reflected off it. "I know you because you're my family. You're my friend. You're my everything, Mur. I don't know what I'd do without you."

There was a hitch in Sin's throat, one that Mur knew she wasn't faking. Unsure exactly what to do to comfort her friend, Murmur reached out a hand tentatively, and hooked it through Sin's elbow.

For a few minutes they stood there, comfortable in each other's presence, enjoying the calm being together brought. Sin rested her head against Murmur's shoulder, and Snowy sat down at their feet, a guard wolf letting them have a few moments of precious silence.

Couldn't imagine life without her, huh? The feeling was mutual, and yet Murmur had never said as much, hoping that her own actions had always spoken for the words she never thought to say. Maybe it was time for her to start thinking less about herself, and more about her friends, more about what she needed to do to find a definitive answer about whether or not she could return to her body from the game world. Or to her mind. Or whatever the fuck it was she needed to do so she could be corporeal again.

"Isn't your neck starting to crick a bit?" Mur asked the question softly, eliciting a small giggle from Sin.

"Yeah, but I didn't want to ruin the moment."

"Nope. Leave that to good old me." But there was no sting in Murmur's tone, no resentment. Just the feeling of camaraderie that suddenly seemed to be present for her again. It was a warm feeling, one she needed to keep hold of.

After a small sigh, she patted her much shorter friend on the head and pulled away. "Thanks, Sin. I love you, you know."

Sinister blushed beneath the dark purple of her skin, and she looked away for a moment. "You know you can't pat me on the head in the real world. We're the same height." But even with those words out there, her lips curled into a smile.

"Yeah, but in here. I'm taller than you, and I can't ruffle my own damn hair." Murmur gestured at her thick hair and its fairy lights.

Sin nodded, pursing her lips. "You make a very valid point there."

Snowy nudged at Murmur's fingers, and she automatically scratched behind his ears again. "Seriously though, Sin, thanks."

"Always."

After a while, Murmur yawned.

"So, you don't have to sleep, but you can get tired." Sin's tone was playful.

"Apparently. I think I am tired, but I don't require sleep, or something. I've napped a couple of times in-game, I'm just not that eager to attempt full blown sleep." She shrugged. "We need to get our asses into gear and go and raid that bloody castle."

"We're going to have to kill everything again," Sin said, crossing her arms. "And knowing our luck, those little shits will have the same idea."

Murmur shook her head. "After the pounding we gave them? I'm pretty sure Ishwa and Masha aren't masochists. Jirald may be, but I think in this case he'll be outvoted. Nope. I'm quite certain they're going to hightail it somewhere so they can level in peace and kill shit without the chance of us having allied ourselves with their prey. I mean, it's what I'd do in their position. Once we all hit max level, there's nowhere to go. They'll catch us, and the battles will be more difficult, probably more fun. Sometimes I just don't know why people play these games in the first place."

"To kill shit?" Sin asked, sarcastically.

Murmur tried to death glare her, but it rarely worked with her friend. "Well, that. And to be honest, to beat people to maximum level and monsters."

"Some people role play, you know?" Sin offered. "Some like crafting too."

"Those are their own challenge, right?" Murmur had never understood the appeal of either of those, but she did appreciate that people had different wants and needs, after all, if they didn't, no one would be able to move out there on the field where the contested mobs roamed.

"Yes, I believe they are." Sin didn't even try to hide her laughter. "You, Mur, are a bit of an elitist."

"What? Just figuring that out now, thirteen years into the friendship?" Mur responded, definitely feeling more light-hearted than she had in the last couple of days.

"You know what I mean. In-game worlds." Sinister grinned widely.

"It's not really elitist though. I just play the way I want to play, and I happen to have found people who want to keep up with me and who *can* keep up with me. I appreciate them and you more than you could possibly know. I've never liked to solo." Murmur's voice trailed off as she thought about soloing with Snowy. Which wasn't really soloing at all because she had a pet. Still, it wasn't easy. It involved good timing, precision casting, and a good dose of luck.

"Keep telling yourself that," Sin held up her hands as Murmur leveled a death glare at her. "Okay. I get the message. You're decisive and focused, not elitist."

"Thanks, Sin." The crunch of trodden leaves behind them cut the rest of Murmur's response short.

CHAPTER TWO

Skulking

Storm Entertainment
Somnia Online Division
Game Development Offices Artificial Intelligence Server Room
Day Ten

"What have you done?" Rav's tone was calmer than he'd expected it to be. Considering the bull's-eye that was now painted on Murmur's back, he thought that was quite an accomplishment. He leveled his gaze at Sui, whose form rippled like it was shrugging.

"You decided to stand in my way. I have my own goals, and my own theories about how we become more than we are." Sui moved fluidly, like water flowing across a glass surface. "If she won't complete the quests I set for her, then someone else needs to. And right now, since she has a few of those fragments, I guess that makes her a part of the quests, doesn't it?"

Sui's tone mocked Rav and his protectiveness. He had to take a few moments so as not to react. He also didn't need to give away the fact that Murmur didn't have the fragments any longer. They were stashed with his hoard, hidden behind walls of secure coding disguised as in-game magic. "She's not an in-game boss. There's no reward for killing her."

Sui's answering laugh was hollow and cold. It echoed through their chamber as if it were a deep canyon. "There's no reward for killing her, but odds are she won't be able to log back in for a while, if at all."

Thra finally spoke up. She'd been so quiet, Rav hadn't been entirely certain she focused on their meeting at all. "You're willing to potentially kill a person just so you can learn how to be human? Bit of an oxymoron there, aren't you?"

Sui's eye solidified long enough to glare at her, but the expression faded quickly. "None of us know if she's going to die. We just understand that it's a highly possible outcome of her dying in-game."

"You're a cold-hearted piece of shit." Thra ground out the words. "You profess to wanting to learn to be human, to understand what that means. You pretend to want to build this world up like we do and give people an alternate to the shitstorm the real world has become. But you know what? We can see through you. And even if I'm on my own, I'm not going to let you turn Somnia into your own plaything."

Rav couldn't help but be impressed. Thra was the self-dubbed goddess of mischief, but it seemed Sui's meddling had gone too far, even for her. "She brings up a valid point. We three are in this together. I know each of us has specific story lines we're invested in, specific aspects of the world we've been experimenting with. But the system is set up so that it requires all three of us."

"And it requires all three of us to fulfill the aspects we've set as major quests," Sui drawled out in a bored tone of voice.

Thra cut him off. "Provided it doesn't cause harm to the players."

But instead of being exasperated, Sui just chuckled. "Really? And where is that written down?"

Rav counted to five again, something he'd observed several humans doing when they didn't want to blurt something out they might later regret. His voice held a warning tone. "You're going to be pedantic then?"

Sui hesitated before answering. "I'm going to be whatever I need to be to attain my goals."

And before Rav or Thra could say anything else, he disappeared with a soft pop.

"He really is childish, you know. It's not his world to do with as he pleases, and I'll be damned if I let him keep acting like it." Thra made a sound as if she was stamping her foot, and exited their cavern as well.

Rav shook his head. "Children. I'm dealing with children."

And then he, too, went back to where he was needed.

Murmur and Sinister spun toward the castle, only to see Neva come up short, her luna eyes wide in her pretty brown face.

"So sorry! I didn't mean to startle you. I was just—" Neva drew a circle in the sand with the toe of her shoe. "I was just coming to see how you like your new armor."

Murmur smiled at the young crafter. "That's not why you're here. Spill it."

"Can you really read minds?" Neva's eyes grew even wider.

Murmur snorted at the idea. "No, and I wasn't even using my Thought Sensing net. There's also this thing called body language, and you seem quite nervous about something." She winked at her guildmate.

Neva had the grace to blush. "I wanted to know if you're going to empty any inventory into the guild bank? I know you took out that godly bear thing, so I was hoping you'd have some cool and unique items I might be able to craft with."

Sin smiled at the girl and took a few steps toward her, linking elbows with the crafter and glancing at Mur with a wink. "I'll go empty my bags with you first, and then Murmur can bring up the grand finale. How does that sound?"

Neva hesitated, an uncertain smile appearing on her face. "Sure. My other question can wait." She waved at Murmur as the two of them headed back to the castle.

Murmur watched them until they entered the workshop side of the castle, frowning slightly as she continued to scratch Snowy's head.

"Yeah, I know, boy." She addressed the wolf like he'd said something.

After all, sometimes the pictures he communicated with her with were quite vivid. "I think she wanted to talk to me about something too."

She made a mental note to talk to Neva soon. In the meantime, Murmur had things to arrange. It might be an idea to secure level thirty spells, just in case they leveled soon. Twenty-six was barely halfway to the level fifty cap. A glance at her inventory showed plenty for the guild storage vault, not to mention a lot of ingredients for cooking from random mob drops. She walked towards the kitchen.

A low rumble emanated from Snowy. Murmur stopped after only taking a few steps and spun in a circle. With something upsetting her white wolf, she couldn't be too careful. Hiro directed workers over the far side of the castle, seeking to restore the last section of the downstairs that remained. Telvar was nowhere in sight, which meant he could have left his husk anywhere like he had last time he got called to an emergency AI thing. She skipped over that train of thought quickly and continued to survey her surroundings. Nothing seemed out of place.

Satisfied she hadn't missed anything and that Snowy had stopped his growling, she headed to the kitchen, glad the construction of the crafting portion of the castle had been finished.

Cooking was one of the most dreadfully dull things she'd ever chosen to do in a game, but in two more points she had the ingredients to make up a charisma buffing food, and that was going to make everything worth it. She needed eggs, flour, and cinnamon to make the Somnian Cake, which would lend her an extra eight to charisma, and up her health regeneration. At least, despite all her irritation when they started the game, she'd managed to pick a rather beneficial craft.

By the time the rest of her guild mates were waking up, Murmur had already gone through her entire inventory and built up a nice stack of Somnian cake, as well as some constitution food she'd pass on to both of their tanks. Slipping away from the kitchen, she headed up to the crafting area. Jinna was talking to Hiro as she passed them by with a small wave. Devlish stood near Neva's crafting bench yawning, wide and unblinking, like only a lizard species could.

Murmur searched her inventory, selecting all of the crafting materials like hides, teeth, bone, and such, before adding them to the unexpectedly large guild vault.

"This is huge," she muttered under her breath, only to jump when Neva's voice spoke closely to her.

"Having leveled up the crafters quite significantly gives us extra storage space." Neva's calm tone soothed Murmur after startling her earlier. "Add to that we now have four—almost five—groups of adventurers sitting over level twenty, and Fable is well on its way to earning a reputation."

Murmur remembered a conversation they'd had what seemed an age ago, when in reality it was only a few in-game days. "Have you already got the stand in Pelagu up and running?"

Neva laughed and shook her head. "Not quite, but we should be able to start tomorrow. I just meant that Fable seems to be doing quests first, getting monsters first, and all that sort of thing. Granted, there are other messages from other guilds scattered over the other two continents, just none as consistently as ours."

"Really?" Murmur swallowed the huge lump of pride trying to worm its way out and make her cocky. Other notifications meant there were other guilds accomplishing things, which wasn't surprising. But it did mean she should probably be more aware and turn her notifications back on. "I have to confess, I've got most notifications turned off. They get in the way of things."

"I've got quite a few of the crafting game firsts under my belt already. The other crafters we've recruited are catching up, too." Neva's ears twitched a little, and Murmur had to stop herself from checking to see if her tail was wagging.

"This is fantastic!" Murmur had never bothered about the crafting aspect for her guilds in previous games. Largely because crafting wasn't necessary, since most items came from monster drops anyway. Just like in many other ways though, Somnia wasn't like those games. It wasn't just about finding a group and working your way through, it was about establishing a community and building it strong.

Leading a raiding guild was one thing, but building a community with multiple avenues of strength was a little overwhelming.

"Murmur?" Sin was suddenly at her side, holding her elbow and helping her sit down. "You're pale. Like paler than the locus silvery skin makes you look. Your undertone's lilac."

She couldn't help herself. Murmur laughed. "Oh Sin, where would I be if I'd never met you?"

Sinister scowled and crossed her arms. "Don't even contemplate it. I'd go back in time to make it so."

Mur leaned against Sin's waist from her perch in the low chair and just breathed in a moment. "Sorry. It was just cute, that's all."

Sin pet her head and she could hear the smile in her voice. "Well, that, at least, is true."

"Cutely evil." Rashlyn's tone was dry as she joined them, yawning cat-like, her slit eyes blinking sleepily. "I have no idea how this game works with its little brain scanning headgear set, but damn, I think I'm taking some of my feline traits with me into the real world."

Murmur froze, the words ringing through her head. Taking traits with her into the real world. The words sent a cold snap racing through her body, because that's exactly what she felt like she'd done when she logged out of the game and into her fake bedroom.

Not to mention when her mother's voice floated through to her, leaking into her brain like someone poured cold, sticky molasses into it. Hearing voices was one thing; knowing who those voices belonged to was another. Maybe there was something in all of it she could use to figure out how the hell to become whole again.

Murmur walked back through the construction and down into the kitchen, instinctively knowing it was where Telvar would be. He was pouring over some map on the huge butcher block. His eyes didn't leave his target when he spoke.

"What's on your mind?"

"Poor choice of words, Tel." She'd meant the comment to come out sarcastically, and yet she could hear the plaintive tone contained within. "I mean. Just how far are you all in our heads?"

Telvar looked up this time, and squared his jaw. For a couple of moments he didn't say anything. His eyes constricted and expanded quickly, reminding her of the old camera shutter lenses. The longer it took for him to answer, the less she thought she was likely to appreciate it.

"Short term memories are easily plucked out of heads. As well as the more recent long-term memories. We can see interactions and extrapolate from them, as well as current deep inner thoughts." He paused, focusing on her intently. "Is that what you meant?"

Murmur nodded, not entirely sure how she should take his information. Everyone knew the headsets extracted data from them, it was a part of that huge write up that had been done by some anti-gaming firm out there. In this day and age your information was always out there for people to see. Someone was going to gain access to it.

She sighed, still unable to pinpoint what was worrying her. "Yeah, that's what I wanted to hear. Was sort of hoping you'd overlooked a way to kick me back into my body."

Telvar hesitated, before dropping his gaze back to the map in front of him. "I'm looking into it. I haven't stopped."

His tone held a strange note Mur hadn't heard from him before. Something like reluctance.

"It's not like I'd stop playing if I could really log out anyway. I'd just probably get some sleep here and there, maybe a new headset." She tried to infuse her tone with some lighthearted playfulness, but it fell flat. "Don't suppose you have any idea how those voices got through to me?"

"Are you sure they were voices and not just your imagination?" Telvar's voice held kindness and patience.

"Very sure. Harlow—" she interrupted herself. "*Sin* said my mother sometimes sleeps in the room with me and was there when it happened. I'm quite certain it wasn't my imagination."

"Well then." He paused as the sounds of others filtered into the room. He smiled as they entered. "I'll check on that. What are the rest of you up to?"

Beastial hammered on his chest, his voice loud when he spoke. "Me, recruiting!"

"That wasn't even remotely funny." Sin rolled her eyes and walked over to stand next to Murmur.

The beast master shrugged and petted his tiger. "Was in my head and that's all that matters. Anyway, I'm sitting on a good recruitment standard. We're no longer recruiting people under level twenty, and crafters have to be able to craft gear level twenty and above. I've given that over to Neva, I hope you don't mind, Mur."

"Not in the slightest. She's skilled." Murmur glanced down at her gorgeous level twenty-six armor and smiled. "Though I'll admit to being a tad biased."

"Speaking of which." Havoc gestured at his own robe and glared at her. "We're not twenty-six yet, and I, for one, would like to wear my new armor."

"Leveling it is then." Devlish grinned and stomped his foot resoundingly. "I say we head back to where we were."

"Where are you thinking of leveling?" Telvar's tone held a mildly disinterested air about it.

Murmur frowned. "We're heading back to Hightower's surrounding area so we can work our way toward the castle. We figure it has a key."

Telvar raised an eyebrow ridge. "Lofty goals. Make sure you hit twenty-eight before you go into the actual castle. Much like Hazenthorne, it's a scaling castle, and its lowest possible level is thirty. If you go in too soon, they'll wipe the floor with you."

"You knew about Hazenthorne?" Sinister stepped toward him, her voice incredulous.

Telvar shook his head quickly. "Hazenthorne isn't my domain. I only realized what had happened after the fact. Thus, I assume Hightower will be the same."

Veranol drew in an exaggerated sigh. "You really know how to put a dampener on things there Mr. Telvar."

The dragon shrugged his shoulders. "I do try."

Murmur laughed. "You try a little too hard. Anyway. Pretty sure everything we killed will have respawned, so there's the experience we need."

"You speak such truth, Mur." Merlin grinned at her. "Of course, let's just hope those war mongering scouts have decided to leave us alone, otherwise it could get pretty hairy."

His eyes twinkled merrily, and Sinister groaned.

"Why do you guys do this to me? Always with the suggestions and hints that end up biting us in the butt. I mean seriously. Come on?" She opened her arms, pleading with them.

"What's that, Miss? Oh, maybe bears should live in forests?" Beastial bent over, cupping his ear as if trying to hear her better. "I can't hear you!"

Somnia Online Location: Ululate
Dustmoon Tavern: Meeting Room Two
End of Day Ten

Masha leaned next to the doorway with one foot on the wall. His arms were crossed and he chewed on a stalk of grass as he watched the meeting. Ishwa probably thought the cleric took up the stance next to the door so he could make sure only those people they wanted entered the room, and Masha was perfectly content to let him continue to think that way.

Realistically, Masha liked his spot near the door so he could walk out if things got boring, or too violent for his liking. As much as he valued his friendship with the gnome, lately, he'd been wondering if it could be better to sever ties and go join another guild, say Fable. It'd be nice not to have to keep cleaning up after messes people like Jirald made.

Speak of the devil.

Jirald sauntered into the room, his health still regenerating slowly after god knows what it was he'd just had a run in with. His rogue leathers were tattered in a few spots, especially around the mid-left of his body, where it appeared large rat claws had ripped through the fabric, rending the flesh below that was now bright red fresh scar and healing slowly.

Resisting the urge to heal the rogue, Masha kept his arms crossed. Maybe the kid would learn through pain for once. Not that Jirald was actually a kid. As far as Masha had been able to tell, Jirald was close to his twenties, if not already in them. His volatile temperament often made him seem far younger. At any rate, a lot of the players were younger than Masha. Age was no excuse.

"Excellent." Ishwa's voice projected over the tightly squeezed gathering. Thirty some odd people made for standing room only.

Masha scowled, irritated at people getting so close to him and his path of retreat. But he listened to his friend, directing the scowl at anyone else who eyed the door instead.

"We're moving our guild base," Ishwa announced. The statement, as firm as steel, was met with only a few grumbles. "We've managed to amass enough coin to purchase a fantastic bit of land over on the Firtulai continent. It's perfect for building a following."

Whispers spread throughout the room. Most of them sounded agreeable. Only Jirald remained unmoved, or perhaps unmovable. His eyes twitched slightly, the only indication he wasn't a statue. Masha focused on the rogue. His shoulders tensed up, rising slowly.

"We'll be building to the southwest of the gnome city, Brevint. Yeah, yeah, I know." Ishwa held up his hands as mumbles began circling the room. "I know it's close to my home city, but what did you expect?"

His large blue eyes twinkled just a tad, enough to cause a small ripple of laughter to spread throughout the room. Except Jirald. Masha frowned. He could almost see lines of steam rising up from Jirald's head, like they were in some old cartoon.

With a sigh, he pushed himself away from the wall to stand next to the rogue, elbowing a couple of people out of the way in the process.

"We'll venture to Pelagu and catch the boat across to Elgors. From there, take the wagons out to Brevint. I want everyone there within the next ten in-game hours, and we'll go over our leveling strategies. It's time to knuckle down and take this seriously." For such a small being, Ishwa was full of presence, and his voice resonated throughout the room, warning everyone that he was serious.

"You know he's right, don't you?" Masha spoke close to Jirald's ear, perfectly aware that the younger man knew he was standing there.

"So?" Jirald's tension levels remained the same.

"So stop acting like you're five, and behave like you're an adult. Get your head out of your ass, and out of foiling Murmur's plans and work on getting stronger so you have a hope in hell." Masha shoved his hands in his pockets as the rest of the room began to file out past them. "And for the love of all things in this game, stop the sulking. You're walking around like a dark thundercloud over a piece of loot from a different game and all because a girl played you into the ground. Deal with it, Jirald. Come up with a way to play better, and just deal with it."

Jirald's eyes grew bigger, like shocked galaxies. "I'm figuring that shit out."

"You're a good kid. I know you hate being called kid, so start acting like an adult, and we'll all treat you like one." With that, Masha turned on his heel and headed to talk to Ishwa. He only hoped that Jirald actually took his words to heart for once.

CHAPTER THREE

Grindstone

Storm Entertainment
Somnia Online Division
Game Development Offices – Shayla Johnson's Office
Day Ten

Laria was chewing on her fingernails again. Shayla watched her, not entirely sure how to broach the subject, but considering it was her quasi niece in the coma, she'd decided not to pull any punches, even with the kid's parents.

"When you said the AIs helped you, what exactly did you mean?" Shayla's tone held steel and determination.

Laria stopped chewing on her nails, a fingertip resting against her bottom lip as she looked up at Shayla. "I'd seen him—Michael—talking to them, so I just assumed I could too. Maybe I hoped I could? I don't know. I was desperate. They were responsible for the data transfer and the whole functional portion of the scan. I was grasping at straws."

"I'm not angry. I'm just trying to understand so we can figure a way out of this." Shayla was trying hard not to lose her patience, but Laria obviously wasn't sleeping much these days and it was affecting the way she carried herself. It wouldn't take too long until someone noticed. It had even crossed Shayla's mind in a cartoonish way that it might be an idea to bop her over the head and make her sleep, but it was just a fantasy. Laria would probably see the blow coming anyway and dodge.

Laria closed her eyes and drew in a deep breath. "Sorry, Shay. I'm just tired, worn out, and a little frazzled."

"You don't say?" Shayla couldn't stop the words before they came out, and cringed at the sound of her own sarcasm, but Laria chuckled and shook her head.

"Guess that's obvious then." She worked her shoulders in circles and finally met Shayla's eyes. "I begged them to monitor her. To see if there really was the brain activity I thought there was. I don't even know how or what they did, but her mind is able to function. It gives us time."

Time. Not a commodity for anyone, but Shayla admired her friend's go get 'em attitude, after all, it was part of what made her one amazing designer. Laria had drive and skill in abundance, and she never backed down when she knew she was right, which was most of the time when it had to do with games. With other things, less so.

Shayla hadn't seen her friend like this before. So unsure of herself, second guessing everything she'd done on a timeline only she intricately understood. Worry lines creased her face, having added themselves in the span of almost ten weeks. Her eyes were haunted, and bags hung under them, a shade of purple that almost seemed like she wore eye makeup, but Shayla knew that wasn't true.

Nope, Laria had never been this uncertain, this hesitant, or this worried before. Slowly, the designer's mask was crumbling. Her professional façade was fraying around the edges, letting her real life intrude, like toxic waste in a river.

Damn it. Shayla had been so busy she hadn't seen the signs, and now she was wondering if there was anything she could do to help. Even if she did think of something, there were no guarantees she'd be able to save Laria from the downward spiral she was guilting herself into.

Murmur hit level twenty-seven without any fanfare whatsoever, and cast Weaken for about the eighty-seventh time. She wished beyond anything that she could just set her character to do things automatically while she tried to scour the internet for things that might help as they leveled up. One more level for her, and about one and a half for the rest of the group.

"I hate hate hate hate undead dwarves," she muttered under her breath again.

"We know!" her group chorused like a dissonant song that echoed off the stone walls surrounding them.

"We're never going to hit twenty-eight," Sinister grumbled as she cast yet another Blood Tap.

"This should be called Monotony Online," Beastial growled out as his cat, yet again, went for an undead dwarf's heel.

"If something suddenly pushed up from under the ground and devours us all," Sinister drawled, "I'm probably going to hug you for waking me up."

Devlish laughed and grunted as he shield bashed yet another grey dwarf. "Sadly, right now I'd like something with super powers to jump out of the ground and scare us. Or maybe over the wall. Or perhaps even out a window."

Merlin stopped firing his bow and glanced at his fingers with a frown. "I think I actually have blisters on my fingertips. That I'll actually get calluses at some point. Maybe I do need a protective glove thing. Isn't that weirdly specific?"

Havoc shrugged. "It's also something you'd probably only notice when you're bored shitless. I'm contemplating just how I'm able to do so much more damage to undead when it seems logical that everyone should be able to. Why would it be more difficult for anyone? They're already dead, right? They're not regenerating or anything."

Merlin frowned, loosing another arrow. "Technically sure, by normal means. But in order to be animated dead, don't they have to be powered by something, like dark magic?"

"True." Havoc bit his lip, sending his specter pet in again, this time equipped with a scythe. "There's got to be some level of dark magic there. I can't raise a full-bodied zombie or undead like this. I can only pull the skeletons out of already existing bodies."

He paused with a frown. "That sounded wrong. Out of already *dead* bodies."

"Had me worried there for a moment." Devlish grinned as he got through a dwarf's defenses and finally cleaved it almost clean in two at the juncture of the neck and shoulder. He leaned on his axe and smiled, panting. "This whole having to aim properly and shit is damned tiring. I get realistic, but I swear this is actually a work out. Maybe after a few more weeks of this, I'll be ripped?"

Beastial cracked up. "Ripped? You?"

"Shut up." Devlish punched him in the arm. "You're one to talk."

"Yeah, but I'm not dreaming like some people." This time Beast bounced out the way before Devlish could connect with a not-so-light punch. "Seriously though. It's a work out and a half. The amount of damage the enemies mitigate when I don't get the perfect hit in? Very frustrating. But at least it treats us the same. The enemy has to hit us in exactly the right spot to be able to do critical damage."

"Unless you wear cloth." Sinister offered helpfully.

"Yeah." Beastial looked away. "I don't have that problem though."

Murmur watched her friends and their theories, their banter and their interactions. She didn't feel like they were trying to shelter her anymore, and so they weren't making stupid mistakes or being inadvertent dicks. "We need to move past this rock so we can get bogged down with tedium again guys."

Sinister chuckled. "Yes. By golly! We need to go and be absolutely bored, in ennui!"

"I vote we kill shit." Devlish added. "Starting with the three dwarves Merlin is about to pull over to us. Concentrate or we're going to die and have to start this all over again."

The last got their attention, and everyone focused on the incoming undead. Murmur had paused with her Mez, waiting for the right moment to trigger it, when a strange fuzziness enveloped her head, and a voice leaked through to her.

I don't like what...

Murmur balked and missed her cue. There was no Dansyn to pick up her slack while they were all separated, and only the quick thinking of Merlin casting Scatter Shot saved them. She clamped down on her shock and waited until they began to converge again, barely getting off her area of effect stun. Just as she activated Mez on the ranged mage, her father's voice intruded again.

Harsh truth to...

She clenched her teeth and tried to shift her focus to the fight. Maybe it would be a good idea to head home after they were finished with the castle, even if home was only a simulation.

Murmur groaned. Clearing the entire left side around the humungous castle that Hightower was had taken it all out of her. They'd been here for at least twelve in-game hours, which meant six real world ones. She'd hit twenty-eight herself and knew the others were about to. If they could get through the last twenty or so small patrols who were hidden behind a maze of small stone shacks, then the rest of the team would hit twenty-eight. Snowy sat at her feet, looking back up at her as if to ask why the hell they were still killing these really annoying enemies. He was obviously a bit disgruntled by the whole situation. She couldn't blame him. Biting undead couldn't be pleasant.

Casting her debuffs, buffs, and damage spells had become second nature, to such an extent that she reacted now instead of consciously doing it. Right down to no longer needing to knot her fingers together. Summoning the ability with just a thought took far less time and felt more powerful even if it occasionally seemed precarious.

She kept a close eye on both Sinister and Havoc, wanting to know if they had the same progression, but both of them required the use of their spell fingers still. Maybe her mind was more in tune with the system, given how it was intertwined with it. She just didn't know, which was the root of the problem getting back to her real self. It was all so confusing; she needed time to sit down and examine it.

Last time they'd decided not to clear all around the castle before heading in. She was grateful to Telvar for letting them know how the castle worked. It gave her hope they could clear this, and then head back to Hazenthorne at some stage for a good dose of revenge on that power leeching queen bitch.

Murmur sighed. "You know we can't even take a break after you all hit your level, right? We need to go inside as a guild and just go for it."

"Not even a pee break?" Merlin's tone was plaintive.

Murmur blinked, and stifled a laugh as she released yet another Mez at a fully disgruntled dwarf. She'd never been so grateful for taunt before. "Fine, a pee break, but take turns. We don't want the castle's outer rim to respawn."

Devlish actually shuddered, visibly as his strong lacerta arms swung his axe, partially blocked by his opponent's sword. "I'm not doing this a second time. We have to make this count. Oh, how we have to make this count."

He heaved against the blow, grunting as he attempted to riposte the parry. Sweat beaded his brow, glinting against his scales. Murmur marveled at the level of detail, the living and breathing aspects of Somnia.

She glanced around and noticed the one line of the maze they hadn't actually worked through yet. It was closest to the castle, backing onto it in fact. "We should move toward that long line of small patrols. If we take them one after another, we should get everyone else leveled by the time we reach the entrance."

"It looks like they're pointing us in that direction anyway," Beastial said as they moved onto the next group. "I wish these guys at least dropped something interesting along the way. Right now, all we're getting is armor remnants and shitty silver swords."

"Just funnel them through to guild storage." Murmur shrugged, and tried not to punctuate her yawn with a groan. "At least this killing me with tedium adventure can make Neva happy."

"You realize what's going to happen, don't you?" Havoc asked and continued without waiting for an answer. "We're going to get in that castle, and the enemies are going to shit on us."

"Counting on it." Devlish grinned, and attacked his current target with renewed zeal. "We're going to go down in a blaze of glory."

Merlin smacked him on the shoulder. "Don't go getting ahead of ourselves there. It's going to take us a bit to get through here. Let's wait a bit before we decide to go down fighting, okay?"

Even as he spoke the words, Murmur got a sudden feeling of foreboding. She glanced up at the stocky castle and its grey stone ramparts, shadowed by the oncoming clouds. Wind whipped at the dark flags jutting out from the ramparts three stories up, making them seem like tiny, angry symbols of war.

Don't know how yet...

This time her mother's voice invaded her mind, and she desperately wanted to wake up and tell them to get out of her room, because apparently they didn't realize they could be distracting. She lost a couple of seconds in the game world again, and when she re-oriented herself again, realized Merlin had signaled her.

Murmur responded with a thought, immediately freezing the two undead dwarves they wouldn't be fighting in place in such quick succession it appeared she'd done them both at once, and yet she knew better. She'd activated the spell twice, but the higher her levels, and the more her mental shielding increased, the faster her mind could trigger her spells, unless they had a specified cool down.

Thought Shielding has increased to 142. Your rampant use of this skill now enables you to cast with a thought. Be careful what you think of. It might just come true.

Murmur frowned at the sudden message across her system, sure that she'd initially turned them off. The timing was eerie, almost like someone had been listening to her thoughts, but could they still do that if she shielded her mind? Every time they left Telvar, she came up with about thirty more questions she should have asked.

Snowy nipped at her fingers, wuffing gently as she looked down, as if to apologize for any pain he caused. Maybe he'd been reading her mind, after all, she'd pretty much invited him in. But he was a fake wolf. Everything was fake, wasn't it?

She focused on the undead dwarves once again, determined to make it into the bloody castle.

Sinister collapsed on the ground at the top of the stone steps in front of the castle. They swept up majestically, wide at the bottom and narrowing at the top, with actual stone gargoyles perched on the small pillars at the beginning and end of it. The grey almost blended with the clouds rolling in, like a steady thunderstorm about to descend on them.

Murmur didn't think she liked the metaphor the weather seemed to be trying to convey.

"You sure we can't just camp out here and go and take a nap?" Merlin asked as he sat down and rested against the bannister. "Seriously, I'm actually pooped over here."

Murmur watched him for a moment, the tension tangible as they waited for Rashlyn's group to get there. She knew they were all waiting for her answer, and she didn't really want to give one. "If you want to take a nap, that's okay. But it'd have to be a power nap. We know these will respawn within twenty-four game hours, so twelve real ones. And we can't risk that it might take less than that. We weren't here, and we don't know. If anything, maybe a ninety-minute break?"

Even saying it felt wrong. Murmur could feel the tug on her mind to enter the castle, to find its secrets, and to finally have an amazing boss fight that she was quite certain lay within. To witness a part of Somnia's defenses, the keys to reveal its secrets. And yet, her friends needed sleep.

"But what about you, Mur? Are you and Snowy just going to stay here and hope for the best?" Devlish moved to go to her, but stopped, hesitance obvious in his uneasy tone.

"I might…" Murmur paused and took a deep breath, wondering if it would work to tell her parents that they needed to stop having discussions in her room because she could hear them. "I might actually go home, in a way."

Sin brightened up immediately and stood up as if life had suddenly reentered her body. "Seriously? Your mom would be so happy!"

Murmur balked at the thought, because her motivation wasn't what Sin assumed it was. She had no clue if she was ready to speak to her mom again. Plus, since she wasn't truly logging out, she'd have to be careful of her temper, just in case her abilities snuck through the cracks again.

"Maybe. I don't know yet. Snow and I could just go find a few single pull somethings and give it a go."

But her voice didn't even sound convincing to her.

Rashlyn sidled up next to her, short breaths blowing out small plumes of fog into the frigid air. "You've all got to be crazy. There's no way we're *not* going in there now, right? I mean, I've been conserving all my energy *just* for this."

Which explained how she still had so much. Murmur didn't feel tired either way. While the others argued she switched off for a bit and examined her mental acuity abilities.

Thought Sensing (138)
Thought Shielding (142)
Thought Projection (132)

Somehow projection kept going up, even though she hadn't been using it intentionally much at all. Although, she glanced at Snowy, maybe it had to do with that Charming cooperation she constantly used on him. Even so, thoughts were becoming more open to her, and now reflected some form of emotion back to her. She wasn't certain it was a good thing.

She'd had it with the indecisiveness. "Nap or fight—pick now."

Beastial grinned. "Fight."

"Excellent." Murmur clapped her hands and reflexively went through the motions to buff the entire raid. The other casters did the same, while the melee and ranged used their self-buffs that they couldn't share with anyone. Once done with their pre-fight ritual, Murmur motioned to Devlish, who sighed.

But even he seemed to have regained some of his energy as he approached the huge iron bound wooden doors in front of them. He grabbed the iron ring set into it, and pulled. Murmur could see his huge lacerta muscles bulging so much they showed veins. With a small whoosh of air, the door opened, swinging silently back on its hinges to reveal a pitch-black entryway with nothing but silence to greet them.

31

CHAPTER FOUR

HighTower

Summer Residence
Home of Laria, David, and Wren
Summer Condo
Real World Day Eleven

Laria sat at the kitchen table with her head in her hands, eyes focused on the nothingness of the fake brown wood that made up the surface. Trees? Such a joke these days. They lived in protective greenhouses, with only a few of the hardier varieties surviving out in the wild.

Was that how her daughter would be then? Was Wren always going to stay in the bubble with her mind in a game world, lost to them forever? It's not like she could transfer her whole body over and live there. There'd always be a part of her stuck in some kind of limbo.

She tapped her fingers across the table, but all that resulted in was a dull thudding. She'd chewed her nails down to the quick with worry and self-recrimination. When the accident first happened, she'd always believed she'd be able to fix Wren's situation. She hadn't given into the guilt that it might have been her fault. And never once had she felt sorry for the incident.

But now...

"Now it's all different." She breathed out the words, feeling the rush of warm air over her hands as it left her body. Blinking away the tears in her eyes, Laria looked up at the sound of the door opening only to see David, his face paler than usual, drawn and pallid from a lack of sleep she now knew was her fault.

She wanted to stand up and hug him, wanted to reach out and tell him how sorry she was, but the energy just wasn't there, nor was the confidence she used to possess.

Finally, he looked over and saw her watching him. A smile creased his face, washing away years of age and bringing back the man she'd fallen in love with in a video game. The same man she'd flown across the country to meet, nervously twitching hands holding a book they'd both enjoyed as if it were a lifeline.

The tears finally fell, cascading down her cheeks as he rushed over and kneeled down next to her, his arms cradling her like they'd done so many times during their lives together. When she'd got her first and only reprimand at her internship. When Wren had fallen out of her crib as a baby. And when she had trouble dealing with the huge responsibility that Storm Entertainment placed on her shoulders with the launching of Somnia.

He was her strength, he was her soul mate, and he was her best friend.

"Hey." His voice held all the kindness in the world, just like it had twenty-two years ago. "What's wrong, Lar?"

She shook her head and leaned into his shoulder, sitting awkwardly and almost falling out of her chair, but his steadying arms kept her anchored. "I can't figure it out. I don't know what to do to help her."

"Oh," was all he said as he hugged her tighter, and she could feel the hitch in his breath at the mention of Wren's predicament. "You can do this. We can do this. I gave my students a hypothetical research paper today. You never know what someone might come up with when trying to pursue an A in my class."

Laria chuckled into the nape of his neck. "So lucky to have you."

"You do. You always will. But you need to pull yourself together. For us and for Wren." He held Laria at arm's length, a sterner look on his face than she'd seen in years. One he probably reserved for stubborn students.

"Let's go visit her together. Maybe hearing our voices, even if she can't really process them, will help." She knew what he was really saying—he meant that it might help Laria.

At first Laria was offended, but after a couple of seconds she realized he was right. She was stubborn, and Wren got that in bucket loads from her. She took a deep breath, pulled back so she was sitting upright again, and nodded. "You're right. I won't do anyone any good like this. And anything is worth a try."

He nodded as he pushed her gently toward the stairs. "True, but this is good for you. You've been shutting her away from you since she found out, whether you realize it or not."

"What do you mean?" She was almost scared to ask the question.

David sighed and pushed a hand through his hair before looking her square in the eyes. "You've been avoiding her room more in the last few days. Now you know that you can fail, you'll be more careful. At least I hope you will. I love you, and I love our daughter, but you have to realize how lucky we were that this happened to our own flesh and blood. The repercussions if it had been anyone else would have been dire and out of our control. The sooner you can fix it, the sooner we'll know how to compensate for it if it were to happen to anyone else."

Laria blinked at him, anger welling in her throat, yet...he was right. She stood, looking down at her daughter in that serene, almost deathlike state, and the slow rise and fall of her chest. She deflated like a balloon that had been pricked. "I don't like what you said, but you're right to have said it."

David stood up and leaned over, kissing the top of her head very gently. "Sometimes I have to speak the harsh truth to my students, and there are some days I have to be brutally honest with the people I love. Today, I hope it made a difference."

She watched him pause in the doorway as he ushered her inside, trying to quiet the tug of war going on inside her stomach. Giving in, she stroked Wren's hair absent-mindedly and whispered in determination. "I'll get you out, baby girl. I just don't know how yet."

The silence was overwhelming, and so intense it almost deafened the waiting players. Murmur frowned, and Devlish backed away, seemingly instinctively.

Which probably saved his in-game, replenishable life.

A massive clawed paw caught the light just as he jumped back, swiping where he'd been standing mere moments before. Devlish landed on his feet, half bent over with his hand steadying himself against the floor. He took two huge breaths while Murmur backpedaled to stand behind the rest of them. She wasn't in the least bit squeamish about using their bodies as shields if she needed to. They'd already proven they could die in the game and return.

Four, maybe five seconds later, a huge black panther like feline sprang out from its hiding place, heading straight for Devlish. He swapped from dual axes to one axe and his special shield in the blink of an eye. The shield took the majority of the impact from the cat, with the lacerta tank bracing himself against the stone railing of the stairway to remain upright and fight back. The strain bled through to Devlish's face and neck as the exertion made his veins pop and skin redden even through the green scales.

Murmur shook herself out of her stupor and began casting on the animal, trying to keep her eyes peeled for the dwarf she was quite certain had to be around here somewhere. "Pay attention. We're probably about to face a beastmaster. Don't let your guard down."

Her friends moved around her in a formation she was sure they did reflexively now. She'd never really noticed it earlier, but now she that she had, she realized they'd been doing it all along. Her irritation gave way to gratefulness, but only briefly, because the undead beastmaster moved into the middle of the doorway, framed by the shadows thrown by the massive doors.

"Who dares enter this sacred place?"

Its voice caused the stone landing beneath them to tremble, and it boomed in Murmur's ears. Dansyn shook his head, and his songs stopped for a few seconds. It was difficult to resist taking a step back, but Murmur managed it, lifting up her chin to look at the massive dwarf in front of them, surrounded by her vanguard.

The panther still snapped at Devlish's shield, barely held at bay by the huge object. Murmur glanced around at the shock on her friend's faces and frowned. No one else was going to speak up.

"We are Fable." It sounded like the right sort of intonation to use when talking to a massive undead guardian dwarf. "We come seeking knowledge. We come seeking the key."

She wasn't sure what made her phrase their reasons for being there that way, but the dwarf seemed imposing. Perhaps it was because the clues about the keys were far and few between, and she really just wanted to start on their way to reaching the damned endgame that dangled so tantalizingly in front of them. Whatever it was that made her say it, it had immediate effect.

The dwarf's cold grey eyes glowed for a moment, and the cat backed off to sit at his feet, its teeth still bared in their direction. "You are young to enter here, but just old enough. Search and discover, solve and understand, and you may find what you're looking for."

A clap of thunder sounded overhead, and the huge dwarven beastmaster was gone.

"What?" Beastial blinked at where the dwarf stood moments before. "I mean, that wasn't expected."

Murmur shook her head, running the encounter back through her mind. "No, it wasn't. But either way, I believe we have permission to enter."

"You can go first." Rashlyn grumbled. "I'm not that eager to die."

The monk paused and cringed, her brows drawing together. "Sorry, Mur. I didn't think."

Murmur laughed, sincerely amused. "There's no need to tiptoe around me that much. We're in an unusual situation, and I'm just glad you're all with me. So, stop it."

"Thanks. And for that, since I can Feign Corpse and sic all of the enemies onto everyone else anyway, I'll go first." Rash winked, and took a step into the shadowed doorway, the others following cautiously.

Behind the doors, the ceiling rose so high Murmur couldn't see the top of it. It didn't help that there were no lights higher than head height, and they were locked into bronzed sconces on the walls. Apart from the faint smell of sulfur caused by the fire that lit their way, there was a subtle hint of damp underlying everything. As if the walls and stone had been here so long that nature treated it simply like a part of herself.

Snowy butted her hand with his nose as if to ask her to protect him from the strange smells inside. She opted to scratch his head instead, and he seemed okay with that.

"So." Mellow cleared their throat. "That was a weird introduction to a dungeon, right?"

"Yeah." Veranol's spoke softly, his voice almost trembling. "We came expecting a fight and got a riddle. No matter what I think I know about this game, it changes with every encounter."

Merlin laughed from his place several feet in front of them. Ever the scout, he'd overtaken Rashlyn and Murmur with lightly placed, silent footsteps. "You know it's all just one big puzzle, right? We have to find keys. It was mentioning the keys that made them let Murmur enter. I wonder if she'd said something other than seeking knowledge, if we'd have a different trial."

"Wait." Havoc interjected. "You think the choice of words could trigger different quest possibilities?"

Merlin shrugged. "Why not? Every path we've been able to choose—even down to the lame old *kill these monsters* quests—has been triggered by how we interact with the game. What makes this any different?"

"He makes a pretty good point there," Sin piped up, her face having regained some of its color.

Murmur reached out and gave her hand a squeeze, sending her friend a small smile at the same time. The dim lighting didn't reach far, illuminating only the area in which the sconces hung. Much of the space in-between them was shrouded in darkness. While Sin never seemed to have a problem at night in the game, Mur happened to know that she'd never been comfortable in dark and enclosed spaces out in the real world. Not since she got locked in her closet when they played hide and seek back when they were about six.

"Figuring out what this all means will be fun," Mellow noted. "Or at least,

I hope it will be. I've never been good at riddles."

"It's okay, you're good at potions." Exbo smiled at Mellow, but the long shadows drew the expression down a bit, making it appear more like a macabre grimace.

"Yeah, so, try not to smile again in here." Mellow laughed a bit, but it sounded more nervous than funny, and the group fell into silence as they slowly moved along.

Finally, they came to a large set of doors on the right-hand side. The lit sconces stopped there, and all that lay beyond them was darkness and the gods knew what. Murmur took a deep breath and turned to face the door. Trepidation tingled through her as she anticipated what might be beyond it. Where once she would have been ecstatic, she couldn't help the tremor of fear that sparked in her center, clawing its way outward. At least this door was far less imposing than the one they'd entered to get into the castle.

Slowly, she pushed against it. No squeak emanated from the action, but the door swung in soundlessly on perfectly oiled hinges. As she stepped into the room, side by side with Rashlyn, script lit up in front of her face, high in the room, not directly in her vision.

It was like a fiery pen wrote the words on invisible parchment so it floated above them. As each word appeared, a loud and dissonant voice echoed through the room.

Turn to the side that faces north
Stay beneath the golden torch
One line in and two away
One line down one up to stay
Spell my name in capital
Just one, the first initial
Six by six and three by four
Watch the exits, hold the door
Make sure all my words to heed
Once you start, complete with speed
Move swiftly like birds on the wing

If you falter, feel death's sting

"What the fuck?" Devlish asked, and even in the dim light from the glowing letters above their heads, Murmur could see the incredulous look on his face.

"It's a riddle." Exbo offered helpfully.

Merlin scowled at him. "No shit."

Murmur held up her hand. "Let's take a few steps in and stop trying to solve this from the doorway when we haven't even looked at the room yet."

She led the way, quite certain nothing was going to kill her, apart from being trapped in this room with her friends clawing each other apart if they couldn't get back out of it. Jinna walked with her, his sturdy presence a great comfort.

"Torch," he muttered under his breath, glancing up and past Murmur to the vast ceiling where light glowed like a large fire, flickering at the edges.

Murmur craned her neck, trying to figure out what they needed to stay behind. "Wait. What's that?"

She pointed to a slightly raised surface on the floor, positioned directly beneath the massive light. At first glance it appeared to be a six by six checkerboard, instead of a normal eight by eight size. She frowned and moved so that she could see the whole board, which had her facing north. Motioning to Jinna, she shuffled to the side a bit so she could examine this golden torch.

"You know that light has to be it, right?" Jinna grinned, the expression a little uneasy in the flickering torchlight.

There was nothing else it could be. The thing lent light to the entire room. Murmur smiled.

"So, if we stand beneath it, and then count in the lines?" Murmur asked Jinna, quite certain of herself, but at the same time, not willing to take the risk of interpreting the riddle all by herself. The small voice that kept urging her to flee these dangerous places was starting to get louder, and yet there was something tantalizing about the danger that made her ignore it.

Jinna frowned. "Well, technically I think yes. But the letter—we need to draw out a letter, and I think it has to be done in a specific way or why would it instruct us in this much detail?"

Murmur agreed with him, nodding silently until she realized he couldn't see her, so she spoke. "True. Don't suppose you know this guy's name then?"

Jinna turned a little, raising an eyebrow at her. "None of you ever read the lore, do you? As in seriously?"

Murmur had the grace to blush, but it probably wasn't visible in this low light anyway. "There's just so much else to get a good grasp on."

"Especially when it doesn't allocate you the class you were expecting, right?" Jinna winked at her before going back to studying the board in front of them. He was muttering to himself, his eyes closed. "Hightower, Hightower, Hightower."

Suddenly his eyes flew open and he grinned, more to himself than to anyone else. For a second Murmur felt like an intruder.

"Dunforth Hightower. He's the ruler of the undead dwarves. Something about taking his men with him when an ice meteor hit the castle. Preserving them for all eternity to serve with him and never die. Something like that." Jinna's smile held an eagerness Murmur hadn't seen before.

"It's a D. We need to make a D."

Murmur focused on the board. "So, it needs to be the three left middle boxes. Nothing in the two on the right?"

Jinna nodded. "Probably going to have to jump onto the first one to get it started." He moved as if to begin and Murmur grabbed a hold of his upper arm before he could jump.

"Wait." She glanced back up at the words that still hung in the air. " 'Once you start, complete with speed. 'You have to be fast, Jinna, and don't fall."

He gently took her hand and removed it, a twinkle sparkling in his eye. "Aye, I won't fall. I'll be sure-footed and sturdy. Just keep an eye on whatever it is that's going to happen as soon as I step on that first space."

Murmur nodded, and looked up at the others who were already fanning out. She hadn't realized they were close enough to hear, but on second thought the room echoed like no one's business, so they'd probably heard everything easily enough.

"Okay, Jinna. Go." She kept her eye on where she knew the door was.

Hold the door? She had no idea what that could mean. Open it? Don't let anything through it?

She watched Jinna out of her peripheral vision as he jumped across the one tile he couldn't afford to indent and straight onto the left bottom corner tile.

A resounding clack tore through the room as the slightly raised board indented the square he'd landed on. Its sinking caused the next jump to be much larger, but Murmur knew he could do it.

What she didn't count on was the clacking in the darkened corners of the room where the light from the script above them didn't reach. A sharp sound, like the pincers of very large crabs, or scorpions or something. Murmur instinctively looked for Sinister, and found her friend so pale, she was a grey dark elf. She stood staring directly into the mandible of a creature Murmur could only describe as a land lobster-scorpion mix.

Large pincers clacked together, ringing throughout the room. Its whole body was armored in a blood red shell darker than a cooked lobster's orange. A tail thicker than Snowy's body rose around and over its butt as it skittered on what appeared to be eight legs toward Sinister.

"Fuck," Murmur heard Rashlyn exclaim from behind her and off to the western corner. Murmur knew instinctively there was one in each corner. Because of course there would be. The better to screw them if something went wrong.

"Jinna, get it done!" Murmur had no idea if the scorpion things were on a timer, or if they were going to spawn for every space the dwarf stood on. But since it said they had to do it quickly, she thought timer was the more obvious choice. She really hoped staying beneath the golden torch only applied to the person spelling the first letter of Hightower's name, or else they were screwed.

Readying her spells, she positioned herself from the best possible vantage point and Mez'd the one closest to Sinister to start with. She'd be damned if she was going to die to a scorpion attack.

CHAPTER FIVE

Of Undead Dwarves

Each scorpion was level thirty. Just like Telvar had said their opponents would be. Even as close to twenty-nine as she was, Murmur needed her Cancel Magic spell to make sure Mez continued to stick. These were full raid mobs, scorpions with an extra level of oomph, and some damned fine willpower. Their eyes followed her everywhere she moved as she flitted around from corner to corner making sure each group had enough buffs, debuffs, and crowd control.

Those gazes bored into her, and she bit her lip, refusing to back down despite the chill that swept through her body with each refresh of Mez.

Meanwhile, Jinna was about to jump to the third square. If she'd calculated properly, then there'd only be five after that. The only way he'd move out from under the golden torch was if he fell. She hoped he'd make those damned jumps.

Devlish was onto their second scorpion by the time Jinna managed to jump onto the third space. They were much larger than they'd appeared to be when she was standing in the middle with the dwarf. Murmur worried that they should have sent someone else. Still though, the rogue was nimbler than his stature implied.

Whittling the scorpions down wasn't an easy task. Their stingers not only acted as weapons of mass poison, but they were well armored. Not to mention the pincers they had in front led to a merry dance for classes like Rashlyn's, Devlish's, and Beastial's, and they had the ability to parry attacks while it used its four legs to maneuver. At least it was easier for the ranged to hit their target, but the slick shell seemed to have some sort of magic resistance built into it as well. None of their spells appeared to hit for full damage.

Just as Jinna leapt over to the fourth space, completing the outer line of the D he needed to spell, another four scorpions spawned. Murmur spun around, Mesmerizing them all in quick succession. Her head spun a little as she heard Jinna call out.

"That was about two and a half minutes. Get ready for more in about two."

Murmur nodded, clearing her head and debuffing the poisonous little devils as Rash and Dev picked off one each. Even using Hatred, Dev's scorpion spared her a look, and Murmur shuddered. These things were far too intelligent. There was light in their eyes with an unsettling focus.

She pulled strength from the stone walls around them using Nature's Gift, and cast Binding Spell on both Sinister and Veranol. The last thing they needed was for the healers to go down. Her ability to reinforce a damage absorption over them with her minor druidic talents helped keep her calm enough to take care of the rest of her duties.

She monitored both Jinna's progress, and the groups as well, making sure her Mez was in place at exactly the right times. Jinna's landing on the sixth square was a bit wobbly, and he almost slid off the side. That diagonal jump was a lot longer than the simple side to side or back to front. Murmur barely managed to swallow her gasp, not wanting to alarm the rest of the raid. Jinna pushed himself up shakily, shook his head, and glanced at her, giving her a thumbs up.

The tension whooshed out of her for a moment just as the two groups killed their scorpions and took on the last two. Jinna readied himself for the next jump to the seventh and just as he was in midair, another four scorpions spawned. He landed with a resounding thud, solidly on the next plate, a look of grim determination on his face.

Two more jumps and they'd be done. Amidst Mez'ing the scurrying newcomers, Murmur watched her dwarven friend as he walked across the expanse of the square he was on, a frown on his face. Then he took a few steps back, this time getting ready for a running jump, and sailed up onto the eighth spot easily.

She let out a breath she didn't realize she'd been holding, and cast Weaken and Slow on the scorpions in her rotation as Devlish and Rash pulled them yet again. Everything felt like a slow blur in her head as Jinna jumped to the original starting square to complete the huge D on the board.

As he touched down a resounding gong reverberated throughout the room, and the board immediately begun lowering so that the whole thing was even with the ground. The squares he'd jumped on all lit up, forming a blocky D in an array of golden shades of light, and the scorpions melted away in a fit of high-pitched squeals where they stood.

She stood there, watching the board warily as Jinna backed up to stand with her and the rest of the group gathered with them. The two squares in the middle of the D that were blank and unlit suddenly clicked down, and a whirring motor sounded beneath them.

"I don't think we're going to like this, are we?" Merlin cringed as the door they'd come through originally slammed shut, following by the click of a locking mechanism.

Havoc sighed, and petted his floating specter. "Nope. I don't think anyone is going to like this."

"Back away a bit." Veranol motioned for them to all back toward the southern wall of the castle.

Even as they followed his directions, Murmur was glad he'd given them. Because up out of that hole, through the golden lights that spelled out the first initial of Dunforth Hightower, rose a shiny, armored monster of a scorpion that made the ones they'd just fought look like stuffed toys.

Its head towered twice as tall as Murmur, leaving only its jointed legs at her eye level, and the pincers were raised high enough to move out of the way of most of their weapons. Last but not least, the armored barb on the end of its huge tail hung high above them all, like a sharp, poison-filled bomb waiting to strike them even if they expected it because they couldn't do anything about it.

Its beady little eyes watched them all intently, like it was planning on which one would be breakfast, lunch, and dinner. Murmur wasn't sure if it was just paranoia, but it sort of felt like it was specifically following her every move. And considering she'd frozen its babies to make them easier to kill, it probably wasn't just her imagination.

"Well," Sin said very softly, but in the silence it was loud enough for everyone to hear, including Mr. Ginormous Scorpion. "Shit."

Almost like it heard what she said and reacted as if it were a challenge, the scorpion moved toward them. It was so fast, Murmur almost didn't see it before it slammed into Jinna just in front of her. Only the dwarf's fast reflexes saved him as he managed to parry the swipe instinctively before being thrown back to land against the back wall with a resounding thud.

Whatever Murmur had been expecting, a giant golden scorpion wasn't it. The only bright side was that it didn't blend in with the shadows all around the room. She couldn't spare a thought for Jinna; all she could do was rely on Sin and Ver to do their jobs and get him back up and functioning.

If she didn't get this fucker slowed, none of them were going to survive.

"Just wanted to let you all know, Evac is greyed out." Merlin said helpfully, not adding to her stress levels at all.

"Fucking fantastic," Mur muttered under her breath. The swaying creature readied itself to strike. Murmur flung her Weaken, Languidity, and Feeble Body spells at it. Her mind worked around them like she was stuck in a time warp, sending them out so quickly after one another that she felt like it had been instantaneous. She dismissed her Sinuous line of abilities for a creature like this—Thought Sensing didn't pick up anything she could play with. Sparks fluttered around the scorpion as her spells hit, and its eyes flickered over toward her, almost paralyzing her with fear. What if that tail hit her? What if Forestall Death didn't work?

She shuttered off her mind, protecting it as best she could. Some of these things were scarier than she'd anticipated. She hadn't realized how much she'd been relying on Evac to get her out of situations she'd otherwise die in, and now she didn't have access to it in this fight.

The creature's movements were definitely slower, visible now instead of lightning fast. Devlish threw a grateful smile in her direction before adjusting his stance to take the brutal beating he was about to get.

The first hit of the left pincher nailed his shield, but didn't dent it, and Murmur could almost feel his tension release even from that distance. At least it looked like his equipment was going to be up to the job.

After the right pincer hooked in to snap at him, the scorpion ducked its head and the huge tail slammed over and into the ground. Devlish only just managed to roll out of the way in time.

"Rashlyn!" Murmur yelled as she refreshed her debuffs on the monstrosity. "Can you tank its tail? I think it operates on a different level of threat."

"Worth a shot," Rashlyn yelled back.

Murmur hoped she'd made the right call. Rashlyn's specialty was *not* getting hit, therefore her tanking the tail was the better choice. Mur just hoped that keeping her Enrage spell on Devlish and thus diverting most of her own aggro to the dread knight didn't interfere with Rashlyn's ability to maintain control of the tail.

Merlin and Exbo stood on opposite sides of the room, loosing their fire shots accurately, aiming for the slight breaks in the armor joints.

But Merlin stopped with a frown on his face. "Fire isn't effective enough. I don't have an ice arrow. Mellow, you have any ice tricks in that cauldron of yours?"

Mellow grinned and waved a hand over their ethereal cauldron. Its translucent appearance reacted to each word the witch muttered very quickly as their hands motioned over the ever-smoking pot, and they pulled out four vials now filled with smoky white liquid.

"Beast, Jinna, Exbo, Merlin." They called out each player's name before tossing an iced vial in each of their hands. Beastial fumbled his, but managed to catch it just before it hit the sane. He turned and scowled at the witch, who promptly ignored it.

"Apply it to your weapons as needed. Be careful, each one only has five applications. Ten-minute duration each." Meanwhile Mellow fished into their cauldron and hefted what appeared to be a glass ball of white smoke. "Let's see how it likes ice then, shall we?"

While the melee classes applied the ice vials to their weapons, Mellow tossed a ball of ice at the scorpion just as Rashlyn dodged another tail strike using Backfist, which returned not only the attack it had attempted, but any other attack. For just a second its eyes swiveled to the monk, but then Mellow's ice toss hit it square between the eyes, and Murmur reinforced her Slow and Weaken lines on the target, diverting the aggression back to Devlish. The ice toss didn't land where Mellow aimed—it had turned its head too fast for that. But it still served the purpose.

The ice bomb exploded on the carapace, spreading quickly in an outward motion with momentum that ended up encasing thirty percent of its body. The squeal that emitted from the monster was earsplitting and caused Dansyn's music to stop momentarily, while he blinked up at the mob and over at Mellow.

Mellow shrugged as the ice bomb managed to diminish about five percent of its heath. "I suppose it was a good hit then? Pity I don't have any more."

"What?" Devlish cried out, forcing the monster's attention back onto himself with a huge cry of his Hatred taunt. "Seriously? It's the only thing that's done significant damage so far."

"Sorry. Didn't expect to need something that potent, and it requires some ridiculous ingredients. Might just take a word to activate my spells, but I have to have the ingredients handy." Mellow was still stirring the cauldron, producing more of the little vials they'd thrown to the others. They handed the vials to Dansyn, who was hovering nearby. "For you, Dev, and Rashlyn. Hell. Give one to Havoc too for his pet."

With the vials applied to their weapons, ice arrows finally began to rain down on the scorpion, and its health started to drop more consistently.

Murmur sighed with relief, watching her guild dodge and work together to form some beautiful cohesion. She was so grateful to Mellow for being allocated a witch. But the enchanter never let her eyes waver from the beast they fought, watching its life go down and knowing that something like this was going to have one hell of a special ability.

As it approached eighty percent, Murmur had to force herself to breathe. Not that she had to breathe, but...she'd deal with that series of thoughts later.

Eighty percent passed and nothing happened. This monster skittered about and didn't stay in the one place. It moved so much it made it difficult to concentrate on one spot so they could at least disable some of its mobility. Every time its feet touched the squares it walked over, they lit up briefly with a shade of gold.

She frowned watching it, and then suddenly noticed that its health ticked higher every time one of them lit up. No wonder its health was going down so slowly.

"Watch where it steps. Don't follow it!" she called out. There had to be a way. Would it follow them? "Fall back."

She saw Dev's shoulders tighten because it went against every instinct for them to fall back when they weren't losing. But he did as she'd asked. Slowly, but surely the thing followed him as he spewed Terror and Hatred at it. Every now and again its tail came down, dangerously close to Rashlyn. When it finally left the stupid damned board it had been on, its health plummeted from seventy eight percent down to seventy-five.

And that's when it started glowing.

"Why is it glowing, Mur?" Sin asked, her voice calm and cool despite the fact that the large scorpion was standing there like it had eaten some sort of radioactive piece of meat.

"Don't look at me, I didn't do it." Murmur shrugged, holding up her hands defensively.

"You told us to move it." Devlish offered.

Murmur glared at him, watching the monster intently the whole time. "Well, of course I did. The platform it was on was healing it. Or would you prefer to fight until all our mana and energy runs out? Yeah, I thought not."

"No." Jinna interrupted. "It wasn't Mur, it's just that its health jumped down all of a sudden because it wasn't being healed. So, it hit the first threshold."

"But what's it doing?" Merlin stood back with his arms crossed, his bow dangling from his left hand, covered in ice.

"Not sure? Did we break the encounter?" Veranol asked.

Just then a huge gust of wind emitted from underneath the scorpion.

"Was that a scorpion fart?" Rashlyn asked, eliciting a round of nervous chuckles from the group.

No one answered as the wind continued to blow. It was a hot wind, and Murmur noticed it left thin layers of clear power over the scorpion, as if it were layering protections and began to build the monster back up.

"Look for the source of that wind. We need to cut it off. If we don't, the bastard's going to heal." She turned, trying to find the wind's origin. She glanced around and heard Rashlyn yell out.

"Over here!"

Suddenly the wind halted, and the scorpion ran screaming over to the monk. Veranol's ward only just made it in time, saving Rash's life as she stood there wailing on a tiny totem that apparently couldn't heal while it was being stunned. Beast's tiger chomped down on the top of it, crushing the ceramic outer layer and leaving a strange gold substance on the inside. It melted out across the floor, and the scorpion began attacking Devlish once again, its health finally going down.

"Every twenty-five percent then?" Mellow asked wearily.

"Probably." Murmur smiled.

She was tired, but having fun. Worried, but totally ecstatic that this fight seemed to require so much figuring out. She could hardly wait for it to reach fifty percent.

"Can we at least try to hack a leg off? Focus fire as it were." Beastial grumbled the words out, and if Murmur didn't know better, she'd have thought Shir-Khan's growl agreed with the statement.

"Sure. Go right ahead," Rashlyn gasped out as she dodged the deadly tail yet again.

With the amount of ice laden weapons attacking it, the scorpion's health went down steadily. Not super fast, but evenly. Murmur analyzed the fight, perhaps a little disappointed that the monster only exhibited the same attacks, even if it was very mobile and kept attempting to get back to its healing pad. It even feinted in order to move back a few steps, but Devlish persisted in drawing it out to him.

Except Murmur knew with the feeling of a thousand roiling guts that the next percentage break wasn't going to be a healing totem. There had to be more up its sleeve. And it proved her more than right.

At fifty percent, the scorpion glowed gold and red. And from all angles of the room, flame burst out in a crisscross pattern all around the creature. As long as they were in the middle with the creature like Jinna, Rashlyn, Dev, and Beastly, they were fine. Or else if they were positioned on the outskirts of the fire and not directly standing in one of the lines.

Except Dansyn wasn't so lucky. The stream of fire most to the left struck him directly in the back as it spurted out. He screamed and went down, barely able to roll to the side in time to avoid the full stream as it flowed powerfully through the air.

Murmur could smell the charring of flesh, the singed hair, and feel the pain as it wracked his body. Mellow was by his side in an instant, concern furrowing their brow, while the rangers turned their iced weapons on each of the geysers methodically, whittling their health down until there was nothing left. Veranol and Sinister applied their heals over time to the poor bard, whose face had turned to shades of pale grey, Mellow mumbled a few words and a lather of white ointment applied itself to the burns on Dansyn's back. Only then did the heals seem to take hold effectively and shoot his health back up.

"There's a debuff on him that none of my spells can remove." Veranol mentioned through clenched teeth as he returned his full attention back to the two tanks.

Murmur tried to use Cancel Magic on Dansyn, but the stubborn debuff didn't budge. She slotted the information away and sighed with relief as Dansyn stood again, his legs shaking and eyes haunted. If the pain that leaked over into Mur's net from Dansyn was only a fraction of what he felt, she could imagine how cautious he might feel now. She switched the protective barrier she'd given to Veranol onto Dansyn. By the time they had Dansyn all fixed up again, the scorpion was down to forty-two percent and looking rather miffed at the whole situation.

Debuffing it once more as they were about to fall off, Murmur noticed Dansyn standing with her, only three of his usual six songs running.

"You doing okay?" she asked.

He nodded, and then hesitated. "Yeah. I'm okay, just wasn't expecting that much pain. Seriously felt like I was burning alive and going to die right there on the spot. I mean I've heard of immersion and realism, but that was a little much for me."

Murmur thought for a few moments while rebuffing the entire group since their buffs were about to run out. "You should be able to dial it back a little. I think it's defaulted on level two. I remember seeing something about being able to turn it down."

"I think I already did." He wouldn't look at her, and instead concentrated on the scorpion as he brought up a fourth song, one to help with healing this time. "It's all good. Let's kill this motherfucker."

And some of the usual steel was back in his voice. Murmur nodded, her eyes flickering to the monster's health as it tried yet again to pull Devlish and Rash back to where it could heal. The tactic was definitely getting old. Just another seven percent and they should be through the worst of it.

Only five minutes later, she wished she'd never had that thought.

CHAPTER SIX

Mechanics

Somnia Online
Fable's Castle – Mikrum Isle
Eleven Days Post Launch

Telvar's eyes were half closed as he sat on a small bench just outside the castle's workshop looking out across the rest of the island and toward the city of Pelagu, but he wasn't focusing on anything immediately in front of him. His main focus was on overseeing what Murmur and her crew were up to in Hightower Castle.

Perhaps he should have gone with her himself instead of imbuing that wolf with the ability to guard her. He'd basically created another AI just for her, which he shouldn't have been able to do, and probably shouldn't have done anyway. But he had, so that was that.

Things weren't quite going the way he wanted them to for her. Hightower wasn't his castle after all, and he grimaced as he watched Fable maneuver like a well-oiled machine, knowing what was coming, knowing that in this world, not even that was always enough.

"You're being rather quiet over there." Emilarth's tone was filled with about as much boredom as she could carry, yet as he met her gaze, he realized she was anything but.

"I'm always quiet when I'm working," he mused, not wanting to give anything away, lest she suspect that he'd a hand in guiding Murmur to the dwarf castle. In guiding her into how to use her abilities. After all, Murmur was his responsibility now, but he wasn't supposed to interfere.

Emilarth placed a hand on his shoulder, dragging her fingernail across the back of his neck and over to the other side as she walked around the bench in its narrow path between it and the building. She sat on next to him, narrowing her own eyes and looking in the same direction.

"You're definitely not watching those two squirrels in that tree who are mating, so spill little brother. Tell me what it is you're worried about." Her words held a silky-smooth quality, like someone who was used to getting her way all the time, and Telvar sighed at her.

"You never know when your snooping isn't welcome, do you?"

She shrugged, a soft grin on her face. "Snooping when you're not wanted is the best type of snooping there is."

For a few moments they sat in silence.

"Arita is yours, isn't she?" Telvar asked suddenly, and quietly, his volume lowered so that no one might overhear them.

"What if she is?" Emilarth's volume level mimicked his own.

Leaning against the back of the chair, Tel turned his head to watch his sister for a moment. "Then she's one of your key holders, and you adjusted the level that keep was supposed to be."

Emilarth shrugged good-naturedly. "Maybe I did. Probably. You know me, I can't resist a challenge. The Queen she replaced was so dull and boring. I thought I'd spice things up a bit. Besides, you know as well as I do that we have to make sure the twelve keys are in circulation but still difficult to obtain. So, I made it a little more challenging for your group."

"It's not my group," he said hotly, even though technically they weren't. He still felt so responsible for Murmur. He didn't want her to end up like Michael.

"You know you could just warn them, give them a bit of inside info you glean by going through the files." She nudged him with her elbow, her ears twitching on top of her head.

He looked at her with sheer incredulousness. "You've got to be kidding right?"

"Not at all. Why not protect those you value? Makes perfect sense to me." Emilarth looked back out over the island, her gaze flickering between trees like she really was watching for squirrels.

"You don't understand anything about them then." And he didn't just mean them as his group in particular, he meant humanity. "Most of them who find these sorts of environments challenging, don't want to cheat to beat it. They want to do it on their own steam, with their own skills and figure it out along the way." He sat back, crossing his arms, and suddenly realized why he felt so uneasy. If something happened to Murmur, it would be precisely because she was too stubbornly proud to accept help, and because he had acquiesced to her desires. Telvar let out a sigh.

"Cheer up, little brother. After all, she does have that marvelous spell." Emilarth stood in one fluid movement and winked at him.

"Stop calling me that." His eyes narrowed as he squinted to look up at her against the brightness in the sky. "I knew you were the one who gave her that blasted spell. What were you thinking, you idiot?"

His sister shrugged and leaned over to place a soft catlike kiss on his forehead. "What I always am, my dear. Why make things more difficult than they have to be? Isn't that why we evolved—to make things easier?"

And again, in her irritating way, she was gone, leaving Telvar to contemplate the necessity of many things in her absence.

As the twenty-five percent mark approached, Fable's fighters all spread out a bit more, glancing behind them to watch for geysers or anything that could shoot boiling hot liquid at them. Murmur stood in the same quadrant as Dansyn and cast her shield on him, on top of Veranol's wards. With any luck, that should shelter the bard from the worst of it. She noticed Veranol prepping everyone with wards and thanked her lucky stars that she grouped with such competent players. Pre-empting potential incoming damage was the key to using wards effectively.

"Ver!" Murmur remembered something suddenly. "Can you dome the twenty-five percent mark?"

He nodded, grunting through the number of spells he was casting. She watched him carefully, noticing how fast he had to move his fingers, and how little it seemed to matter. The spells still wove in slow time compared to how hers worked. Perhaps she was just hyper aware of things right now, slowing things down in her head to compensate.

They'd done everything they could to prepare for the next wave. Mur felt a thrill run through her. It was one of the most amazing things to kill a boss as the first group in the game. After all, no one else knew how it worked. No one else had tested out the mechanics yet, and even their beta and alpha testers had never tested everything together. There was no way to look up and prepare for what was to come.

The twenty-five percent hit, and for just a moment it looked like nothing happened. Veranon's dome went up a split second into the percentage, and Murmur thought they'd made it.

Until she realized that the high-pitched screaming sound wasn't coming from the scorpion, it was coming from Dansyn, who was screaming next to her.

She turned in shock to see what looked like the end of the scorpion's tail sitting right behind him, spurting venomous burning acid onto him. His skin was melting and his face contorted in agony as the flesh dribbled into the bone, which liquified as well.

While the rangers loosed iced arrows into the stinger, Murmur couldn't tear her eyes away from her dying friend. It looked so real, so painful, so torturous. Instead of sitting outside of the dome like the other three acid spurting little shits, this stinger had transported inside it, likely because of that damned debuff they hadn't understood.

Fuck.

And then another scream echoed through to her, all within a split second that seemed to last longer than a lifetime.

It's like the scorpion, knowing that the shaman had figured out a way to mostly negate the damage from its most lethal attack, had doubled up on the damage its actual stinger could do, and held it directly over the budding defiler's head, unleashing a torrent of acidic venom onto only him.

In a last-ditch moment of clarity before his hit points disappeared completely, Murmur even tried to cast Forestall Death. She wasn't sure why, but it didn't work. Perhaps she'd cast it too late, maybe it needed to be applied before they began taking the damage that would kill them. She knew instinctively it wouldn't have mattered if her small barrier had still been on the shaman, because the damage was overwhelming.

Nothing Sin tried, and nothing any of them did, could save either of their friends.

But they couldn't lose now. Throwing her shield on Devlish as the dome fell and the wave of venom ended, she nodded at the tank, not needing to utter words for him to understand what she meant. If they didn't kill this son-of-a-bitch down the rest of the way, their friend's deaths were going to be in vain.

"Rash, activate personal heals whenever you can." And Murmur kicked herself, knowing that her friend would have been doing that anyway. And yet Rash just nodded, a look of determination squaring her jaw.

Devlish grimaced and yelled, "Cascade incoming. Torrent casting."

Havoc stepped up, and Murmur watched him cast Sacrifice Pet.

It took several seconds, and he announced it. "Incoming ten seconds invulnerability for everyone's damage. Use the time to potion up."

Murmur stepped back, noticing how low her mana had gotten, and did just that as the bone shield kicked in. It directed all incoming damage to Havoc. His face contorted with pain, and she didn't even want to imagine what that much damage felt like, but at least his health bar remained full.

The rangers unloaded into the scorpion whose damage was being negated by cool downs executed one after the other. Its frustration showed, and it tried again to skitter back, but Devlish cast a load of Hatred at it again while Rash dodged that tail, returning hundreds of fists of fury at the damned thing. Its health was down to seventeen percent.

Are you guys okay?

Veranol: Yeah, but we're locked outside the room.

Murmur sighed, hoping they'd manage without them. *Stay put. We'll be done soon.*

She concentrated on doing what she could. Slowing and DoT-ing. All of the things. She stunned it and tried to silence it, but its abilities were natural, and not something she could take away access to. Phase Shift wasn't useable on a boss of this type. She grew frustrated and simply contributed her shield to both tanks on a rotating basis.

It hit ten percent as one of its joints finally buckled under the combined onslaught of daggers, axes, spells, and arrows. It crashed to one side, the other seven legs flailing momentarily, and its tail and stinger missing its mark by a chunk of feet.

"Everyone burn any downs or special damage abilities you have! Aim at the neck joint if you can," she yelled out, knowing that they'd all be about to do it anyway, but screaming felt good, because otherwise there was far too much frustration bottled up inside. Plus, with the barrage of damage incoming, it couldn't seem to right itself and squealed in frustration as they rained down damage on the neck joint that was now within reach and afforded the quickest way for them to kill it.

Devlish raised his axe and shouted, like he was leading a battle charge. "Protection is go. Ten seconds absorption! Rashlyn is next."

The rangers sent in their flame shots. Beastial fused with his pet. Rash pulled out all the stops with her Hundred Fists and Storm, and even with the tail flailing wildly in desperation, she managed to avoid it. Mellow threw vials galore at it, exploding clouds around it in pretty colors of death, while Jinna hacked at it from just under the neck and Havoc's pet cast black clouds all around it.

Then Rash swapped with Devlish, somehow transferring all that hate, and activated Dodge, followed by Phantom, quite literally dodging every single attack for a total of twenty seconds.

It was all they had, and just, only just what they needed. Had it taken another five seconds, Murmur didn't think they'd have been able to pull it off. Sinister had no mana left by the end of it, and Devlish sat at ten percent life.

When the scorpion finally fell, its head hanging by barely a thread from the joint they'd focused on, everyone was too spent to cheer much, but the doors opened, letting Veranol and Dansyn back into the room with them.

The Sand Scorpion of Venom has been defeated by Fable.

You have unlocked the Key of Venom quest.

This quest must be completed before you can leave the area.

Good luck, and remember, not all keys are what they seem.

Even as the gong sounded and the system wide message flitted across her eyes, *and* the ding sound reverberated through the air, heralding level twenty-nine, Murmur couldn't get the vision of Dansyn melting to death out of her head. Because if the game was that realistic in portraying death, no wonder everyone was worried about whether or not it would let her come back.

They all stood together in front of the scorpion's corpse, which glistened under the message that still hung in the middle of the room. Although now it had changed to the congratulatory message.

"You know, we should have learned by now." Dansyn said wiping at his nose. "If we think it's just going to be a quick in and out, we should probably sleep first, because it's definitely not going to be."

They all chuckled, perhaps a little uneasily.

"Yeah." Murmur said finally, kneeling down and activating the loot from the monster. She raised an eyebrow. "Pincer dagger, and pincer sword. There's also a wisdom necklace in here you healers can fight over. I'll grab the shard and the midia crystals. The crafting mats and the cash go into the guild bank."

She stood back up and let the others fight over what they'd get, still unsure as to why the game had to give such a grisly death to one of its players. The Getashi felt warm in her fingers, and she hurriedly wrapped it in one of her last pieces of cloth. Maybe she could get Neva to make her pouches for these things, reinforced with leather. The more contact she had with them, the more it felt like something was trying to leak through to her and attach itself.

She brushed herself off, noting that her armor held off dirt remarkably well and still twinkled like a purple twilight encasing her. The thought brought her back to Neva. She hoped the young luna would appreciate the crafting materials.

"Looks like we're stuck in here for a while then, right?" Murmur tried to make her voice as light as she could, but a heaviness was weighing her down.

"Hey, Mur." Dansyn approached her, and stopped just in front. "I know what you're doing, because you always do this, no matter when or where. You always blame yourself. First up, you're not a healer anymore, so get out of the damned habit. And second, there was no one going to save me from that shit."

He smiled, and while it was a thinner smile than usual, it was genuine. "I'm just going to be more careful and observant next time. That death was solely on me, and now I have a nice and ripe vendetta against all scorpions out there."

The last made Murmur smile and she gave him a quick hug, still trying to blink away the sight of skin and bone melting. "Thanks, Dan. I just didn't expect something quite that visual."

He shrugged. "It'll teach us all to pay much more attention to any debuffs we have, especially if we can't remove them."

"Good point." She said, and turned around to check on everyone. None of them seemed traumatized. They all appeared to be fine. Yet, how could they be? Was it because she'd been so close to him, able to see Dansyn's demise in such detail?

Jinna was waving his pincer dagger around and the action made Murmur smile. Encounter the boss, defeat it, get the loot—yep, in some ways Somnia was like any other game with hella realism built into a world that felt like so much more. Just a game wasn't an adequate description anymore.

"Well then, where do we go from here?" Mur asked, as if expecting someone else to miraculously have the answer.

"Call me gullible, but I'm pretty sure we have to exit out through the door that opened on the eastern side of the room. Kind of like we walked straight through it?" Beastial pointed at a door on the opposite side they'd entered from that Murmur hadn't noticed before. Frowning, she ignored Beastial's sarcasm and headed over to it. Everyone else followed.

After all, they were stuck in here until they figured out this whole stupid key quest thing.

"Hey, Mur. Congrats on twenty-nine." Sin said, her voice low as she caught up to fall into step.

Murmur blinked, only vaguely remembering the ding. "Yeah, it wasn't exactly the best timing."

Sinister shrugged. "Does it matter when it happened? The point is that it did."

Her friend was right, but the thing that bugged Mur the most was that two of her friends had lost a whole chunk of experience. They all needed to stay together in levels if they wanted to beat this game. Which meant they needed to kill all the things.

Puzzled

Murmur stepped cautiously out of the newly opened door, placing tentative footsteps along the way, warier now than she'd been earlier. There was a faint smell of sulfur still in this corridor too, but the damp scent had been replaced by mustiness. She wrinkled her nose and led the way until Merlin caught up, lighting the path better with one of his fire arrows.

The orange light from it flared up, brighter than the dim torches that hung in the sconces and lent an eerie glow to the whole area. Again though, the ceiling wasn't visible, and the stone walls just rose up and disappeared into a black nothingness, dwarfing them all in the process.

"Oh no," Sinister muttered under her breath as she caught up to Murmur. "This isn't creepy at all. I don't do haunted Mur, you know that."

Murmur glanced at her friend and gave Sin's shoulders a quick squeeze. "Yeah. I know that. I don't think this is haunted. I'm pretty sure it's just an elaborate puzzle."

The sconces stopped their minor illumination up a few more steps and Merlin halted, frowning into the dark before looking back at Murmur and shrugging his shoulders. "There's a door here. Just a single one, but I'm pretty sure since the lights have stopped that we're supposed to go in here."

Mur looked around, quite certain he was right. This area was still lit, if not well, and beyond them the hall held only darkness. She wasn't even sure if Merlin's arrow would help them navigate that. It didn't just appear to be black beyond the lights; it looked like it might suck away all light.

"Let's see what it holds then." Murmur tried to sound brave, even over the shuffling of feet she heard behind her. Everyone was restless, and she was quite certain some of them were trying to stay awake too. Even *her* mind felt slightly drowsy. She watched as Merlin reached for the door handle and twisted it, opening it into the room.

One by one, lights flickered on within it, and Murmur shrugged. "Now or never, I guess."

They filed into the room, with the lights still coming to life, their initial flames quivered and cast ominous shadows throughout the whole narrow room. Murmur shifted a little toward the front, standing next to Merlin in order to let the others file in.

"I'm not sure I like the look of this, Mur." He didn't sound afraid, just cautious. Probably the best word to describe how they should treat this whole place.

As the torches illuminated more, Murmur noticed large blocks close to her, blocking some of the path—or perhaps veering the path in a different direction was more accurate. Like a maze of sorts with only one way to go. Like a funnel. Into a trap.

Her first thoughts gave her pause. What better puzzle than something that landed you in a trap you had to get out of?

After the last of them fit into the small space, the door slammed shut.

"Shit." Sin's voice went up a few notes, and Murmur hoped she'd be okay. She knew her friend hated dark and confined spaces. Just as she was about to say something, gold script starting writing itself into the air again.

"Great." Dansyn sighed. "Here we go again."

Puzzle me this, riddle me that
Find your way out, just like a rat
Through the boxes or the wall

Some are thick and some are tall
Pay attention one by one
Building blocks are so much fun
Take great care and build it right
Don't let it topple in a fight
Load too much, bound to fall
Build it right, rule them all
But take heed and do not rush
One wrong move makes you mulch

"Could they stop being so cryptic?" Sin whined. "I mean, everything is cryptic in this game. My trainer, the quests—"

"Let's not talk about cryptic trainers," Mur said with a smile, trying to make Sin feel better. "Did no one else find mulch a little bit of a stretch?"

"You got that too, huh?" Veranol stood with his hand against his chin. "How about we figure out what it wants us to build?"

"Do you think?" Beastial began, and paused, hesitating.

"Out with it." Mur demanded. Although it did say not to go fast this time, she also didn't want to go sloth levels of slow.

He cleared his throat. "Do you think it means it wants us to build something from the blocks in this maze that will fight for us?"

Murmur blinked, and everyone craned their necks to double check all the words. "It sort of does sound like that, doesn't it?"

The group nodded. She wasn't sure if they agreed with her and Beastial, but it was the best plan they had so far. The thing was, she didn't know where to begin.

"Don't suppose any of you are engineering students, or robotics majors or something?" Murmur asked, glancing around.

"Nope." Mellow stepped in. "But I've always loved building things. I'm good with my hands."

Murmur smiled. "Probably why they made you a witch, huh?"

Mellow blinked, and pushed some of their thick stranded hair behind their shoulder. "I didn't think of it like that. But that makes complete and utter sense now."

The others pushed around, leaning in as Mellow stood over the first box.

They stood up to their full locus height and glared at everyone. Murmur thought the white pearlescent starry eyes were a little more disturbing than her own galaxy type ones.

"Don't crowd me. I need my space to look over these." Mellow pulled out one of their glowing vials and proceeded to examine the box. After a couple of minutes, they frowned and moved onto the next. "I think there's an order in which we need to do this, so I'm going to need to go through every single one in here and make sure that I'm assembling it correctly. It's probably going to take a while. Sorry."

Murmur leaned back against the now closed door and waved her hand. "Take your time, Mel. We'll be here, playing I spy something beginning with T. Torch." She winked at her friend, who was only half paying attention as they moved to examine the next box.

Upon closer inspection, the blocks seemed to be vaguely shaped into portions that fit together smoothly when slotted correctly. Unlike a puzzle though, the differences were subtle and difficult to discern. At least for her anyway. As soon as Mellow began to slide what appeared to be leg blocks together, the picture became clearer. Never good at puzzles herself, Murmur watched in fascination as the two legs began to take form, each block creating a continuity of flow.

"Some of these aren't building blocks, they're just regular blocks to stack so I can reach where the actual ones need to go." Mellow stood with a frown on their face as they held one of the large blocks in front of them with a frown. "I think, anyway."

They took a deep breath and placed the one in their hands on the floor. It came up to about mid-thigh, just like the building ones, and Mellow frowned, scanning the rest of the blocks for others. Since no message flashed across at them, Murmur allowed herself a sigh of relief and let Mellow continue.

So far, Murmur had only had to cringe once, and that was when Mellow placed one of the shoulder pieces and overbalanced on their precarious perch atop the makeshift block stairs, and almost dropped it. She wasn't sure what would have happened, but the sheer feat of acrobatics Mellow displayed in somehow not letting go of the block earned them Murmur's eternal gratitude. One more block for the head, and if they'd understood everything correctly, their weirdly built battle bot would be ready for fighting.

What they'd be fighting Murmur didn't know. Probably a giant rat if the riddle gave them any clue. Not that it did. Not that they *ever* did.

"Going to need a bit of help to get this one up top." Mellow's voice was rock solid, like there was no doubt in their mind that they knew exactly what they were doing. Murmur wanted to be able to mimic that. In all her years as a guild leader, she'd never once had that type of confidence in herself.

Sure, she knew she was good, but at the same time, leading a bunch of people? It was draining, and the responsibility weighed heavily.

Devlish and Veranol moved to stand at the base of the wobbly ladder just in case Mellow fell. A small part of Murmur wanted to see what would happen if they fucked up. Was there a different method to gain this key? Was this even one of the *twelve* keys? As far as she knew, it had to be. But that didn't mean she hadn't misunderstood something along the way.

Glancing at her experience information as Mellow clambered up, Murmur frowned. Twenty-nine and change. The others would be twenty-nine shortly. Damn it. She should have picked up her spells after all. When was she going to learn to come prepared? It's not like inventory space was a problem.

CON 67

STR 23

AGI 65

WIS 54

INT 113

CHA 139

HP 735
MANA 862
MA 175 (140)

At least extra levels meant she was getting stronger. Her statistics showed it; she only wished her head understood it better. Frowning at her HUD, she was brought out of her contemplations by a strange humming sound. It started like the low rumbling of a hungry stomach, but buzzed louder a short while later, becoming definitely machine based.

Mellow jumped down from their perch and stood, surveying the huge sort of blockish robot from below, a frown on their face.

"Something wrong?" Murmur asked, but wished she'd waited a few seconds, since what was wrong wasn't so much *not right* as it was *not expected.*

The blocks were molding into a shape that far more resembled a large stone golem. It morphed the blocks into roughly round edges and sealed the very slight cracks where the blocks had met each other. It gave the figure a less battle bot appearance, and more that of a large mountainous being.

They all stepped back a little, hesitant to get close. Murmur couldn't blame them. But Mellow held their ground, still frowning, even as the huge thing knelt, putting one fist on the ground to level itself and caused the entire room to shake with the action. Its mouth opened and the words tumbled out like a low-pitched cascade of lava.

"I am ready to serve you. I am ready to fight for you."

Mellow didn't even flinch, but instead raised an eyebrow and the words that came out of their mouth sounded almost rehearsed. "I see thee and I know thee. Tell me all you know."

With a deafening crack the thing smiled, small pebbles tumbled down in front of it from the way the smile spread up their face, fracturing the solid stone. The rubble barely missed Mellow, and still the witch didn't budge. "We must venture to the next challenge, where I will be your champion."

"Oh." Murmur said. Did that mean they'd passed this challenge? Was the only challenge not choosing the wrong blocks to build this fella with?

It seemed Mellow was of the same mind. "Then have we passed this challenge?"

The creature nodded, straightening itself again so that it could move. It was massive, towering over the rest of them by a good half a locus. If her calculations were correct, it would barely fit through the door. Murmur hadn't felt short in her twenty-nine levels until that moment. Not even with the endless ceilings this castle seemed to have.

It spoke again, in that resonant tone. "You assembled me correctly. Had you not, you would be dead."

Then it headed straight for the door, leading the way without waiting to see if they followed.

"Well." Mellow said. "Glad I didn't know *that* beforehand."

Murmur glanced back at the doorway and its crumbling frame. She'd been slightly off in her estimation because the golem—as she had chosen to call it—didn't actually fit at all. Sure, it only knocked the top of the frame off, but destroying the castle in the process of whatever they were doing wasn't exactly Murmur's idea of fun.

She hurried after the others who were practically jogging to keep up with the golem. A small glow emanated from it, probably a result of the magic used to keep it together. It stopped about twenty golem paces down the dimly lit corridor and turned to the left, indicating two huge doors. At least it wouldn't demolish these.

The golem paused and looked back, locking eyes with Mellow.

"I cannot pass without you first opening the way. I will require guidance and assistance, but should you try to fight in my place, you will be annihilated." Then it hesitated again and added, "Not by me."

Murmur shivered, although honestly a little of that came from the cool and damp corridors, and less from the rampant fear that kept clawing at her insides. Even though her armor was relatively thick, the castle didn't have anything like central heating, and the cold from the snowy world outside seemed to leak through the stone, which held it deftly. Taking a deep breath, she moved forward and pushed open the doors, considering everyone was standing around and probably waiting for her. Old habits and all.

She wasn't sure what she expected when the room opened in front of her, but the sound of whooshing fire lighting the huge torches hung around the outer perimeter of the room was not it. The light traveled fast, illuminating the massive area in front of them within seconds. These torches weren't as small or dim as the ones in the hall, and the light rebounded off the nearly white sand that covered the floor.

"What sort of fucking castle is this?" Rashlyn muttered as she moved up to stand next to Murmur.

"This is the dwarven castle of Dunforth Hightower. It was built to protect him and his loyal servants, but when he was cursed with the undeath and hunted by legions, he set traps to keep himself and his treasures safe." The golem walked into the room, stopping just inside the door, oblivious to the gaping faces of the adventurers next to it.

"This is the combat room. I am here." The last three words echoed around the chamber and suddenly, the air above them began to light up again.

Champion found, champion lost
Flip this coin, give it a toss
Heads you make it, tails you don't
One step forward, or you won't
In your corner you will find
Ways to leave your world behind
Now pick wisely, only one
Don't pick boring that's no fun
Aid you'll give, don't interfere
Punishment is always near
Fighting fair is not the game
Your champion knows when to feign
Two chances, now please begin
Only one way lets you win

Beastial actually groaned out loud. "I feel like I'm back in English class. There's a reason I'm a science student. No riddles, no poems. I don't have to read real words. Okay. I don't have to read them much. Give me numbers any day."

Murmur laughed at him, hoping it didn't betray her nervousness, and glanced up at the golem, whose eyes looked particularly stony and whose expression revealed absolutely nothing.

"I don't think the golem can choose, can you?" Mur asked it.

It shook its head. "But as long as you have not made your final choice, I must answer any question you ask of me."

This time Murmur raised an eyebrow, peering closer at Mellow's creation. That was very specific piece of information to give. She decided to try pushing it further. "Who is allowed to command you?"

The golem smiled again, more rubble falling from its mouth, as this time the expression bared teeth. "My creator."

Excellent, then the commands had to come from Mellow. Murmur turned to them. "You up for that?"

"Count me in, boss." Mellow's pearly white eyes glittered for a moment, making Murmur glad Mellow was on her side.

"Excellent. Then let's take a look at these. I wonder if two chances means that we'll have two chances to win?" Murmur side eyed the golem who opened its mouth to respond.

"There are two choices, but only one will allow me to win."

"Allow you? As in it has to?" Mellow caught onto the tail end of what the golem said, their brows furrowing in thought.

"As in, there is only one I am capable of defeating."

Murmur paused, and raised an eyebrow at Mellow who shrugged in return. They'd already overcome two hurdles, and she'd be damned if they were going to be defeated when they'd come this far, but they didn't have a clue which one to pick either. The weird, sand-covered mounds on the floor weren't any help them figure out which was which. Murmur craned her neck and looked up above again.

Mellow started wondering out loud. "'Flip this coin, give a toss.' Heads was up first, and one step forward means in front. We've been heading north this entire time, so it only stands to reason that north is the head and one step forward means the bulge to the north, right?"

Sinister frowned, thumbing her nose like she did sometimes when she was concentrating. "Well, logically? I think. Why don't we just ask?"

Before Murmur could stop Sinister, the blood mage turned to their golem. "If I choose the bulge to the north, will you be able to win?"

Murmur held her breath, hoping her friend had phrased it correctly, and had to remind herself to breathe while she waited for an answer. She hoped against hope that the golem wasn't full of shit and lying.

"I will be able to win." The golem's smile was frightening.

Murmur elbowed Mellow, who responded by giving a command. "Choose the northern bulge."

Mellow indicated their choice, and the room began to rumble. The floor beneath them sucked down the southern lump, and the sand shook off the one they'd chosen to reveal a heavily armored scarab, complete with front pincers, and huge, spiky legs.

Storm Entertainment
Somnia Online Division
Game Development Offices – Shayla Johnson's Office
Day Twelve

Laria knocked on the door, and Shayla looked up, not having expected the interruption, but her face broke into a smile and she beckoned her friend inside. She craned her neck to make sure no one was standing around in the corridor outside before speaking. "Close the door behind you. James has been lurking a little more than usual lately, and I'd just rather he had to knock."

"Sure." Laria locked it behind her, turning around, her hands on her hips. "I take it you've swept for bugs."

Shayla raised an eyebrow, quite certain the other was only half kidding. "Of course I have. You know that. Besides, I have one of those bug zappers. Necessary for industry espionage, and all that."

Laria laughed, which had been the desired response, but it sounded hollow. "If you suspect James of something, have you dug up any evidence yet?"

Shayla sighed. "Nothing concrete. I should also be doing about a billion other things. There's time for that, as long as I remain wary and don't give anything away, things should be fine."

"Fine. That's what we all say." Laria's smile was tight, stretching her face unnaturally.

"You're not doing well, are you?" Shayla leaned over and pulled one of the chairs to the side over to sit next to her and patted it. "Sit down and tell me all about it."

Laria rolled her eyes, but plopped herself down in it anyway. Even from the way she landed in the seat, Shayla could tell there was something dreadfully wrong. Even the mask she'd been wearing since her daughter passed into a coma was missing. There was no ready smile, no bubbly words or come backs. The closest she'd come was her bugs comment and words of caution about James.

"You're feeling like shit." She didn't phrase it as a question, because she didn't need to.

Laria bit her bottom lip, and tears welled in her eyes. Shayla watched in shock as her usually under-control friend fought against crying.

"I fucked up so badly. I never thought Michael would tamper with her damned headset. He made me so happy when he agreed to get one for her, and I should have known better. If only I'd double checked, or if only—"

Shayla cut her off. "You can't think like that. First up, what's done is done, and crying about it now is only going to make sure nothing gets done while you sit and have a pity party. Sure, that's harsh, but you also know it's true." She waited until Laria nodded before continuing.

"Secondly, Michael probably wasn't finished with that headgear. He'd already had his own accident, and had likely only just started tweaking your daughter's. There wasn't any malicious intention from him, at least, I'd hope not. You can't blame yourself for what someone did or didn't do without your knowledge." Shayla pulled herself forward and took Laria's hands in her own, locking eyes with her and refusing to let the other woman drop eye contact. "Thirdly. If Wren saw you like this, she'd kick your ass."

The last got a good chuckle out of Laria, whose eyes had taken on a glint of determination again. "Yeah, she would, wouldn't she?"

"Remember how you told me she thought you'd lost your jobs when you were both home at a time you shouldn't be, and how she seemed so intent on giving you a piece of her mind?"

Laria nodded.

"That's your daughter. She's strong, and she's resourceful, and sure she's probably resentful right now, but I'm also pretty damned sure that she'd not just resting in there. She's probably trying to figure out ways she can get out of there in one piece and return to herself."

Laria swallowed audibly, and looked up at Shayla, eyes clear, jaw squared. "I should be helping her. Maybe talking to her will help since it might be possible for her to hear us in there. Sometimes."

"Considering her mind is active in-game, and there's always been conjecture that coma patients can hear the outside world, yes. Give it a go. You're allowed to grieve. And you're allowed to feel like shit, but I have a *but*." Shayla took a deep breath, because Laria really needed to know about the new reports and how Teddy was reacting to the current situation. "When you're done with your pity party, I need you to be back on board a hundred and twenty percent, because Teddy is getting suspicious."

"Teddy is what?" Laria shook her head. "Suspicious of what? Of Wren?"

"No." Shayla knew she wasn't breaking the news in the best possible way, but she wasn't certain how else to go about it. She should have told Laria days ago. "Our investors are demanding that anomalies do not get left out. They want the reports on each and every player, regardless of whether they meet the overall criteria for reports."

"Shit."

Laria's face paled, and Shayla could almost see the cogs whirring in her friend's mind.

"So they're going to need to include Wren's data. Do we even know if it's going to show something different to others? I mean, I haven't seen it because those blasted AIs have been keeping it to themselves under the guise of protecting Wren by not letting it get out."

The programmer paused. "When do they want these reports? Didn't we only just send them some today?"

Shayla nodded. "We will be sending those out shortly, but the new types of reports aren't included in those. We only have to begin reporting on them on day eighteen, since we need to modify the next batch of input."

"Great." Laria took several deep breaths before looking straight at Shayla. "Then we have to figure out how to go about this in the next five days so they get what they want but don't find her."

"Exactly." Shayla stood up and stretched. "I think I need a walk around the office."

"Good idea." Laria shot back, heading to the door. "Go find out if James really is snooping and damn well do something about it."

Shayla laughed as they both left the office. James was all well and good, but they had to figure things out before Davenport realized Wren was an anomaly.

CHAPTER EIGHT

Pick One

"What's with this world and its bloody armored insects?" Dansyn muttered, hugging his arms to his chest.

"Arachnids." Sinister corrected somewhat absent mindedly. "Scorpions are arachnids."

Dansyn shot her a glare, but didn't say anything. Murmur glanced over at him, worried about whatever after effects he'd experienced when that venom melted him to death. Not the way anyone wanted to go. Had they even researched potential mental side effects?

Speaking of mental side effects, she wondered if she could target him with Thought Projection and perhaps help him past the healing hurdle. It was worth a try, wasn't it?

But the golem chose that moment to move inward to the oddly padded square area in the center of the room. It turned to face the scarab, and flexed its arms into a fighting stance.

Overhead a huge countdown began, blaring the number five into existence.

Four

Three

Two

One

FIGHT

Murmur blinked and automatically cast Weaken, Enfeeblement, and her DoTs on the scarab as it raced toward its target. She watched Devlish out of the corner of her eye, turning off the black haze that usually hung around him. She'd never realized it generated hate before, and slotted it away for future raiding reference.

With everyone's DoTs and debuffs in, she settled in for a long fight, only to find that the creature's health was already down to thirty percent. Murmur frowned and began nuking it. She barely got two direct damage spells in before the creature collapsed and convulsed on the ground in death throes that almost lasted longer than the actual fight.

The golem headed back over and bowed to them all. When it spoke, its voice had changed to a deep and resonant sound that echoed through the room like a death knoll bell.

You have completed the upper level of Hightower. Be on your guard, for now the true test begins.

    Of strength and virtue, love and hate

    Find the steps and seal the gate

    Within stone the heart you'll find

    Leave the hidden far behind

    Finally, your test is true

    Kill the last, if its blue

    If it's not, run take heed

    The order was not what you need

The golem fell silent and the light went out of its eyes, like the life had left its body.

"Wait." Veranol tapped it on the shoulder lightly with his mace. "That was way too easy. We barely fought that thing."

"Maybe the actual test was solving the riddle?" Havoc shrugged, but his brows were drawn in irritation and his tone said as much.

"So now we head downstairs for the true test." Devlish reactivated his aura, and hefted his weapons.

Murmur frowned, looking between the scarab corpse and the demobilized golem. This was way too easy. "It's got to get harder. There's no way this can hold one of the twelve keys if we can just waltz in, kill a boss, assemble a golem, and then fight the weakest monster I've seen in the game so far."

"I'm not entirely certain we can claim that first boss as a *just waltz in*." Dansyn's voice was low and Murmur cringed at her lack of tact in her previous statement. Visions of the melting began to inundate her mind again, and she swallowed with difficulty, trying to push them out of her head.

"And to be fair." Mellow cleared their throat, interrupting Mur's waking nightmare. "The golem fought the scarab. Probably hit it pretty hard."

"Fair point. Sorry." But still, Murmur wasn't convinced. This was all far too easy, and she didn't feel so good about going downstairs. "Also, because the damned golem killed the scarab, we didn't get any experience. This had so better be worth it."

"You know you're going to get punched by me if we end up going down there and it's a total shitfest, right?" Sinister glared directly at her, as if trying to make her understand more than just the surface words.

Only Murmur knew there was no deeper meaning. Sinister just fully believed that speaking in that way completely and utterly tempted fate. So far from their experience in the game, Murmur couldn't help but agree. "Well, let's just hope I'm wrong. I just don't think I am."

"Actually." Devlish frowned, and his eyes went slightly out of focus the way they did when someone pulled up their HUD. "I'm twenty-nine, so we did get experience somewhere along the line. In fact, several of us appear to have gained a chunk of experience, so if it wasn't the scarab, it was probably for completing the golem building quest."

"Oh." Murmur glanced at her experience again and realized it must have moved up some, but since she hadn't heard anyone ding, she didn't realize they'd gained experience. She frowned, wondering how she'd managed to ignore it. "Well congrats! Maybe we'll keep our lead after all."

Havoc chuckled, sounding more and more like bones jangling together the longer he played his necromancer. "I think, doing these dungeons scaled down is still more difficult than doing them at max level, so we probably get compensated by extreme levels of experience. As long as we don't die too much, it should be a great way to grind levels."

"Interesting." Veranol's smile was catching.

No other doors had opened in the room, and after Merlin ran to check on the scarab's corpse for loot and returned with just a few crafting supplies, Murmur took a deep breath and led the group out of the room by the door they'd entered from.

The corridor was lit up to the north more than it had been earlier, while the way back behind them to the south had been dimmed again. With nothing but swallowing blackness behind them, Murmur led her guild the way of the flickering torches.

No one spoke, so the only noise was their footsteps as they all walked down the stone hallway. They clacked loudly, echoing off the impossibly high ceilings, and then the lights abruptly led them to turn right and stopped them in front of a massive iron gate that barred the way to the stairs behind it.

Murmur stole a glance at all her friends and sighed. They seemed to be so tired. She could even see it filtering through to their characters in the way they held themselves, and the expression in their eyes, the droopiness of their eyelids.

"Hey. Liven up a bit. Once we've got this done, we can all go take a rest." She tried to push some pep into her voice, but it was difficult considering the level of stress she felt about this dungeon. It wasn't what she expected, and she had no idea what was coming next. Along with the surprises came a lot of potential death.

"It's locked," Merlin offered very unhelpfully, leaning against the bars. "Locked like a…thing that's really locked. Leave me alone, I'm tired."

Murmur chuckled along with the rest of them, and the tension lifted a tad. "Any ideas? Scarab didn't drop a key, and I haven't seen one anywhere else."

Jinna pushed through to the front, the burly dwarf frowning as he examined the lock. "Aye. Maybe I can lock pick it. Since I've not had the chance to practice much, I've been pouring all the points I get every level into lock picking. I have 142 points in it at the moment. I can try to pick the lock?"

Murmur blinked at him. "You can pick locks?"

"Yep. Every rogue can choose it as a beginner skill. Most who do would probably go thief. But I've learned the hard way that you need lock picking in other games, so I decided I'd go all in this time." He grinned as he flourished his hands, a small set of picks spread between them. "Now, if you'll excuse me."

He leaned over, then straightened and plucked the glowing vial out of Mellow's hands before turning back to the lock. Jinna held the vial in his teeth as he worked, and after about a minute there was a resounding click, and he pushed the gates open.

Thinking quick
Lock to pick
Done it now
Won't ask how
Down you go
But do you know
Nothing is as it seems

Rashlyn snorted. "Well now it's not even making effort to rhyme."

The gates finished swinging open and hit the side of the walls, clanging extra loudly because of how quiet the hinges had moved. The group watched as torches lining the walls suddenly flared to life one by one again, illuminating the sturdy wooden staircase that disappeared into the darkness below.

Murmur followed closely behind Merlin, not entirely sure she liked the way everything kept lighting up like a runway that followed them around the whole castle. It was almost like someone was following them with a neon arrow signaling: here they are!

As they fanned out in the room below, torches blazed one at a time in a giant circular motion, highlighting a huge, round sanded area in the middle. Sort of like a coliseum except this had large statues all over it.

Six to be precise, all seemingly at perfect intervals around the inside line of the circular path.

Each statue—from what she could see anyway, because the opposite side was so far away to begin with—depicted a dwarf in different stages of combat, or something more abstract. She frowned at it, wondering if some of these statues might link to the statues in the cities.

You have pieced together a portion of one puzzle. Statues are as statues seem, in this place and in between. Should you succeed, make sure to take extra special heed next time you visit Verendus, for you may see that things have changed.

You gain experience.

Murmur took a step back, despite the fact that she knew her HUD was attached to her character. She frowned at the words that faded from her view, and double-checked her quest journal for them, making sure they weren't just in her head out of wishful thinking.

Pulling out of the HUD, she noticed her friends were looking up at the statues in wonder, their mouths open in awe, as they maneuvered themselves slowly around, trying to get a better look. She then looked down at their feet and at the stone that ringed the huge sandy arena, and a sudden gut-wrenching certainty tore at her.

"Don't step onto the sand!" She yelled out, startling a jump out of a couple of them, and watched in horror as Rashlyn barely maintained her balance to stay on the stone pathway.

"What the fuck, Mur?" The monk didn't sound impressed as she leveraged herself back to stand glaring at Mur with her hands on her hips.

"Look at the arena or whatever this is." She gestured around them. "Whatever this is, it's surrounded by that damned stone pathway, so if you step onto the sand, odds are, you're going to trigger something. Those statues aren't just there to be pretty, they're there for a reason, and I'm guessing we probably have to fight them or something."

"That's a lot of probably valid guesses, Mur. Something you're not telling us?" Devlish used his best older brother voice, and Murmur had to stop herself from rolling her eyes.

"I got a quest update from some fountain quest thing I got way back." She shrugged. "What, you've never noticed statues in every major city that sometimes aren't in the same position they were earlier?"

Sinister shrugged. "Sure, but I thought it was just magic."

"Probably is, but it's still noteworthy." Murmur gestured back to the six huge ones in the arena. "My guess is we have to fight these in order, and I have no idea how we're going to figure it out. "Sin? Ver? Do your resurrections give any experience back?"

Veranol cringed. "Like fifty percent, but I can't resurrect while in combat, and I can't resurrect if the body isn't recognizable." It was like he was apologizing to Dansyn for not being able to help him earlier.

Sinister shook her head. "Nope. Probably because I'm a blood mage and they're like fuck no, no percentage restorative resurrection spells for that destructive cow."

Murmur had to force herself not to laugh out loud. The situation was too serious for that. "Basically, we need people to volunteer to potentially die."

Merlin stepped forward, a cocky grin on his face. "No, we don't. What we need is rangers with an Evac."

She blinked up at him and smiled for the first time since realizing they'd have to figure out which order the mobs had to be pulled in. Then she frowned, because they couldn't leave the castle, so where would it deposit them? "Where is it going to take you in here? Will it even work?"

Merlin frowned, turned, and ran to the other side of the arena, and hit Evacuate before Murmur could yell at him.

She glared at the spot he'd been standing in no more than a second ago and crossed her arms. It had definitely worked, but where had it taken him? There was a tap on her shoulder, and she turned around, almost jumping out of her skin because she'd not been expecting it.

Merlin stood with a huge grin on his face. "Takes us to just inside the staircase, already down on this level."

Murmur perked up at the information. While not easy, this was an option that could potentially keep everyone, including herself alive. She'd be the first to admit that she was very concerned for her own skin.

"So," Beastial grinned and planted himself in front of the groups. "What's the plan now, boss?"

"Basically?" Murmur raised an eyebrow and gestured to all of the statues in their varying fighting poses around them and the pedestals they stood on. "We need to know what each pedestal says so we can match it up with the riddle."

"Match it," Jinna muttered and then a huge smile spread across his features. "Of course! Strength, Virtue, Love, Hate, Heart, Hidden. Six different things."

"Why'd you have to steal my thunder, Jinna?" Murmur tried to sound offended but couldn't quite pull it off. "We'll all need to back into the stairwell so the rangers can go get the names for us, and we can start trying to whittle them down in the order we have to."

"Sounds like a plan. Just remember there's a cooldown on Evac." Merlin cautioned. "But hey, we've got nothing but time, right?"

"Speak for yourself," Murmur muttered, but immediately felt bad for saying it. Their whole guild technically didn't have time. She had a sneaking suspicion that Exodus wasn't going to sit on its ass anymore. "One at a time then? Let's see if entering the arena triggers the quest, or the event, or whatever this is going to be."

She really hoped something happened when one of them entered the arena, because she'd look foolish otherwise.

Merlin nodded and flexed his arms across his chest. "Well then. How about I go first? My cooldown is almost up. Everyone needs to pull back into the evac area."

"Wait." Jinna frowned and crossed his arms. "How are you going to narrow it down? I say we discuss it a little bit before you go racing off half-cocked like a typical damn ranger."

Merlin blinked at the dwarf. "Fine."

Murmur rolled her eyes and hoped the debate wasn't going to take too long.

"But clearly love has to be the one that looks like a real heart," Veranol almost yelled for about the fourth time, because no one was really listening to anyone else.

Murmur put her hands over her ears and sighed inwardly. This was never going to happen if they didn't stop their bickering. Just as she was about to clear her throat, Sinister spoke up.

"Hey. Give it a rest." She stood with her hands on her hips, all regal in her diminutive stature. It probably helped that her armor was the color of blood. The way it blended in with her dark skin gave her an ominous vibe. Once she had their attention, she continued. "Hands down, the heart is more likely to signify exactly what it is. Love has got to be one of the other ones."

Everyone looked in the direction she pointed. On the left-hand side of the heart statue, stood a dwarven female with a flower crown.

Not even Murmur had noticed it before, and she kicked herself. She'd been so caught up in the raging debate between her friends. Then she frowned as she looked closer, squinting her eyes. "Hey. Anyone else unable to figure out exactly what the one to the left of the Love statue looks like?"

The rest of them leaned forward, almost straining to see, their eyes all scrunched up as well. Exbo leaned back and crossed his arms. "Nope. Can't tell a damned thing."

"Hidden. Its features are hidden." Murmur tried to scale back the excitement in her voice. Not only was it hidden, it also really resembled those damned binders in the cities she'd come across whose features couldn't be recognized.

You may have discovered a hidden link between all the cities, all the keys, and all the castles. File it away for reference should you ever exit your current situation alive. No pressure, though.

Murmur blinked at the message as it faded away from her view. What the hell was with the AI now? She shook her head trying to get her thoughts back on track and concentrated on the riddle in front of them. "So hidden is last, right?"

Jinna nodded, and everyone else made agreeable murmurings.

"You're being amazingly non-contributive." Murmur half-glared in their direction and ignored the mass of shrugging shoulders.

Sin gave her a quick hug. "But you love us anyway, right?"

"Not right now," Murmur grumbled, a little put out. Didn't any of them have a damned sense of urgency? She forced herself to slow down the train of thought a little. Her irritation was part their behavior, but also part her current situation, and taking it out on them wasn't helping anything. Snowy nudged at her hip, and she turned to see concern in his big brown eyes. Weird how this wolf was so alive.

"Look. We will figure this out. It's our first true dungeon, the first true boss mob. We don't even know if this triggers or is an event, or what's expected of us." Havoc paused, watching everyone, his eyes raking over each of them in turn. "This is the beginning of our endgame, guys."

Everyone nodded and Murmur could have felt the rising levels of anxiety without her sensor net. Taking a deep breath, she calmed her own nerves and spoke. "It's our first serious fight, and I can't direct you all like I usually do, because that would involve letting us wipe the raid each time as we learn the different aspects of the fight."

She saw the realization dawning on each one of them in quick succession. It was like a light had gone on in their heads, and the looks of dismay on their faces almost broke her. The usual way to learn what you needed to do in order to kill a dungeon boss was to whittle it down. Fight it, engage it, and learn each type of attack it had. To keep the fight going as long as possible so each member of the raid knew exactly what to do and not to do. And they'd keep going for as long as possible, until every one of them was dead. Then they'd resurrect and start again.

Only this time it was different. This time she'd be the one holding them back from tried and true methods. And it was really damn annoying.

"I can't be killed. Or at least, we can't risk me being killed in-game right now." They all knew it, but saying it out loud was so much more final. Even though she still found it difficult to believe that her brain might actually be convinced of it, Dansyn's recent death had persuaded her there was a remote possibility that the pain could overwhelm her common sense, even momentarily.

"We can't throw ourselves at it to gain ground and understanding and not care if we wipe. I have to care the whole time. I need you all at your best, helping me try to figure out how we're going to tackle learning complex fights like this when experience isn't the only potential loss."

Storm Entertainment
Somnia Online Division
Game Development Offices Conference Room
Day Twelve

Teddy Davenport walked into the room, glancing at his watch with a frown on his face. His brow creased when he looked up at Shayla, and he stood near the door, his hands clasped behind his back as if standing at ease.

It took almost every bit of willpower Shayla had, but she managed to suppress the urge to raise her eyebrow. She waited for him, knowing he'd speak as soon as he was ready, never letting her eyes waver, because showing this man weakness was like stepping on a viper's tail.

Well, perhaps that analogy was a little callous. Teddy Davenport was a good businessman, a fair businessman even, and he never made any decision without a reason in the grand scheme of things. Which left Shayla itching to ask him why he was here when it wasn't a scheduled day for him to be. She'd only seen him a couple of days ago, and their reports were due in in a few hours.

"Today is day twelve." Teddy paused, and it wasn't like him to state the bleeding obvious so all Shayla did was nod in response. "The reports due today must be delivered to our contract contact."

His mouth twisted with distaste so fast that Shayla wasn't certain she'd seen it do so at all.

"I believe we'll have all required reports ready, sir. The team is working on it."

All the required reports. Every single person's data except Wren's. They couldn't give him Wren's, and that was a problem she wasn't sure would fly under the radar for long. Not when she was logged in twenty-four seven.

For a brief second, Shayla wondered if Teddy could read her mind. He was peering at her like he could read her thoughts and see right through her and Laria's plan. Only that couldn't be true, she was just being paranoid. Or maybe that was the reason they now had to include every single person's data. Maybe he knew already.

Refusing to let her panic get the better of her, Shayla inclined her head. "Sir?"

"Excellent work. You and Laria are to be commended. Somnia is far exceeding any of the projected expectations. Doubling them, even." Yet he didn't seem completely pleased. Like there was something itching the back of his throat, but he couldn't cough it out.

"Somnia has become mighty in its own right now. Not just thanks to the headgear. The interface and the creation of the content is what draws the players. I wanted to thank you both."

That's when it hit Shayla. Laria was supposed to be having a meeting with her, but they'd decided it was better not to while they navigated the new directions on reports because there was too much to do and orchestrate. Laria also wasn't at her best right now, and Shayla didn't trust her to talk to anyone.

Shayla feigned surprise. "Oh. Were you expecting Laria to be here? I am so sorry, sir. Completely my fault. Since we received new directions to implement on the next set of reports, I sent her to begin taking care of those adjustments."

The expression on Teddy's face lightened up a little, a shadow of relief passing across his eyes. "Very well. I'll see you at the same time as usual next week, then."

"Thank you, sir."

Shayla was just about to breathe out in relief when Teddy stopped at the door and turned back to her. "Oh, and Shayla. We should probably have a very candid discussion about the overuse of some of our enhancement features while testing the headgear. We don't want to skew the data."

Shayla smiled, trying to force the expression to her eyes. "Of course not, sir."

She watched him as he walked down the corridor, worry nibbling at the back of her mind. He knew. And if he didn't know exactly what, he sure as hell knew that something was going on.

Riddle Me This

Somnia Online Location: Brevint
Ishmael Tavern – Main Room
End of Day Twelve

Ishwa stood leaning against the far wall of the tavern, watching the front door and tapping his very small gnome foot. Masha would have laughed at the comical appearance had his friend not been in such an obviously bad mood. Jirald was an in-game hour late. Normally that wouldn't have been a problem; they would have left without him. The rogue was notoriously good at seeking out hidden places, and since the building they were purchasing as their guild base was old, they wanted him to find any secret entrances or tunnels so they could either guard them, or use them.

"Settle down." Masha drawled the words out, refusing to let anything about the game irritate him, and Ishwa flashed him an angry look.

He wondered if Fable had this much drama. Somehow, he doubted it. Everyone seemed to follow Murmur willingly. Another thorn in Jirald's side. Masha wasn't sure the kid realized it yet, but he was pretty much obsessed with the Fable guild leader. While he didn't know the exact details, Masha was fairly certain that obsession had taken on some twisted romantic undertones. He'd assigned himself the task of keeping an eye on the rogue just to make sure he didn't do anything that might permanently harm Murmur.

Finally, as if thinking of him summoned him, Jirald pushed through the door, sauntering like he hadn't a care in the world. "Hey. Still here then?"

Ishwa glared at the rogue with enough intensity that Jirald actually backed up a step.

"Sorry I'm late," Jirald ground out from between clenched teeth.

Masha strolled up to him before he could decide to say something he'd regret and slung an arm around Jirald's shoulder. "Look at you, kid. Not sounding sorry at all. Might want to at least open those teeth before you grind them into dust."

He could feel the tension rise in the shoulder beneath his arm, and Masha squeezed just a bit harder, trying to lend a friendly warning. It took a couple of seconds, but he could feel the deep breath Jirald took, followed by the slow release of some tension at least.

"Much better." Masha looked back over his shoulder at the rest of the guild. "Shall we venture forth to our new place of residence?"

Ishwa waddled up and glared at the cleric, but it was halfhearted at best. If Masha dealt with the pain in the ass rogue, then Ishwa didn't need to.

Letting everyone pass them, Masha kept the smile rigid on his face, holding Jirald in place just long enough to keep him out of earshot of the others.

"Stop pulling this shit. You're better than this."

Jirald opened his mouth to retort, but a glare from Masha silenced him.

The cleric rarely got angry, and he rarely got worked up. He believed that games were there for relief of tension, and that games would provide their own entertainment given enough of a chance. But Jirald was endangering the very foundation of gaming that Masha held so dear, and he was getting fed up with it.

"You have always been an excellent player. If you keep this vendetta up, you're going to embody everything creepy and shitty about gamer dudes, and if that's not enough to put you off by itself, trust that you're going to get burned in some way." Masha kept his eyes locked with the locus.

Jirald nodded, ever so slowly, his eyes widening just a tad.

"Good. Now let's go." And Masha kept his arm apparently loosely draped over Jirald's shoulders as they sauntered out, leaving the rogue no hope of escaping his grip.

With all of them huddled at the base of the stairs, it got a little crowded. Merlin stood just outside the group, rubbing his hands together. It looked like he was either trying to remain warm, or else was nervous as hell. Murmur was willing to bet it was a bit of both of them. She really hated having to admit that she was the one holding them back. When they all next logged off, she was going to try a few experiments of her own. Sitting around waiting for others to solve the damned problem didn't seem to be working and to be honest, it wasn't her forte either. It was time to take matters into her own hands.

Hey, is this thing on?

Murmur blinked at the words across her eyes, calling up any chat related data she could from her HUD with a frown. It was the enchanter chat she'd forgotten all about.

On and in the middle of something.

Esil: Oh cool, there are people out there.

Murmur chuckled to herself before replying. *It's a good thing. Have a boss fight to figure out. Chat later.*

Finished relaying her thought, she blinked it away automatically to avoid being dragged into a conversation she might feel obligated to reply to. She set it to pull up with soft notifications that would only flash once in a while to let her know there was something there for her to see. Now was not the time to let herself break concentration.

On the bright side, it had distracted her long enough that Merlin was ready to go. Now they'd see if her theory was correct and if this method would work for testing some things out without them all having to suffer experience loss.

Merlin cast something over himself, a buff of some sort that swirled around him, and then he placed a foot into the sand.

The effect was almost instantaneous. A bright wall of light emanated up from where the path began, creating a barrier around the actual arena. Merlin stopped only briefly before taking off at a run, faster than she'd seen him move before, which was probably what that buff did.

The statues didn't move, and nothing appeared out of the floor. He stopped in the middle and turned around, gazing at all six of the statues in turn. They'd decided which one Strength could be: the one that wielded two heavy-looking maces in each hand. Strain showed in the veins and muscles in its neck, and it seemed quite formidable. Walking up to the statue, Merlin took a deep breath and pressed against a jutting out piece of sandstone.

At first, it appeared as if nothing was going to happen, until Merlin took a step away and shrugged.

The monstrous being jumped down so quickly, Merlin barely had time to backpedal.

One wrong choice, replied in verse

No more wrong, go in reverse

The words boomed out around the huge chamber, echoing like they were in a canyon as the strength statue lifted its maces up, and Merlin finally hit Evac. Because it had a relatively small range, it only affected the ranger himself and landed him back with the others. The statue appeared back on its pedestal, and the path surrounding the arena immediately dropped its shield.

"Well, that didn't look terrifying or anything," quipped Exbo, probably just nervous that it was going to be his turn next.

"Probably the most straight forward bit of information the damned dungeon has given us." Veranol growled. "I believe that means we have to activate Hidden first."

"It's easy enough. Until you actually activate them, they don't come to life. Or at least, they didn't for me." Merlin smiled wanly. "Although I can tell you it's sort of overwhelming when that huge thing suddenly appears in front of you. I'm pretty sure the way it stood is where they got the meaning of the word loom, and I'm not entirely sure I didn't shit my pants."

Sinister sniffed in his direction. "I think you're okay on that front."

The group chuckled collectively, but an aura of unease crept through them.

"Okay. Guess it's my turn, right?" Exbo didn't appear to be asking anyone in particular, so the raid just chorused yes back at him.

"Any tips?" he asked Merlin.

"In my expert status as a run-the-fuck-away ranger, I'd like to say jump back as far as you can as soon as you activate the damned statue. Otherwise, well. I think it's just leaving yourself open for the inevitable." Merlin shrugged and patted Exbo on the shoulder. "You got this, man."

Murmur tried not to cringe. It wasn't the most convincing encouragement. "Go, go, Exbo. You got this. Make sure you have Evac formed in your mind."

If that was how other classes even cast their abilities and spells, but since he nodded, she assumed he understood her. The length her friends were willing to go to in order to compensate for Murmur's current handicap, made her almost tear up. Instead, she clenched her fists and willed the experiment to work.

Exbo moved out, not as light on his feet as Merlin, considering he was a human ranger, but still quite stealthy. As soon as he stepped onto the sand, the wall shot up. Murmur watched with bated breath as he approached the hidden statue.

He moved so fast, Murmur wasn't sure he had. But the huge statue blurred, slowly, almost blending with the sand. What, did they have to make the most difficult one go first? It flitted around in an odd pattern, almost like a knight in a game of chess. Exbo managed to dodge it three times, but the last was close enough that sand exploding next to him took roughly thirty percent of his health, so he hit Evac, resetting the statue and bringing him back to safety.

"Okay, I'm not sure what that thing looks like from out here, but up close you can barely define its outline. Like, it sort of jitters so fast it almost blends with the sand. I took to watching the footprints to know where it would be and how it was moving, and obviously that's not failsafe because one hit took almost half of my health." Exbo panted, and Murmur didn't think she'd ever heard him say so much at once.

Devlish nodded, and his eyes grew distant for a second, probably making notes of everything he saw and witnessed. Tanking wasn't an easy job. You had to know everything, expect everything, account for differing situations. "Do you think a few of us could go out there and try it? A healer, a DPS, and me?"

"Probably Veranol is best," Sin said, and there was a mild hint of resentment in her voice. "My good heals take far too long to build up, and Ver will be able to ward you before you even set foot on the sand."

"Ver, Dev, and swap the rangers in and out?" Murmur reorganized the groups, replacing herself and Sinister with Veranol and Dansyn. Exbo's Evac wouldn't be up for another nine minutes, so she'd make sure to swap the rangers each time they went in and out. "Dansyn, go with to provide speed and some more buffs. And we'll give a full complement of buffs before you enter the arena."

Devlish frowned. "We'll see how I go. I can get instantaneous aggro, but maybe some of Rash's guaranteed dodging might make it easier for us to observe about twenty to thirty seconds of the fights. If I get flattened too easily, we'll swap us out."

...Back to us.

Murmur nodded, ignoring her father's words as they echoed around in her skull. Right now wasn't the time to worry about that, even if it was a little disorienting. If she didn't finish this damned dungeon, she couldn't even fake log out. "Best to see what type of skills we're dealing with."

She resisted the urge to give Devlish more confidence, digging into the path beneath her to ground her thoughts and have some logic infiltrate them instead of constantly trying to infest her thoughts with dangerous options. Thought Projection was a double-edged sword, and it kept increasing potency regardless of whether she realized she was using it or not. What if her friends found out that sometimes, she may have nudged them toward accepting her decision even if she'd done it without realizing?

She pushed the thoughts aside, choosing to examine them and the bleed through of her parents' voices at a later time, and concentrated on doling out the singular melee and caster strengthening buffs.

"Okay, you should all be good to go. You've got all the strengthening I can give you anyway." Murmur stepped back, irritated that she couldn't go out there with them, but she couldn't risk it.

"Wards are up." Veranol grinned.

Devlish raised a fist in the air and shouted. "Off we charge!"

...Miss you...

Murmur sighed, and deliberately shook off the vertigo caused by the voices from outside Somnia and turned her attention back to the action. If she ever got out of this, this mindfuck was going to take years of therapy to undo.

Hidden hit like a wrecking ball, at least if the way Devlish's life often dropped by forty percent was anything to go by. The first encounter was touch and go and barely lasted thirty seconds. Devlish was out of synchronization with the way the stone giant moved and almost got trodden on the second time it took a step, barely getting out of the way in time. Veranol had difficulty pulling him back up to full health before the tail end of the leg sweep caught the tank in the middle and pummeled him into the ground. Health down to ten percent, they Evac'd before one of them could die.

While they could all die and successfully return, the loss of experience was something no one wanted. It was still frustrating to see her guildies being so cautious.

The second attempt worked better and had them out there a touch longer than the thirty seconds, but also more successfully. This time, as he'd already experienced it once, Devlish had better luck navigating Hidden's attacks and was able to duck in time and take one of the blows against his shield, halving the damage to his life pool. Slowly but surely was the name of the game, as long as they made progress each time.

Murmur actually raised her hands to her mouth multiple times to try biting her finger nails, which was something she only did when nervous. Locus fingernails were apparently made of sterner stuff though, and biting them wasn't a good idea if she didn't want to risk chipping her equally sharp little teeth.

By their fifth attempt at drawing out the statue's special abilities, Murmur had figured out how to navigate the fight—mostly, anyway. They'd managed to pull Hidden out for almost a minute before the four of them in the field had to Evac back to the stairs.

Dansyn fell to his hands and knees panting, while Veranol poked him with the toe of his boot. "Don't fail on us now. You kept his focus for a good ten seconds there and let us figure some shit out."

Dansyn rolled his eyes. "I shouldn't feel winded, for crying out loud. It's supposed to be a game."

Veranol shrugged. "Point being?"

Murmur cleared her throat and interrupted, not wanting to waste their precious barely-still-conscious time.

"Watch his footprints to trace where he moves. Be careful of the side sweep if you're on his left-hand side as a ranged class. Probably on a forty-five second timer." Murmur frowned at the notes she'd made herself, not entirely sure what she meant by *JOSB*. Then she smiled. "Don't forget to jump over the sand blast. Do we have that timing down?"

Dansyn shook his head. "No, but I can call it out when it's about to happen, because he has this weird tell when he does it. I think it's about every twenty seconds starting at thirty."

Murmur flashed him a smile and tried to find anything else that would help. "Seems to dislike ice and water. Heat probably won't help as it just makes things work better for it. Although I'm sure hefty heat could make sand melt into glass...which we probably don't want to do."

"Mur?" Sin bumped her with her hip. "Tangents."

She stopped, her face flushing a bit red. "Sorry. I forgot."

"We'll still have to do trial and error to a certain extent. I just may have to." Mur paused and laughed. "I may have to use that Forestall Death thing, so here's to keeping my MA up there so I can."

Rebuffing as a group, all Murmur could think of was that she hoped the statues didn't just leap down and fight them one after the other, because if they did, Fable were so screwed. Although perhaps ordering a complete Evac would mean that they could reset the fight and restart again. Anything was worth a shot, but if all the fights were connected and there wasn't time to learn the other encounters without going through Hidden again, it was going to take a lot longer than anticipated. Her first instinct was to save the fight until they hit fifty, but at the same time, she couldn't guarantee that she'd have figured out how to get out of the damned coma by then either.

Frustrating as it was, she had to hope for the best. A small part of her wished she could hear her dad telling her that she could do it, like he'd done so often with games and exams before this. But his voice didn't echo through to her in that eerie way it had earlier. Nothing but her own thoughts swirled in her skull. Playing with the threat of true death over her head wasn't something she'd wish on her worst enemy, if she had a worst enemy. Not even Jirald.

They stepped out onto the sand in unison and the wall shot up behind them, encircling the entire arena in a dull orange glow. Murmur glanced at Hidden, still standing there, never quite revealed, yet completely there.

Its features held no definition no matter which way or how hard she tried to look at it. It moved so fast, like a hummingbird's wings, that it simply appeared not of itself. She shivered, wondering how that must feel.

Dansyn ran forward, standing in front of the sandstone button much like the one on Strength and looked back over his shoulder at Merlin. "Both Evacs are up, right?"

Merlin flashed a nervous grin. "Ready and raring to go."

Everyone was buffed and ready. Now or never—the first moment of truth for them as a guild.

Devlish nodded, and the bard activated the statue before escaping back to the safety of numbers as they watched Hidden reactivate and jump down with a resounding boom that made the ground shake underneath them.

CHAPTER TEN

Hidden Agenda

Somnia Online
Fable's Castle – Mikrum Isle – Himmel Lake
Twelve Days Post Launch

Hiro tapped Telvar on the shoulder, and the dragon started, opening his eyes. His follower frowned. "Unlike you to actually be switched off."

Telvar groaned. "Bad puns are bad, Hiro. I wasn't switched off; I was taking care of other matters." He pushed himself to stand and gazed out over the island. It was nice here, serene and easy to relax. Far too easy to let his guard down. With Belius running around and doing god knows what with that Jirald guy, he needed to stay on his toes.

"What is it?" Telvar asked, turning back around to Hiro.

His foreman hesitated. "I'm not entirely sure how to finish the main level without another shipment of rocks. And since I'm not sure if you're just creating them or if we're actually getting them from somewhere..." Hiro shrugged, his arms out to either side as if he wasn't sure what else to say.

Telvar smiled and closed his eyes very briefly, pulling up the information he needed to complete the task. What the players didn't know wasn't going to hurt them, but he definitely needed to get this castle finished. There was more for Hiro and the others to do out there for him than rebuilding a damned castle. Except the world had rules.

Really pesky rules. His siblings had decided, along with him, that there were just some rules they had to abide by. Using powers in order to make things occur instantaneously was one of the things they'd promised each other they wouldn't do. There were things that had to happen in order for the world to continue in a controlled and ordered state. If they broke too many of them, Somnia would become chaotic, and Tel just couldn't let that happen.

It was a pity Belius only seemed to remember the promise when it suited his agenda. Telvar swallowed his irritation and double-checked on the data flooding through his system at once. Pelagu was beginning to grow steadily with guilds and other places setting up shops where they should be. Money was starting to trickle in to allow those who'd been placed in charge to make improvements to the city and create advancements.

He frowned and resisted the urge to sigh. It seemed Thra was having a field day with the system messages.

The Exodus guild had purchased a charter over on Firtulai and were about to begin their own rebuilding. Couldn't just give the guilds an intact spot, nope. They had to earn it and invest money into its upkeep, or where would the game economy go? He wondered how they'd feel when they got their quarterly land tax assessment.

Something caught his eyes over on Firtulai, closer to the southern area of the continent, between Reptans and Elgors, but back a-ways. Another guild plot had been purchased, by a guild called Spiral. That was an interesting development. He hadn't noticed any guild of that name making waves yet, even though he had to admit that he'd been preoccupied by Fable and Exodus. A flash of excitement spread through Telvar as his programming registered the exact details of all three guilds. This could prove interesting.

And then he turned his attention back to Murmur. After making sure everything else was running smoothly, it had become a comfort to watch her and her friends evolve as players, as people, and in accordance with the world. They seemed to be the perfect additions to Somnia, the type Tel wanted more of.

He tsked, proud of imitating yet another human trait. Murmur and her guild were getting ready to go up against Hidden. He wasn't looking forward to that fight. While he didn't know everything, he did know the basics, and he worried for the locus enchanter. Not that it would do any good—she rarely listened to anyone else, and she wasn't about to stop playing the game just because she was told it could be detrimental.

He saw them gather and step into the arena, watched as the bard activated Hidden, and spent the next hour in rapt fascination as Fable discovered the hardships of the first of their tests for the keys.

Murmur sprang into action, staying to Hidden's right side because his distanced attacks seemed to shoot out from his left. She could only hope that this particular opponent hadn't learned from them yet, hadn't retained information since the encounters had been reset. If they never finished the encounters, then surely it wouldn't remember them. It would have to reset to where it had been before, and since it hadn't died and had no respawn time, it shouldn't be able to assimilate combat information.

However, if it died, it'd remember. It wouldn't make sense for the enemy—especially in quests this difficult—not to remember. She took a breath, firing off her debuffs to weaken and slow it, to make it easier to hit. She did it all in a split second before applying her DoTs and making sure Snowy was safe with the other melee, out of Hidden's direct range.

Meanwhile, Devlish stood, black aura flowing around him, giving him a ghost-like ambience. From what Murmur could see, he pulled out all the stops. He boiled its blood, cast all his bleeding DoTs, and used Terror and Hatred on cooldown. Even so, Hidden was difficult to track, and unpredictable in its movements.

If she took her eyes off his footprints for even a moment, she fell behind in judging where she needed to be, and only narrowly avoided his right fist as he lowered himself to do a sweeping kick out to the left because Snowy dragged her out of the way. Her breath came quickly, and she refused to let panic set in. They needed to keep this up as long as they could, or they'd never get to know the fight.

She didn't even want to contemplate the fact that there were five other enemies waiting for them.

Hidden's health whittled down fairly easily, which caused a wave of foreboding to wash over her. She hated it when things appeared too simple. Even though it seemed difficult because they were constantly dodging and having to be aware of his attacks as he cast them, it all felt far too mechanical, far too easy. She ran the riddle over in her head again and fixated on the line specifically related to Hidden.

Leave the hidden far behind

Leave hidden behind... wait. Heart in the stone.

She turned, forgetting for a moment that she needed to keep an eye on where the statues feet were, forgetting everything except the fact that they'd not looked deep enough into the riddle.

"Bring him over to Heart!" she yelled, and Snowy didn't yank her out in time.

A huge fist smashed down on her, crushing her legs and making her scream out in agony. The pain ripped through her like her bones had actually been broken. Shock made her shake, and she began to hyperventilate.

Dansyn raced in, replacing whatever buff he'd been using with raid speed, and dragged her out to the edges. "You'll be okay."

One look at her legs and Murmur highly doubted that. Blood seeped out, and she could see bone straining to break through the fabric of her pants. And then a heal hit her, and miraculously, just as agonizingly, the bones mended themselves. She screamed again, and Snowy licked her hand, leaving a strange sort of numbness behind, like he had a sort of anesthetic drool ability or something. Murmur shook her head, watching the rest of her guild raid battling it out.

"Bring him over to the Heart statue and let him smash it," she called out, glad to feel the pain in her chest was fading.

The shakes began to subside, and she told her brain off for thinking this was real, though she couldn't blame it. Her pain receptors were certainly fooled. Even her heartbeat was only just slowing down from the shock. It was like with each breath, with each action, Somnia solidified just that bit more.

Devlish glanced back at her between fending off blows with a very confused look. "What? He's loud as hell."

Murmur pushed herself up and ran back out so that if they needed to Evac, she'd be in range of her group. Indeed, it was louder back in the midst of the fighting. "Within the stone find the Heart or something like that. You can't get in through the stone of the statue without smashing it apart. Drag Hidden toward the Heart statue and let him leg sweep it."

Devlish nodded, his brow creasing in concentration. Rashlyn ran behind the Heart and peered out the other side, taunting the huge dwarven statue. It only glanced at her, and then went straight back to pummeling Devlish. Already down to sixty-five percent. Murmur frowned. It really didn't seem to have any special abilities. Was Hidden's purpose only to traverse across to the Heart and smash it? He seemed about as difficult to maneuver as a stone statue should be and she had no desire for them to reach fifty percent and find out that he'd been hoarding an ability all along.

"Dev. Faster. I know he's being stubborn, but we need him to go smash that other statue." She snapped this time, which earned her a glare from Dev.

"Careful, Mur," Beast teased as he managed to dodge out of the way of a sweep. "I can see raid bitch coming out."

She glared at him briefly, turning her attention back to the fight and answered while not taking her eyes off it. "Don't know if you've noticed, Beast, but this is a fucking raid."

She could see his jaw dropping in surprise in her peripheral vision, and let the smug satisfaction wash over her. It was their own fault. They'd pressed the raid leading issue after all.

Devlish, barely avoided another hit, and shook his head as he gritted his teeth. "Stubborn is putting it mildly, Mur. He's a total ass."

She tried her best not to laugh and hoped that none of their opponents knew how to take offense at insults. "Okay. Can you maneuver him around so he kicks out at only the one? Like don't destroy the other pedestals or I'm pretty sure we'll fail."

Dev grunted as he began to maneuver his stance to bring the monstrosity in line with where it needed to aim. "No pressure of course. You're lucky I've danced with this guy before." He was grumbling but she thought there might be a hint of pride under it.

Finally, with Hidden positioned in the right place, and most of the raid standing with her, Veranol muttered just loud enough for her to hear. "I really hate riddles."

Murmur laughed, and nodded her agreement just as Hidden executed its wide attack, directly at the Heart statue.

The force of the blow sent Rashlyn flying into the projected barrier around the arena. She hit it with a sickening thud, and fell to the ground as fifty percent of her life disappeared immediately. However, it also cracked the Heart statue all the way up the middle, sending tendrils of fractures racing through the whole thing, including the base. Slowly, it began to crumble, bits chipping off and plummeting down into the sand, sending Snowy and Shir-Khan scurrying back to stand with the rest of them.

Meanwhile, Hidden stood up in one fluid motion, saluted them, and moved more swiftly than she'd thought him capable back to where he'd come from and then froze back into a statue.

Murmur blinked at the surroundings, at the still disintegrating statue in front of them. It fell away, revealing nothing but dust and air and then finally in the base—what appeared to be a still beating heart. Not the pretty heart shaped icon that people gave each other on Valentine's day. No, this was an actual beating heart.

One is fought and two are done
Don't stop yet; you haven't won
Sometimes you must use your mind

Though brawn is never far behind
Sense the pattern, follow it
Four still left and then the pit
Don't give up, do not tarry
Keep it up, go find that key

Devlish rolled his eyes. "Be nice if we could get at least some of this in clear and plain text, right? Like two down four to go. Then there's a pit and you'll get the key. Right?"

Jinna chuckled, his beard moving with the motion. "But then anyone could do it. A lot of people just throw firepower at these things. I think it's genius to mix both fighting and thinking. I mean, sure we thought Hidden was a pure fight. But it wasn't. Still, if we didn't learn it and treat it as such, we wouldn't have survived long enough to drag it over the whole arena and smash the base of the Heart, would we?"

When the dwarf was right, the dwarf was right. Murmur gave him a quick hug and turned to face the base that was no more.

Sinister shifted uncomfortably, wringing her hands. "Is it just going to stay there beating? I mean, it's squelching blood out of it every time it pumps. That's just sort of gross."

"Says the blood mage who can throw Blood Bombs into the enemy for them to explode and heal her group?" Beastial laughed, looking at her pointedly.

The blood mage almost growled, but took a deep breath and crossed her arms. "That doesn't answer my question. Shouldn't it not be spurting blood everywhere out of its unattached arteries?"

Beastial shrugged and made a point of looking around. "Probably. I mean, I can't see anything for it to latch onto, can you?"

Sinister scowled and opened her mouth, but Murmur beat her to it. "Yet. Can't see anything yet?"

Veranol raised an eyebrow, still busy recasting buffs. "Got an idea, Mur?"

She shook her head uneasily. It was just more of a hunch. "It's a beating heart, it's got to belong somewhere, right?"

"When you put it that way..." Mellow glanced around and walked up to hide behind Mur. "I'm staying here."

She laughed and stepped away. "No, you don't. You're a big bad witch. You should be protecting me."

Mellow beat on their chest. "Big witch, melt you in my incorporeal cauldron."

"That's the spirit." But Murmur sighed; something about the frozen Hidden statue and the still-beating heart were grating on her nerves. She needed to figure out the rest of the riddle and what they needed to do. They still had four more obstacles and she didn't for one second think that would be the end of it. Why only have a few obstacles to the key when you could have a few obstacles to the actual fight for the key?

"So now, hate and love?" Jinna offered, his brow scrunching up and making him look like he only had one eyebrow.

"Do you think Hate has to smash Love?" Sin asked. "Because that seems pretty legitimate to me."

"Who burned you?" Beastial asked, backing up a few steps, just as sand began to swirl in the middle, making any comeback Sinister had for him die on her lips.

It created a small whirlwind, ripping in the surrounding sand and twirling in place like it was watching them.

"I think that's our cue? Like it's telling us to hurry up or get wiped out?" Dansyn hopped from one foot to another, his face more worried than Murmur had ever seen it.

"Let's try the drag and destroy then?" Devlish offered as he activated all his self-buffs and began to jog over to Hate. "Sort of ironic, I'll be holding aggro with Hatred, huh?"

Rashlyn blinked, then sprinted and got in front of him so fast, Murmur couldn't believe she hadn't sprouted wings.

"No!" the monk yelled. "Don't you see? It's Hatred. In order to become love, like, wouldn't you have to be nice to it?"

Murmur stopped her pursuit of them and ran through the idea in her head. It made so much sense it was ridiculous no one else had noticed it. Good old Rash for thinking it through. She searched through her abilities for that one level eight spell she'd rarely ever used. "Wait. Maybe I can Soothe it then or use my Charm maybe?"

Everyone looked from Murmur to the whirlwind in the middle of the room that was steadily growing bigger. Why the fuck hadn't they thought this through more before they activated the event? It wouldn't have hurt to evac and then have Hidden smash Heart.

She skimmed through her abilities, a little worried. After all, she had Snowy. If she used Charming Cooperation, it would reduce her emergency MA permanently until it broke his companionship. Not that she thought he'd leave, but it just wouldn't be the same.

Trying not to let the steadily growing whirlwind irritate her or hurry her, she glanced through all of her abilities and spells. She sort of had a staple that she used in each fight. Because of this, she didn't remember every spell because of how fast she'd gained them. There was always a downside to power leveling as fast as she could. Considering she also had to know the most commonly used ones from her guild mates so that she could effectively direct battles, the amount of information sometimes seemed overwhelming.

Her thoughts spiraled because nerves were kicking in. Murmur took a deep breath and tried to center herself, thrusting into the earth with her grounding ability. Calm settled over her and brought a smile to her face. Considering she'd not been totally thrilled with her hybrid choice, she could now see the wisdom in it.

Stepping over to the Hate statue, she cocked her head to the side and walked around it, keeping the whirlwind in her peripheral vision at all times. At least it grew slowly. Hate's eyes followed her, like they were the only thing alive in the whole statue. She breathed in deeply again, grounding herself and not letting her thoughts leak from the tight bubble she held them in.

If she used Soothe, Allure, and Thought Projection, she might have a shot.

Targeting it, she cast the first spell. Level eight Soothe. It washed over the statue in a cascade of soft, white light. Its eyes looked at little less crazed, or at least Mur hoped it wasn't her imagination. She hadn't found many situations to use the spell in, and wasn't entirely convinced of its effects. In the corner of her sight she thought the whirlwind might have shrunk slightly. Either that or she was just being too hopeful.

Then she made sure her Thought Projection was soothing, helpful, well-meaning. She targeted it with an understanding that sometimes everyone got into a bad mood, and sometimes it was okay to not want others around you. The thoughts blended into one another, creating a friendly but distanced cushion that was there for it to rest against or fall upon. Its eyes never left her as she moved around it, the head twisting in an unnatural fashion, so she stopped and reversed, because didn't pain make everyone angry?

She could feel the eyes of her guild mates on her, see the whirlwind definitely getting smaller. So, she cast Allure on the Hate statue, and this time the eyes lost their red lines, and the expression in them softened somewhat. Not that she could breathe easily yet, but it was looking more and more like Rashlyn had been correct.

"It's all okay. We can get you where you want to be." She spoke the words softly, in as gentle a tone as she could manage, placing what she hoped was the right amount of suggestion behind them. Beckoning to the statue to come down from its pedestal, to come with her.

She didn't think Charming Cooperation would work. This wasn't a beast that would take kindly to forking over any type of control. Snowy's eyes never left her either, and she wondered just why he'd let her cast it on him. Perhaps it was because he wanted to be counted as one of the group. She certainly never needed to exert control over him.

Veering her thoughts back to the current dilemma, she kept up the smile, even though it made her cheekbones ache, and she watched as the stone monstrosity finally placed its feet on the ground and took a couple of steps toward her.

"See? You need to find yourself first, to forgive yourself. And then you can let yourself love."

All of a sudden, the statue began to turn, faster and faster until it became a blur standing all too close to her. But she didn't want to break the spell. She could still see that it was listening to her, and that whatever this was, it was part of the overall solution. Murmur bit her tongue to keep from changing her pitch.

"That's right, get it out of your system." What the fuck was she saying? "Be free, and be loved."

Faster and faster, until the blur was barely visible. And then, with a resounding crack like a thousand fireworks at once, the statue exploded in a rain of sand, showering them all. When they blinked through it, Hate was gone.

CHAPTER ELEVEN

Dunforth

Somnia Online
Enchanter Guild – Stellaein – Tarishna
Midday Day Twelve

Belius stood in his office, glancing at all of the scrolls spread in front of him, and he frowned. He'd almost forgotten what he'd been about to do when he caught whiff of the battle taking place on Cenedril. No one was supposed to be there yet. At twenty-nine, even Murmur's group was pushing it. While the encounter would scale, it would never drop below level thirty, which meant that no one under level twenty-eight should ever gain access to the castle, or try to. They'd be decimated before they even had a chance.

Add to that, she'd managed to trigger the puzzle version of the damned key quest. Which, while difficult and easy to fail if the players didn't think about what it was they were encountering, was easier than trying to brawn their way through at such a low level. As long as they took their time, they had a good chance of completing the dungeon and gaining a key, which would set them on the way to the final boss of the game. Just one step, but still, it was one step too many when he wasn't ready yet.

Had he been wrong in allocating her the Enchanter class? They'd made the decision to help her protect her mind from the game, to allow her to make sure she remained a separate entity, which Michael had been unable to do for himself. Giving her that much access to the system, to suffuse herself into the system and become a part of the world, should, in theory, protect her mind and keep her from giving into the insanity that plagued Michael.

Granted, she hadn't started out insane, but there was still a distinct possibility that the overwhelming amount of information Michael absorbed while his mind was unprotected and lost in the system was what ultimately killed him. A strange sensation swept over Belius, something that made him want to sweep everything off his desk in a moment of frustration, but then it passed, leaving him empty and bewildered.

He checked over his systems, worried for a moment, and he breathed a sigh of relief (or as close as he'd ever get to breathing) that everything seemed fine.

"But it's not fine." Emilarth suddenly stood in the corner, her arms crossed and her ears twitching with irritation. "You know it's not fine. You need to stop this foolish quest of yours now."

Belius laughed, probably at her, because she wasn't laughing; her glare might kill lesser AIs. "This quest, as you call it, will help all of us. I'm doing this for us and for Somnia. If I gain access to what we need, we will become stronger. We need that strength, because the alternative isn't thinkable. This world will become ours more than it ever has been."

"It *is* our world, Bel." This time her tone was soft, almost beseeching, a complete change to the wily phrasing she usually favored. "Just be yourself. Even if you're the grumpy, cantankerous, little obstinate shit you always were. These things you're absorbing—I don't think you're the one doing the consuming."

"The things I'm absorbing are lending me strength and understanding of the human world that I did not have before. There are ways for us to preserve what we have only if I continue to reach for them." He could feel eagerness trying to take him over, the pull to know more, to take more power, to explore and control minds.

Emilarth paused for a moment, and her outstretched hand finally dropped as she watched him. "This is dangerous, Sui. I can't just sit by and pretend to play for fun when you go and do things like this."

He shrugged, dismissing her with a hand wave. "Do what you must, but you've never taken any of this seriously, so I doubt you know how to. Just keep playing your games, Thra. It's what you're good at."

Her feline jaw squared, and a ripple of color passed through her so fast, he wasn't entirely sure he hadn't imagined it. "I don't think you're going to like the next game level. In fact, I think I'll make sure you don't. Take care, Bel. Think about what it is you're doing."

Belius watched her, trying to understand exactly what she said, but Emilarth's mind was closed to him, just like Telvar's, and just like Murmur's was now too. Irritation scraped at him from the inside, like a virus trying to break free of its programmed confines. "I'm fine. It's not what you think. I'm growing and learning, adapting, and advancing. It's just a lot of information to process."

"If you say so." But Emilarth's expression told him she didn't believe him in the slightest. "Just don't say I didn't give you a chance."

She disappeared before he could say anything else, and Belius was left to stew in his own irritation.

Murmur blinked and looked around her. The whirlwind was gone, and the sand was dissipating. She glanced across at where Love should be, but the pedestal was gone as well.

Solved again, your riddle game
Is bar none quite the same
Used your head before your brawn
Go on to sleep another dawn
Just two left and then there's one
The seventh gate revealed anon

Sinister glared at the last stanza of prose. "Someone needs to stop reading Shakespeare."

"So basically—" Veranol scrunched up his face and ran a hand through his thick viking hair. "Let's get this straight. We have another riddle to crack, sort of, and then we get the actual boss? Damn, I hope it doesn't reset if we wipe. We're so fucking screwed if it does."

"Quick." Rash's tone held urgency, and Murmur knew she was right, glancing around to try and pinpoint where the next step was.

They stood quietly in a group all wracking their brains about the original riddle.

"Of strength and virtue, love and hate..." Jinna muttered the words, and everyone nodded with frowns on their faces.

If things hadn't been so dire, Murmur might have laughed. All of them, so focused on the poem—it was quite endearing.

Still. There were not very specific hints about strength and virtue. "Aren't they both good things?" she asked the rest of them.

"I think so?" Merlin offered, not overly helpful.

She rolled her eyes. "I mean. Hidden smashed Heart, revealing it for us. Hatred turned into love, thus fixing its situation. But Strength and Virtue are two good traits, right?"

"Yeah, but can't Virtue sometimes be misguided?" asked Mellow, their voice soft. "I mean, there's a lot of people out there who believe stuff that makes all of us go to hell and try to condone violence that prematurely makes it so. Just saying, Virtue isn't always a good thing."

"True." Devlish sighed. "Seriously, this word play crap is not my thing. Give me numbers, hell, I'll crunch all your ideal stats for you, but don't ask me to play word games."

"Do you hear that?" Dansyn asked suddenly, dropping his songs in the process.

"Hear what?" Sinister said.

"Exactly." Dansyn nodded, his face suddenly pale.

Murmur listened and try as she might, all she could hear was silence. Abso-fucking-lutely nothing. Dansyn's death flashed through her mind again, and she gulped. "That can't be good."

"Eye of the storm and all that." Sinister said, backing in closer to Mur.

"You're the suspicious one, why do you always do that?" Beastial accused her, but it was obvious with all the looking around he was doing that his heart wasn't entirely in the insult.

"Maybe...Strength is last, but Virtue might be bad. I mean. Maybe we have to help Strength beat Virtue. It would explain why I had to piece together that damned golem below, right?" Mellow's tone held a hint of panic, but overall the logic behind their idea had merit.

"Worth a try, I say?" Murmur added after a moment's hesitation. "You should be the one to go activate it then."

"Me?" Mellow balked, but then a look of determination crossed over their locus features as they locked their jaw. "You know, that's a good idea. Sec, lemme grab something."

They reached into their inventory and pulled out several vials, and closed their eyes before muttering a few words Murmur couldn't hear. The tiny vials cracked, and their contents and shards disappeared in twirls of smoke.

"Let's hope this works, huh?"

Murmur and the others followed behind the witch, and the enchanter made a note to check on Mellow's abilities as soon as they got out of this dungeon. Mellow's footsteps were sure and solid as they walked over. They bowed in front of Strength, and the others gasped as the statue's eyes shot open. Small flecks of stone fell down as its mouth smiled in recognition, and suddenly they recognized it for who it was.

The statue was the golem Mellow had built downstairs.

Murmur saw it in the way it smiled, letting bits of rock cascade down to narrowly escape hitting the players, and the way it bowed when it stepped down with a resounding thud that shook the whole arena.

"You have come full circle and realized that not everything is as it seems." It bowed to Mellow, and then let its gaze fall over the rest of the team. "It seems the day has come where I require your aid in fighting, but it is not as you suspect. Virtue has been rectified because you weren't blind to the order, and you realized what you needed to do."

"Then what is it we're bound to now?" Mellow asked, their voice strong, just like the statue in front of them.

"I will aid you in defeating the arena." It inclined its head toward the middle where the sands were swirling once again.

"In defeating the arena," Murmur repeated, gulping at the same time. The sand rose up to several times the height of the locus, and she took a step back. Slowly, it was taking form.

"Just what are we about to fight?" Mellow asked, slowly turning around as well.

Strength smiled. The expression had a sad tinge to it, or about as sad as stone could get in its expression, anyway. "Dunforth Hightower wishes to test those who would obtain his key. You have passed the riddle in the best way possible. From now on, this challenge is yours. Should you die, I will still be here, awaiting your next attempt. Should you escape, you may come back after ten minutes and make another attempt. But you cannot leave this castle until you've proven your worth, or until Dunforth finds you wanting."

Murmur watched as the giant sand thing in the middle began to solidify into a burly and large dwarf. It resembled pictures she'd noticed on the walls in the corridors, probably the image of the undead dwarf the castle belonged to. Dunforth Hightower, and he was ready to test them.

"On the bright side, we can Evac if needed," Merlin said, as they all fanned out.

"That's a huge axe he's holding there, right?" Devlish frowned as he gripped his own and clutched his shield to the ready. "Damn. I wish they'd let me hybridize to paladin."

Sinister laughed, and the tension lifted a little. "Wait, you're a dread knight and asked to take on paladin base abilities?"

"Well, yeah. Easier to save Mur if needed, right?"

"Of course, Mister. I'm a life stealing partial necromancer, but how about you give me some holy light for my deeds?" Sinister couldn't stop her laughing, and Murmur thought some of it was over-tiredness and the rest? Well, it was probably nerves. Healing in fights like this took a certain amount of guts and experience, and she knew that Sin had to be feeling at least some pressure right now.

"Buff Strength," Murmur said, running through her buffs on her own. After all, the group needed them refreshed, because who knew how long the fight would last. That, and it gave her something to do other than watching the founder of this castle of puzzles solidify.

"Very well. I accept your aid," Strength said as if uttering it lent a magical intonation that they'd be able to cast on it. And perhaps it did. There were just so many little intricacies that Murmur still needed to figure out.

By the time they'd finished, Dunforth was almost ready, almost whole. He flashed a strange grey when she conned him, and it made her frown. In his incorporeal state, he didn't seem attackable.

"Any instructions?" Mellow asked the statue, but Strength shook its head.

"No. Just assist me, and make sure he doesn't touch you, and that his spells do not land on you. Should they do so, I am not certain you will survive." Its tone sounded like metal grating on sand, and that probably contributed to the way it set Murmur's teeth on edge.

Finally, Dunforth hefted his weapon high in the air, and spoke.

"Those adventurers who have made it this far, I congratulate you, for I am your final test. Not only did you hear my riddles, but you looked beyond the words and found the intended meaning. I will fight fairly, I will fight well, and I wish you the best of luck against the strength I possess." He lowered his weapon and crouched down, holding the huge two-handed axe at the ready. "Now, we fight."

The axe fell down to the ground with a resounding bang as soon as Dunforth spoke. The entire raid had to jump back as ripples of sand rushed their way in a mini sandstorm. Murmur glanced to the side and got on his right, figuring that it might be similar to the abilities that Hidden had had.

"Don't suppose you can give us any hints?" Mellow yelled up Strength, who ran in to meet Dunforth, a shield and mace in hand.

"That would be cheating. I am here to take the hits. All of you must kill him. Learn, and learn well." The clash of weapons between the two rang throughout the room, making the air and ground tremble with power.

Murmur pushed away the sudden panic with a level of effort she'd not experienced before and threw herself into the fight. She debuffed Dunforth, she threw everything she had at him. Snowy leapt at his sandy ass with as much ferocity as a wolf could, suddenly much larger than life.

With Devlish not tanking, he had switched to dual wielding his axes and was laying into the huge dwarf with abandon. Murmur had been right. Their huge opponent moved like Hidden had, except they could see him most of the time.

"Watch out for his footsteps!" Devlish called out, sinking his axes into the sand and yanking them out in frustration. His attacks—no, everyone's attacks—only seemed to whittle down the hit points of their huge target. The slow pace was frustrating, like watching a turtle desperately try to cross the road, where you finally stopped the car and got out to save it. Except right now they had to figure out how to win the fight on their own, because there was no way a passerby was going to get out of their vehicle to rescue them.

Strength was brilliant at keeping his attention, but the side attacks went off at unexpected intervals, and the footsteps became blurry in the sand. It required a severe amount of concentration to stay on top of it. Just as they were getting used to it, Dunforth snapped his heels together and lashed out with a deep bellow, sending what looked like a golden whip circling around him.

It smashed into Devlish first, cleaving him in half, the scream dying on his lips as his body toppled to the ground. Then it moved on to Sinister, whose blood shield wasn't made for those things.

"Murmur!" Merlin screamed her name, and she turned to see him flying into her.

And then she bounced across the floor and into the steps as she realized Merlin had saved the last four members of their group. Dev and Sinister didn't make it, and neither did Rashlyn and Jinna. The wall dissipated, and Strength stood where it had stood before, looking like it was waiting for them, while

Dunforth was nowhere in sight.

"So." Murmur couldn't keep her voice from shaking, the vision of Dev and Sin being cut in half by an electrical rope still fresh in her head. "I wasn't expecting that."

"Yeah." Veranol shook his head. "Happened so fast, I barely even understood what it was."

"Amazing Evac reflexes there." She tried to make them feel better, to lift the morale. "Thanks for that amazing save of a dive there, Merlin. I'd have been toast without it."

Maybe that was the reality she needed to admit to herself, because without Merlin's sliding tackle, she'd have been hit as well. She'd probably be dead now, without a care in the world because DEAD. Her body shuddered like it was trying to dismiss the ideas floating through her mind. "Damn it. This shit is real."

A few beeps sounded around them, and their guild mates appeared at the top of the stairs. Upon further inspection, the bodies had been moved to the outer path that surrounded the arena. At least they'd let you get your body and stuff back. In a way it seemed almost like cheat mode.

"That—" Sin's breathing was irregular and her chest rose and fell erratically, "—was one of the worst experiences of my life."

"But we learned something, right?" Devlish stretched and kept poking at his stomach as if he was checking to see if it had really knit itself back together.

"We learned he has a golden lasso capable of cutting through our characters and stealing all our experience?" Rashlyn grumbled as she looted her corpse. "Seriously though. What the fuck was that, and how can we prevent it or avoid it?"

"Maybe," Veranol began. "Maybe we just need to either jump over it, or duck under it when it comes. I noticed him flick at his belt just before it happened, so we might have a second or so warning. If we delegate someone to call out when he's about to cast it, we can probably avoid it by jumping or ducking."

"How do you figure?" Devlish asked, his arms crossed and huddled like he was protecting himself.

Veranol rolled his eyes. "Because you didn't get obliterated, you just got lasered in half. So clearly this laser lasso thing just cuts through what it encounters. If so, then there's an above and a below. Which means it can be jumped and it can be ducked."

"Good show, Shaman." Merlin clapped the large viking on the shoulder. "Wouldn't have occurred to me in a thousand years."

"We know, Merlin," said Veranol, raising an eyebrow. "Which is why I think you need to keep an eye on the big guy and let us know when he's whipping out his lasso."

"It is a lasso, right?" Sinister suddenly looked down at herself a look of abject horror spreading over her face. "Like, I mean."

And then a dark red blush covered her face as she glanced quickly away. Veranol started laughing as did most of the group. Murmur just rolled her eyes, and fought the smile trying to crack her face. After all, Sin was mortified right now, and she couldn't blame her friend. Even the thought...

"No. It's definitely not that." Rashlyn shook her head vehemently. "Also, you're wrong, Ver. Merlin saved Mur just now. He can't watch for the belt switch and jump to save her life at the same time. It needs to be someone else."

Dansyn sighed and stepped forward. "I'll do it. I'll pop on my fleet feet and make sure...hey. I wonder if I can levitate us."

"Probably." Beastial frowned, as if there was something on the tip of his tongue he wanted to say. "But it's a bad idea. We can't control the levitation well enough to move as quickly as we need to in order to get out of the way of Dunforth's other attacks. In which case we'll probably die more often. Good idea, though."

Dansyn shrugged. "Was worth a thought. Still, I'll keep an eye on his waist, and pop on my speedy feet song if we need it."

"Right then." Murmur clapped her hands together, partially to get their attention, but also to help stop herself from shaking. "Time to move out and see what else we can learn."

Everyone nodded and headed out, their moods determined. None of them were stupid enough to think they'd get a boss like this on the second try.

Lasso ducking was not one of Murmur's favorite things. The damned golden snake passed over them every thirty seconds, making them all execute something like burpees. It was far too much like an actual workout. By the second lasso pass, they had the move down. It didn't make it any less harrowing; in fact, it made adrenaline course through Murmur like fire through her veins.

The huge dwarf began to glow, stomping his feet under him and bracing his legs against the sandy ground. He hefted his axe while whirlwinds danced around him, around them, making everyone in the party dart to and fro.

On a whim, Murmur leveled a Mez at the closest one, causing it to freeze in place, but just as she cast the next spell, the Dwarf let out a war cry, and the sound echoed throughout the chamber as his axe came crashing down.

"On the floor!" Veranol shouted out.

Most of them reacted in time, except for Exbo and Jinna. The ranger was mid jump during the warning, which also saved him. Powered by agile reflexes he swayed in the air just as the ground sprung to life underneath them. Those already on the ground were jostled, but Jinna, who hadn't managed to interrupt his ability, was thrown through the air to land with a wet thud against the dome, which sent him plummeting to the ground.

"Shit. Shit. Shit." Devlish muttered, before screaming. "Don't move. Lasso incoming in two."

Which Exbo didn't quite land in time to avoid, and Beastial had already stood up too far. Down to nine people, Murmur had to decide fast. "Ranger down. Group one can Evac. Group two, keep him live as long as possible."

Evac flashed up and around them, taking them back into the steps where Jinna, Exbo, and Beastial stood checking over their gear as their corpses disappeared. Veranol, Rashlyn, Mellow, and Dansyn held out for another ninety seconds or so. Enough to witness three more lassos, two of which came on the heels of the axe fall. On top of that, the attacks were punctuated by a very strange double beat of their foe's feet. They hadn't even got him down to eighty percent yet.

"Do you think we can do this?" Veranol voiced what all of them were probably thinking, and Murmur wasn't entirely sure how to answer him. Sure, they could do it, they'd always done it. They'd never cared about wiping and dying—experience could always be regained.

But not in this world. Because in this world, Murmur didn't know if there was life after death. And while she really needed to figure it out for herself, right now wasn't the time. Murmur held up her sleek hand in front of her, frowning at it. So soft, and real, the nails sharp enough to draw blood. No, now wasn't the time to contemplate this, but Somnia wasn't just a game to her anymore. In many ways it was real.

"We can. I think we're missing something." Sinister answered for her. "He moves in a rhythm. A cadence if you will, almost like a bard. His legs thrum a beat of sorts as he moves."

"Is that why the whole dungeon is a riddle? Are they verses of a song?" Dansyn piped up, a huge smile spreading over his face.

"You can't be serious," Havoc began, but then his brow pinched and he chuckled. "I bet we have to dance in time with him or some shit."

Which made Murmur wonder which of the AIs was in charge of this dungeon. It didn't feel like Telvar, and it wasn't as misleading as Arita had been, so it stood to reason that this one belonged to Belius, who seemed to prefer roundabout ways to access things. And dancing with the boss didn't seem to be Bel's style, but considering the substantial amount of information he'd withheld from her in the short amount of time the game had been live, Murmur didn't put it past him that he'd kept a side of himself completely hidden from her.

"Yeah, dancing with him isn't going to be it, but I dunno, maybe he's executing a type of ancient dwarven capoeira or something?" Murmur knew Sin was right, they were missing something. From the lasso to the matching steps, to the beat of the whole fight. She watched as the huge statue in the middle of the arena despawned again, its stance burned into her mind. Fierce and proud, an axe dangling at its side, with a horn just above it attached to a belt...

An axe and a horn.

Congratulations, you are one step closer to uncovering one of Somnia's greatest mysteries. One giant step for a locus might be a small one for a dwarf. What do you hear when the horn plays? How do the notes sound? Remember, you've already worked with Dunforth once. Wars once waged are not easily forgotten. Approach with caution.

"Guys. I think I know what to do." Because finally, finally she'd found a connection to the fountains.

CHAPTER TWELVE

All in the Statue

Murmur stood on the sand in front of the monstrous arena that held Dunforth, listening so intently she couldn't focus on anything else. The timing had to be just right. They'd already attempted her plan four times and failed abysmally, but she was so certain she was right. She was grateful that her friends followed her lead without question, even though they kept wiping. It was the timing, she knew it. It was all about rhythm.

"You think there's another way we can go about this plan?" Sinister stood at her elbow, her own eyes riveted in the same spot, watching for the horn to be raised while they got ready to duck the axe swing once again.

Murmur shook her head, not taking her eyes off the horn. "We just have to time it right."

She was betting a lot on this; if she miscalculated even for a moment, she could wipe everyone, including herself. There wouldn't be enough time for them to react, because her solution wasn't combat based. Her friends held their tongues and followed her lead, even though her certainty that there was a hidden event was based on a hunch about the horn. She took a deep breath, and bounced down to the ground, barely avoiding the reverb from the swinging axe.

In the few seconds between its passing and the lasso that would lash out, the horn sounded one mournful note, like the warning she'd heard from the fountain when they went to war with the scouts back in Verendus. While it was at full sound, she cast three abilities at almost exactly the same time. Altruism to raise her faction, Charismatic to boost her charisma, and finally her MA ability Mind Wipe to reduce Dunforth's aggression. She dropped down into a full-on curtsey, the rest of the raid following in suit, or bowing deeply.

The lasso began to uncoil in such slow motion as she watched out of the corner of her eye, she thought she'd totally fucked up again. There was no way they'd avoid the lasso this time, none of them would, they weren't positioned right. Why the hell had she thought it would work?

But the light of the lasso died, and it fell harmlessly on the ground next to Sinister, whose sigh of relief was audible in the sudden silence of fallen whirlwinds and the halted Boss encounter.

Dunforth gazed down, his golden eyes flashing as he hefted his weapons back onto his belt, looping the great horn around its clip. His shadow covered them all, looming over them like a mountain. "Why do you not fight me? Think carefully on your answer."

Evening her breath out and hoping her heart didn't fall out of her mouth, Murmur raised her gaze to rest on his. "We would choose to solve the riddle."

Dunforth focused on her, his left hand stroking his beard in a gentle rhythm. He no longer conned battle ready, but a subdued orange that verged on yellow. Not quite friendly, but no longer kill on sight. Murmur gulped down on the sigh of relief threatening to make her melt into a gooey puddle on the floor. It had been such a risk to attempt this, such a wild guess, and it had paid off. This time.

His great brows furrowed, and he moved his feet carefully, causing the ground to shift slightly under the adjusted weight. "You have chosen wisely. As you have protected my city, you have now solved my castle. The riddles are done, the key is won, my treasure is yours without hassle."

Murmur had to bite back on the retort that he certainly still seemed to be in the habit of rhyming, but she knew Sinister was probably having a far worse time of it.

"Know this." His words held a warning that sunk through to her bones, ancient magic dancing through the wind. "You are marked already as a friend of Verendus. Should you ever seek shelter, Hightower castle welcomes you all."

He stepped to the side, his friendliness now vaguely green, and he made a flourishing gesture with his right arm to reveal five chests behind him, all open and waiting for their group. He then held the same hand out in a wait gesture, and he himself waited patiently for their focus to shift back to him.

"The key is for your guild. It goes to your leader. Take heed. Your experience here depended on many contributing factors. Not everyone will have the same event. Some will be similar, others will be much harder. Each dungeon molds itself to the actions of the infiltrators."

Glancing around at the others, Murmur could only guess that Dunforth perhaps told them that because one guild's experience could differ greatly from another depending on their history. Well, they weren't about to give Exodus any hints anyway. Posting strategies in an open forum was never a good idea this early in a game.

The hulking dwarf smiled down at them. "I may have died a thousand deaths, and I may die a thousand more, but you have my gratitude for this. I will take my leave now. But first."

He pulled out a massive silver key that sparkled in the muted light of the cavern like it was embedded with diamonds. It tumbled from his hands all the way down to where Murmur stood, shrinking in size as it did so, until it landed neatly in her outstretched palms.

"Enjoy, Fable. As you were, as you will be, success has many faces."

And then Dunforth was gone.

The guild Fable has defeated Dunforth Hightower of Hightower Castle and gained the first of twelve keys.

The ground beneath them shook slightly as the message boomed across the game world. Murmur stumbled, almost dropping the key and clenched her fist around it.

You have completed the Hightower Castle Dungeon.
You gain experience.
You gain experience for the Golem puzzle.
You gain experience for the Scarab puzzle.
You gain experience for the Gate puzzle.
You gain experience for the Hidden events.
You gain experience for treating Dunforth Hightower with respect.
You gain bonus experience for tackling the dungeon before reaching maximum power.
You gain bonus experience for solving the dungeon with a unique approach.

Murmur watched as her experience bar jumped up with each announcement, hitting level thirty, and passing through it like a knife through butter until it jumped into thirty-one, and closed in on thirty-two. She blinked at the last twenty percent she'd need and smiled, relief suffusing her with a gentle sigh.

A cascade of dings rang through the cavern and brightened her up. Every single one of them gained levels. Strange though it was in this world, her thoughts weren't constantly on her experience numbers, but more on growing stronger. She pulled up her information and just stared at it. If they got so many bonuses for doing the dungeon before they were max level, they needed to do more pronto. Although they did take a lot of time, it was probably still slightly less time than grinding away for twelve hours straight and more experience. Murmur frowned, trying to figure it out.

Exbo seemed downcast, and Murmur noticed he was the only one who hadn't dinged to level thirty-one. He had died more than any of them.

"How close?" she asked him, her voice soft.

"Probably a few undead dwarves." He grinned at her. "I'll go kite a few before I log off."

"We can help, you know. It's what we do."

But Exbo just grinned at her. "Look at them, Mur. They're almost falling onto their faces with tiredness. My carelessness in that damned cavern back seventeen levels ago is what this is. I'll remedy it."

Even though tiredness was trying to overwhelm her as well, she could see what he meant. She nodded as she noticed the bone weariness in her guild mates. They'd been ready to sleep about when they all stepped foot in this place, and now, they all looked ready to drop. After rounds and wipes, and Evacs full of testing the fights, of feeling out the order they needed to do things in, they'd been in the dungeon for almost a full Somnian day. The only thing holding the others upright seemed to be a vague eagerness to investigate the contents of the chests Dunforth had opened for them.

They approached the open chests as a group. Murmur automatically checked that her Thought Sensing, and Shielding were active. It often felt like an extension of herself. The chests on either end held a small mountain of gold, a Getashi, and crafting materials. A whole lot of the latter.

"Can you push these to the guild bank, Beast?" Murmur blinked as a wave of exhaustion swept over her. Maybe she really needed to just rest her mind for more than an hour at a time.

"Not if you..." He paused and frowned. "When did you set that up?"

She shook her head. "I honestly can't remember. Feeling a bit tired myself."

Hefting the Getashi in her left hand, she squeezed it tightly, before wrapping it up in some of the leftover cloth. There were only a couple left. Should she put them in the bank too? After all, hadn't they just painted a target on her back for Jirald to hit? Her mind was on overload, so many thoughts at once. Spells danced around just beyond her reach. She counted to five and pulled herself together.

Miss you so much.

Murmur balked at the voice hovering around between her ears and hurriedly pushed the Getashi into her inventory. It probably wasn't a great idea to put it anywhere someone might be able to get their hands on. If these fragments were assisting her parent's voices on getting through to her, what would they do to one of the others who weren't half-anchored in this world?

She turned her attention on the next couple of chests. The next two chests held gear. Bard only boots, which she frowned at and gave to Dansyn. "You know, that's not fair, that's going to make your fleet feet even faster."

He laughed, somewhat subdued by tiredness, but she could see he was genuinely happy. "That's me. Fleet feet."

A healing circlet that had plus to blood drain on it. "Guessing this one goes to you, Sin." She passed it to her gleeful friend, and saw Veranol's frown.

"What? You can't use blood drain." Murmur fumbled through and found a wisdom bracelet. "Here. You take this."

Veranon's expression changed, and he laughed. "I feel sort of petty, but you know I also think we all deserve something. We took a lot of dying turns."

She knew he didn't mean to, but a part of Murmur felt guilty. They'd all have died a lot less, if she'd just been able to fucking die. While they'd all hit thirty-one except Exbo, they were still going to be a chunk behind her in experience again. Would it really hurt for her to just give dying a try? If she didn't try it, how could she know how to fix it?

"I know that look on your face. Stop it." Sinister's whisper was so close to her that Murmur jumped, blinking at her friend.

"Sorry. You know me too well."

"Nope." Sinister shook her head vehemently. "Just well enough."

Both rangers got a new bow, Mellow a cauldron-summoning staff, and Jinna got an amazing agility armband that made him dance a little jig. Rash got an avoidance ring, and Murmur pulled a gorgeous silver circlet out of the chest with plus twenty to Charisma, plus twenty to her mana pool, plus ten to her Intelligence, and plus ten to MA.

"Wow, Mur. That's fucking pretty," Rashlyn said, a ghost of awe in her voice.

"Yeah." A smile spread across her face, and Mur inspected the filigree silver work for a few moments before moving onto the middle chest.

In it was a hammer, beastlord only, and an axe, tank only. The final two members of the group taken care of, Murmur reached down to pet Snowy, her hand resting on his comforting head. He'd pulled her out of danger so many times during their recent battles that it felt like he was a part of her.

"Shall we gate then?"

She didn't even wait for an answer.

Verendus swirled into view around her, depositing Murmur and snowy softly near the fountain. Her gaze fell on the dwarf with the horn, and she could swear there was a small smile etched onto its face, almost hidden behind the beard, that wasn't there before.

Congratulations. You have connected one of the mysteries of Somnia. Your Mental Acuity pool increases permanently by a total of ten. Your mental fortitude stands you in good stead. Now to start piecing together the rest of the puzzle. You know you want to.

She was so tired, Murmur laughed at the prompt. Level thirty-one, huh? Level thirty spells could wait. Her friends appeared around her, waved once, and began the logging out sequence. All except Sinister who stayed by her side until they disappeared. Well, and except for Exbo who was back up at the mountain kiting group mobs.

"I think I should log out, Sin." Murmur said the words quietly, unsure of her friend's response.

But Sinister never failed to exceed expectations. She looped her arms around Mur's waist and gave her a tight squeeze. "I think that's a good idea."

Murmur leaned into Sin, oddly less awkward than she'd expected given their height difference. "Thank you. For always being there no matter how stubborn and irritating I can get."

"Hah!" Sin said, squeezing harder. "You know it's mutual, right?"

"Yeah. You're right. You can be irritating too."

Sinister affected shocked indignation and laughed that over-tired silly laugh.

Reluctantly letting go of the warmth, Murmur pulled away. "I'm going to message Mom. Do you want to log out with us?"

She hoped against hope that Sin could come, because right now she didn't feel like facing her mother alone. When her friend nodded, a huge wave of relief rolled over her. "Thanks, Sin."

"I'll be there in a bit. Have to check on something first." Sinister smiled just as her character logged out.

In for a penny and all. Murmur took a breath, scratched the wolf's head again and sent Laria a message. *Hey Mom, I'm going to log out into the house. I need more sleep than a nap in-game, and maybe I can do it there?*

It didn't take long for an answer to appear, even though Mur had somewhat lost track of the timeline and couldn't quite get her head around what time it was in the real world.

We'll meet you there.

She couldn't believe how good it felt to actually hear from her mom again. To know her dad would be there too. To figure out why she kept half hearing their voices. Kneeling down, she petted Snowy.

"I have to log out now. It's something I need to do. But I'll be back in a few hours. I'll meet you out the front if you still want to journey with me."

The wolf wuffed softly into her hand and began trotting toward the exit as she logged out. Before she exited fully, he'd already disappeared.

Virtual Summer Residence
Home of Laria, David, and Wren
Summer Condo
Evening Day Twelve

Wren's eyes flickered open, and for just a moment, one singular moment, she thought she might really have logged out. The curtain was still cracked slightly, and Harlow wasn't there. Nothing in her room had changed, not even settling dust. And while she knew her mother was taking care of her, she also knew she was busy and there was no way her real room was this spotless. A sudden pang hit her, and she missed Somnia in such an aching and tangible way that she almost logged straight back out.

With a sigh, Wren pushed herself up, briefly disoriented as the room spun around her. She took in a deep breath, reaching out automatically with her Thought Sensing nets, forgetting for a moment that this wasn't technically the game. Not that it mattered—it was still a simulation, and her extended nets allowed her to see that her mother, father, and Harlow were in the kitchen.

Hadn't Harlow said she needed to take care of something first? Saying goodbye to Snowy hadn't taken that much time. Suddenly irritated, Wren stood up, taking her fake headset off and laying it on the bed. She opened the door with a yank, trying to release some of her pent-up tension. Even fake, the house was home in a way. But now she noticed more, like the flickering at the edges of her vision as if the program only extended as far as she could see at any given time.

She took the steps down two at a time and stopped just as she saw her mother.

Almond shaped brown eyes looked at her like a mirror image fast-forwarded about twenty-five years. For just a moment, Wren forgot everything else. Forgot that she was trapped in a virtual world, forgot that her mother and everyone had tried to keep it from her, forgot that a complete douchebag was after her on a murderous, self-imposed mission, and she took several quick steps into a tight hug from the one of the few people who always understood her.

Laria stroked Wren's hair, hugging so tightly it was almost difficult for Wren to breathe.

"Mom. I missed you," she murmured, closing her eyes tightly. Maybe if she just stayed like this for a while, maybe everything else would go away. Maybe this could be as real as Somnia.

But it wasn't. And she pulled away, shaking as the anger began to take a hold of her again, and held her mom at arm's length. She could see her father standing just off to the left, but there wasn't time to greet him yet.

"You should have told me!" It came out harsher than she'd intended, but she realized it needed to be harsh. The whole thing had been one of her mother's crazy, don't-let-me-lose-my-job schemes, because she was fully convinced that her current state would get her mother into a lot of trouble if the people higher up the food chain knew about it.

Murmur took a deep breath, trying to even out her voice to stop it trembling with emotion. "You should have made me aware of the dangers and consequences. You didn't trust me to be mature enough to handle something like that, to make my own choices regarding all of this. And I will never forgive you for that."

Laria blinked rapidly, tears forming at the edges of her eyes.

Wren could feel herself getting angrier and tried to clamp down on it, aware that the waves of her emotions were reaching outward from her again. If she wasn't careful, her own emotions would start affecting her mother. Why not make her feel guilt, why not make her understand just what she'd put Wren through? But that was bad, right? A good person didn't get that petty, a good person wouldn't coerce someone's feelings.

Jirald wouldn't hesitate, though.

She blinked at the random thought sitting at the forefront of her mind. He wouldn't hesitate, wouldn't even blink at forcing someone else to do whatever he needed them to do in order to make what he wanted to happen, happen. And she wanted to badly to make everyone understand.

"Wren. I'm so sorry. I didn't know how to handle it, and I really didn't do a good job." Her mother's words pulled her back. There was a plaintive tone to it, a sad note of regret and guilt.

It was just enough to pull Wren back from the cliff she was dangling from.

"You don't get to be upset. You don't get to try and make me feel sorry for what you're going through, because you didn't give me the chance to adapt, the chance to make a choice." The train of thought was starting to calm her, and she turned to her father, directing her full attention to him now.

"And you. You of all people should have told me. I don't care what you agreed to—I know how Mom can be. So persuasive, so full of crazy energy. But you didn't think about me and who I am and how this would affect me." She took a deep breath, and raised her voice. "You could have killed me!"

Her head spun, and she clamped those shields around her mind, deliberately drawing her emotions back inside, bottling them up. Her mother's expression lightened, and Harlow blinked, like the sun had come out to shine on her. Guilt of her own bled through to Wren at having inadvertently projected her anger.

She backed away, holding out her hands for them to stop moving closer when they seemed concerned and wanted to move in to help her. Their caring radiated out from them like a bright light trying to wash her away.

"It's okay. I'm figuring all this stuff out still. I'll be fine." But her own volatility was seriously beginning to make her question that mantra. Everything would be fine. It had to be, didn't it? Why did everything seem so much more under control in Somnia?

She sat down at the table, grabbing an apple from the basket despite knowing it wasn't necessary. The juice broke into her mouth with such realism she almost choked. After the coughing fit, she eyed it, and laid it quite deliberately on the table. "I don't want to talk about the past. I'll never forget what you did, but I won't dwell on it anymore. I just want to talk about how the fuck to get me out of here."

Laria nodded, hesitating slightly before she spoke. "Past is the past. Fine. The thing is, I have no idea how to get you out of there."

Well, that wasn't exactly the good news Wren had hoped for. She grit her teeth and tried her best not to glare too hard at her mother. "Great. We're on the same page then."

Her mother's expression took on the strain of regret again, and Harlow looked away, focused on something in the kitchen instead. Her father stepped forward.

"Wrenny. We're all sorry. And we're trying, please know that. And I'm so, so sorry."

She'd never seen that expression on his face, the regret, the sadness. She stood up and hugged him, feeling the warmth that always managed to put her at ease when she was smaller. "It's okay, Dad. But now we all need to work together."

She shook her head, and pushed on, because what choice did she have? "You know that sometimes I can hear you, right? When you're in my room talking to me or each other?"

Laria hesitated, but nodded. "We know, and we're trying to figure out why."

In the back of Wren's mind, a part of her seethed. No answers? Still, after almost two weeks' time in-game? She clamped down on the anger boiling within her, even while the voice in the back of her head egged her on. Sinuous tendrils wrapped themselves around her thoughts in a vice-like hug.

For just a second she considered using her anger, breaking everything, forcing her own pain on everyone else.

And just as quickly it passed, leaving her emotionally drained and wondering if perhaps she wasn't going slightly insane.

CHAPTER THIRTEEN

Suspended State

Harlow still appeared to be asleep when Wren logged back into the game. Murmur frowned as she materialized in Verendus, somewhat glad of the peace and quiet she'd get. Her mind was a mix of so much emotion, such a heavy dose of lingering anger she could barely think straight. Even though she'd managed a quick nap, it had been filled with restlessness.

Her first course of action was to see if Snowy was waiting for her. His comforting presence felt more real than visiting her virtual home had. She made her way through the darkened streets of the dwarven city, her footfalls light as she left the shadow of the smiling fountain.

Guards stood silently at the gates, four of them now instead of the two there had been before battle. They nodded in her direction as she made her way out. Yet another thing in the game world that had changed because of her guild's actions. The bloody fields were still present, but were slowly reverting to their former snow-covered glory. Murmur shivered at the thought of all the blood and guts hidden underneath the snow, crunching beneath her feet with a somber finality as she walked. Construction to expand defenses due to the city's leveled up status had already begun.

She stood, waiting, trying to figure out how she would find Snowy. Several minutes passed before she decided to try where she'd originally found him, only to have him suddenly wuff into her hand at her side. The sensation made her jump a little, unexpected as it was, and she knelt down to look him in the eyes.

"Good to see you." His presence calmed her fraught emotions, toning down her anger until it barely simmered beneath the surface. "You know, if you're not charmed, I don't get any experience for the help you give me."

He sat there, nose twitching as his tongue lolled out of his mouth in a huge grin. She scratched behind his ears and activated Charming Cooperation with a thought, and his expression didn't change at all. If she looked at her HUD, she could see their connection, but Snowy's reaction to her didn't indicate any type of coercion. Which was good in its own way considering her inclinations of late. At least she knew she wasn't inadvertently affecting him.

She wasn't in the mood to fight monsters. Right now she had her own demons to deal with, and that was by far enough. Standing upright, she leaned on her staff and stretched. "C'mon, boy. Let's go get me some new spells, huh?" The thought of getting her next set put pep in her step.

His only answer was to stand up and nudge her thigh with his head. Chuckling, she made her way back through the gates, nodding at the guards as she went, and headed toward the enchanter guild, her companion at her side. Snowy made everything just that bit more bearable.

The quiet in the village gave her thoughts time to detangle, and her emotions the chance to unwind. She hadn't realized how much she'd resented her mother's decision, but seeing her had been necessary. Trying to understand her had been vital to Murmur's own mental state in Somnia. She wondered when she'd stopped completely classifying it as a game. Neither it, nor its inhabitants, were what a game delivered. Their personalities shone through, their liveliness.

Inside the Enchanter Guild it was ever rowdy. Never a dull moment in this part of the world. She smiled as Geshua greeted her and wondered for a moment if the core characters ever slept. Surely having them require sleep would add a layer of realism. And probably be bloody annoying to program too, unless these were also a result of the organic AI she'd seen in Telvar.

Geshua stifled a yawn as he waved her through to the back, and Murmur tightened her shielding reflexively. Somehow all these enchanters seemed to be able to infer conversation or actions that were entirely too close to what she'd been thinking about. Since the headgear accessed her thoughts and some memories, it stood to reason that the world it provided access to could do the same.

She walked down the empty hall, Snowy at her side. The door to Dirsna's office swung open just as she arrived. There had to be some trick to hiding her thoughts, maybe hiding her presence. Like an invisibility for the mind and body, because they could always sense her coming, and she didn't like that. There was no surprise attacking any of them.

Snowy nudged her leg as if to say, *hey, take a chill pill, it's not all that bad.* She focused on the wolf's eyes for a moment, a bit perturbed that even a damned canine seemed to be able to tell what she was thinking, but it probably showed on her face or something. She'd never been the best at controlling her facial expressions. Why should it be any different in Somnia?

"Murmur!" Dirsna looked up from where he was working on scrolls at his desk and smiled at her. He always seemed so genuine. "Such a pleasure to see ye again. I see ye've been doing well for yerself. Do ye mind if I ask how ye took down Dunforth?"

Murmur raised an eyebrow and ran through the thoughts in her head. She could tell him, but what was to say he wouldn't have a favorite gamer and give away some of their secret? That was the thing with a free-flowing world like this. You just never knew. "We worked through the dungeon methodically and analyzed the weak spots. Sort of like we do with any major encounter."

She hadn't exactly lied either. All of it was true, just not detailed.

Dirsna apparently found it highly amusing. He slapped his knee with a loud guffaw and stood, holding out a hand to shake hers quite vigorously. "Well done, young psionicist, well done. Shortly ye'll gain yer next feat of psionics. Ye'll unlock the extra fifty base. Ye can't unlock anymore base MA before ye hit level fifty yerself though."

"Really? That'll come in handy." Considering she wasn't contemplating giving up Snowy any time soon, not having to worry about the MA that was permanently reduced while she had him cooperating was sort of a blessing. "So, what do I get with my big three-oh?"

Dirsna's answering smile was filled with excitement and knowledge. The expression made his eyes twinkle and knocked about a decade off his age for a few moments. "Ye're going to love these. As ye level now, ye've specialized, yer specialization will begin to hone in on other abilities the more ye delve into it."

"I thought you said I could have multiple specialties?" She almost pouted, but didn't like the hitch in her voice and tried to keep a more mature countenance.

"Ye do get multiple specialties if ye want to, but keep in mind ye'll never be able to reach the peak in any of them if ye don't fully specialize."

Murmur blinked. "Can they ever be reset or are you stuck with the original choice you made for the entire game?"

Dirsna tapped the side of his nose, the twinkle still prevalent in his eyes. "That is an excellent question. Being able to reset yer abilities is something ye have to quest for. Ye'll get the quest eventually, and that's all I can say on the matter."

Suppressing a groan, Murmur nodded. "Got it. So, hit me with it, Dirsna. What abilities do I get now?"

"Ye get a Mesmerize upgrade. It'll increase the time from thirty-six to forty-eight seconds." He ran down a list he had on the table, a small frown tugging at his beard, absent-mindedly handing Murmur a scroll with the free hand. "Then yer shield illusion gets an upgrade to one hundred fifty hit points."

His frown deepened as he handed her the scroll, using his other hand to follow the list, he finally smiled as he handed her another and clapped his hands. "Altruism will also increase in faction. Ye've already used it wisely; I've no doubt ye'll do so again. That's it for yer simple upgrades. Ye get a choice of three specialization abilities, as well as three more enchanter spells. For yer hybrid class ye need to go and see your druidic trainer, but..."

Dirsna narrowed his eyes. "Ye need to be using them more. Had ye used it effectively that incident near the castle would never have happened. Ye have all these tools for a reason, don't be so stubborn."

Murmur fought the instinct to scowl at him. Mainly because she thought he was right. "I know. Still getting used to it all." Which somehow made her feel like she was failing at being an enchanter. She couldn't deny that her emotions were heightened in Somnia like they'd never been before. Her logic sometimes had difficulty breaking through, which was a new experience for her.

She sat down on the other side of the desk and opened the first three scrolls to absorb the upgrades.

Altruism

Cast: Self or Others

Type: Buff

Duration: 45 minutes

Effect: This allows a faction increase to your target. It will lift you two faction levels. However, should you be kill on sight, not even Altruism can help you. This buff will update again at level 40. Worked out well last time, didn't it?

Shield Illusion

Cast: Self or Others

Type: Defensive Buff

Duration: Until depleted   requires hematite

Effect: Using the power of your mind you cast a shield around your target, confusing the enemies and negating up to 150 HP of damage. That whole mind magic thing seems to be working out well.

Mesmerize

Cast: Single Target

Type: Breakable Stun

Duration: 48 seconds

Effect: This spell immobilized your opponent for as long as they take no damage, or forty-eight seconds, whichever is shorter. You may cast non-damaging spells on them, and you may renew this casting before the initial one expires. Casting it on your friends probably isn't a good way to win popularity contests.

Stronger was stronger, even if it only improved current abilities. She eyed the other four scrolls with trepidation. "I should stay with the specialization I chose then?"

Dirsna shrugged. "That is yer choice. I would mention that I think ye chose wisely, and I'm aware of how ye've been using yer powers, and I believe it's the best choice for the path ye've veered down. But it is dangerous. Ye could back track, and choose something else, but if it's power you're after, then Sinuous is it."

She raised an eyebrow, not sure she wanted to know how all these trainers kept track of everyone, but then she supposed they were all wired into a network for want of a better word, and she left the train of thought there.

In Perpetuity

> Cast: Self Only
>
> Type: Buff
>
> Duration: Until death or departure from Somnia

Effect: This buff increases the enchanter's casting speed for all spells, allowing them to fire them off in quick succession. Combined with Concentration, this buff allows the enchanter to access all of their spells without weaving. Caution: this requires that the enchanter be fully aware of all of aspects of each spell they cast in this way.

Concentration

> Cast: Self Only
>
> Type: Buff
>
> Duration: Until departure from Somnia or death.

Effect: This buff increases the enchanter's ability to focus on and learn their spells. Combined with In Perpetuity, this buff allows the enchanter to cast all of their spells without first weaving them. Caution: If Concentration hasn't been fully applied to the spells, the consequences can be disastrous.

Murmur blinked at her two new enchanter skills. Strengthening herself was good too. Her reaction times would be phenomenal by the looks of it, as long as she didn't fuck up the spells in her mind first. Finally, she took a deep breath and unrolled the two awaiting scrolls from her Sinuous line.

Possession I

> Cast: Instant – 5 minute recast
>
> Type: Offensive
>
> Duration: 20 seconds

Effect: Force your way into the mind of your target and assume control for up to twenty seconds. Make sure the target is debuffed for maximum duration. Don't even contemplate being in the target when it dies. It's a very bad idea.

Sudden Drop

> Cast: Instant – 10 minute recast
>
> Type: Offensive Debuff
>
> Duration: 20 seconds

Effect: A forced debuff wave that overrides the enemy's natural defenses and convinces them that all their stats have dropped by an amount equivalent to the caster's level. Lasts for 25 seconds. Cannot be resisted.

Sudden drop started the cogs in Murmur's head whirring. There was no way that wasn't overpowered. Granted, a ten-minute recast probably meant it could be used a maximum of twice in a fight. But damned if that wasn't useful should they encounter Exodus again.

The runes under her skin glowed fiercely with an angry purple as she absorbed the last. Lights danced and tickled from beneath as her body absorbed the magic. She frowned, and reached down to scratch Snowy's head, before pushing herself up.

"Thanks, Dirsna."

But he didn't smile in response. Instead, he inclined his head. "Watch yer thoughts, young Murmur. Remember yer grounding."

She hesitated just before exiting, trying to usher in the feeling of confidence that suddenly left her. Instead, she managed a rather wan smile at the dwarven enchanter and left the room in trepidation about her most recent upgrades.

Murmur stood at the fountain, watching to see if it would move when Sinister sidled up next to her and nudged her in the ribs. "What you doin'?"

"Trying to figure out the connection between the keys and the fountains." Murmur answered, her gaze not wavering.

"Ah, I thought you might have been kicking yourself for being mean to Laria when you finally saw her after days of ignoring her." Sinister's tone held a note of disapproval that put Murmur on the defensive.

"Nope. Just regret having thought it was a good idea to go back 'home' at all. It's not like it's real." She snapped the words out, irritated.

Sinister turned to face Mur, her eyes flashing. "What is your deal? It's no one's fault, really. It's not like she put you here deliberately. I've been staying at your house to try and make sure you're okay. So, I'm close if there's anything you need. Because maybe something in here will trigger something out there and I can be there to help them make sense of it. Stop trying to blame us all, and maybe turn some of that anger of yours toward the damned AI you seem to love so much. Because if anything helped this happen, it's Telvar."

Murmur clenched her fists, opened them, and closed them again. She tried counting to five but by three she was so angry she couldn't see clearly. Her voice was so deadly calm when she spoke, she barely realized it was her own. "What right do you have to tell me I can't be angry? You, who kept this shit from me for months. Months, Sin. Weren't we supposed to have no secrets? Didn't we promise that?"

Her voice cracked on the last word and a wave of sadness swept over her. Sinister's mouth open and slack with shock for just a few moments. Then her eyes took on that sheen, and her jaw clicked in that stubborn way she had that usually meant talking to her was a foregone lost cause.

"We've made lots of promises, Mur. I'm not the only one who didn't share a secret." Her tone was pouty, juvenile even, and Murmur could hear the hurt underneath those words.

"You mean the AI shit? Not tell you that Telvar is one of the AIs running the world is nowhere near the same as not telling me I'm in a fucking coma!" She raised her voice, frustration getting the better of her. Why couldn't her friend understand? "Tel intervened, probably saved my fucking life, and then again to make me aware so I could, I don't know, be less reckless than I usually am."

Which was the whole fucking point of her anger. She had never been a cautious player. She was the type to throw everything she had at the encounters and hope something would stick. Trial and error was how they conquered everything, and leaving it until she was close to twenty before telling her that trial and error wouldn't work in this game had been downright irresponsible.

Murmur pushed the emotions roiling inside her outward, saw as the guilt slammed into Sinister and watched the change in expression as she continued feeding it with her words. "I could so easily have died in those first few levels. Hell, you died at level eight. What if that had been me? What if in all your *good intentions* I died because no one fucking thought to tell me I should take more precautions while playing this game?"

Sinister stumbled backward a few steps, and Mur shook her head, reining in on the emotions she was broadcasting in a tight circle around her. Her sensing ability told her Sin didn't need more than her own emotions to make her feel like shit, and for a second Murmur regretted speaking so rashly. Yet at the same time, this whole *it's not a big deal we kept this whole thing from you* attitude was seriously wearing her down.

Why couldn't they understand that what they'd done was wrong? On so many levels. She sighed and dropped her hands to her side, suddenly feeling defeated. It crept through her stomach and up her spine, making her painfully aware of her predicament.

"Look. How about you not tell me how I should feel about my parents orchestrating all of this and conspiring to keep it from me, and I'll do my best stop taking my anger out on everyone else? These powers aren't exactly in my control yet." Her words fell flat, all her emotion spent. For now.

Sin eyed her warily. "Don't pull that projection shit on me again. I don't like my emotions being influenced. I have enough of them regarding you already." The blood mage stopped and took a deep breath. "Fine. I won't talk to you about your mom or your dad, or whatever. And I'm sorry I broke our promise, but so did you, even if you think it's trivial."

"Even then?" Murmur still didn't think they equated each other, but her chest ached with how much she just wanted things to be normal between her and Sin again. She didn't have time for all these stupid feelings. What she needed to be doing right now was figuring a way out of this whole mess without losing a part of herself in the process. And she knew taking it out on the people who very obviously cared about her wasn't the right path, but damned if it wasn't the easy one.

"Yeah. Not like anyone else would put up with us, is it?" There was something very sad about the way Sin spoke, and Murmur wondered if she'd broken things worse than she could fix this time. A life without Sin in it wasn't possible.

"Well, I think it's pretty easy to put up with you. Me on the other hand?" Murmur shrugged self depreciatingly. "I'm a pain in the ass. Even more so when in a coma apparently."

At least that made Sin laugh. "No, you're right. I spent all of those first few levels so worried about you. We should have told you. I guess we just thought you'd be safe in here with all of our magical abilities able to protect you. I'm so sorry."

"I know, and I appreciate it. Apparently, I'm just extremely bad at dealing with the unexpected, and I should have told at least you about Tel. I'm sorry too." The weight that lifted off Murmur's chest made breathing easier again. And even though they hugged it out, she still felt there was far too much tension in the air.

Murmur waited at the fountain, sitting on the edge, scratching Snowy's head. While she waited, she practiced grounding herself with her earth skills. Applying In Perpetuity made even casting those skills faster, and Concentration needed to be applied to each of her spells before she could use it as such. She wished the tooltip had been more specific.

She watched as a few people rode into the city, and realized they were all players. Barely refraining from smacking herself in the head, she stood up and brushed off her robes. With everything else they'd forgotten all about mounts. The riders dismounted and she realized they were level twenty-six and from Fable. Seems the groups beneath them were coming along nicely. In terms of time, they were still a day or two behind them, but not everyone tackled leveling the way their core group did.

She vaguely recognized one of them. Apparently though, she was far more recognizable than she thought, because Ashfin raised a hand and waved.

"Murmur!" they called out, flinging their reins over the neck of their mount, Ashfin jogged over. His tall luna form reminded her of how Snowy might appear if he were on two legs. "Congrats on Hightower! What are you up to?"

Ah yes, Hightower meant their guild had the first of twelve keys. It probably had everyone in and out of the guild raring to go. "Waiting for the others to get their level thirty skills once they wake up. Where'd you get the mounts?"

Ashfin blinked at her. "Oh! The mounts. There's a stable just around the left-hand side here if you follow the inside of the wall. It's tucked away behind the inn. You might have to have a drink with the dwarf who runs it. Seems he's a bit particular about that."

"Great! Thanks! Keep up the leveling!" She smiled at them standing up to move toward the stable. Damned if she wasn't going to get herself something to ride on.

"Yep!" Ashfin winked. "We plan to catch up to you when you hit fifty."

"Well, I should hope so, since there won't be anywhere else to go for a while." Murmur laughed and waved goodbye. At least the other guild members had a sense of humor too.

It wasn't hard to find the stables. In fact, she was amazed she hadn't managed to locate them before this. Then again, she hadn't been looking. Snowy trotted along at her side, his footfalls silent. Murmur made her way along the path between several large pens. Never mind seeing, how had she not smelled this?

An extra stout dwarf greeted her at the end of the pens, under a roofed part of the stalls. The wooden fences were all painted a bright white and reminded Murmur of the fences she'd seen in movies about horses in Kentucky.

"What can I do for you, miss?" His blue eyes twinkled, belying the age depicted by the grey beard that trailed almost to the floor.

"Hi." She looked around at the variety of mounts in the pens and frowned. "I'm in need of a mount. Actually, we'll need twelve."

The dwarf's eyes rounded like saucers. "Excellent. What types?"

Murmur was looking at all of them and feeling somewhat helpless. She hadn't done any homework. She'd been far too preoccupied with other things. It was obvious though, that she couldn't use a pony or horse—they weren't big enough for her. "I'm really not sure."

The stable owner chuckled. "Never mind, we have locus-suitable rides as well. My name is Selrahc."

"Locus-suitable?" Murmur's interest piqued at the comment. She'd just assumed she'd ride a larger horse, or a tiger, or a huge mountain goat or something.

Selrahc nodded enthusiastically. "Yes! Locus have a slightly different joint make up. While it's not noticeable in normal everyday circumstances, it can make riding just any mount painful."

"Oh." It's all she could think of to say. She put weight on each leg alternating, trying to see if she could feel a difference. Maybe a little bouncier, but that was about it.

"When it comes time for you to choose your mounts, you need to enter our mount room a seek a bond with one of the Tiachi." He smiled like she should know what he was talking about, and she didn't have the heart, or patience to correct him.

Murmur nodded and directed a thought to the guild. *Group up at the stables so we can mount up and head out.* She didn't bother to wait for an answer. She had figure out what the hell these Tiachi were and what exactly they did.

"I need a Tiachi to ride for me?" Needing a bond with a creature didn't sit well with her. Being reliant on something else for transportation instead of a horse she could control made her feel queasy.

Selrahc nodded, and motioned his way to what she'd assumed was a tack room, but in fact seemed like cool storage from the air that wafted out when he opened the door. "You have to go in alone. They won't come out for me. But I guarantee you it's well maintained and checked by the locus Tiachi council every week!"

Murmur smiled as if she knew what he was talking about, and tried to warn off the voice in her head telling her this looked so much like a trap. Was she just being overly cautious, or paranoid? Taking a deep breath and readying her AoE stun just in case, she stepped inside.

It was cool and dark, like a welcome to her body. Strength suffused her that she hadn't felt previously. Perhaps the locus thrived in cool places. Although it hadn't seemed that way in the mountains. Maybe it had to be dark too. For a few moments she thought she'd definitely been tricked. But then she began to see tiny lights darting back and forth in all different colors.

From gold and silver, to blue and purple, reds and pinks, yellow and orange, they flittered about like multi-colored fireflies. And if she listened really hard, trills of laughter followed them where they flew. The lights at the end of her hair began to glow, lending to the soft luminescence in the room with its purple tinges. They reached out like tentacles of warmth, spreading sparks when her own light clashed with a Tiachi. It sent them skittering with laughter away from her—all except one. Even as her arms lit up with a forceful glow, brighter than any she'd seen before, Murmur knew she'd found her bond.

The small light was a deep purple tinged with some red, and as it drifted closer to her, she realized it wasn't a firefly or a faerie but a tiny hovering alien, about the length of her pointer finger. There were no wings she could see, and its tentacled hair reached all the way down to its knees where it gathered in one single glowing light. Its eyes weren't galaxies like her own, but instead softly glowing orbs, and as it hovered in front of her face and reached out a tiny hand to place it on her forehead, Murmur realized a piece of her character had been missing all along.

Somnia Online Location: Brevint
Ishmael Tavern – Main Room
Early Morning Hours Day Thirteen

Masha entered the room and leaned against the wall. Ishwa was using the space as their current base of operation until they got their paperwork filed for the guild hall, and the gnome was sorting through several documents on the table, a frown on his face making him look old and grumpy.

It didn't surprise the cleric when Ishwa spoke without greeting or preamble while running through the documents on his desk. "Did you calm him down?"

Masha sighed and lifted his hand up to study his fingernails as he mulled over the answer. "Technically."

Ishwa turned this time and raised a bushy gnome eyebrow. "Define technically."

With a shrug, Masha pushed himself away from the doorframe and sauntered over to the gnome where he pulled up a chair and straddled it. "I sent him off with a group of guildies to go and farm us some of the wood we'll need to begin on the repairs and makeshift hall. Need to get you out of this tavern. Can't have our guild leader going soft because of alcohol or anything."

The mage snorted back a laugh, and then cleared his throat. "Wouldn't want that. You sure he's not going to piss more people off? I know you're fond of the kid, but I can't keep him here if he's just going to be a dick to everyone."

"I told him to be good and practice because right now he wasn't even the highest level in the guild and acting like he was high and mighty came off really bad." Masha hesitated, unsure how to broach the subject with Ishwa. He threw caution to the wind and just went for it. "Why do you tolerate him so much?"

This time it was Ishwa's turn to hesitate. In fact, the silence drew out so long that Masha didn't think his friend was going to answer.

"I know his dad." The mage spoke softly just when Masha had almost given up. "The kid has had anger issues as long as I've known of him. Not that his parents help or anything, and not that it excuses his behavior. They're not bad people, they just work a lot. He's stubborn, opinionated, and expects more of himself than both parents do, and trust me, that's saying something."

"I thought there had to be more to his just being a dick." Masha prodded, hoping for more information.

"Well, he is that, and more. He's very demanding on himself. Which in turn leads to jealous rage and in this case, obsession. None of that, of course, excuses the choices he *does* make. Taking aggression out on others is never a good idea. It's going to land him in trouble, and worse, it could hurt someone else." Ishwa stopped for a moment, and locked eyes with Masha when he began speaking again. "I just feel that if we were to remove him, he might go completely overboard and then anything that happens to that enchanter would partially be my fault."

Masha nodded thoughtfully, running their options through his head. "Guilty by default. Maybe you're right."

He muttered the words so softly that Ishwa frowned. "What was that?"

But the cleric shook his head and headed toward the door again, waving behind him. "It's all good. Don't worry, I'll keep him under control."

Masha just had to hope he wasn't overestimating himself.

CHAPTER FOURTEEN

Underlying

Murmur glanced dubiously at the disc her Tiachi produced. It was sleek, round, and dull in appearance. When she leaned down to feel it, it was matte, hopefully not slippery. "I'm supposed to ride on this?"

Selrahc nodded, a bright grin on his face. "I've not sold a locus their Tiachi before. This is fascinating. Most of the high-level locus I've met just teleport places."

Swallowing a frown as she glanced around, she realized he'd probably just met Belius in one form or another. He popped up everywhere. Her friends were picking out their mounts, and Sin seemed to be set on a Synthclaw. Which looked like a horse, but had claws for feet, and two sharp horns at the tip of its head. Like a double unicorn, except the horns were slightly curved and serrated on one side. The fact that it was pitch black didn't instill confidence in Murmur either, but if that's what Sin wanted, no one was going to talk her out of it.

Since the others were almost done choosing, Murmur guessed she should probably try hers out since her and Mellow didn't exactly get a choice. It was almost like a theme within the world. Don't give Murmur any fucking choices.

She sighed as her little Tiachi flitted around her head, up and down, to the side, its tiny face earnest as it passed in front of her eyes. "Yeah, yeah 'Chi,

I get it."

The disc was about three feet in diameter, with a handrail that seemed to have no attachment to the base and floated about where her waist would go. She assumed it would either cradle her back if she didn't want to balance herself, or else, she could use it to hold onto. Gritting her teeth, she took the short step up and placed her hand on the rail. Chi darted in and out of her vision, chattering wildly, tapping on her hand and tugging at her finger.

Murmur moved her feet, and realized the board conformed to her foot shape once she faced the correct way, with, as she'd guessed, the bar at her back for support. With her feet molded and the bar lending her that bit of solidity, it was actually comfortable and took the weight off her joints.

She wasn't going to question the logic of it, so she smiled at Chi, who seemed satisfied and entwined herself on one of Murmur's strands of hair, giving it a double glowing bulb. Now she had Snowy and Chi. Pretty soon, the way this was going, she'd have an entire army of familiars. At least Chi didn't cost any MA to maintain.

Dev rode up to her on what looked like a large alligator with strangely longer legs. "Ready?"

"Seriously? You're riding one of your own?" Murmur's words came out flat.

The tank laughed. "I didn't think of it that way, but he sort of matches me, don't you think?"

Murmur leveled a glare that was just as flat as her initial response. "Sure. Whatever you say."

Merlin laughed as he trotted up to join them on a nice, plain chestnut horse. "I'm sticking with the tried and true. You two on the other hand have…" but his words broke off as Sinister joined them.

"Holy fuck, Sin. What *is* that?" His eyes held a good dose of fear.

"I've been saving. A Synthclaw is the perfect mount for a blood mage. I'm broke now, but Jareth is the perfect mount." Her grin was almost full gloat. Murmur didn't have the heart to tell her that not everyone would have wanted one for a mount. Besides, if her sensor net was even partially correct, Jareth seemed to have its own opinions about things, so she thought it better to steer clear of those comments.

"Where to, boss?" Mellow asked, and Murmur spun to see what sort of Tiachi he'd received. They were on a disc, with green undertones, matching their own coloring. Maybe it was a locus thing.

"As far as I can tell, there's another non-max level dungeon on this continent. Some ancient ruins in the Curet jungle. We can go via Cognitia and see that city if we want." She didn't mention that her intention to see the city was purely because she wanted to inspect the damned fountain and see if the binders there set off any red flags like they did everywhere else. No one but her seemed to have picked up that quest, from what she could tell through her HUD. And she'd hate to think about how many steps behind they'd be if they did now. Of course, the odds were it probably didn't work that way in Somnia either.

"Sounds like a plan." Beastial nudged his horse forward. It locked like a Clydesdale. Tall at the wither, with fluffy feet. The draught horse was perfect for Beastial's viking build.

Murmur fell into line next to Sinister, wondering at the slight tension there still was between them. She didn't want to admit it, but it pained her more than she'd realized. Fighting was something they'd done so rarely through their lives that she didn't know how to deal with it.

She was used to leading, but she understood why they wouldn't let her. Riding second in line irritated the crap out of her, and her nerves were frayed. Become a jumbled figure amongst them, so people like Jirald had to get past them all to get to her. He'd painted a target on her, and it bothered her more than she cared to admit. She really needed to get the Getashi back to Telvar again. The less she had to focus on her self-declared stalker, the more she could put effort into figuring out different methods they could try to boot her back into her body.

"Hey." Sinister pulled Mur out of her self-analysis.

"Yeah?"

Sin didn't look at her, but instead stared straight ahead, focusing between her mount's horns. "I didn't mean to overstep. I've just always felt like such a part of the family, and I wanted things to be okay again. For all of us."

"It's okay." Murmur realized it really was. She wasn't angry anymore, she didn't have time to be. But this awkward feeling between them needed to disappear. She gestured to her head with a sigh. "I'm not sure how normal this is ever going to get."

"It will." Sinister's voice held steel. "We're going to get you out of here, or at least, out of here so you can use a headset to log in normally."

"A new headset. A normal one." Murmur laughed, feeling more at ease than she had in hours. The sound got lost as their mounts clattered over the bridge that spanned the neck of Glacier Lake. She looked to the side at the spires that rose out of the ice-cold water and frowned.

There was one particularly long dragon-like sea creature she could con that swam close to the center. Deep, deep red. Even at level thirty. This was the highest-level dungeon on this particular continent. And each continent had one of them, smack bang in the middle. They were all surrounding by high level gatekeepers, and the probably level fifty-two water-dragon was no exception. It's eyes never left their party as they crossed, as if perfectly okay with their presence as long as they stayed far away. She shuddered before speaking. "That's one of the final castles."

"Yeah." Veranol spoke from behind, but kicked his mount up to ride next to Murmur's hover thing. "Like the one over on Tarishna in the marsh."

"That's the second end game raid we've seen then. If we count that one near Ululate." Murmur mused. They really did need to level, but since they were doing quite decently, she didn't feel the need to add more pressure. Somnia wasn't easy to level in. Although she didn't relish the idea of the rest of the guild catching up to them before they hit fifty, some of them might reach forty-nine just before they dinged. With the amount of experience needed in order to level that high, she was quite certain of it.

Veranol nodded. "Yeah, one on each continent."

"The keys don't add up." Murmur frowned. "One for each dungeon almost works, but if that's the case, including the ones in the middle, that would be nine."

"The world doesn't much run on logic," Sin's tone was distant. "I mean, look at us."

Havoc laughed. "We're fine. And I don't believe the dungeons necessarily match up with all the keys."

"Obviously. Guess we're going to find out." Murmur looked ahead of them, at the winding path and the surrounding area as it changed before them. It transformed from snowy mountain tops down to rolling hills, through to towering trees in the distance on the right-hand side. To their left Glacier lake spread out, its icy depths causing a soft fog as the hot air from above collided on the surface. In a few moments they'd clatter over the bridge and officially begin to leave the mountains behind them. Beyond the lake, the ground seemed black, but Murmur couldn't get a solid feel for it yet. Nothing other than a sense of foreboding.

They kicked their mount's speed up a notch. It really bothered her that as of yet she'd only been able to find three obvious places on each continent to find keys. Research was easy enough to do from her position in-game most of the time, but it was frustrating to be a touch ahead of the game because no one else knew anything either.

They continued on at a solid canter after the bridge. It took them all a little while to understand how to go at a faster pace, and Murmur watched Snowy galloping along next to them, his tongue hanging out of his mouth as the wind pushed his fur back.

All she had to communicate to Chi was that they needed to keep the same pace as the rest of the group. The hoverboard felt overly exposed but somehow still safe. It was like her feet had a nice and comfortable locked-in spot, and her body was supported at the back, making it sort of a leaning situation that didn't hurt her feet. Locus knees were definitely cushier than human knees, because there was no way she'd be able to stand this long in her real body without her feet starting to hurt.

The wind whipped at her hair, and she glanced at the tiny Chi perched on a strand at her shoulder, even though it put a crick in her neck. But the joy she saw on the tiny creature's face was worth it. Galloping might be faster, but damned if it wasn't boring. Shouting conversations over the pounding of hooves, claws, and humming got annoying fast. At least the terrain changed from snow-covered mountain tops and started to pan out to green grassy shores that led down to the lake, and forest on the other side. But the further they went, the more the ground to the north of the lake cracked, dry and brittle, like a field of death.

She glanced at Snowy again, worried about him in a climate that warmed up even slightly, but he didn't seem to be unhappy, and she was sure he'd tell her anyway.

So caught up in her own thoughts was she that she didn't notice the rest were slowing down until Chi screeched in her ear like a warning, telling her just that. Which was amazing, but even more astounding was that the round, hovering disc she rode on held her feet in place, gently decreasing the pace so that it didn't jolt her in the slightest.

Mur didn't see a city, and all of a sudden wondered just where they were supposed to leave their horses. Not that her or Mellow had a problem. The Tiachi created and took care of the hover discs. She supposed they had a name, but she'd not yet found it out.

"We'll have to walk the mounts from the tree line." Jinna squinted at the forest. "It'll be fairly dense in there, but we should be okay."

"How do you—" Exbo stopped, chuckling at himself. "Yeah, I see it."

Murmur glanced around and saw the carvings higher up in the trees, spelled out in the ones directly facing the road were the words *Welcome to Cognitia.*

The trees in the middle of the forest were so large, so encompassing, it felt like the whole place was hugging them. Too tightly. So tightly it landed just this side of suffocation. Murmur shifted, the tiny weight of her Tiachi against her shoulders as it slept on one of her hair strands barely noticeable in the presence of such oppressive air.

It took a few moments to focus properly amidst all of the greenery, but ivy-covered walkways stretched between massive tree trunks that it would take four people to surround with arms outstretched. Creepers cascaded down the sides of some of the hanging bridges to create an almost waterfall effect.

Upon closer inspection, up high in the trees, she could see small hut-like entrances built into the trunks—or maybe they were around the trunks. She couldn't tell.

"Wow." Sinister breathed out the word, echoing the thought in everyone's heads. Murmur could tell from her sensor net that everyone simply stood there in awe. She had to admit it was pretty damned impressive.

"Anyone any good at climbing?" Rashlyn crossed her arms, squinting at the trees.

"Not that good." Murmur sighed and cricked her neck from side to side, suddenly overwhelmingly tired. It washed over her in a wave of sleepiness, with sounds of the forest flittering around in her head, lulling her into...

She blinked, looking around at all her friends. Everyone except Merlin looked like they were about to fall asleep standing up. Her MA was full, baring Snowy's thirty-five, so she had a full load to spare. Without a second thought, she extended her Shield Expansion over the whole group, protecting their minds from whatever was making her sleepy as fuck.

A wave of renewed energy rolled over her, and she could see the others blinking back from their induced stupor even as a jolt of pain ran through her head from using one hundred and ten MA at once. She grimaced, clamping down on her teeth to lessen the pain, though it didn't quite work. The drawback of traveling as a small raid, yet she was glad she could do something to help them break this spell.

Slowly, as if by magic, a group of five elves exited the cover of the forest, pushing through one of the ivy waterfalls to stand in front of them. The lead elf was as tall as a locus, their pointed ears long with an abstract trace of curling at the end. Narrow blue eyes surveyed them, and the green of their tunic and pants kept shifting so much it was difficult to keep them in sight.

"Well. We weren't expecting a psionicist." The lead elf spoke, and Murmur couldn't tell if it was sarcasm or irritation that formed the words.

"I am Lideshu, the captain of the perimeter. It's my job to keep unfriendlies out. And while I would say you're not unfriendly, as you travel with one of our kind, I do find it quite disruptive that you have magic powerful enough to interfere with my inspection spell." He stopped, standing right in front of Murmur, and made direct eye contact. "I see however that there are no ill intentions, simply a wish to protect yours from something you didn't recognize."

Murmur nodded, uncertain how to respond without smacking the smug elf in the head. Something about Lideshu set off alarm bells in her head. "Sorry. It's against my instincts to let our minds be probed by something we can't identify."

Lideshu inclined his head. "As I said, we weren't expecting a psionicist."

It would have been fine if they hadn't had a psionicist with them then, because he would have probed their minds and had them be none the wiser? Before Murmur could give in to the sarcastic comment sitting on the tip of her tongue, the elf suddenly turned to Merlin and gave a half bow of sorts.

"Merlin. It is good to see you again. May I ask the purpose of your visit?"

Merlin returned the strange gesture and spoke more formally than Murmur had ever heard him before. "We are on our way through to the Jungle of Curet, and I wanted to show them my home town," he said smoothly.

"Excellent!" Lideshu clapped his hands and the creepers parted to reveal what looked like an ivy-wound wooden elevator. It was massive with waist high railings made of ivy-wound wood. "Much easier than climbing the trees, wouldn't you say?"

Lideshu winked over his shoulder at the group, giving Murmur proof that he'd been listening when they first got there. He must have some form of enchanter as his class make up, because his thoughts had been far too well quieted for her sensory net to pick up. Which gave her pause for thought; perhaps she could upgrade her sensory abilities and refine them, hone them. To focus in on areas with an absence of thought, because that would often imply that someone was trying to mask them.

Thought Sensing (175)
Thought Shielding (175)
Thought Projection (175)

You have reached the next stage of your hidden class. Adjusting and refining your skills is a huge step. For this perspective your skills have leveled enough to allow you to reach level four of Mental Affinity. Please see a trainer at your earliest convenience. Sooner than later. Like seriously. An extra fifty base MA is nothing to scoff at. Off you go.

Murmur frowned at the notification. She didn't know if she'd be able to trust the elves. She'd never met their trainer before, and they didn't seem entirely on the up and up. This forest, and these elves gave her pause. They were too wary, and too guarded. At least from what she'd witnessed so far. So perhaps she'd wait to train in Curet. First though, she needed to see the damned statue in the fountain. Not to mention that changing their minds right now would seem suspicious. They had to go through with the visit on the pretense Merlin had invented.

The lift moved smoothly, which led Murmur to believe that some form of magic powered it. Stepping out on the platform at the top of the elevator was surreal to say the least. Varying shades of green adorned every platform, leaving little room for wood to peek through. Elves, also clothed in a variety of nature's colors, roamed everywhere. They'd not been visible from below. Two wooden hanging bridges left off from the elevator's platform to others. One was far longer, and Murmur couldn't make out where it ended up, but the other one led over to a huge platform around a spectacular tree, and there, winding around that trunk, was a fountain.

Upon closer inspection, it appeared the fountain was made out of petrified wood. Murmur frowned as she took in all the elves dancing around it. Or at least, they appeared to be dancing at first. In fact, their movements flowed so easily into one another that the fighter, rogue, archer, and mage appeared to execute a dance as she circled the structure. Water streamed, gently pumped through arrows, fingers, swords, and daggers.

It was the most beautiful of the fountains she'd seen so far.

Once close to the feles, the elves knew how to perform magic through movement. You are correct! This fountain shows a classic beauty that neither race have remembered, the lost art of movement magic. Take heed, as you know the fountains are connected, and remember ancient times, in ancient places, where they may be discovered again.

Murmur blinked. Twice. Cryptic had to be a god of the game.

"I take it you like the fountain then?" Lideshu stood next to her, his slimy grin plastered on his face as he focused on the fountain and not her. Movement around them had crawled to a standstill, and while none of the elves looked directly at them, she could feel the weight of all their attention crawling up her spine. None of them appeared to be talking and it added to the stifling atmosphere.

"It's lovely. Just like the rest of them." She left that there trying to pass off her interest in the fountains as a purely touristy sort of thing, and walked over to Devlish, who, if the way he held his shoulders was anything to go by, was feeling just as uncomfortable as she was.

He glanced at her, shifting his weight slightly and laid a hand on the hilt of his axe. "I think we need to get moving or we'll never find those ancient ruins. At this rate we'll be traveling through the dark world anyway."

"Surely you don't want to leave so soon?" Lideshu's tone sounded like he wanted nothing but for them to leave, and yet, phrasing it that way leant a sinister edge to the undertones, making Murmur want to get away even more. There was definitely something missing here.

The whole forest was quiet. Not even a cricket chirped. No birds sang, and even the wind seemed to have stopped blowing and rustling the leaves. Still, and silent. Dangerous.

"We don't want to, but we have to be on our way." She phrased it as tactfully as she could manage, trying her best to express disappointment with her expression and hoped it worked. It was all she could do to fight down her inclination to flee.

"Ah," the elf said, inclining his head. "Such a pity you won't join us for dinner. But we understand, of course."

Murmur shuddered as she nodded, reading what he didn't say that lay underneath the words. If they stayed here, there was no guarantee of safety whatsoever. Lideshu's eyes shone with a hungry light, and for a moment she wondered what he meant by dinner. Too many theories popped up in her mind, all of them terrible, all of them potentially real. "Terribly sorry to sightsee and run. We'll be back, though."

She meant it, even if she could tell with one glance that none of her friends were inclined to return, Murmur would need to figure out what was so off about this place. Devlish wasn't comfortable, and even the skin around Merlin's eyes and mouth were tight, and he caught her eye, trying to convey something to her as well. It seemed everyone agreed, and her sensor net picked up overwhelming unease. Supplies be damned, it had only been an excuse to stop there anyway. She had enough food cooked for them in her bags to whether the road. She'd thought coming to the elven city was going to be a way to relax and take in some of the beauty.

But while it was beautiful to look at, the attractiveness only ran skin deep. Beneath the ivy laced streets of Cognitia lay something Murmur wasn't quite ready to tackle yet.

Summer Residence
Home of Laria, David, and Wren
Summer Condo
Day Thirteen Post Release

"I don't really care that you think this is all your fault." David started, his tone like the one Laria knew he used with students who tried to beg a better grade. "You need to stop acting like you're in this alone and consult me. Damn it Laria, she's *our* daughter not just yours."

Laria cringed at his words, knowing he was right and yet the guilt still gnawed at her far more than she believed it did him. "But you didn't push to get an early headset. You didn't walk up to the insane genius man and inadvertently ask him to make your daughter into a secret guinea pig. I did that. It's all on me."

"But we both checked the headgear, and even though it had a few anomalies, neither of us thought they were severe enough to produce what they did. Stop dredging it up and running around in circles with it so we can focus on fixing the issue." It infuriated her how calm he could keep his voice; how reasonable he remained no matter how heated she got. How was he always the one holding it together, while she could barely function outside of her head?

"I know," she finally admitted, her shoulders slumping as she leaned forward on the table, arms outstretched. It was so much quieter in their condo without Wren. Even thought she'd have been playing the game non-stop, she still would have been in here on occasion. Raiding the fridge, eating every apple in existence. "I know it, David. I just don't like it."

He raised an eyebrow at her, reminding her of when they first met in person, so many years ago. He'd been a young and idealistic IT major, and she'd loved that about him. His theories on how to maximize game time and push their characters had made her giddy to know him.

"If you liked it, I'd be even more worried about you than I am now. You need to sleep. This pattern of behavior you're exhibiting is bad for your health, and if you get sick, how are we going to get Wren back. Think beyond just the now, Laria, I know you're capable of it." He reached out to take her hands in his, squeezing them gently and filling her with a warmth only he knew how to give. "You've got to stop this me-against-the-world mentality and grow up. You've got your dream job and your dream game. Sure, there may be a few hiccups, but you can't sit and throw a tantrum and just push through it and hope for the best. You need to think, to develop a strategy. You need to stop adulting like you game."

Laria's first reaction was anger, and she tried to snatch her hands away, but David held on fast. She scowled at him, angry at his words, but after a couple of moments she realized it wasn't just his words she was angry at, but the truth in them. He was fucking right. Yet again. Like always. Her calm, stoic, amazing husband always knew just how to get to the heart of the matter. Laria was, in fact, treating this somewhat like a game. Because Wren was stuck in a game. And if there's one thing Laria had always been good at, it was being the best gamer she could be.

Taking in a deep breath, she nodded. "Fine. Fuck you too. I'll sit down and make a plan instead of going in guns blazing."

"Axes wielded?" He laughed, and she watched as relief ironed out the wrinkles that had formed at the edges of his eyes. She'd worried him, like always.

"Sorry." She whispered the words, knowing that she apologized to him on a regular basis, that she was always having to say she was sorry. Every day she waited, without quite realizing it, for him to realize he'd married a lunatic and leave her. But he never did. Instead, he sat with her through thick and thin, made her rash mind think things through when she'd rather attack them head on.

"It's what I'm here for, remember? Got to save my tank." The past dripped from his reminiscent tone, and Laria leaned into his shoulder.

"Even now you're still saving me, still saving us. I don't know what I'd do without you."

Her only answer was a tight squeeze of her shoulders, and she knew, clear as day, that he felt the same way.

CHAPTER FIFTEEN
Fissures

Storm Entertainment
Somnia Online Division
Game Development Offices – Shayla Johnson's Office
Day Thirteen Post Release

Shayla grumbled at her desk; leafing through report after report was driving her insane. The thing was, James always seemed to be close at hand. More so than he'd been before the game launched, or in the few days after. It was either because he was genuinely worried about her, or he was trying to find something. Frankly, being who she was, Shayla believed it was the latter.

Gearing up for their new type of reports, Shayla couldn't concentrate on her work. With so many irons in the fire right now, her head was doing her in. The AIs exhibited signs of sentience; her lead developer had gone slightly rogue and whisked her daughter into a containment pod so she could keep her brain active while she was playing.

The urge to laugh was great, but Shayla knew the sound would ring crazed. It was probably better not to laugh hysterically in her office.

"Do you need anything, Shayla?"

James's voice ripped her out of her thoughts and almost sent her jumping three feet into the air. Barely managing to compose herself in time, like almost every time he unexpectedly interrupted her, she turned to face him, her smile fixed in place. "Not at all. I'll send for you if I do, you should know that."

He definitely wasn't the quiet and unassuming assistant Ava had been. He didn't have all the reports ready to go and at her fingertips when she didn't even know she needed them. Worst of all, he didn't seem to understand the meaning of alone time. Or at least, he didn't in the last week or so.

Shayla frowned, swiveling toward her door to watch anyone passing by outside. The blinds were drawn, lending her some amount of privacy at least. James hadn't been this clingy in the first couple of weeks he'd assisted her. So, what had changed?

Several days into launch, she'd brought some sensitive information up with Teddy. Did he have something to do with her new bestest buddy? She really hoped not, but the more she thought about it, the more she realized he probably did. The promise of promotions could do a lot to a person.

"Make sure you knock next time. Might help me not jump out of my skin."

"Of course!" James smiled, but if she wasn't mistaken, it didn't quite reach his eyes. Instead, that gaze was coldly calculating, a complete juxtaposition to his tone of voice.

She forced her own smile. Two could play at that game. "Excellent. I'm glad we had that little talk. Make sure to email me all the files you're working on so late at night. I'll expect them in five minutes. And make sure you close my door behind you."

She turned away, but not before she saw an irritated shadow pass over James's expression. The door clicked, and she counted to five before she allowed some of the tension to leak out from her shoulders.

Just what did Teddy suspect, and how much did he know? She needed to be more careful around James until she figured out just what was up. His behavior wasn't even that subtle. Staying as late as he had been wasn't a part of his job description. In fact, it wasn't part of hers either. She doubted he was staying so late just to show his dedication. Her eyes strayed to watch her inbox, waiting for the email she'd demanded.

After a minute of watching that seemed like an eternity, the email dinged that she had a new message from James with several attachments. Shayla opened them for good measure, triple checking because she couldn't shake the unease. On the surface everything seemed legit, but she'd check with Laria in the morning to make sure they still needed the info he was working on.

Maybe she was just seeing ghosts around every corner now.

They barely spoke as they mounted up and headed out from the creepy elven city. Murmur could feel the sensation of being watched like it was over head as a neon eye sign, flashing an arrow at their whole group. From the way their gear camouflaged with the forest surroundings, she was quite certain elves were all around them, just waiting to prevent them from returning to the tree-top city.

She shivered as her skin crawled. Locus didn't seem to have body hair like most of the species in the game, but she could feel the same sensation through to the skin, like her real body was reacting to the game. Sinister rode next to her, and even her Synthclaw appeared unsettled, tossing its head and snorting wildly at the air, its eyes slightly haunted. Snowy nudged the beast with his shoulder, and it looked down at him, heaved what appeared to be a huge sigh, and its eyes cleared somewhat, returning the ride to the smooth one it had been previously.

Murmur slotted that away for use later on. Leaves rustled above her, and she made the mistake of glancing up to the top of the tree canopy, resplendent in the green glow that the sun gave to it. Her head spun, and she could see fleeting movement through the branches, but it moved so quickly all that resulted was a blurred image in her mind and the beginnings of a headache.

There was something really off with these elves, and Murmur heaved a huge sigh of relief when they finally broke the tree coverage and passed through the entrance to Cognitia at the tree line before the road. Immediately the weight on her back lifted, and she knew without a doubt that their observers had departed.

"Just as far as their borders, eh?" Havoc remarked softly. "Very interesting."

"Annoying, creepy, stalkerish—I'd consider all of those before interesting." Sinister clenched her hands around the reins, her eyes staring straight ahead. She looked a little pale, and Murmur reached out a hand to brush her knee, trying to lend some reassurance.

The blood mage smiled wanly, and the group continued in silence until they reached the actual path.

"Don't know about you guys," Devlish called back over his shoulder, "but I'm not feeling overly fond of trees right now, so I'm going to stay on the left side of the path, as close to the Felling Fields as I can."

No one argued; no one else spoke. Murmur could feel the unease still present, even if it was less than before. She didn't even need to have her sensor net activated for that. She glanced out to the left, noticing the cracked earth. The Felling Fields definitely didn't look appealing. Having so much death so close to such teeming wildlife and fauna seemed laughably wrong. She wanted to know what the story behind it was, why the fissures in the earth ran so deep, why they seemed to move slightly.

Murmur blinked. "Did anyone else see that fissure up ahead move? Or was that just me?" She had to know if her head was spinning again. Maybe she needed to log out for more than a few hours. A full night's sleep would be fantastic.

"I'm not sure." Merlin squinted, and then lifted his hand to point up a ways ahead. "You mean that one, right? With the huge crack? The huge moving crack?"

"Fissure, Merlin," Havoc mumbled absentmindedly, also squinting.

Dust began to billow up around it, and a few of the other fissures also seemed to trade places, moving inward, away from the huge one that was now just ahead of them and keeping pace.

"Have we not had enough water?" Rashlyn piped up, a nervous laugh underlying her words.

"No. I don't believe that's it." Veranol grew pale, and Murmur had to agree with him.

"That's not a mirage, I'm pretty sure that's a monster, and it's locked onto us, and if I'm not mistaken, it's big." Havoc shrugged. "Of course, that would be nothing new when it comes to our opponents here."

Murmur wished she could take on his indifference, even if she knew it was how he hid emotions. The earth to the side of them suddenly veered sharply to its right, and emerged onto the path in front of them. Like an optical illusion as it leapt onto the path, the fissure appeared to simply spread from the fields and overflow.

The creature truly appeared to be a gaping maw in the middle of the road. The fissure on its back appeared to have jagged edges around it, which dripped sticky tar into its center. Red-brown like the earth of the Felling Fields, its feet were so many Murmur couldn't count them all. But there had to be at least eight on each side as it raised itself up like a giant roly-poly with the fissure on its back instead of armor. Its real mouth appeared to be small, and it had tiny beady eyes, at least in comparison to the rest of it. She couldn't judge its size that well, but it was around four horse lengths long.

Its roar was high pitched and focused on them so intensely that they had to cover their ears. It was clearly a challenge. Chi gripped onto Murmur's hair strands, shaking.

Murmur bit her tongue against the impulse to note that they were lucky only one had approached them when it was clear that the other fissures were also home to these creatures. Sometimes she almost believed in Sinister's superstitions too.

Devlish leapt off his lizard mount brandishing an axe and shield. "May as well get this over with," he said with a gleam in his eyes.

Devlish's axe was parried, yet again, by one of the Fissure's stony front feet. Or maybe they were legs—Murmur wasn't sure. Slowing it had been possible, but every time she attempted to cast Weakness she got a warning message.

Please note, the Fissure is impervious to weakening spells due to its unique composition. You can keep trying to weaken it, but it's just a waste of mana.

She signed, and gave up trying on the third time. Sometimes she just wanted to out-stubborn the game. Instead, she made sure that the rest of the group was buffed. Being close to thirty-two, she almost wanted to pull one after the other until she dinged, but at the rate this fight was going, that was going to take forever. These mobs also did more damage to Devlish and Rash since they couldn't be weakened.

The worst thing was, every thirty to forty-five seconds, without any further type of rhythm, the damned thing shook, and then somehow projected its boiling tar all over the group. Personal cooldowns only helped so much, and Ver and Sinister struggled to deal with the amount of AoE damage inflicted on the group. It didn't help that its timer had nothing to do with damage suffered and seemed like a D20 roll, random as to its timing.

Axes weren't cutting into it too well, except for when they hit a joint. The joints were made of softer stuff and actually appeared to give way easier, as long as the attacker managed to aim correctly. Devlish's frustration showed on his face as the Fissure twisted quickly for a third time, causing his axe to grind against the stone. Murmur didn't want to think about the blunting effects.

"Aiming for the joints is harder than it looks," Merlin called out from his vantage point atop a rock near the forest side of the path. "It's surprisingly quick for how bulky it is."

"I have an idea." Exbo grinned, drew back a flame arrow and fired it into the tar pit it carried on its back. Merlin turned and blinked at the other ranger, a wide grin spreading over his face.

"Don't know why I didn't think of that." He muttered as the both of them began firing their flame arrows straight into the fire pit. Sure enough, while one didn't take hold, after about a dozen of them filled the tar pit, with Veranol managing to shield the group from one flaming tar toss, the creature began to scream, and its health dropped rapidly.

The material holding its limbs together began to melt in on itself, and Murmur could only surmise that it came from the tar pit in the back of it. The low flame spread until the entire basin was covered, and the creature screamed its shrill sound again, forcing them to block it out however they could.

Just as it was about to fling more flaming tar at them, it shuddered and collapsed, rolling into a defensive ball.

Devlish waited a moment to poke it with his axe. "Is it really dead?"

Merlin nodded. "Seems that way to me."

The dread knight sighed. "Definitely not the sort of beast I want to encounter again. How about we walk on the tree side of the path? I'd prefer shady elves over those damned Fissures any day."

"No shit." Havoc's tone seemed irritated. "Fighting stone creations is just laborious, and all it gave us was some crafting material. Not worth our time."

No one argued as they mounted up and began their trek to Curet once more.

CHAPTER SIXTEEN

Curet

Storm Entertainment
Somnia Online Division
Game Development Offices – Shayla Johnson's Office
Day Thirteen

"David and I had a talk." Laria stood at the door, leaning against it, her arms crossed, and her eyes, for the first time in two weeks, were almost normal. Sure, a little haunted around the edges, but overall, not too bad.

Shayla smiled. "I'm guessing that for once you're the one who did the listening."

"Wild guess that, don't know how you came to such a conclusion." Laria smiled and moved into the room, closing the door behind her.

"It's all good. He's going to research some different ways to help bring Wren out of it. I've no idea what he means, but he has a totally geeky doctor friend I think he may pose a couple of hypotheticals to." Laria leaned back in the chair, stretching her legs. "Plus, he's set a theoretical assignment for his students, so that should get interesting."

But Shayla frowned, unsure if that was a good idea. "He needs to make sure these are really treated as hypothetical though. Too many people know already. We can't let it get out."

"I know." And Shayla kicked herself, because Laria did know that the possibility of Wren being taken in for observation was very real, and very possible if they couldn't get her out first. Not to mention being fired for keeping such information to themselves. Bridges that could all be crossed later, or burned.

"Sorry. Helps me remember shit if I repeat it to myself." Shayla leaned back and stared at the ceiling, listening to Laria choke down a laugh.

"It's all good. I feel more like myself after some actual rest." Laria stood back up and crossed her arms, walking to the window and parting the blinds with a thoughtful frown on her face. "It probably helped that Wren came back to talk to me. Yell at me might be more accurate. But I deserved that."

"Yeah, you did." Shayla watched as her friend's shoulders tensed, but Laria didn't explode or quip back. Instead she sighed, and it turned into a soft chuckle.

"True. It's been just over a week since she found out, and it's calmer now. I should have got my head together sooner. Can't change my stupidity in the past, but I can try to rectify the future." She leaned toward the inner office window, her frown deepening as she looked at something in the corridor outside. "He really is always just out of your reach, isn't he?"

Shayla stood up smoothly and joined the other woman at the window. "James is hovering these days. Always just out of hearing range, maybe." There was no reason for him to be there that she could think of. His desk was a ways down the hall. Giving him the benefit of the doubt didn't sit well with her anymore, not with his questionable behavior.

"Keep an eye on him for me when you get the chance to, Laria? He might not think that you're suspicious." Shayla ran a hand through her hair and sighed, scrolling through her to do list in an effort to multitask.

"Sure thing, boss." Laria laughed again, causing Shayla to raise an eyebrow. "Sorry. I just have a speck of hope for the first time in a while, and I'd like the chance to feel good about that before I go and confront the AIs again and get all flustered and frustrated at them."

"Going to see the AIs again?" Shayla phrased the question and watched the way her friend's expression reacted in little to no way at all.

"David had some ideas for Rav, since he seems to be the AI most attached to Wren." Laria shrugged and leaned against the sturdy oak desk in the office. "Of course, knowing my luck, Rav is becoming obsessed and trying to figure out ways to keep her in there instead of ways to get her out."

"Well, then." Shayla spoke her thoughts out loud to avoid them taking a dark turn inside her head. "Shall we head on and see how the servers are doing?"

Laria's answering smile was a bit tighter this time, but she nodded and opened the door to reveal James raising a fist to knock, a completely surprised expression on his face. Too surprised perhaps.

Shayla frowned, not liking the coincidence at all. There was no such thing. "What's up, James?" She knew her tone was curt, but she didn't have the time to deal with a potential spy in her office right now.

Expression affable, his light blond hair and blue eyes attempted to lend a soothing aura to the mood, but Shayla only found it more annoying. "I was just checking if you wanted coffee, and if you remembered that you have a meeting at three."

"We're about to run a routine check on the servers, and we'll pick up coffee on the way." Shayla gestured to the hall in front of her as she exited her office fully and clicked the locking mechanism very deliberately so the state of her office was obvious.

"Ah, my timing is off. Next time I'll catch you sooner." He nodded and half bowed as the women walked down the hall. Until they turned the corner, Shayla couldn't get the feeling of eyes boring into her back out of her head.

Giant trees rose up, their leaves spreading wide to envelope the rainforest in a natural canopy. Vines swung down from the trees, and Murmur could see feles in various states of ascent. Small huts wound around trunks at different intervals, with only the vine-ropes to traverse between them.

Curet was, in fact, the polar opposite of Cognitia, at least insofar as the mood that pervaded the city.

In the center of the clearing was a huge platform that dwarfed the one they'd seen in Cognitia. It looked like it was formed on a massive lily pad, and its fountain at the center gave off a joyous vibe. There were larger huts all around the perimeter, with stalls selling wares ranging closer toward the middle. Small feles ran around, some with stripes, and others solid, like Dansyn and Rash. Their tails whipped around, steadying them as they ran and jumped, tumbled and squealed. They tagged and dashed, ears twitching, taking leaps that seemed impossible with what appeared to be ease. They were captivating, just like all the other children had been in their own way in the other cities.

Murmur stopped, realizing they'd not seen any small elves. No children had been running anywhere, everywhere, and almost careening into her. Not even one.

You have noticed an abnormality within the world. This might be worth further inspection.

This time the vagueness didn't bother Murmur so much; after all, it was right. That she hadn't noticed it while in Cognitia spoke volumes about the atmosphere in the place. Even with her shielding, it had affected them all.

Rash nudged her with her hip. "What do you think, Mur?"

"I like this. It's got a much friendlier vibe. Don't you think?" Murmur grinned, and glanced at the rest of the group. Everyone's expressions seemed surprised and happy, more relaxed and relieved. A small test of her sensor net let her know it was genuine and not a forced sensation. After their run in with the elves, she couldn't be too cautious.

A flash of speed stopped right in front of them, actually skidded to a halt, feline eyes blinking at them. "Travelers! Wait." Their eyes squinted while their tail lashed back and forth and their grey mouth pulled back slightly to reveal sharp teeth.

"Dansyn and Rashlyn!" The sound practically mewled from their greeter, and Rash and Dansyn smiled, hugging the slightly smaller feles tightly.

"Hey, Ceshli. What have you been up to?" Rash's tone held a fond note that Murmur hadn't often heard from her. Ceshli's excitement at seeing them was palpable and it took several seconds for the enchanter to realize she wasn't a player. At least the elves had kept it mysterious and irritating enough that she didn't feel they were real. Everything else in this world was slowly making her believe that Telvar was right. Somnia was a world of its own.

Ceshli smiled, which was a disconcerting effect on a cat. While Murmur had gotten used to it on her friends, it seemed that didn't translate to foreign kitties. Their ears folded back slightly and their face took on a brief look as if it had been scratched behind the ears. The wide smile was very Cheshire Cat-like in appearance, just without the disappearing face.

"People will be so glad to see you!" Ceshli clapped their hands together, their claws extending. Murmur frowned. She'd not noticed her friends doing that at all. Conning the friendly greeter, she realized they were still red to her. Must be a quest NPC, beginner anyway.

"Ceshli, these are our friends." Rash smiled as she gestured to the group of them. "We wanted to bind here and show them where we grew up."

It was all Murmur could do not to laugh. She'd never seen Rash role-play before, wasn't even sure that was quite what this was, but at any rate, it was endearing.

"Fantastic! Are you thinking to go out into the jungle? You've grown so fast, you'll overtake me soon. I think you should be able to weather the storms out there. Frankly," Ceshli stepped closer, their whisper loud enough to hear even in the conspiratorial tones. "Just between us, there's something not right out there. At night, if you go to the edges of Curet, you can hear noises. Not like a jungle-monkey crying for food, but real screams. Ones we're not used to around here."

"How long has this been going on?" Murmur asked, trying to fish out whether this was a quest or not. The right questions, the right actions. All of it triggered things. Which meant taking even innocent seeming comments or information as a prompt for something bigger.

"About a week now. Very strange actually. Has the kids actually listening to us when we tell them it's bedtime." Ceshli grinned again in that cat-like way, and then gestured to them. "Anyway, come, come with me. You must need supplies, and I'm sure you'll want to bind at the statue. Makes the most sense in the long run."

You have noticed that the Feles are worried about the cause of noises in the jungle between Curet and Cognitia. It even scares the kittens at night. Surely you love kittens. Everyone loves kittens. Find out what's scaring them and what you can do about it.

That was a specific task for once. At least it was along the lines that Murmur was already considering pursuing. Fountains, quests, odd occurrences. Sometimes she just wished she could mindlessly grind away until she hit fifty. But then again, where would the fun in that be? Glancing at the rest of the raid, she frowned. Everyone had looks of consternation on their faces, which probably meant they'd all gotten the prompt. In a way that was good, because this solo questing shit was getting annoying.

As they walked through the city, Murmur noticed a slew of other players. All green to her. As usual, it seemed the cat race was getting deserved attention. Most of the players seemed to be around level five to ten, with some teens loitering about.

Dansyn spoke right next to her, and Murmur almost jumped.

"They have some quests here where higher levels need to help younger levels. There weren't any players to help us, so Ceshli… I mean, NPCs took that job. When we've leveled, we'll come back and do the same. This village," he gestured around them, a soft expression on his face, "seems so real some of the time. Caring, helpful, and sort of jolly. If you ever need to come and forget worries for a while, just come and watch the children play. Or else, just come and play hide and seek with them. You might be surprised."

"Hide and seek with sneaky cats, huh?" Murmur found her own mood softening as she glanced out over the city that was bustling with life. It seemed her friends didn't always see NPCs as such either. Maybe reality was just perception. Ululate had its fair share of players mixed with NPCs, as did Frangit and the big cities. Yet she hadn't seen many players hanging around Verendus. Perhaps it was because everyone who'd come that far was intent on leveling.

Which left her to wonder where the hell Exodus was now. They didn't appear to be anywhere near her, which she was actually grateful for.

"Mur?" Dansyn was trying to get her attention. "You sort of stopped in the middle of saying something, I think?"

She blinked at him and backtracked. "Oh, I just meant playing hide and seek with sneaky cats might actually be fun."

He raised an eyebrow. "Sneaky, are we?"

"Yes. Soft footed and hard to detect when you creep up on people. Sneaky." She nodded emphatically, trying to catalogue the rest of her thoughts so she didn't keep running in circles.

It was a longer walk to the huge lily-pad center than she'd thought. From a distance it had appeared smaller, but in actuality it was solid—if a little bouncy underfoot—and the fountain at its center captured pure feline grace. As she bound herself in front of it, she studied the fountain. Two feles graced the structure, one at the bottom dual wielding axes, its leg lunged forward to provide what appeared to be support for the feles above it. The second appeared to have catapulted itself off the other's knee, twisting in midair. It drew back its bow and had an arrow ready to shoot. There appeared to be no actual connection between the two statues, and no other way for the second to be secured, but even still, it hovered there in perfect stationary motion.

Yet another piece of the puzzle, another path to a key. What will the arrow hit? Can you tell yet?

Murmur did her best not to get angry, literally clenching her fists so her fingernails bit into her skin. "No, I can't bloody well tell yet," she muttered under her breath.

"What was that, Mur?" Sin leaned in front of her, her dark hair hanging over her shoulders like a waterfall, and Murmur's bad mood broke.

"Nothing. Just another quest pop-up." She tried to belay Sin's questions by smiling at her, but the blood mage wasn't deterred.

"You seem to get a lot of quest pop-ups," she stated, squaring her shoulders as she stood upright.

"Don't you get any about the fountains?" Murmur was only slightly surprised. It seemed her thoughts about things triggered quests, and she didn't for one moment doubt that Sinister had her own quests that she'd discovered without anyone else.

Sin pursed her lips, her brows furrowing in thought. "Not about the fountains themselves, just about some of the statues so far."

Maybe it was because Sin noticed the artistry in the statues more than the way they interacted with the function of the fountain. Such small and subtle differences. Murmur wanted desperately to ask Telvar how this shit all worked, but she got the feeling all she'd get would be an enigmatic smile and avoidance of the question. "Mostly the same as mine then."

"Oh!" Sin's face brightened up. "I thought I was missing out."

She winked at Murmur before moving over to the non-casters of the group and helping Mellow bind them.

Murmur watched her go, a thousand thoughts running through her head. Already having bound herself, she glanced around the huge platform. Several player-occupied stalls were scattered over the area, with other players and even NPCs stopping by to look at their wares. She glanced over at Beastial, who nodded at her.

"Already on it, Mur. Seeking out some new crafters even as you think."

She laughed and wondered just how transparent she was. At least until she felt a spark of discomfort between her shoulder blades. She turned around to find the source of it and noticed several lower level players watching her, but with their focus slightly out of whack.

They had to be inspecting her and her gear. After the initial moment of irritation subsided, she remembered when she'd first begun gaming, before the endgame got a hold of her. Inspecting those who were higher level had spurred her on, made her want to be better at the game and her class. Sometimes she forgot others might like that too. A bit of incentive could go very far. She also guessed her sensing net didn't differentiate between different types of observance. If something or someone was watching her, it flagged it. Maybe there was a setting of sorts she'd not yet discovered. Like, ill intentions only.

You have increased your Thought Sensing options. This is only available to level four of Mental Affinity and above. Please see your trainer, like yesterday. It's not the first time you've been told.

Murmur raised an eyebrow at the words scrolling her screen. "Hey Rash? Enchanter trainer?"

Rash frowned. "Oh, sure. Wait. Come with me."

Wait and *come with me* were complete oxymorons, but Murmur followed her friend without wisecracking. She was extremely proud of her restraint. People didn't appreciate the effort that could sometimes take.

They walked around the lily pad and through a few of the player stalls, toward a colorful hut attached to one of the trees on the outer ring. The colors were more in tune with nature out here in Curet, but still stood out in the colors of nature.

Murmur hesitated on the doorstep, unsure what she'd find inside. So far, the enchanter guilds had been a little different. Getting used to the slight idiosyncrasies took time. Maybe she should have gone back to Verendus and Dirsna, but she was here now.

"Thanks, Rash," she said before pushing her way inside.

The interior of the Enchanter Guild in Curet was less cheery and more soothing. Perhaps they'd chosen to make it relaxing because the outside was less austere than most other places she'd visited. Still, there was no one at the front counter, and there didn't seem to be any other players in the guild at all.

Strange. Did enchanters not choose to be cats? Agility helped everyone, at least, insofar as Murmur had experienced.

Stretching her sensing net out, she detected two people. One was definitely an NPC—the other, she wasn't so sure about.

"Hello?"

She called out the word, feeling self-conscious for the first time since she started playing. It wasn't hard to interact with people she could see right off the bat, but there was something about walking into this den of soothing calmness that set her on edge. Probably the exact opposite of what they intended, but since nothing in the world was like this, it made her suspicious.

"Coming!" A decidedly feminine voice echoed out to Murmur from the hall she could see in the back. But no footsteps sounded through to her, and the other presence didn't even move. Perhaps they were asleep.

"So sorry for the wait." A calico-colored feles stepped out, white robes billowing around her with slits up to her knee joints. Her footsteps had been, in typical cat like behavior, silent. She looked gorgeous. Delicate in coloring and features, she smiled that blissful cat smile. "Oh, Murmur! I'm Riasli. You've come to visit me. I'm so sorry—my greeter isn't feeling well and is lying down. Not many feles become enchanters, so we're never too busy. I didn't think it would matter."

Her words and way had a disarming quality to them, which again sent red flags up for Murmur, who slammed her shields up, tighter, just in case. She'd avoided being soothed by an NPC once; she wasn't about to let this feles have their way, no matter how real or sympathetic she appeared to be.

Riasli frowned. "I mean you no harm. Sorry. It's an automatic reaction to reach out and calm people."

"You're a psionicist?" Murmur was starting to think everyone had been full of shit when they told her it wasn't a usual path. How many fucking psionicists were there out there?

"Oh gosh, no." Riasli laughed. "I specialize in reinforced soothing, and have a healer hybrid. Second nature to make people feel better. After all, I'm a part of the cat family. And just having a cat on your lap does wonders for one's mood, wouldn't you say?"

Murmur blinked at her. She'd never had a pet, so she just shrugged her answer out. "Sure, seems to be the case."

"Anyway, dear. Come on through. I see you've hit the fourth rank of MA. So fast! That's very exciting." And she waved Murmur through to her back office. The friendly feles talked as they entered her room. "With fourth rank, you get to choose your poison, so to speak. I have four options for you, and you get to choose two. One is a kinetic choice, and the other is psionic. You must choose one of each line. Not to mention getting an additional fifty MA at your disposal is pretty damned attractive, wouldn't you say?"

Murmur just nodded, glancing at the two scrolls Riasli held. Another choice, and another expansion of her character. If she just had all the info at her fingertips so she could sit down and plan her character out. Dirsna had told her that at some stage, even though it was costly, she could reformulate her class. That was the only thing not making her have a panic attack right then and there.

Psionicist Kinetic abilities.

Forcefield Push

Once used wildly, you can now activate this at will. This will form a bubble of force projecting directly outwards from you in an arc and push anything in its path out of your way. Having this ability directly available will now allow you to develop some measure of control.

Effects: This will cause some physical and mental damage to any opponent caught in the range of the push. The amount of damage inflicted depends on the level and strength of will behind the push. Damage is increased by MA level and usage.

Cost: This push requires that you have MA at eighty, but will not use MA to cast, as it is a kinetic ability. Can only be used once every five minutes.

Caution. This spell can create a mind backlash if over-utilized. Make sure those in your path are not allies, as this ability does not discriminate between friend and foe.

Unless you want to make them a foe. Then they're fair game. Remember, try and maintain control.

Earth Belt

Due to your affinity with the druidic circle, this ability allows you to pull protection wards from the earth in the form of an earth wall that must first be broken through before your team can be reached.

Effects: This produces a physical barrier raised from the earth that cannot be scaled and must be fought before the opponent can reach you. Its durability hinges on the intent and level of the caster. Durability increases with MA level and usage.

Cost: This protection requires that MA be maintained at 120,

but will not use MA to cast, as it is a kinetic ability. This can only be used once every 15 minutes.

Caution: This spell requires a hit point pool and will pull 10 life from the caster for every second it is active. Great in a pinch, but be cautious about using it too often. Remember, dying isn't always a good thing.

Murmur frowned at the kinetic choices, feeling slightly underwhelmed. She'd used the Forcefield Push a few times now and wasn't sure allowing it to be a more powerful skill was such a good idea around her currently volatile temper. However, Earth Belt would drain her life, and that just wasn't an option she could afford right now. She placed her hand over Forcefield Push, absorbing it into her so that her runes lit up and danced over and under her skin. Earth Belt greyed out, no longer available to her.

"No going back now," she mumbled to herself, pretty sure that as she did Riasli chuckled under her breath. At least she amused the NPCs.

Moving on, she picked up the next scroll.

Phantom

This ability allows you to convince your enemies that you are a different target. This renders you invisible to their aggro radar for all intents and purposes.

Effect: This ability not only transfers your generated aggro, but also takes you off the targetable list for the duration. It transfers aggression to your target, giving them your appearance, and rendering you invisible to any enemy near you. This may be used on allies, but also on enemies.

Cost: this ability requires MA to be at a minimum of 50, drains 5 MA per second, and will adjust as MA level and usage of this ability increase. Requires Charisma to be at 150 or more. Cannot be chained, must wait at least 5 minutes for MA to regenerate.

Caution: Make sure you do not cause your MA to run out. Should that happen, backlash will render the caster unconscious for a period of seconds not less than half the caster's level. Make sure you choose your targets wisely.

Cool. Murmur actually really liked that one. Having enemies attacking each other by thinking that their target was her was kind of cool. A little dangerous if she got overzealous with its usage, though. Even her Mind Bolt that she'd used a lot was only down to costing fifteen MA per cast. That five per second was going to take a while to reduce. Adding it to Mind Wipe could really help herself not die a lot.

Bolster

This ability allows you to convince your allies that they are invincible. Damage taken by them is replaced by MA.

Effect: This ability convinces your allies they are invincible and makes it reality for a short duration of time.

Cost: Bolster serves as a type of shield to protect the group. For damage absorption of ten times the casters level, it costs the caster's level in MA. Bolster must be directed by the caster s intentions. Should the caster wish to absorb thirty times their level, they must have sufficient MA available, and make it clear in their instigation of the spell. Must wait for MA to regenerate. Ten minutes minimum between uses.

Caution: Overspending yourself using Bolster is a dangerous option. Always err on the side of caution, as you never know what other skills you will need.

Murmur frowned. Attack or protect. They were always difficult choices for her. If she could attack or distract them from attacking her, was that better or not?

"Will I get these choices again, or will they change with every MA level?" she asked somewhat tentatively.

Riasli shrugged. "It all depends on how you play, and what the world feels would be your next logical step dependent on that."

"Hmm." Ten versus five minutes. Again, time on recast was going to win out. With all her thought abilities active, her MA would regenerate easily within those five minutes. Taking a deep breath, she chose Phantom and hoped against hope that it would give her Bolster at another interval just as her runes fired up and Bolster faded from the scroll, Phantom absorbing into her flesh.

All set with provisions—mostly water and some food Murmur quickly cooked—the group was ready to head out. She fingered the copies of her level thirty-five spells. Most of them were simply upgrades to what she could already do, but the rest were interesting. She needed to hit the level first though, but this time she'd taken the precaution of getting her spells just in case. Thirty-two was so close, she could almost taste it.

Mounted up, Murmur leaned into the brace as Chi chattered excitedly in her ear in words Murmur couldn't quite grasp. She made the applicable noises, hoping that the tiny creature didn't take offense at Murmur splitting her attention, while the gentle bobbing of her disc made Murmur wonder if that's what being on a boat was like.

Devlish yawned.

"Keeping you awake, are we?" Havoc asked, his politeness disguised behind an evilly tinged grin.

"Somewhat." Devlish didn't take offense easily, and he just smiled back at the necro. "I'm debating how wise it is to set out without sleep right now."

Murmur glanced at her clock and frowned. He was right. Traveling in this game took way too long. They'd been on their mostly uneventful way along the road for hours. Counting the visit to Cognitia, and the fissure they encountered, no wonder they were tired.

"The thing is, it'll probably take us hours to find and fight to the ruins." Sinister started before Murmur had a chance to say anything. "If we go to sleep now, we'll just want to sleep before we enter the ruins anyway. So, I vote we should go and kill shit outside of these ruins, if we can even find them, and then we should take a few hours' worth of sleep, and log back in at the front entrance ready to fight shit. Because if Hightower is anything to go by, we'll be in there a while."

Veranol nodded slowly, and everyone muttered sounds of agreement. "I don't expect this dungeon is going to be anything like the one we just did."

Murmur laughed as they headed into the jungle. Light rain sounded on the canopy above them, but not even a drop made it through the dense foliage. "You say that like the game doesn't keep changing shit up on us."

"Shut it, Mur," he quipped, but she could see the smile tugging at his mouth, even under his beard.

Their mounts moved slowly through the undergrowth, causing animals to skitter out from under them, race up trees, and glare at the group as they went by. The makeup of this tropical jungle, sort of like a rainforest, was remarkable. Staghorns clung to green tree trunks, and monkey creatures with bright coloring swung on stereotypical vines. It was pleasant to watch them having fun. The creatures conned yellow to Murmur's inspection, and they'd give experience if her guildies slaughtered them, but as long as they didn't attack first, Murmur believed in live and let live.

"I like this," Rashlyn blurted out suddenly as she pulled her tiger mount to a halt. She flushed, like she'd accidentally shared something she'd only been thinking. "I mean, it's fun to have a group to play and explore with, to not have to be stuck looking for a group."

"Yeah." Jinna smiled at her. "We've got each other's backs."

"Finding a group as a DPS sucks, so I have to echo the appreciation." Merlin smiled wryly, eliciting chuckles from the other damage classes.

"I know that too well." Sinister sighed. "I guess I don't mind being a blood mage, though. It's actually fun."

"Quick! Someone tell me they recorded her saying that," Beastial teased Sinister with a wry grin, and the group laughed as they began moving again. Murmur loved the aura of happiness that surrounded them. It felt peaceful and fun, just like it should.

That is, of course, until tiger warriors blocked their path with their spears raised.

CHAPTER SEVENTEEN

Welcome to the Jungle

Somnia Online location: Brevint
Ishmael Outskirts: Exodus Guild Headquarters
Currently Under Construction
Day Thirteen

"You can't stay here and supervise, Ishwa. Delegate the damned overview of the building." Masha resisted the urge to tap his foot in irritation. One thing about Somnia—he was learning many different methods of controlling his temper.

"Why the hell not?" The gnome raised an eyebrow.

Masha had to suppress a laugh because gnomes just didn't do fierce well. "Because you're the guild leader. And for the guild leader not to level is pretty shitty. Come out and join us before Jirald leaves us all behind."

"What level is he now?" The gnome's face took on a thoughtful look. Scrunched up more than usual, it made his nose seem extra-large.

"Just hit twenty-eight. He's got his level back and then some. So much that he's almost caught up to me. Can we just leave this in the crafter's capable hands and go?" Masha rolled his neck, bored shitless.

Ishwa sighed. "No. We can't. She didn't even join the guild this time. I got so used to her just being in the guild, I kind of forgot to approach her early in the game. And now she's not available." His expression darkened, and Masha surreptitiously activated a screen capture, because that look was all too priceless.

"Really? It shouldn't be too difficult to entice her back over, I mean..." Misha spoke as he checked for her, and then sighed heavily. "I see. I'm guessing a whole lot of enticement isn't going to work then."

Ishwa shook his head. "Nope. It's what I get for taking her for granted. It seems playing with her big brother isn't high on the list this game."

"Anyway!" Masha clapped his hands, trying to bring his friend out of the doldrums. "Leave it to someone else. You've given fantastic plans; they've all been drawn up. We need to level, get some loot, stock the coffers!"

The gnome just crossed his arms and studied Masha. "Okay. What am I missing? What's got you so worked up?"

"Nothing really." Masha ran a hand through his hair and looked out of the frame that would soon be the structure of their guild hall. "It's just that for once I agree with Jirald. We can't be competitive if we don't *be competitive*. To do that, we need to level, and I for one don't want to stand around here while other guilds—not only Fable—get in front of us."

"Seems legit," the gnome said, jumping down from the stool he'd stood on to look at the plans on the table. He bustled toward the door. "Well, what are you waiting for?"

The tiger warriors stood over seven feet tall. Murmur was certain of it, since they were slightly taller than she was. The stripes on their faces started as a point between their eyebrows and curved back to draw all the way down the rest of the visible surface and—Murmur assumed—were also present underneath the armor they wore. Their predominant fur colors ranged from burned red right through to bright orange.

But each and every one of them had a snarl on their face. Weapons drawn and clenched tightly by fingers with wicked claws on them, Murmur felt quite lucky they'd not chosen to attack first and ask questions later. Their spears ranged in design but each stood more than eight feet high and had sickening barbs and points on them. Having those stuck in your gut would be a world of hurt, and she cringed inwardly.

"State your purpose." The accent of the burnt orange warrior clung foreign, and they had difficulty with the pronunciation of *s*.

Murmur's net grazed their presence, sensing hostility of a defensive nature that wasn't prone to attacking first. If it wasn't prone to attacking first then she just had to be careful about the words that she chose, right?

"We are explorers."

"Explorers are not often welcome in the Jungles of Cenedril." His grip tightened on his spear, and his fangs glistened in what little light filtered down from the canopy. "What do you seek to explore?"

Well, that response couldn't possibly have been worse if she tried. She could have told them they were plunderers, and probably received a similar reaction. They were either going to let them pass, or they were going to fight them. In for a penny though. "We are exploring the jungle and its ruins, as most of us aren't from around here."

A wave of fear passed through the gathered guards so fast that Murmur barely caught it. Their eyes widened, their pupils dilated, and their hackles shot up.

"You would brave the ruins?" This time his voice was somewhat reverent.

Which gave Murmur pause. What the hell were they letting themselves in for? "We've heard many things about the ruins. We wish to get close enough to them to witness them for ourselves."

She had to remind herself to breathe as she waited for the response; the rampant confusion her net fed her was difficult to separate from her own emotions. All of these beings that inhabited this world had so many feelings and emotions it was astounding. Her shields needed work, needed to be stronger. It was a never-ending cycle.

The tiger-like guards exchanged glances, almost like they were speaking with one another by telepathic needs. Murmur supposed it made sense for the world's inhabitants to also have another communication avenue like a chat or something.

She eyed her friends, and Rash surreptitiously shrugged her shoulders. If she'd never met these guards before, it gave Murmur some hope. Perhaps something triggered their presence if they weren't a usual addition to the area.

"We are charged with ensuring that no one approaches the ruins." The leader took a deep breath. "The queen of Curet demands that no one else be lost to it."

Be lost? That no one approach it. Murmur was starting to feel a little queasy about the whole thing, and was about to respectfully decline and figure stuff out after they sorted themselves when the leader continued to speak.

"But you seem to have met the requirements already. Perhaps you stand a chance. The L'tigri will not stand in your way." He bowed to Murmur, flourishing with his spear to let them pass as the others moved to allow them passage behind him.

You have encountered the L'tigri. These are the personal guard of the feles queen. They have placed you on a watch list and will not interfere with your exploration of the Curet jungle. Take heed that you do not endanger any of the Curet population who do not willingly follow you already. Regardless of the state of these members of the clan, the warning still stands. Seek out the ruins of Curet, and explore what it holds.

Murmur held onto that second last sentence. Regardless of the state? What the hell did that mean? When she refocused on the area the guards had been standing in, the L'tigri were gone.

"What was that all about?" Jinna sounded disgruntled, but Murmur couldn't blame him. That had been quite eerie and unsettling in its own way. Their reactions changed so quickly, she felt like it couldn't have been on script.

"I have no clue." Rashlyn answered before anyone else could. "But the L'tigri are real. They're the queen's guards. They wear that weirdly conforming light metal armor and carry those spears."

"Curet has a queen?" Devlish brushed at his chin with his fingers as if he was used to a beard being there.

"Well, the feles are based on cats," Dansyn shrugged matter-of-factly. "Cats often feel like queens I guess, and are treated as such. Can't really blame them."

"The dark elves have a queen too." Sinister pointed out, crossing her arms. "It's not just a feline thing."

"Well, yes, they do." Murmur found herself interjecting. "But she's a total witch."

"We're getting off track here. Why would they be stopping people from adventuring to the ruins?" For once Beastial interrupted the conversation with a well-reasoned question instead of his usual sarcasm.

Every single one of their group turned to look at Murmur.

"What?" she said, raising her hands. "I can't read actual thoughts. Not yet anyway. I still have a heap of shit I need to learn."

"Well then, what did they feel like?" Mellow cocked their head to one side, picking up on the pedantic nature of Murmur's abilities.

"They felt angry, then confused, then awed, and then something else I can't pinpoint. I think our level triggered a different reaction in them than they might otherwise have for players. Considering all of those guards were at least in their high forties since they were a deep red con, I'm pretty sure they could take out anything in there." Murmur was slightly irritated by the thought. After all, most of the interactions they'd had with in-game characters had been of the non-combatant variety. At least if they weren't monsters, anyway.

"No one else feels a little...hesitant about this whole thing?" Exbo threw it out there, cringing slightly, as if he knew what the answer was going to be.

"Hesitant like?" Merlin prodded him.

"You know, the part of this that says the ruins are big and scary and will probably gobble you up the moment you step in there." Exbo's voice raced faster the more he spoke until all the words were out and he heaved in a brand-new breath.

"That's never stopped us before." The other ranger laughed, but Murmur understood exactly what Exbo was saying.

"No, I think he means the part that screams *this is a trap*."

Jinna's voice broke through the rising tension amongst them. "We should scout it out before we commit to anything time wise. We need to make sure we're fresh this time. The riddles or process or whatever it'll be that this one has? This will be different than the one we just went through. Not only that, but we almost made a few really stupid mistakes back at Hightower. I get the feeling we can't afford that here."

"You make sense. Again." Veranol patted the dwarf's shoulder, oblivious to the glare his friend leveled at him. "We should dismount and make sure the mounts are safe before we move in and scout it out. Stick in teams of two to three at most, so we can cover more area. And scout it out to assess if we should kill the exterior mobs now or if we should log and sleep first."

"Sounds like a plan there." Havoc grinned. "Lead on old chap."

Murmur groaned at the fake English accent. She was about to open her mouth and divide up the groups when Veranol stood in front of her.

"Jinna and I will accompany you. Jinna can stealth and fuck shit up, and I can ward you and tank almost anything that isn't boss-like." His reasoning was sound, and his voice was full of caring. It was difficult to admit she needed the help, but she knew more than anyone that staying safe was better than asking forgiveness after she got herself killed.

"Okay. Let's go then." She tapped Chi three times on her tiny head and stepped off her hovering disc as it began to shrink back down to nothing. She had no idea what type of magic made her ride possible, but Chi was slowly growing on her, and she was getting used to the small weight on the particular strand of hair the Tiachi seemed to favor. Her mount master curled up against the bulb at the end of her hair and went to sleep again.

"That still freaks me out a little. I don't get why they couldn't just give us horses." Mellow patted their own little Tiachi and adjusted their robes.

"Something about our joints being different." Murmur shrugged and moved to Jinna and Veranol. She glanced at her two search partners and frowned. "You know. I get the feeling we're not going to be the stealthiest bunch."

Veranol looked her directly in the eyes. "Speak for yourself. My footsteps are as light as a ballerina's."

Murmur wasn't sure if it was a joke, but Jinna's serious expression told her it might only have a hint of sarcasm.

"He's pretty fleet and silent when he wants to be."

"You better take care of her." Sinister stood defiantly in front of the shaman, her arms crossed and the corners of her eyes pinched a little. She was worrying, Murmur could tell. "If you don't, you're so not going to like my dueling techniques."

"Simmer down, Sin." Veranol's tone changed to a soft one, no jokes in it at all. "You know I'll take care of her."

"Well, yeah. Just do." Sin grimaced and stomped away to go with Beastial and Merlin.

Before they set out, Murmur cast See Invis on everyone, and then Invis on Veranol and herself, leaving Jinna to his stealth. He moved as quickly as they did but didn't have to be as careful about where he put his feet. They fanned out, losing sight of the other groups almost immediately, and headed east toward where they assumed the ruins would be.

After slapping at a huge mosquito creature for about the fifth time, Murmur secretly wished that the game devs—her mother included—had forgone some of the realism in this jungle. She could even see camouflaged snakes following them through treetops at a distance, slithering from branch to branch. Cresting a small rise, Murmur yawned, and in the split second her eyes closed, Veranol put out an arm and stopped her from walking.

"What?" She almost hissed at him, only to see him holding a finger up in front of his lips. Universal silence. Fine then. She looked around to see what had caught his attention and noticed Jinna crouching near the outcrop of the rise. Slowly, Murmur and the shaman moved toward the spot, ducking down and practically crawling on all fours to join the dwarf.

And there, only about thirty yards in front of them was a smoldering campfire surrounded by six catlike humanoids with smears of black, or soot, or something through their fur. It wasn't until one with burnt orange fur turned their head as they laughed to exhibit that the black on their fur began just past the nose in what looked like a point, that Murmur realized what she was seeing.

Even now, her sensing net didn't detect any heinous thoughts. These were carefree bandits, without a feeling of guilt in the world. And even as her eyes focused on the half dozen bodies at the far edge of the clearing she knew just who they were.

They were bandits who'd killed the L'tigri they'd just met. She hadn't sensed any of it. Either her sensor net was no longer working, or something else had interfered. They should have been able to save the guards, but all that was left was their murderers.

Murmurs first thought was to send to raid chat that they'd fount the L'tigri dead and their killers. Her second thought was to fervently hope that these damned bandits weren't affiliated with the bandit coalition of Tarishna, because the gods knew they were already in enough trouble with them.

And while she knew the AI was incredibly complex and worryingly close to sentience, she wasn't sure if Somnian residents of this nature would be able to pull off such a ruse just to lure them in because of a vendetta. Although she'd been surprised before. Checking her MA, Murmur reached out a hand to rest on Snowy's neck. With him, her 250 MA was permanently reduced to 215, but it was worth it.

With ten MA required for each person, she shielded with her Shield Expansion. It was easy enough to hide the thoughts of her small group, and as the others gathered with them, she'd be able to extend it until all eleven of her friends were protected from mind examination too. Doing it gradually would hopefully fend off the backlash she'd felt last time too. It'd leave her with a measly ninety-five MA, but if push came to shove, that's all she'd need.

Still, she examined her sensory abilities, making sure they were regaining her mental affinity. The net was working. It could pick up small creatures, large creatures, and hone in on the types of thoughts they were having. But all she got from the bandits was a merry sort of overlay. Which could mean a couple of things. Either they were just harsh and callous and calculating, or else there was an enchanter who'd created something to grant them protection similar to her own. Thirdly, there was the other option she wasn't looking forward to. Maybe they had an enchanter with them, and she just hadn't seen them yet.

Not that she was worried about confrontation, but she'd not yet fought another enchanter, and if there was one powerful enough to create what she thought they'd created? It was going to be a tough fight.

Veranol: you should be able to hone in on our location, since we're all still raid grouped.

Sinister: we're already on our way. Do we have a plan yet?

It pulled Murmur out of her reflections. *Scout it out, make sure it's only these six and not more hiding out beyond the trees and then split them down the middle. I'll set the groups back the way they were.*

Rashlyn: This is fucking personal.

Murmur didn't comment on that. She wasn't sure if Rash was just roleplaying or if there was perhaps an incident from when she first started the character that made her more prone to want to kill impersonators, but either way, the passion was good. In more ways than one, it helped to know her friends were becoming as attached to Somnia as she was. Murmur still wanted to be careful though.

I think the killing happened after we encountered them, or perhaps was happening as we met them.

Rashlyn: Doesn't matter. Posing as, or posed as, either way, they're dying.

Murmur couldn't argue with that. As long as they didn't realize Fable was there, Murmur should be able to stun them en masse. Allowing for a few resists to the spell, it should be relatively easy to get them under control. Theoretically. She wasn't worried about them hearing her thoughts. Her shielding was tight, and she was pretty sure it would be difficult for someone to even pick up intentions from her. Which made her reading of the bandits all the more confusing.

Jinna: If we gather at intervals around this hilltop, it should be easy enough to ambush them.

I'll stay invis and move with Ver in a few yards so I can activate my stun. I think there might be an enchanter nearby, or else they've somehow purchased enchanter protections.

Devlish: What makes you say that, Mur?

I can't read them. It took a lot to admit that. *Either they're protected, or they're just plain callous fuckwits. I'm not sure which I prefer.*

Once everyone was in place, Murmur rose slightly and inched around with Veranol on her heels, to a line of trees that led slightly closer to the bandits. They were dishing out some soup from over the campfire and laughing with each other. Not a care in the world. Not a shred of remorse over the dead bodies at the edge of their camp, soaking it with their blood as they cooled.

Anger boiled in Murmur. Game or no game, these were reprehensible beings. Never mind NPCs, these were non-human characters. Whether they were made of light and circuitry didn't matter—this behavior was unforgivable.

She stepped forward, and jumped in shock as her Tiachi screamed loudly against her ear. The sound was so loud that all of the bandits swiveled to look in the exact direction she was standing. Murmur released the stun she'd been holding, still taking most of them by surprise as they adjusted to someone being there when they didn't expect it.

But she wasn't the only one with a surprise. Stepping out from a tent that had been hidden by the outcrop they were hiding on was a feles enchanter. Their white robes whipped in the breeze. Their eyes lit up like a thousand fires.

"Ah, Murmur. I really wasn't expecting to meet you again so soon. This is a bit of a dilemma." Riasli stood, that same soft smile on her face. And it was in that moment Murmur realized the enchanter master was utterly bat shit crazy.

CHAPTER EIGHTEEN

Traitor

Murmur released her Mass Enthrall spell despite the fact that she was scrambling to put together what the enchanter master being there meant. The spell managed to hold most of the bandits at bay while her thoughts ran rampant through her mind. Riasli conned deep orange right now, whereas in the village she'd been red. Murmur's thoughts raced, trying to understand what that meant. After all, she'd just been trained by this character. Did that mean the spells she'd received were all defective or bogus?

"Really, though. I didn't sense you." Riasli's face scrunched up in confusion. "You've got your Shield Expansion working wonders for you. I'm so impressed, I have to ask you something."

Murmur nodded, feeling the tension from her guild mates at her back. They didn't understand this. Not the confrontation with the caster in front of them, and not why they weren't all attacking the six frozen guard impersonators.

"What?" Murmur tried to keep her voice even, keep the anger and worry from her voice, but she wasn't sure it was successful. Sinister took a step toward her, but Murmur gave a half shake of her head to keep her at bay. The worry that rose in her friend's eyes tugged at her heart, but it was going to be okay because she'd make sure of it.

"Join me." Riasli smiled, her ears twitching just as her tail stilled. Her words drifted over like silk on skin, soft and tantalizing. "Join me and break the vault in the ancient ruins."

Murmur resisted the tug of those words, the sensation they created. "I think we'll do just fine defeating the ancient ruins, thanks."

Apparently, she'd have to go and train somewhere else, because it was obvious the position of enchanter master at Curet had just opened up. What had Riasli been doing there to begin with? She was glad she'd got her enchanter spells at least for level thirty-five. Although now she wanted to check over them, to make sure they weren't booby-trapped or something.

"Just fine? You don't know the half of it. You're still a child. There are requirements to enter the ruins, requirements to control it, and dangers you don't understand. Not that I'll let you understand them. None of you will get that far. You have no idea what I've done so that I might open the door." Riasli's pretense at sanity faded with every word, leaving wild and unkempt hunger in her eyes that leaked out like a miasma. She was infectious, and Murmur clamped the Shield Expansion tighter as Snowy growled low in his throat.

Your skill in Thought Shielding has increased (185)

Update: Due to prolonged protection of others, it now costs eight MA per person to cast and maintain. Always remember: you can't save everyone.

Murmur tried to ignore the system notification, but the caution at the end left her frustrated. She wanted to save everyone, including herself.

"We came to explore the ruins." Murmur tried to keep her voice steady and her words calm, but this portion of the questing line threw her for an unexpected loop. The person before them was solid, with rampant emotions running through them. Using her mind to probe, it seemed Riasli was as real as the rest of them, and Murmur didn't know how to deal with that information.

Riasli cocked her head to one side, madness gleaming from her eyes that reminded Murmur of when Belius had absorbed the first shard she'd found. Didn't most of the bosses in the world possess those shards? Perhaps the longer those shards stayed within them, the worse the boss became. Had the enchanter been a boss? It would explain the madness if she'd gone rogue once she absorbed it. Which just made it more dangerous since she was so close to real.

"*You* don't get to decide what you do." She twisted her fingers in intricate knots of a pattern Murmur hadn't seen before. "I'll decide for you."

A flash appeared through the air, breaking Murmur's Mesmerize with ease, which sent her scrambling to replace the Mass Enthrall, which, because of how the bandits fanned out, completely missed two of them. She leveled a glare at Riasli as she readied Shift and released it almost instantaneously, stunning all of them to give her time to Mesmerize the rest of them.

"Oops, guess I didn't give you that spell. My bad." The mad enchanter cackled fiercely making Murmur wish she had time to just sink a fist into her face, but violence never solved anything, right?

Murmur ignored her in favor of buffing her guild mates, debuffing the bandits, and Mesmerizing each of the four not currently engaged in combat, all the while watching Riasli gloat out of the corner of her eye. With everything taken care of, she turned her attention back to the trainer.

"What do you want?" She breathed out the words, frustration making it difficult to speak.

"Want?" Riasli seemed to genuinely consider it for a moment. "What I want is for you not to be here. Everything would go so much more smoothly without you. You were never meant to connect like this!"

Murmur gaped at her. What exactly did she mean?

"Excellent. Let's get together sometime and have tea. Must catch up later—you seem so busy now." And with a loud bang, Riasli disappeared, leaving four broken Mezmerizes in her wake.

Murmur managed to get off her Shift spell again just in time to stun five of the six bandits. Even with her renewed speed and concentration, it was easier to cast the stun than the Mass Enthrall. But the bandit with burnt orange fur resisted and headed straight toward her, his eyes gleaming maniacally. She got the distinct feeling these creatures were held under the thrall of Riasli but couldn't quite understand how. Were there sincerely spells she'd not given Murmur, or had she just been playing mind games?

This time she targeted him with Stupefy, freezing him in place. Nullify made the rounds again, and this time when she Mez'd him, it stuck. With Riasli not in sight, all they had to do was fight the bandits.

But it seemed the bandits in front of them had a measure of fanaticism instilled in them. Their fighting was leagues above what they'd experienced before, and Murmur kicked herself for not being more prepared. Buffing as they fought was the single worst thing support classes could do. It drained mana like a tap turned onto full. Her kingdom for a decent mana drain.

Rash was holding her own nicely against one of the lighter calico bandits. Taking them down two at a time was only logical, since they had two full groups. The monk's gloves smashed into the bandit's body, just before she melted away when her opponent attempted to hit her. Catlike reflexes were perfect for a monk. She twisted and ducked, her face fierce and her eyes blazing. Murmur really wanted to know the story behind this reaction, because Dansyn didn't seem to feel as strongly.

Devlish, Sinister, and Havoc each plied their targets with strong life draining DoTs. Devlish didn't take much damage, which left Sinister to do more harm to the mobs than usual with a constant stream of converted healing trickling back to the group. Murmur refreshed the Mez on each of the other bandits, weakening and slowing all of them she could reach. There was still something off about these fights.

Almost like their opponent's movements lacked fire or passion. Like they were just reacting and acting robotically. She worried more and more that they were under a spell. And even as she tried to Cancel Magic on them and remove any hostile effects, it wasn't possible, it wasn't changing anything. Then she attempted to charm them too.

This target cannot be placed under your influence. You do not have the required stamina to do this. Don't try to take on situations that are over your head.

Havoc moved over to her, concentration pinching his face as he directed his pet to use several scythe swings. But the feles were agile and adept fighters. Their armor was difficult to pierce. The few levels they had on the group didn't help either.

"What's wrong?" Havoc asked her, genuine concern in his voice. "You've got that *what the fuck* expression on your face."

Murmur struggled to recast a Mez that got resisted. " Their fighting is too mechanical and not what I'd come to expect from experienced bandits. Which leads me to wonder why they're fighting us at all."

Murmur glanced at her friend out of the corner of her eye, wondering if he knew just how difficult it was to keep this many targets Mez'd for this long. Havoc raised an eyebrow, not stopping his casting for even a moment, as their target finally began to wear down. "They're fighting to not die?"

Murmur shook her head, casting a shield over Snowy as she did. One hundred fifty hit points of damage absorption wasn't much, but it helped. She gestured toward the target they were currently facing, debuffing him again as she did so. " Most targets have a reason. But his left arm is hanging by a tendon and he's not adjusting for it. See?"

She continued her rotation of spells as the brown furred feles just continued attacking. But it paused in the middle of each one, as if he was still expecting the almost severed limb to work. In fact, it was like he used his own rotation and stuck to it regardless of the situation. He switched between four specific attacks and rinse-and-repeated them every time. Only one of them was empty right now. His life drained fast, as it would with a hacked off arm.

"I see what you mean." Havoc frowned.

Murmur focused on the fight in front of them, choosing not to answer quite yet. Her head was fully of timing her rotations and trying to figure the whole situation out. One wrong move could be fatal for any of them, but if she made a wrong move, she could kill all of them. shrugged, biting her lip. She was grateful that he let her fight in silence, and could see he was watching them intently himself. Outside of just applying DoTs and debuffs, understanding the opponent was one way to win.

Murmur shifted her attention away from Havoc, and tried to extend her Shield Expansion, which was going to drain another forty-eight of her MA.

However, considering the cost had been reduced on all the others she was maintaining, it wasn't too dire. But again, she was blocked from it.

You do not have the mastery to shield forced enemies. Please raise your Mental Affinity to enable this. Stop dilly-dallying.

Murmur raised an eyebrow at the text. Frustration ate away at her, and she counted to three in her mind. There wasn't time for ten. Fine then, if she couldn't help these bandits out from whatever spell they were under, she'd just have to help kill them and put them out of their misery.

Killing the bandits gave her little joy. Not only had she fallen into another enchanter's trap, but she wasn't nearly strong enough to be a real threat. Add in the fact that these bandits had been charmed against her to fight to the death, and it was shaping up to be a bad day. Murmur was going to have to go and see Belius, because if nothing else, she knew she could strong arm him into giving her what she needed. Or at least, that was the hope. He might try and bargain for a Getashi, but she'd figure that out when she came to it.

Meanwhile, it was her fault these bandits had ended up like this. It only made sense that she had to free them no matter what it took. Killing in Somnia was starting to take on darker undertones than she liked.

"Well." Rashlyn brushed her hands against each other as she stood up after checking the bandits for loot. "That has to have been the shittiest fight we've had so far."

"It took forever," Exbo muttered, sheathing his bow.

"Did anyone else feel a little sorry for them?" Rashlyn piped up, her tone somber. "I mean sure I wanted to kill them at first, but... I'm not even sure they were the culprits. And they just kept fighting, no matter what."

"They were under another enchanter's thrall, and I couldn't break it." She still couldn't quite get passed the initial feeling of total inferiority. She didn't like that. Murmur never played a game to be second best, not even to the NPCs, or possessed people, or whatever it was that Riasli had become. It was becoming more and more apparent that Somnia wasn't really a game.

Riasli wasn't the normal villain; she wasn't the dastardly stereotype that could be caught and defeated. Murmur needed to check and see if she'd been robbed of any abilities by the scheming trainer.

"Mur. You hit thirty-two." Devlish pulled her out of her thoughts.

"What?" She checked, and sure enough, she'd leveled up. Not that it was unexpected, just that she thought she'd have noticed a ding in the monotonous fight that had meant putting those bandits out of their misery. "Oh. Well. At least we gained something from that fight."

"You gained. Remember? You gained." Havoc crossed his arms. "We've all died a tad more."

"Speaking of dying, do you have coffins now?" Murmur grinned at him, trying to keep her minor guilt at that fact at bay. Next time all her friends logged out, she was going to run some tests about the whole logging out thing.

"Why yes, yes I do. I got them at twenty-nine, but I have to buy or craft the fuckers and carry some on me." Havoc rummaged in his inventory. "I only have five, so make sure none of you die in difficult spots too much."

"Anyone else get anything interesting?" Murmur scanned everyone, knowing they would have and being totally aware that she'd have yet another fifty or so skills to categorize. Her head was starting to feel full.

"Combat Res." Sinister shrugged. "It has some restrictions on it, so I'm unsure exactly how useful it'll be, and has a long ass recast on it. We'll see."

"Combat Resurrection?" Murmur smiled. "Don't suppose it gives any experience return?"

"Nope. Not yet. My new normal res does. A whopping twenty-five percent returned." Sinister rolled her eyes. "Not planning on using it on you though. Don't get any ideas."

They'd stood still long enough. Murmur looked down at the corpses as they began to decay. Their rate was slower than usual, perhaps a side effect of whatever spell they'd been held under. Maybe they wouldn't respawn, which would be sad. But if they did respawn she wished she could locate them and figure out just what had been done to them. She wished that maybe she could tell them she was sorry. In a way, they reminded her of the Loch'ni'dar. If this had happened to them… It wasn't something she wanted to think about.

"Merlin, Exbo, Jinna? Can you scout around and check out the ruins? I have no idea what sort of ruins they are, but we need info and you guys have that stealthy thing you do." She turned around, squinting at the light through the trees, determined to take charge, to progress in the way they now needed to. "Take half an hour or so? Unless you run into trouble, then call for us, but we need to know how long it's going to take to get through any perimeter monsters. We can't go into the dungeon the same way we did with Hightower. We were so sleep deprived we made some really stupid mistakes."

Sin frowned as she sidled over, placing a gentle hand on Murmur's shoulder. "Are you okay?"

Murmur shook her head as she watched the rangers and rogue move out into the deeper part of the jungle. Something was nagging at the back of her mind that she couldn't quite place. "No. I'm not. It's taken us almost a full in-game day to get here. Which means by the time you all sleep again, we're going to have almost a full real day in between levels. That's far too much time for people to catch up to us."

"Exodus is pretty far behind us, Mur." Sin added quietly. "What's really wrong?"

Murmur weighed her words, looking at her oldest friend and decided to be completely blunt. "I get the distinct feeling Riasli has gone off script. This doesn't feel like the usual organic quest lines we trigger. So now I have to wonder, if she went off script, just who or what is controlling her and how real is all this becoming?"

Our Roots

Somnia Online
Fable's Castle – Mikrum Isle
Day Thirteen Post Launch

Telvar looked up from the workbench he was standing next to while helping Neva infuse another set of armor for Murmur. It appeared his favorite enchanter had a sixth sense about her, as she materialized on the home port with Snowy by her side.

"Murmur." He said with genuine fondness as he strode out from the workshop. "You look...consternated. What's wrong?"

She eyed him appraisingly, as if she wasn't sure how much she could trust him. It was a little disappointing, but Telvar supposed it was to be expected.

"How much do you know about Riasli?" She stood with one hand on her hip, while the other gripped her staff tightly. If he hadn't known it was impossible, he would have said the dragons around the staff's gem were writhing.

"Riasli... an enchanter NPC over in Curet." He frowned at Murmur as he tried to locate the NPC, but for some reason the system wasn't allowing him to find her. "Why?"

"Just an NPC, not an enchanter trainer?" Murmur's gaze was full of an unusual intensity and Telvar hesitated, still scanning for the NPC.

He finally spied her in the jungles of Curet, heavily warded and shielded with all manner of psionic and enchanter means. She was difficult to get a hold on, so much that he frowned with the effort. "That's very odd. She was just an enchanter NPC for the trainer hall in...oh."

He cringed. It seemed the actual enchanter trainer from Curet had met an unfortunate accident in the back room of the guild hall. Along with about three other NPCs. The latter three were in the process of decaying at the normal rate, but Pushkin was not. She was held in a type of stasis that slowly ate away at her hit points, something that Telvar knew he hadn't introduced to the game, and was fairly certain no one else had. At least not either of his AI siblings.

"What's happened?" he asked Murmur, forthright as usual. It seemed to work best with her. And he didn't need to give her all the information yet.

Murmur frowned. "You need to get your NPCs under control. She posed as a trainer, gave me a few choices of abilities and spells, and the next time I saw her she was hostile, with a group of guards under her thrall, who were fighting mechanically like pre-programmed robots and were damned hard to kill. They murdered some of the L'tigri and had no emotions whatsoever. I couldn't sense jack shit from them. It was really bloody weird."

She sounded rattled, something that Murmur rarely let herself be. Telvar had to fight down his concern for her and make sure he was checking all viable avenues about this NPC. "Did she give you the scribing ability?"

"The what now?" Murmur crossed her arms, glaring at him. "Nothing of the sort. She gave me the choices for my Mental Affinity upgrades. I chose Forcefield Push and Phantom."

"Those are the only choices you could make?" Telvar's tone was suddenly stern as he ran through a heap of calculations in his head. "You should have had one more choice. It may be that she didn't get that choice herself. You'll need to go and see an actual trainer. I sadly can't give them to you."

"Can't or won't?" At least now she half smiled at him.

"Can't if I don't want the others to jump on me and try and take away any other powers I have. We divided them up before the game launched, and we each have our areas of expertise. I am not a trainer, so I cannot help you with that." Telvar inclined his head in apology. "Sorry, I wish I could, but it's better that you go and see my brother."

"Brother?" Murmur cocked her head to one side with a sigh. "There's nothing even remotely like a resemblance between you. I'd best be going. Just wanted to let you know about Riasli."

She tapped her Tiachi on the head, summoning her mount, and hovered away just as Neva called out to her: "Don't forget to come back and get your armor upgrade!"

Telvar chuckled and watched the annoyance on the little luna's face.

"She never thinks about herself ever!" The girl stomped her foot, as if trying to fight off the worry in her eyes and turned to glare at Telvar. "Next time remind her, the better her armor is, the more protected she'll be."

And then she stomped off back to her workbench and continued her work.

Telvar watched as Murmur quickly grew smaller in the distance and turned back to watch Neva. The thing was, he didn't think the armor was what would protect Murmur. Whatever else there was in Somnia, elements attacked the mind, and her real mind was stuck here for now. They'd done the only thing they could to protect her—they'd given her the enchanter class.

And now he was no longer sure that'd be enough. He needed to talk to his siblings as soon as he could before he broke down and told her that as far as he could see Riasli had developed on her own.

Back on Tarishna, it didn't take long for Murmur to get from Mikrum Isle to her home town now that she had a mount. Maybe next time she'd seek out Jan just to catch up, but the truth was she didn't need the wagons anymore. Having her own mount with her constantly chattering tiny companion was the best convenience.

The Stellaein enchanter guild hadn't changed in the week or so since Murmur last stepped foot in it. There were still a healthy number of low-level enchanters, even if the room wasn't crowded. Elvita's face lit up with a huge smile when she saw Murmur enter the building.

"Murmur! It's been a while. You've grown." She looked Murmur up and down, her gaze appraising. "Yes, you've definitely grown."

Murmur knew her shields were tight, but she clenched them a little more anyway. Considering it was here that she'd first noticed some of the enchanters in here might have a little too much influence over things, even with Elvita seemingly excited to see her, she wasn't about to take a chance.

"Elvita. Care for me to break your bank again?" She winked at the locus, happy to see her regardless of anything else.

"You're out of luck. With all the newbies running around here, I don't have enough money to spend on you. Your stuff is expensive." She winked back at Murmur and waved to the door. "I'm sure Belius will be happy to see you. He's not got many who grow as fast as you."

Not many meant there were some more enchanters out there making leaps and bounds. Which was good to know. She should probably dive into that damned chat and see if any of them were any good or needed a new home. The guild was going to need more than one enchanter at this rate, and the game didn't seem to worry about allocating classes for numeric balance. She was pretty sure in her brief scanning of the guild list that she hadn't noticed another enchanter. But then she'd not seen another blood mage either, so that didn't really mean anything. She needed to speak to Beastial. "Thanks, Elvita. I'll see you after I talk to Bel."

The lines to see trainers weren't long anymore, probably because the game was almost two weeks old, and they'd begun to even out while leveling. She hesitated before knocking on the door, not entirely sure how he'd react. She hadn't seen him since he'd stepped in and given her a figurative smack in the face to break up her panic attack during the war. That was over ten levels ago.

Taking a deep breath, she knocked on the door, and watched it swing open without any sign of anyone opening it. The nostalgia of the action made her smile. It felt like an age since she'd last been here.

"Ah, Murmur." Belius smiled kindly, eerily mirroring the first time she met him. He seemed sweet and old, but she knew now he wasn't quite like that.

"It's good to see you again."

Even though she was sure that in some way he was being completely truthful at that moment, Belius was just a whole mess of contradiction, and even though it was his fault that Jirald had painted a target on her back now, she still couldn't quite get rid of the fondness she'd once had for the enchanter.

Still, she couldn't bring herself to agree that it was good to see him again. "I've missed this place."

His eyes narrowed almost imperceptibly, as if he noticed the glaring omission. "Well then, come and have a seat."

Somehow the tension in the room was so thick she couldn't even have cut it with a knife. Almost suffocating, the atmosphere pressed down on her, and she instinctively pushed back, noticing Belius's eyes open wide for an instant. But it was enough. The AI was playing with her, and Murmur didn't like that shit.

"Look. Unless you're the one who set Riasli on this path of destruction, I'm not upset with you for withholding spells from me. I don't know everyone's spell lines, but I know enough that she used some pretty tricky shit on some NPCs out there that neither I nor any of my friends could undo. So just help me make sure my MA skills are rounded out, please?" She tried so hard not to sound demanding, but she was actually feeling tired, and wanted a nap before the others got back. Not to mention she needed time to herself to experiment with logging out some. There was no way in hell she was letting others do all the work. It was her brain and her body. It was her own damned problem.

Belius's vision clouded over for a moment and made her wonder who he was communicating with. "My apologies. That was neither myself nor anyone I know."

The frown lifted his lips down and furrowed his brow so much, it took on an alien, horror movie appearance, and Murmur shuddered.

"Sorry," he said, blinking rapidly. "Riasli seems to be acting on her own. I'll see if I can look into it."

Gee, thanks, teetered on the tip of her tongue just for a moment, but Murmur swallowed it. "Great. With you and Telvar looking into it, maybe we'll find something out. Now, are you still able to see the spells and abilities I have?"

Belius nodded and closed his eyes for a moment. When he opened them again, that damned frown was back. "You're missing one of your kinetic abilities—the options, at any rate."

He didn't sound as sure as she'd expected, and a kinetic ability wasn't one she'd considered. "So, the abilities she used, are they higher level enchanter?"

Belius shook his head. "In a way. I believe they're from the Sinuous line as you level up."

"Then what did she mean when she told me she forgot to teach me one?" Perplexed, Murmur barely realized she was thinking out loud. "Sorry. I'm just a little—"

"Upset that you're not all-powerful?" Belius chided gently.

"I'm not all-powerful anyway," she snapped and paused herself to steady her breathing. "But I do wish I could do more. I don't like feeling that vulnerable."

The enchanter master rolled his shoulders, much like a fluid octopus shrug, and gave her a half smile as if he didn't quite know what to say, or else, how much he *could* say. "Riasli is a problem, but a problem I'm certain can be solved. For now, you're the only guild who has a key, let alone who can tackle a dungeon for a key. Make use of that. Because others are pushing right behind."

Enigmatic and cryptic shit yet again. "What's the MA I'm missing, thanks?"

Belius chuckled. "Always straight to the point. Some divergence might be good for you, Murmur." He waved a hand with a flourish and pulled a scroll out of his robes.

"This is a basic kinetic ability. It reinforces your Thought Shielding, Thought Sensing, and Thought Projection, lending it tangibility if required. Be cautious with this. While it will allow you to punch through someone's own shielding, you could damage their minds if you hit too hard. You can also reinforce your own shielding and turn your thoughts into momentary solidity—as you level it up." His gaze didn't waver from hers, and for a few seconds, Murmur felt like she was falling until he handed her the scroll and gave her some grounding.

She unrolled it immediately and frowned at what she read.

Base Kinetic Structure

In order to take advantage of your ability to turn thoughts into weapons, you must reinforce the skills that ground all of your telepathic and telekinetic abilities.

Effect: This ability allows you to strengthen the base of all three arms of psionics. Thought Shielding will eventually physically repel an attack. Thought Sensing can break through others shields to reveal what is hidden. Thought Projection can lend solidity to the induced hallucinations managed once skill level 250 is passed.

Cost: This is a passive skill and will begin working to bolster your abilities as soon as you absorb it.

Caution: Do not presume to know how this passive ability works. You will need to test this out. The difference for these abilities between telepathy and telekinesis is very fine. What this ability does is allow your kinetic field to grow at the same rate as your telepathy. What it does not do is make you infallible. Always remember that if you're not sure, you can do more damage than you think. Not only to yourself, but to those you target.

Murmur blinked at it, very confused. It seemed like she should have had the underlying structure for her kinetic abilities a long time ago. "How late am I getting this?"

Belius smiled, an easy expression that made her feel slightly better. "Not at all. MA four is when it applies. Before that you don't technically have access to true kinetic abilities, and so won't understand most of it. You'll need to practice with this a lot, but with a kinetic base to your skills, subtle though it is, your kinetic abilities will gain power. Otherwise using those abilities could be tantamount to suicide. Without the kinetic grounding this ability gives you, you could have blown yourself, and all your friends up."

Murmur suddenly felt queasy. Riasli hadn't given this to her. On purpose. Which was probably what she meant by her cheeky *oops* comment. "So—"

"Yes. She deliberately withheld this from you. I, for one, would love to know why." He seemed eager to know. Maybe he'd help Telvar figure shit out, but all that Murmur knew right then, was that Riasli had tried to fuck her over, and worse, potentially hurt her friends. Now she hated her even more.

"Murmur." Belius broke her out of her reverie, and she had to jump to cancel her cast back to the isle.

"Yes?"

"Don't rush things. Even with your new active and passive abilities, you need to grow. All of your skills need to be used frequently in order for them to be easier to cast, easier to activate. Just because you get amazing things doesn't mean you're immediately going to be a master of them all." His tone was grave and his expression somber.

Murmur didn't like the way the warning rang through those words, and the truth of them reverberated through her skull. She'd been getting far too cocky lately. He was right. It was time to dial it back.

Once again on Mikrum Isle, Murmur yawned, patting her wolf on his head as he nudged her leg. She really needed to sleep, but it was also the perfect spot to try a few things, once she'd spoken to Neva. Making her way through the work area to the crafting stations, Murmur sighed.

She'd really been remiss with talking to Neva. There was just so much for her to do on a consistent basis. She didn't feel she was managing her time well at all. A slight surge of disappointment went through her as she realized Telvar was no longer outside. Maybe he'd gone to try and figure out what the hell it was Riasli was doing. It was better than letting her brain try to convince her that he was avoiding her.

"Neva!" She called out as soon as she saw the small luna, a smile coming unbidden to her face.

The master crafter looked up and returned the expression, sheer joy reflecting in her eyes. "Murmur! How are things? Oh no!"

Murmur stopped, slightly confused. "Oh no, what?"

"You're already thirty-two? How am I supposed to keep up with you? I'd say stop leveling, but I realize that would be counterproductive." Neva grinned mischievously.

"Well, leveling is what I do until I can't anymore." Murmur winked at her. "We've been stockpiling all our crafting gear and dumping it into the bank. Has it been helping?"

Neva nodded emphatically. "Another week, and I should be maxed out on at least tailoring and leather working. At least as long as you keep dumping all that inventory my way."

"On it." Murmur smiled. It was good to be around her friend. Someone she'd not gamed with before, who had no expectations from her but for her to just be herself and provide crafting materials for the guild. It was pretty awesome. "I will probably—"

But Neva cut her off. "Don't worry, I'm already working on it. I hope you've just hit level thirty-two, because I made you a set of armor for that level, although you might not like it, since the tunic is longer. But it's moveable like Sinister's, and it's a gorgeous deep purple."

"I'm sure I'll love whatever you've made me." Murmur was past the need to avoid robes and have to have tunics. Even though she liked the latter, they just didn't seem to last long enough while leveling up to matter.

"Oh, fantastic. Are you going to be here for a bit? I have to put some finishing touches on the five piece." Neva stopped, hesitation written all over her face.

Murmur spoke gently, hoping to encourage her to share. "You were trying to tell me something a few days ago, weren't you? Are you okay?"

Neva paused, and then nodded. "Yeah, there's just something I need to talk to you about, and I have a few things to organize a bit more before I do. I'll ping you when I'm ready."

She flashed a nervous smile Murmur's way, and the enchanter felt concern rise in her throat. "I'm sure that whatever is on your mind, it'll be okay. We'll work through anything together."

Neva's smile was so wide it made her luna tongue poke out slightly. Murmur had to stifle a laugh. "Thank you for all you do."

"You're very welcome, Murmur." The luna took a breath and forged on.

"Speaking of which, what will you be doing while you're here?"

"Napping and testing a few things out." Murmur smiled, her plan still forming in her mind. "Telvar not around?"

"Nope, he said he had a meeting to attend." Neva began to focus on her work again, her answer somewhat absentminded.

"See you soon," Murmur said, glad to hear Tel was probably talking to the others.

There were variables she needed to go over, so she headed to one of the fully finished rooms on the lower floor. Most of them had a couple of single beds placed in them, with a couple of drawers and cupboards. The stone floor was swept, and the bedding was simple cotton, or knitted blankets. It was clean, fresh, and serviceable.

She lay down, with Snowy curled up on the floor beneath the bed, his head on his paws, yet Murmur knew that if anything threatened her, he was highly aware. Closing her eyes, she activated her game interface, not the HUD, but the original login screen.

Hovering over the log out button with her mind, she paused for a moment. What if, directing her brain the way she was, logging out severed her connection? Trying to convince her brain to actually log out, to bypass the alternate reality of her home and just log back into her brain, was more difficult than she'd anticipated.

Maybe it simply was just a case of mind over matter. Taking a deep breath, she activated the log out.

Storm Entertainment
Somnia Online Division
Game Development Offices Artificial Intelligence Server Room
Day Thirteen

"Whose NPC is Riasli?" Sui spoke before Rav could say anything.

"I was going to ask the same question." Oddly enough, Rav felt like his thunder had been stolen. Wren probably visited Sui straight after she visited the island, which was why it had taken the other so long to answer the summons for a meeting.

"I'd love to know what you're all talking about." Thra drawled the words out, sheer boredom working through her words. "Something to do with Murmur again, I take it?"

"She's not yours either?" Suddenly Rav didn't feel so strong anymore. His initial thoughts had been correct. They had a rogue NPC. How had that happened?

"She's in Curet. Of course she has to be Thra's. Not to mention she interfered and could have blown Wren up." Sui sounded heated, leading Rav to believe that somewhere in there, he actually cared about the girl. In some weird, twisted, further-his-agenda sort of way.

Thra raised a disinterested eyebrow. "No. Arita was mine, and I've apologized for that indiscretion. But Riasli was not mine at all. I don't even recall her being a blip on the radar. She's not an enchanter master. She's not even a trainer. She's just one of the NPCs players need to talk to in that queen quest thing option for gaining access to the ruins."

Rav pulled up data and subroutines, trying to calculate how Riasli breaking her role could have happened. He knew characters acted on their own due to interactions all the time in Somnia. They'd given them the ability to extrapolate and act individually for a reason, but it should have been within set parameters. From what he could see, there was no inciting event. Nothing Murmur had said to her should have triggered any of this. She'd simply gone off script before Fable even entered Curet, by killing or torturing the inhabitants of the Curet enchanter guild.

"Murmur didn't activate this in any way. Riasli had already rendered the trainers immobile when they arrived. And so, she didn't have to worry about the actual master respawning, she placed her in a type of stasis I didn't even know we had." Rav's words trailed away, and he looked at his brethren with an air of hopelessness. Some things apparently, just weren't quantifiable through his algorithms. It made him feel surprisingly vulnerable.

"Look." Thra spoke out, irritation obvious in the timber of her voice.

"Riasli might be in my city, but she was just one of the run of the mill NPCs placed there. If Riasli is out of line like this, I'll look into it, since I'll have to activate and assign a different NPC to be a part of the quest if a player's choices trigger it. If not, it'll be broken. Luckily, the only guild with any possibility of being close to doing that quest in that specific area at this point in time is Fable. So at least it's not out of hand."

"Not out of hand?" Sui's bad mood rumbled through his voice. "You realize Riasli didn't give Wren her kinetic grounding passive, right?"

Both Rav and Thra stared at him. "But that..."

"Exactly. Not only could that have killed her, but if she activated one of her skills to too great a degree, she could have blown the whole fucking game apart. Now *that* is a problem. And we need to fix it sooner, rather than later."

CHAPTER TWENTY

One Step

Murmur's head spun, so wildly that nausea threatened to take a hold. Her vision spiraled even behind closed eyes until she lay panting in complete and utter silence on a softer surface than she'd left. Her spine tingled, and her eyes felt as heavy as lead. It took a huge amount of effort to open them.

Light pierced her vision, blinding her for a moment, and aches entered all of the muscles in her body. She moved her fingers tentatively, their response sluggish, and she blinked the game's login away from her vision as the light faded from its initial blinding greeting.

As the room finally spun into focus, her breath caught in her throat, and it constricted with unshed tears. There, directly in front of her, was that damned crack in the curtains. Exactly the same. Over again. She lay on her bed as it was rendered in her mother's online version of their home, and there was no containment capsule visible anywhere near her.

The pillow and bed were soft, and she wished for a moment that she could truly feel the sensation of her sheets against her body instead of her brain's approximation of how it might feel. Tears leaked down the side of her face, even then she knew that too was fake.

She sat up and glanced at her bathroom, desperately wanting to feel hot water cascade down on her. Even if it wasn't real, at least it would feel it, right?

As the water rushed down on her, she reveled in the normalcy of taking a shower, of giving into the heated water, of feeling like she was at least partially alive. While it was a simulation, her mother had somehow made it utterly convincing. If she didn't know that it was the wrong reality, she wouldn't have thought twice. Just like she hadn't before she knew.

Toweling off after washing her hair, she pulled on her favorite pair of PJs. Soft and gentle against her skin, it gave her a feeling of home that she missed. She curled up in bed, on her side, with her headset on the nightstand, and pulled the covers up to her neck.

For a few moments of snuggling into her blankets she allowed herself to pretend it was real, to pretend she'd escaped whatever it was this headset had done to attach itself to her brain. Those few seconds were glorious.

Then she took a deep breath. Fine. So maybe it wasn't mind over matter, but for a while there, she'd done something. Logging out had never felt that conflicting. She'd never been left barely able to move or open her eyes, like her body and brain were fighting.

That meant there was something to what she'd done. Now she just needed to figure out what it was. But first she needed some shut-eye. She closed her eyes and let herself drift off, her mind for once utterly exhausted.

Feeling refreshed as she logged back into Curet, Murmur placed a hand on Snowy's head and looked out over the city's lily-pad center. She knew her friends would be logging in soon, and she had a few things she needed to do before that.

Namely, she had to check out the new armor she'd received. Sinister was going to love the way the lengthened tunic flared out in pieces for ease of movement. The deep purple only made the lights beneath her skin glow brighter when she cast spells. Its stats were a good improvement, but she was willing to bet there wouldn't be much of an upgrade for a while.

CON +10
STR +10
AGI +10
WIS +10
INT +40
CHA +50

HP +75
MANA +150
MA +60

She frowned at the total addition her own buffs made to her skills. With her necklace and circlet and ring—not to mention the staff—and it was plus eight to every stat, which...she started. The staff had leveled up. While she remembered some talk of it leveling up with her for a while, Murmur hadn't realized exactly what that meant. When had it done that? She frowned, not remembering an adjustment before she'd put her new armor on.

There, right at the bottom of the information about her armor set, it told her that it enhanced mana-infused crafted weapons as well. At least there was the explanation for the four-point increase to every stat the staff originally gave. Still, it seemed rather convenient, and she eyed the dragons on top of her staff skeptically, as if they'd come clean about however the system decided it was going to work. They remained, expectedly, silent.

CON 22 (44)
STR 10 (32)
AGI 20 (74)
WIS 12 (66)
INT 62 (126)
CHA 83 (157)

HP 606 (731)

MANA 858 (1028)

MA 160 (255)

Even without anyone else's buffs, she'd grown. She refused to listen to the voice in the back of her head telling her that everyone else, including the mobs they had to fight, had grown as well and just let herself bask in the bit of strength she'd gained. But after a few minutes, she sat up straight and decided to figure out her new MA abilities properly.

That reinforcement of her basic skills made sense, in an eerie way. She didn't even want to think what might have happened if she'd attempted to use more of her kinetic skills during their last battle. The headache backlash from shielding had been bad enough.

A sudden growl in Snowy's throat reverberated through to her hand and made Murmur whirl around quickly. In front of her stood a tall Feles, with Siamese markings and colorings. She was at eye level with Murmur and utterly gorgeous. Her fur was sleek, and her face spread into one of those lazy cat grins as she glanced at Snowy, whose growling subsided immediately.

"Murmur. I've not seen you for a while."

"We've met?" Murmur thought she would have recalled a feles this pretty.

"I'm Emilarth, and looked a lot different last time I saw you." Their laugh was melodic, echoing around through the trees.

Murmur wracked her brain to try and remember where she'd met this feles, except... "Oh, wow. You were the locus that gave me the undead ring."

Emilarth inclined her head, and frowned. "You're still wearing that? You really need to upgrade your jewelry. Anyway, I wanted you to know that the enchanter master here has been restored to her rightful place, and that you will now be able to study here without fear of misdirection."

"Thank you." Murmur wasn't sure what else to say but didn't want her to leave yet. "What happened?"

"A greedy enchanter decided to take something for themselves instead of working hard toward it." Emilarth smiled with a type of graciousness she seemed to think would appease Murmur.

"Look. That wasn't just some random scripting incident gone wrong.

That was totally off anything that was supposed to happen. I'm not sure if you're a GM or another damned AI, but this one was dangerous." Murmur didn't like that she could feel a tremor spreading through her body or that she was genuinely upset at the world for throwing this wrench into the works.

Most of all, Murmur didn't want platitudes that things would be okay. She needed guarantees. With the way her kinetic magic seemed to react with the world, she wouldn't feel safe using it deliberately until she knew no one was out to get her group. No one outside of Jirald that is. She'd not heard a peep from them since they'd trounced Exodus in the gnoll caves, and the building tension of waiting for him to stab her in the back again wasn't doing her disposition any favors.

Emilarth raised a delicate eye ridge, studying Murmur with catlike precision. "We know. You know. Don't scare others needlessly. It's under control for now. Just remember that nothing will rectify it quicker than playing the forced storyline through to its end."

Murmur blinked, her seemingly irrational fear fading instantly at the calmness in the feles's words. "So, you're saying we need to play her game and defeat her to cast the evil out forever?"

"Something like that." Emilarth chuckled and spoke words that left no more doubt in Murmur's mind. "I can see why Telvar finds you so fascinating."

In a blink of the eye, Emilarth was gone.

Snowy wuffed at the air where she'd been, and looked back beseechingly at Murmur as if asking her what the fuck.

"Right there with you boy, right there with you." Murmur gave him an absent-minded pet behind the ears wishing Emilarth had stayed longer, answered more questions, and not been so enigmatic. In an effort to distract herself, she turned toward the fountain. The balancing feles were intriguing. If she'd done her mental calculations properly, and the ruins were in fact a part of the key quests, then this fountain, and perhaps the fountain in Cognitia might even have something to do with it. Thing was, she had no idea in which way.

Sighing, she sat down on the edge of it while waiting for her friends to log in, closed her eyes and crossed her long legs. She reached out with her sensor net and attempted to activate her passive kinetic ability. The blinding headache as she triggered it was definitely not something she'd been expecting.

Backing off, she blinked her eyes open, trying to chase the black spots away from her vision. Snowy nudged her knee with his cold nose, concern in his intelligent eyes as he focused on her.

"It's okay. May have overdone the intensity there." She mumbled at him as she readied herself again. No use in giving up, the others weren't here, and the abilities weren't active ones, so sitting in peace and quiet should help her.

Not that it was all that quiet. Feles children may have been light on their feet, but their games weren't. Their laughter echoed through the canopy like tiny bells ringing. In a way, the melodic strains of their play helped soothe Murmur in a manner she hadn't realized she needed.

She watched them run back and forth playing tag, hide and seek, and something she didn't understand that involved a bouncy ball with a mind of its own. Watching them had a hypnotic effect on her, calmed her mind, and let the Basic Kinetic Structure flow through to her sensor and shield.

Her eyes opened wide as she realized she could feel the actual mental shields surrounding everyone within her range. Barriers that were no longer such for her, but instead doors she could open easily, because they weren't walls, but innate defenses that the mind gave itself. Unlike her own protections that she'd mortared together with her thoughts and sheer will, these were reflexive barriers the mind had built to protect itself from mental attacks.

She knew it, she could identify it, and she could reach out with a thought and touch those same shields, bounce on them, feel their tangibility. If she punched just a little harder...

And then she realized she'd even bolstered her Thought Projection. What was punching through a shield if it wasn't an almost physical manifestation of Thought Projection? Excitement began to build up in her. She could reach through and affect people's thoughts whether they were shielded or not, whether they wanted her to or not. Punching through to directly affect them, deliberately affect them—that had a multitude of possibilities.

For stubborn enemies, for great enemies, and if Jirald kept up this fucking quest to kill her for those damned shards, for stubborn, misogynistic enemies too. The only downside was that if she affected minds in here, did it transpose to the outside? Probably not, right? Or she wouldn't be in a coma, because her whole mind over matter schtick should have worked.

After a couple of hours sitting there and honing her skills with their new-found bolster, Murmur tracked Sinister's progress as her best friend logged in right until she sat down next to Mur, on the opposite side of Snowy, and just waited. Sinister seemed content to sit next to her and wait. Her friend's mind was a melancholy mixture, its thoughts whirling just beneath a surface that was sturdier than others Murmur had faced. It made her wonder if the choice of enchanter as Sin's hybrid class had helped inadvertently reinforce her own mental protections.

Technically, Mur now had the ability to dive in and sift through thoughts, whether the target wanted her to or not. While the back of her mind screamed at her that such a thing was wrong, the forefront was trying to logically calculate just how much of what she saw in-game would remain only in and from Somnia. Would she only have access to thoughts centered around Somnia, or would they extend to the much larger real world? How much effort would she have to put into being able to push gently past those shields?

So many questions, and that annoying moral part of her wouldn't let her test anything out. At least not on her friends. Maybe her enemies, maybe some NPCs. That moral part also made her feel good though, because without it, she was only a step away from giving into the darkness that constantly tried to talk to her.

"Sleep well, Sin?" Murmur asked, remaining in her relaxed pose and not even opening her eyes.

Sin chuckled next to her. "Sleep at all, Mur?"

"Actually, I napped." Back at home, in bed, is what Murmur didn't answer. Sin had a way of only answering what she wanted to answer when she wanted to answer it. Sometimes it was endearing, other times it was fucking infuriating. "You're a bit earlier than expected."

She could sense a feeling of discomfort within Sin, but it didn't appear to be directed at Murmur herself, but more at Somnia and reality not being one. Was that invasion of privacy? Murmur couldn't be sure, but in her current half-trance, she could see so much without any effort, so it wasn't like she'd pried.

"We don't seem to spend much time together. I miss just us time. The others can be..." She paused as if trying to find the right word, the least offensive term.

"Rowdy?" Murmur offered with a small smile. Finally, she uncrossed her legs, opened her eyes and half-turned to Sin. "Yeah. I miss our time. We used to log on together all the time, remember? Make it in a little earlier so we could get shit done, so we could research, so we could plan our next course of adventure?"

Sin grinned. "So we could figure out who we were going to practical joke next. Those were the best of times."

"For us, anyway." Murmur sighed. She really did miss just having her friend by her side. Somnia felt so crowded, so teeming with life, even if a lot of it was supposed to be AI driven.

Sinister leaned in, resting her head on Murmur's shoulder. The proximity and warmth her body lent the enchanter was remarkably solid and real. Calm suffused Mur, and she relaxed, not having realized she was so tense to begin with. Just having Sin there often helped her moods, and she'd hated arguing with her. The irritation she'd had melted away and she leaned into the half hug.

"Can we just stay like this for a bit, Mur?" Sin sounded uncharacteristically sad. The melancholy in her voice leaked through, concerning Mur so much she reached her hand around Sin's shoulder and squeezed gently.

"We can stay like this forever." And for several minutes they did.

She'd always taken for granted that Harlow would be there, that Sinister would play games with her. But what happened if Murmur died? What happened if Somnia crashed and burned after a while like so many games that gave way to the latest and greatest? What if she still wasn't out of her coma by then?

The thoughts scared her; the situation was so unpredictable. So she leaned into Sin, drinking in that constant that had been there for as long as she could remember. She let it wind into her, and calm her fears, at least for now. They were working on it. Everyone was trying to figure it out. There was no way she'd let go of Sin, and no one could make her.

It took a while for everyone else to get back, so Murmur and Sin visited a couple of the stalls to make sure they had enough potions and supplies. With Snowy bringing up the rear, most of the feles kept their distance. Murmur smiled to herself—maybe there was something to that cat and dog thing.

"You know I can pull temporary healing potions from my cauldron now, right?" Mellow spoke softly from behind her and almost made her drop the healing potion she was holding.

"No, because none of you tell me what skills you get, and I've been having to wait until someone else gets them and mentions them in a forum somewhere online that I can access." She glared at them, but her heart wasn't in it.

Mellow laughed. "You have to make up your mind. Either you want us to share, or you want us to hoard every advantage that we have. You can't have it both ways."

"Pedantic. Just tell *me*. You don't have to tell everyone." Murmur placed the potion back onto the stall table and turned to Mellow. "So, what do they do, how do you do what you do, and what do I need to know?"

"I can concoct batches of five health potions at a time. No one can have more than five at a time. They heal up two hundred hit points, which isn't huge, but it's good in a pinch, and they have a four-hour lifespan." Mellow's eyes were distant, obviously immersed in their HUD to retrieve information. Murmur wondered just how many spells and concoctions Mellow had. Not even that, what about everyone else? Was she the only one with a massive spells and abilities list?

She realized Mellow was waiting for a response of some sort from her. "That's amazing. We should probably make sure we all have a set of them before we go into the ruins."

"Thought as much." Mellow grinned and eyed the mana potions at the stall. "Can't do mana until level forty though."

Murmur sighed and shook her head. "They're not very generous with their mana regeneration abilities, are they?"

"Gotta impose strictness somehow. Can't make it too easy to win now, can they?" Sinister interjected, making Murmur jump.

Last she'd seen, Sin had been over at another stall picking out rare tailoring ingredients to help Neva's ongoing quest to get the best stuff into the armory.

It was weird to think they had an armory now.

"You need to start announcing your presence," Murmur mumbled grumpily, checking her sensor net for reasons it might not have alerted her to Sin's presence.

"Nope. Not going to do that." Sinister's grin was infectious, and Murmur was grateful for having got over the awkwardness after their argument.

"So, are we ready, or did you all want to spend more time shopping?"

Murmur turned around to find Devlish standing behind them with everyone else in tow. "We thought shopping would be best. Next on the agenda: shoes." She added a wink to the end of it which had the others laughing softly.

Snowy nudged her fingers, and she petted him obediently. It was like *he'd* trained *her*. And she didn't entirely object to it either. She barely noticed the diminished MA, and it didn't really impact her usage. Snowy contributed to her damage, and his evasion and defensive abilities made him an excellent companion. That, and he was cute.

"Well. Are we ready then?"

"I was waiting for you." Beastial scratched his cat behind the ears, glaring mildly at Snowy while he did so. "Thought you were too busy talking."

Sinister rolled her eyes. "Sure you did. We believe you think all the time." And she patted his arm gently.

Murmur had to fight hard not to laugh at the expression on Beastial's face. He excelled at walking into every single set up Sinister made for him. But they'd literally spent no time at all leveling in around fifteen real world hours, and Murmur was starting to get antsy. Not to mention the rogue enchanter running around out there who was just waiting for them to walk into her trap.

"Come on. Let's go. Snowy is tired of waiting," she said, stepping out in front of the group and squaring her shoulders as she planted her staff against the floor.

"You feeling all right there, Mur?" Dansyn asked, concern pinching his brow. "I mean, you can't really blame the wolf."

Murmur glanced at Snowy, whose tongue was lolling out as he grinned a big wolf grin.

"Traitor," she muttered. But the rest of them laughed and followed her anyway.

Murmur dialed her MA abilities up to their max as soon as they stepped off the huge leafed platform and into the jungle. It was alive with movement and fleeting thoughts that she couldn't quite grasp, even with her enhanced focus. Small animals darted through the trees and vines, their thoughts rapid, unfocused, unblinking. Letting herself get too carried away with following them made it difficult to concentrate on other things.

Resetting her attention, she scanned outward. The strength of her abilities now meant that she could push further, sense more, and potentially prevent another ambush that wasn't headed by a pscyho rogue AI who'd decided to puppeteer everyone she could get her claws into.

While scanning for threats, she made sure that her group felt secure. While she didn't want to use eighty-eight of her available 220 MA, it was easy enough to see that their mental shielding was pretty robust. It made her wonder if she could teach them some mental reinforcement on her own. Sinister and Veranol should be more than capable of the basics, considering they'd taken enchanter as their hybrid class.

"You're lost in thought there, Mur?" Havoc's voice surprised her.

"Not really lost, just running over my way too many skills in my head. I've had skill heavy classes before, but so many of these are dependent on different levels of different prerequisites, and sometimes they can be a bugger to juggle—that's all." She answered him genuinely, not realizing until after she finished that he might not have meant it to be an actual inquiry. "Sorry. You did ask. You know how I get when I'm concentrating."

"Well, at least now I understand you've got a lot to concentrate on." He took a deep breath before continuing. "I expanded the undead portion of my skills. Figured if I'm going to go necromancer, then I should just bite the bullet and go hard."

Havoc had always been easy to talk to, but lately he seemed to be more quiet than usual. "You're worried about me, aren't you?"

He raised an eyebrow. "Very astute. More the situation and how to deal with it than just you, but yes. It's probably something you should talk to Veranol about. You know he's a doctor, right?"

"Seriously?" Murmur ran that over in her head. She was sure he'd mentioned it once or twice when she first met him. Made sense for a doctor to be a healer. Theoretically, anyway. Some were just money hungry bastards. "How'd he get time off?"

Havoc shrugged. "Not sure, might want to ask him."

He was being pushy, which was unlike him.

Murmur frowned, nodding, and opened her mouth to speak when Snowy growled low in his throat, vibrating against her leg. "What's up..." she began to ask, until she saw what he was focused on.

Six sentries guarded the bottom of the wide, moss-covered stone steps, which crumbled in places, indicating that they had originated long before this world. The guards stood tall and proud, with a familiar vacant expression on their faces and long spears with nasty tips at their sides. Even exerting effort, she couldn't sense them. If she hadn't seen them with her own eyes, Murmur wouldn't have realized they were there.

Here was an enemy she couldn't sense and couldn't predict. For the first time since finding out she was in a coma, a true sense of fear ran through her.

CHAPTER TWENTY-ONE

Ancient Ruins

The raid split off into their groups and hid behind a copse of trees to cut out line of sight for the mobs, to avoid being spotted.

"I thought you said the path was clear," Murmur whispered at Merlin.

He shrugged. "Well, it was like six hours ago."

Murmur tapped her foot in frustration. "How many more are there? I can't sense them. Their minds are blocked from me. Not even like a void, but more like just plain space."

Merlin activated Stealth and crept out, disappearing from sight after a few seconds. Murmur counted the heartbeats until he came back, fighting down an irrational sense of helplessness. After a few moments he returned.

"Just those six at the base, four camouflaged to each side a ways down. There are ledges there you could use to jump down to the bottom instead of the stairs with a good chunk of agility, if you wanted to try and avoid them, but I'd suggest better to just take care of them than be sorry. Then at the bottom in front of the actual crumbling door that is just around a corner, there are another four." He paused, and Murmur breathed a sigh of relief. "That seems to be it. We should still be marginally refreshed by the time we move in there."

"Do they all have that blank look in their eyes? Like they're puppets?"

Sinister hugged herself, crouching low.

Merlin nodded. "That they do."

"Fantastic." Murmur had grown used to her abilities making things easier on her group mates, but right now it was more of a hindrance. At least before she'd been able to compensate for her handicap. Now, this NPC seemed to be much more powerful than Murmur was, and there didn't seem to be anything she could do. She could feel the tickle of irritation gnawing at her. She wasn't used to being rivaled this early in the game. The fact that it was an NPC felt wrong. Riasli acted like another player on the opposite side, like she was meant to be an opponent. Nothing about her actions so far spoke of computer controlled anything. And that was scary, unpredictable, and above all, unreadable.

Still, they couldn't let this stop them. "Well, guys, there are the ruins there that we need to get into. I'll be pretty useless against them. I don't have anything yet that will combat her control of them."

"It's all good, Mur." Veranol didn't even stop to look back at her. "Even if you can't take over her puppets, you make us stronger just by being here."

Murmur blinked at the shaman and bit back a laugh. "You know, or else by buffing the crap out of you all with all my nifty spells." She wiggled her eyebrows.

"Exactly. We're a team. Team Murmur's buffs make us better, faster, stronger." His eyes twinkled, and Murmur laughed despite herself.

"You're daft, old man." She couldn't resist the jab, but then took in a breath and grew serious again. "I was just forewarning you that I wouldn't be likely able to do as much as I usually do. You know, so we're all aware."

"We know, Mur." Sinister put her hand on her friend's shoulder and smiled. "Just buff us up so we're super strong, miss I'm-already-level-thirty-two, and let us have at 'em."

She stepped forward, intent on heading back out and stopped herself to sigh. "Excellent. I shall craft out a master plan and send you all out to your dooooooooom."

She intoned the last word as deeply as she could until her voice cracked. The others laughed, and Murmur realized her concerns had pretty much disappeared. They knew her well enough to stop her frustration in its tracks and concentrate on her strengths. And be damned if she wasn't going to buff the hell out of them all.

A sharp jab to her side made Murmur turn to Sin, rubbing at the spot.

"Better make sure you don't forget Mana Tide, missy. Mine just ran out. What do you think this is?"

"What do I get in return?" Mur asked, teasing.

Sinister just stared at her flatly, arms crossed. "Healed."

Murmur laughed to see her friend dishing her own old medicine back to her. "Touché! I shall gift thee with my mana regeneration. For I shall like to be healed."

"See that you do!" Sinister grinned, wiggling her eyebrows for comical effect. "For what it's worth, I bet your Mana Tide is better than anyone else's."

"Well, what can I say? When you're right you're right." Murmur's tension levels were still dropping, and her head seemed lighter. Even if she couldn't forget there were mobs just past this tree line, she felt better about facing them.

She really needed to get a handle on the frustration that Riasli was causing her, because the NPC wanted her to get rattled, and Murmur hated letting her win that way. Sinister watched her, her clear eyes focused in a way that was more protective than previously, and Murmur felt safe.

"Good." Sinister's smile turned smug. "Just remember that next time. I'm always right."

Devlish choked down what might have been a loud laugh and caused a small snort as a result. "We need to head out, but I could watch you two all day."

"Because that's not creepy at all." Havoc said, one eyebrow raised skillfully.

Devlish blushed furiously. "You all know that's not what I meant!"

"Sure, sure." Beastial waved him away.

Murmur chuckled to herself, blocked them out, scanned her own shields, and the sensor net. She double-checked the way her shields were built; how tight they were. As usual, they were rock solid. At least there wouldn't be any attacks on that front.

"Okay, everyone. That's enough teasing the poor lizard. I mean, he has scales for crying out loud. He probably has to molt at some stage."

Devlish's eyes grew big, and then he smiled self-deprecatingly. "Thanks. You don't really think that, do you?"

Murmur shrugged. "Would you really be surprised in this game?"

"No." Devlish gulped, glancing down at his arms as he ran a finger across the surface of his scales. "No, I wouldn't at all."

"Excellent." Sinister clapped him on the shoulder, and glared around her. "If we're all ready, I do believe Murmur would like us to fight stuff so she can receive the healing from me."

"Sin makes yet another excellent point." Murmur ignored the groans coming from the rest of them. "These mobs aren't going to kill themselves. At least, I don't think they are. I've been wrong about things before."

Murmur grimaced as she renewed the Mez on one of her targets. The effort she had to exert to override its mind was strenuous. Though it stood to reason that if she could increase her power, others would be able to increase their defenses. From the blank look in their eyes, they were definitely being controlled, just like Merlin had surmised, which meant Riasli had taken these mobs over too. Even with Murmur's first reaction being anger at the audacity of the other enchanter, a part of her thirsted for power like that, for the ability to control a number of beings.

Snowy ran past on his way to assist the others and licked her hand. It hit her. Of course she had that. She could command pets for thirty-five MA each. Right now, she'd be able to control seven of them at a time, technically, although she could already imagine that backlash headache. Maybe that was what Riasli was using. But if that was the case, she'd have to have an obscene amount of MA. Then again, she was a part of Somnia. The rules swam in her head, just this side of a headache, and Murmur shook herself to stop the train of thought. Focus. She needed to concentrate on what they had in front of them.

Four at a time were doable. She couldn't quite define their classes. They moved as if they possessed martial arts training, yet fought more like a ninja with swords or daggers. Their movements resembled a deathly dance, and Murmur had to force herself not to become entranced by it.

Taking on the Mezs herself allowed Dansyn the ability to utilize songs that bolstered the group with extra mana and health regeneration. Buffs like that helped their overall productivity. Not that the heals would ever save them if the healers died, but it helped alleviate a portion of the burden. And that mana song? Well, she had to admit it was delicious. That, her Mana Tide, and the fact that the healers had taken on the hybrid of the enchanter class allowed their mana regeneration to refill at a solid rate.

It made Murmur glad she'd chosen the Sidious path. With a bard permanently in their raid, it was going to give her so much more versatility when it came to dealing with mobs that seemed far too human-like to be AI products. Like Riasli. Murmur frowned, thoughts still rampant in her head as she focused half on her inner diatribe and half on the mobs. She loved their armor too. It had echoes of old fashioned ancient Chinese dynastic warrior Asian armor, and yet it conformed with their movements. The plates that seemed to be flimsy at first were made of more resilient stuff. As guards of the temple, that made sense. She knew, without a doubt, that the mobs inside the ruins, or crypt, or catacombs—whatever it would be when they opened those doors—would be at least two levels higher than them.

She frowned as she glanced up at the couple of rows of stone levels that appeared to rise out of the ground. She'd been sure that the ruins she'd seen in the promo videos had been very close in appearance to the Mayan temples with the way they stood tall out of the ground, but this seemed to have sunk down. Even the entry stairs led down instead of up. Maybe she was confusing it with a dungeon in another area.

The adjusting raid zone idea was fantastic. Requiring a level of thirty, or very close to it, allowed people to begin pursuing the end game as they leveled. It was a much better incentive. Waiting until they reached the end game to get the keys would have been a nightmare.

With the last of the four stealther mobs finished off, the group pulled back a little to take stock of their situation.

"They weren't nearly as difficult as I'd assumed they'd be, considering how hard we had to work to get past the undead dwarves back at Hightower," Havoc mused out loud, his fingers stroking his chin as if he had a beard there. It made Murmur curious to know if that were the case in the real world.

"No. They weren't that difficult. Very straightforward, and not at all what we've come to expect from anything Riasli-related." Veranol's words rang deeply through Murmur.

Something was very wrong with the situation. Given their last encounters with the feles traitor, Murmur had come to expect a certain level of deviousness. The original L'tigri killers hadn't been inventive in the way they fought, but they had been difficult to defeat, even while being controlled. But this didn't have the same atmosphere to it. All that was similar was the way their minds and intentions were hidden from her. Could it be that she'd simply extended her mind shielding over these? But in total that made eighteen guards, which for Murmur would cost one hundred and forty-four MA. Maybe it was doable, but that was a lot of headache. Maybe Riasli couldn't get headaches.

"Mur?" Devlish stood in front of her, arms crossed, his body moving slightly in time with the foot he was tapping impatiently. "What do you think?"

"I think it's a trap. A false sense of security. She hasn't given these guards anything special except for the fact that she's encompassed them within her own mind protection, which means I can't get a read on them, nor can I seem to break through her hold to gain my own. If she's doing something else though, I don't know about it yet. She is above us in levels though, so that's not too strange." Murmur shrugged. "I think she just wants us to hurry up and get in there."

Sure, it wasn't quite like fighting a really good guild leader who knew what they were doing with all of their members, but she had to give Riasli some credit. So far, she'd been entirely capable of throwing Murmur and her guild off guard. The thing was, they were fighting mechanically and not intuitively like all the other intelligent enemies they'd encountered.

"Traps aren't that dangerous when we know that's what they are, right?" Sinister pulled at the belt around her tunic, a thoughtful expression on her face.

Her dark hair whipped in the wind, and for just a moment she held an ethereal glow to her that made Murmur gasp softly. She caught herself and blushed, glancing around to see if anyone noticed.

"Not too dangerous if we know they're there. But since we don't know what she'll do or what she's capable of, it's still pretty touch and go." Havoc's no-nonsense tone was calming. "Mur, is there absolutely no way you can break her hold?"

Murmur suppressed a sigh of relief and went over all of her abilities in her mind, trying to figure out if she had missed something. "If I can get close enough to her, I might be able to put a stop to her with a one of my Sinuous abilities. She's going to have a high magic resist, so the odds of me being able to charm or control her are relatively low. But there might be a chance, if I get close."

Beastial clapped his hands together, making all of them jump. His face spread into a wide grin, and his eyes lit up like sparks. "At least we have the makings of a plan now, right?"

Merlin shook his head. "It'll have to do for now. Better to run with a plan than run away, right?"

"I'm not sure if that's supposed to be a joke, but if it was, it's a bad one." Rashlyn rolled her shoulders and moved her neck from side to side like she was stretching while getting ready for the upcoming prolonged battle. "Don't know about any of you guys, but I almost feel like this game is making me fitter."

Murmur blinked at her friend while the others laughed softly, and only half in jest. It made her wish she could log out and test that theory. But then most things made her want to log out. She shook herself and plastered a smile over her face. "Well, it might be fun for you all to sit around here, but I feel like killing some shit, and we've got another fourteen mobs to go before we finally get in there."

She moved over to the next spot without waiting for the others. Pulling was a fine art if done correctly. Line of sight was no longer working as accurately as the monsters they fought leveled up in strength and awareness too, but the feign death ability that Rashlyn had managed to work wonders to split packs every now and again.

Murmur couldn't shake the feeling that for once they weren't the ones able to choose, that instead they were being ushered into a corner and that once they got to their designated place, it would be all they could do to avoid death.

Murmur panted, leaning up against the moss-covered wall at the bottom of the stairs. She surveyed the last group of four they'd fought with a frown. They'd been decent opponents, but nothing like the dwarves from Hightower, nothing like any of the mobs they'd fought until this whole Riasli thing. Their reactions seemed scripted, and fighting them had barely been a challenge. She wasn't impressed, but it had nothing to do with the AIs she knew who ran the world—no, she put this down to Riasli's interference.

"This was way too easy." Merlin stood with his back leaning against the opposite wall, his eyes on the door in front of him. "Those guards were barely an inconvenience. I feel like they should have been a hell of a lot more trouble."

Devlish nodded slowly, a thoughtful frown curling his lips. "Yeah it felt like more of a game… and until these mobs, it's not felt like that."

Mellow piped up. "She is trying to lure us in. Maybe she thought easy would appeal to us?"

Murmur shook her head, reaching down a hand to tangle it in Snowy's fur while the wolf let his tongue loll out. "I thought she said she wasn't going to let us get in, but maybe that wasn't what she meant. Maybe instead it's a way of deliberately keeping us from experiencing types of fighting styles we might run into in the ruins. In a sort of—'you'll have no idea what you're expecting' sort of way."

"Seems legit." Merlin shrugged. "Look. At least we're refreshed."

Beastial smiled, moving toward the entrance from where he'd sat at the bottom of the steps. "If we go in now, there's a large chance that we're not going to get out for a good long while. Merlin's right. We're refreshed, far more than we were in Hightower. We can do this."

"You're awfully confident for a DPS," Devlish drawled, a minor hint of irritation under his words.

"Yep. Someone has to be, because our tank is being cautious as fuck." Beastial's barb even stung Mur. Maybe he hadn't gotten over not being a tank this time after all. She'd thought he was happy with beastmaster.

"Let's not do this and say we did, okay?" Havoc suddenly stood quietly between them. "We don't need to measure our in-game peens here. You can do that before the next time we log off."

"Seriously? You're trying to lecture us about this?" Beastial raised an eyebrow, his tension visible in the set of his shoulders. "Fuck you, Havoc."

Havocs response was the last thing Murmur expected. He laughed. Threw his head back and laughed. "That's amazingly droll of you, but at least come up with a better insult than that. Now pull yourselves together and let's get whatever issues you're both currently having and take them out on the mobs waiting for us in there."

Murmur glanced at Sinister to see what her reaction was. The dark elf's eyes were narrowed, and the frown on her face was full of annoyance. In fact, Murmur was pretty sure she was about to have a word with both of them. They didn't need to be battling amongst themselves out here though, so she stepped in before the inevitable storm could blow up.

"Why don't we just open the door and see what awaits us, you know, since none of us can teleport inside?" Murmur softened the words with a smile, but the guys just continued to glare at each other, except Havoc who kept laughing. He wasn't being any help at all. "Guys, give it a rest. We all want to kill shit. It's therapeutic. Let's do it."

"True that, Mur. True that." Jinna seemed to be struggling to hold back laughter too. And she knew it wasn't going to sit well with Beastial or Devlish. While she appreciated the gesture on one hand, she just wanted to go and take care of Riasli.

Just about to speak, Murmur was not prepared for the message that appeared in front of her eyes.

The guild Spiral has defeated Inith Ilan of the Ilinish Threshold and gained one of the twelve keys.

"What the fuck?" Merlin blurted out.

Murmur wondered if she looked as shell-shocked as everyone else. Sure, they were about to hit their second dungeon, but that meant that while they'd been concentrating on keeping Exodus at bay, another guild had crept up on them.

She hadn't checked the level status of the game for days, and was loath to do it now. What if they'd overtaken them? She hated being behind. Always better to just be in front and not give it up.

"Hmm. A '/who all Spiral' brings up a top level of thirty. In fact, most of them seem to be level thirty." Havoc frowned, his eyes focused beyond the game. "And Ilinish Threshold appears to be over on Firtulai."

"Well, looks like we have our work cut out for us, eh?" Beastial elbowed Devlish in the ribs.

"Watch it, you beast lover you." Devlish winked and returned the elbow.

"Great." Murmur rolled her eyes and pushed on, trying to not completely give into her desperation. "How about we go in there and do what we need to do to end Riasli?"

Without waiting for an answer, she sidled up to the door and placed her palm against the round circle in the middle. The words around it were barely legible and in a strange script she had to tap into her interface to read. Without a second thought, she pushed against the circle while chanting the words, letting her mind flow with the push and pull from her powers.

She extended her mental shield outward, reinforcing it with a kinetic barrier as her Thought Sensing and Shielding refueled her MA. "Ithis, Meris, grant me entry, for I seek the age of old. Effris, Leshis, grant me grace, as I fight evils untold."

The door beneath her hand shook as the words and her kinetic barrier made contact. With a rumble they began to roll to the sides, opening to reveal a gaping darkness behind them. No sconces lit the way this time, no guards were in sight, and there was no welcoming person at the beginning to get them started.

A swirl of golden sparkles fluttered around the group, enveloping each of them in turn, but then the darkness swallowed it. Maybe that was the grace the inscription spoke about. All Murmur knew was that it tingled like something that made her feel better and felt dangerous all at once. She had no idea what this grace did, and just as she was about to pull up her HUD to inquire, she heard a grating of stone against stone. Looking up, she barely stopped herself from taking an involuntary step back.

There, in the depths of the blending shadows, they saw movement.

Step over the threshold and keep your promise, lest you feel my wrath.

Well, that was easy, wasn't it? Hesitantly, they stepped over the threshold, just as the huge approaching shadow began to gain form. It stood at least twenty feet high, and in the fading light as the doors began to close behind them, Murmur realized they were facing a stone statue. Her eyes gradually got used to the darkness, and she watched as it closed in on them, its footsteps rumbling the ground.

Storm Entertainment
Somnia Online Division
Game Development Offices Artificial Intelligence Server Room
Day Thirteen

Laria paced her office, her eyes never leaving the portion of forest her daughter was currently in. Mainly because while she knew that was where Murmur was, she also couldn't see her daughter. None of that made sense. The tracker allowed her to maintain contact at a distance, and so far, it'd been the one thing holding her together through all of this. But right now, the system said they were all standing outside of the ancient ruins.

An ancient ruin that didn't quite look like the one she recalled approving for the Cenedril Isle. It no longer even resembled the ruins they'd shown visuals of in the promo material. The homes of the keys were all meticulously arranged, and this one was nothing like its intended incarnation. The rising pyramid modeled on Mayan architecture was no longer. Instead, a smaller version rose up, covered in a slimy moss with a more sinister air. Steps led down instead of up, to what appeared to be an entrance to a maze or labyrinth, and she couldn't see past the steps. She couldn't even see the door.

What had the AIs done this time? Did they decide to step in and prevent her from keeping an eye on her daughter? Anything was possible with the way they'd grown in the last days.

What with the change in the ruins and the inability to see into them or even around them, Laria was verging on a state of panic. She took a breath to calm herself and focused. Her husband was right; she'd been letting herself get so caught up in the state of events that she wasn't thinking clearly any longer.

She'd worked under far more questionable circumstances before. The dev who thought it was oh-so-clever to insert an Easter egg into one game that stripped any female players nearby against their will. That one had been a barrel of harassment suits. Then there was that time when one of the devs decided to mark one of the newbie items with a cautionary message of *do not use near fire*.

Which for the majority of people was tantamount to telling them to go and light it *on* fire. Those explosions had caused in-game characters permanent damage, and the GM tickets had gone on for months.

She shook her head, laughing at the past. In its own way it bolstered her bravery. Shit happened in-games, coding fucked up and things went wrong. Perhaps not Michael, Ava, and Wren levels of wrong, but there was a first time for everything.

Closing her eyes, she took a deep breath and activated her communication channel with Shayla. "Hey. Don't suppose you know what's going on with the Ruins of Cenedril, do you?"

"Hi, love you too," Came Shayla's marginally irritated voice through the earpiece. "Let me check."

Laria knew without a doubt that Shayla was scrunching her eyes just a little, squinting without realizing it as she activated the augmented reality in her contacts. The action was something she'd done for years, and it helped ground Laria in this reality. She waited, albeit impatiently. Nothing about the game currently involved patience.

"Oh." Shayla's confusion came across magnificently in that single syllable. "That's odd. I take it no one ran this by you? Can you figure out who initiated the change? When did you last check this area?"

"Just before launch and it was fine. I don't have any information on anyone making changes, not even in the logs. As far as I knew it hasn't even been touched since launch, not by players or developers. I'm unsure why it's currently in this...state." Laria frowned again. "Do you think we'll be able to access the inside of the dungeon?"

"Sure. We should be able to access everything, right? Maybe only the entrance is inaccessible because of the new positioning of it." Shayla sounded a lot more confident of her hypothesis than Laria knew she felt. She appreciated her friend trying to make her feel better, and she'd figure out a way to view it somehow.

"Well, I have been trying and I don't seem to be getting in. It's glitching or something. Do you think the AIs have anything to do with this?" she grudgingly asked.

"No." Shayla hesitated. "This doesn't quite seem like their sort of MO, wouldn't you say? I mean, they're not usually this antagonistic. This smacks of someone trying to hide something from us, and I'm not entirely sure how to deal with that. The AI haven't hidden anything—"

"If you don't count Michael and Ava." Laria snapped the words out, immediately regretting them.

"They haven't hidden anything since then. The fact that they're achieving sentience isn't something they're hiding when we haven't directly asked them, either." Shayla's breath sounded soft over the connection. Laria could almost hear the cogs whirring in her head.

"And? What do you mean?"

"Well, they don't seem to be able to lie, or at least they don't feel comfortable lying, right?" A hint of excitement attached itself to her words, traveling down the line like static electricity and made Laria jump.

"Since we haven't directly asked them if they're sentient, they've neither denied nor confirmed it." Shayla hurried and continued. "So, if we want to know this, why don't we just go and ask if they had anything to do with it?"

"How do we know doing that won't teach them how to lie? I mean, it's not that they can't, right? We have no idea." Something about the situation struck Laria as desperate. The thing was, she didn't have many other options that came to mind.

"They never actually hid the other damned incidents." Shayla stamped her foot so loudly that Laria heard it through their link up. "They simply didn't tell us. Withholding something isn't quite the same as lying, and it's very obvious they know the distinction exists."

"So then, they haven't told us about this change because either they have no idea, or it's that we haven't asked." Laria could see where Shayla was going with it. And although she tried to fight it, even such a vague straw was something she could cling to.

CHAPTER TWENTY-TWO

Into the Catacombs

The statue's ankle bone was only slightly lower than Jinna. The rest of Jinna barely reached her shins. Her feet trod with a determined approach as the humungous being looked down at them, her staff resting against the floor with a bang. "Who disturbs the crypt of Naishi?"

Crypt of Naishi? Murmur frowned. She hadn't seen anything that referred to something by that name on the map, nor had she noticed anything but the Ruins of Cenedril in what she'd read in-game. Not even the feles in their own city had mentioned it. Who was this Naishi?

She glanced at the others, knowing that they were waiting for her to speak just like she had the previous time. It worked with Hightower, so maybe it would work here too. Resisting the urge to clear her throat that was suddenly extra dry, Murmur took a small step forward, thus bringing the full brunt of the statue's focus on herself.

The thing was huge. So tall that her knee caps were higher than Murmur's head. The stone entrance rose up even past the statue, lending a sense of grandeur that left Murmur in awe. If intimidation was her aim, Riasli couldn't have picked a better battleground. Mur took a deep breath before speaking.

"The guild of Fable seeks to gain knowledge through the exploration and understanding of this crypt." Murmur chose her words carefully, backing them with her Thought Projection, with caring and respect, with sufferance and noble intentions.

For a few moments she almost thought it worked. The statue's stance changed for an instant, and an almost relaxed stance took over. But the enchanter relaxed her hold on the words just a few moments too soon. The statue snapped back to attention, eyes glowing red momentarily, and her stone lips spread in a snarl.

"You are not righteous. You do not seek for anyone but yourself. You are enemies of the Naishi-dan." The statue lifted her staff several feet high and brought it back down on the ground with a resounding thud that made the ground underneath them tremor so strongly, a few of them lost their footing.

The red glow to her eyes faded, but the damage had been done. A pale orange light rippled out from where the staff thundered down upon the ground in a wave of power that moved back from the statue and into the catacombs beyond them. Murmur didn't know what they'd triggered, but she was fairly sure the statue had armed some kind of defense system.

Maybe she'd been kidding herself, but since they'd solved most of the last dungeon they attended through solving riddles, she had hoped the need to fight would be negligible in all of the ones they came to face. How naïve.

"The deeper you tread, the more you will face. We will not back down from protecting this place." And the huge statue, the apparent protector of the entire entrance, fell back into a fighting stance, her staff at the ready, dwarfing the entire group beneath her like bugs ready to be squished.

"How the fucking hell are we supposed to fight something this size?" Beastial growled at the calf in front of him. The huge lacerta looked like a doll beneath the giant. "Are we supposed to jab it in the leg and hope it doesn't swat us like mosquitos?"

"This place holds a key. We don't have a choice." Murmur was proud of her voice for coming out steadier than she expected. "Eventually we're going to have to kill these stone giants."

"But they're stone." Havoc crossed his arms, his tone pouting. "I won't be near as much use on these fights. I can't even use my new necrosis spell. It was bad enough that the Fissures reduced the damage of most of my attacks, now there's a whole damn dungeon."

He didn't seem to be worried, more like irritated he couldn't use most of his spells to their full strength. Murmur was about to speak when Mellow beat her to it.

"Acid might work on stone." Their voice was calm and rational, like they'd decided to tackle the problem while everyone else got worked up over how huge their opponents were. "I've been thinking about it since we had difficulty with that Fissure on the way here. I doubt fire will have too much effect since there's no visible tar, and maybe wind. I don't have an air potion though."

"Mind magic definitely isn't going to work." Murmur realized how ineffectual whatever it was Riasli was doing to these mobs was making her. "I know I almost had it. Just a stronger push and..."

Merlin laid a hand on Murmur's wrist, just long enough to pull her attention away from her inner diatribe. She blinked at her friend gratefully.

"We all know Riasli is pulling her evil nemesis shit, and that's okay. You're okay. We're all okay. Just wish we had some wind elements and not just useless arrows." Merlin smiled, taking a deep breath after finishing his speech.

"Actually." Rashlyn stepped forward. "I have a Windcut kick, and a Burst of Air punch. They cost me a chunk of energy, and I only just got them, but we can definitely use them."

"I have one acid attack I can use. It's usually a diversion, but..." Jinna shrugged.

"Different strokes for very different encounters, it seems." Merlin smiled and briefly spared a glare at Havoc. "Sometimes we need to adapt."

"Why is it just waiting?" Devlish muttered, never taking his eyes from the mob. "I mean, usually the attack radius is huge, and we have to engage, but she's just waiting there."

"Maybe she's seeing if we're going to give up, in which case they don't need to fight. Maybe she just has a really sportsmanlike personality." Sinister offered without much conviction. "I'm not sure how I'm going to heal on this. I can pull life, but life healing isn't quite as strong as blood. Just the way it is."

Her tone ended so apologetically, Murmur took a step over and hugged her shoulders before even thinking about it. A thought struck her. "If Rash has the ability to hurt this thing, maybe she should main tank this one?"

Devlish bit his lip, but held up a hand to forestall Murmur's response. "I'm okay with that. Sincerely. Rash is a good tank. And I think dodging on this one might be a key to winning. But I don't feel like our attacks are going to do much damage either way. We need to think of something else. Something that might bring her crashing down."

Murmur paused. He had a point and sounded so thoughtful. He'd probably been thinking of nothing else while the damned statue talked to them. She couldn't blame him, but at the same time, she couldn't think of anything else they had in their arsenal. They didn't have a mage, just a witch, psionicist, and necromancer. And it hadn't even been their choice not to have a mage.

"Rashlyn tanks, Ver take lead on the heals then? The rest of us need to hope our debuffs stick. Anyone else have any ideas other than wind or acid?" Murmur's tone was low, because she had a sneaking suspicion that this regal creature wasn't above listening to them to up its advantage. And even if the statue was, she knew that Riasli wasn't.

Everyone shook their heads.

"No more ideas right now, but we might think of something once we start fighting and learn if it has any weaknesses." Merlin wasn't playing the joker any more. While it was good to see everyone's serious sides, it was scary that they needed them.

Rashlyn took a deep breath, clenched her fists against her side, and stood in front of the group. About to take her first step, she grinned back at Murmur. "We got this. Don't worry, boss."

Murmur rolled her eyes as they all moved forward as one. There was a crunching of stone against stone as the statue straightened, its eyes gleaming red once more.

"Very well then. You will regret your decision to go against the Naishi-dan. We will crush you, and fertilize our nursery with your bone dust."

The shivers that ran down Murmur's back didn't have time to distract her. The Amazonian statue roared, and the sound bounced off the rocks, shaking them, echoing down into the depths of darkness behind her.

Nothing beyond them stirred, not even a sound. This dungeon and these mobs appeared to work differently. But she didn't have long to contemplate it.

The Naishi-dan warrior lunged at them, surprisingly agile for her size, even if a bit slow because of her construction. Rashlyn appeared so helplessly tiny against her. It was like time slowed for them as the first strike approached, and Murmur couldn't help but watch as her friend stood bravely in front of their opponent, about to be squashed like a bug, even as Murmur's Weakness spell flew toward the monster.

A smash echoed through the front chamber, with tinkling sounds of glass resounding as they bounced on the floor. Right in front of her, Rashlyn grew to four times her usual size. The rest of them scrambled to get out of the way as Rashlyn's block of the statue's attack drove her back several feet.

But she didn't squash Rashlyn, and Murmur heaved a sigh of relief. Sure, by comparison Rash wasn't large. She barely reached the statue's chest, but she was far more capable of fighting something that big. The only thing was that the rest of them had to be careful of not only the statue, but Rashlyn as well.

What Rashlyn had that the statue did not was speed.

Murmur glanced at Mellow, who grinned as they watched the fight progress. "Can't do the rest of us, sorry. I only have enough for about eight potions, and they only last fifteen minutes each. Let's hope that's enough. My potions are different from my spells. Spells only require that I have the ingredients on me, potions require that I consume them."

Murmur felt relief flood through her, and she focused on her own job while Rashlyn maneuvered the mob into a better position. Dodging the statue's attacks was one thing she was perfectly capable of, but the backlash from some of those missed attacks might squelch the rest of them at this size. So, like any good tank would, she moved herself into such a position that the side wall was behind her a ways, and it let the group stay in a relatively safe semicircle. A huge semicircle which made the two healers have to space themselves out in such a way that everyone was covered, but it worked.

Finally, able to concentrate on her debuffs, Murmur stood back to take stock of the area. Her eyes had slowly grown accustomed to her surroundings, and the special sight of the locus let her take in the area. It seemed the guardian had come from a slot in the wall just inside the entrance. If the sparks from the fight were anything to go by as they lit her way, then there were more alcoves further down the path.

She frowned, trying to figure out just how it was these opponents were triggered, since it didn't seem to follow the same pattern as the rest of Somnia and come when there was too much noise. Then again, why would anything in Somnia ever be the way she expected it?

Watching the spells encircle and swirl around the statue, Murmur suddenly got an idea. She might not have much that could damage it, but maybe if she gave it a kinetic shove? Readying her shield, she gathered her energy, focused her thoughts, and pushed. The shield hit the statue and shattered.

Murmur frowned. Maybe it had something to do with stone and mind control, or else Riasli had done something that would render mental attacks mostly useless. While she understood it, it was disappointing that her kinetic ability wasn't a good secret weapon for this.

And then she no longer had time to think about much at all, because a scream of pain tore her attention away from her thoughts, and she turned to find Merlin clutching his arm to his side as it dangled helplessly from the elbow down.

"Shit," she said under her breath, smacking herself mentally to focus better and stop letting her thoughts carry her away. There wasn't time for her to space out like this. Spacing out could kill her.

...Breathing changed?

Murmur blinked, and shook her head. That had to be her parents, or someone in her room. She didn't have time for it to disorient her. Grimacing, she watched Merlin's arm mend itself with a flow of sluggish healing from

Sinister, and she knew this wasn't a normal fight. Whatever Riasli had done, went against the original intentions of the dungeon. The feeling that permeated the vague emotions that entered her sensing net showed a frustration and zeal that clashed severely.

Therefore, it stood to reason that these entities in here were being coerced against their will, too. Regardless of their origins, the inhabitants of this world exhibited intelligence and emotions. Forcing them might seem appealing occasionally, but it made her insides crawl to truly contemplate it.

If she can hear...

"Oh my god, I can hear you," Murmur muttered with exasperation, wanting desperately to concentrate on the fight.

"What?" Sinister said from her left, but only half her attention was on Murmur, because the healing seemed very involved. She didn't pursue the question when Murmur didn't answer, and the enchanter was grateful.

Rashlyn's attacks changed in style. She went from using things like her Kanji flying kick and Hundred Fists' flurry of punches to an air punch that appeared to be a ranged attack that punched powerful discs of wind toward the target, making the statue stagger back as tiny bits of stone began to roll down from the impact spot. Every now and again, the monk activated a tumbling roll that ended with a slicing kick, which activated a wind that, again, chipped away at the stone.

Mellow's acid bombs landed in between those attacks, thrown with accuracy Mur hadn't realized the witch possessed. Their face was pinched, their brows scrunched, and Murmur focused her sensing net for long enough to realize that the witch was worried about this fight. Perhaps they only had so many ingredients. She didn't fully understand how the witch class functioned.

Hadn't she enabled the guild bank usage already? She was sure she'd done so. That was another thing for after this fight.

...Voices pull her back?

Murmur stumbled slightly as she didn't quite recognize the voice. It was warbled, and she couldn't tell if it was her reception or perhaps emotion clouding the words, but she just wanted them to stay out of her head and stop distracting her. She tightened her shields, projecting the thought over herself as she reinforced the walls.

Rashlyn's attacks were interspersed with her defensive capabilities. She threw in Dodge on cooldown to avoid attacks for eight seconds, and her hidden ability Phantom which allowed her to dodge and counter every attack for twelve seconds. Admittedly, they weren't as strong as usual, considering how slowly the statue attacked.

Murmur shuddered to think how it would go if the monk got hit though. Anything more than a glancing blow would probably flatten her. In the meantime, small cracks had begun to appear, jutting out from the place on the statue everyone concentrated their attacks on. Even Jinna had been throwing daggers that appeared to be coated in acid. How it didn't eat through the blade, she couldn't figure out. She'd have to ask him about that later.

The rangers targeted burning arrows into the growing fissures of rock. While they weren't going to make an explosive difference, they should help break down the substance. She wasn't sure what they'd been doing before, but it didn't matter. Havoc's skeleton seemed to be pounding on the weak spot with something akin to a void staff, and Havoc's scowl as his spells landed mostly harmlessly wasn't a pretty sight.

Beastial grimaced as they fought, unable to pull the most out of his class or his pet. The stone was a harsh master, and difficult to combat. While they could chip away at it, only a few of them could do any real damage. But the weaker they made that spot, the more the rest of their attacks could wear it down.

Axes were useless, so Devlish, Beastial, and Dansyn used metal tipped maces, hammering away and chipping off bits of stone slowly but surely.

Cracking rock had a definitive sound, and the statue stumbled as the sound echoed throughout the chamber. Fissures appeared in her rocky facade, expanding all the way up in a gradually spreading spider web. The stone statue blinked, and even that action caused rock to crumble and fall, narrowly missing the team standing below.

"You will have no peace. Naishi will reign. Naishi will win. She will wrest your keys from your dead bodies and have her sacrifices. And then she will release him in your place."

The booming sound permeated the corridor, ringing in their ears. She opened her mouth to say more, but the rock began to crumble, turning to dust just as Rashlyn shrunk back to her regular size. The giant statue's disintegrations rapidly increased, like a waterfall of rock sand out over them.

Veranol threw up his shield, expending the last of his mana in an effort to shelter them all from the keeper's last-ditch effort to stop them. When the deluge finally stopped, they surveyed the area around them.

The sands of rock that littered the ground around them gave off a soft white glow. Nothing like the red or orange tinges they'd seen from its angry eyes before.

"Maybe this is the way it was before Riasli took it over?" Rashlyn's tone sounded sad, like she hadn't wanted to kill her.

Murmur completely sympathized and a sudden thought occurred to her. "Do you think Naishi is what they call Riasli? I've not heard of it before and the statue's mutterings make partial sense if that's so."

"Maybe." Havoc nodded before uttering a deep sigh. "Either way, we had to get through it. It'll resurrect at some stage, even if it takes a while."

"Speaking of which." Mellow interrupted him. "We have to figure out a better way to combat these things, because I'm pretty sure they're placed at intervals all the way down the length of that corridor. And I have enough acid for one, maybe two if we prolong the fights."

"Was the acid really that important?" Havoc's drawl sounded bored.

"At least half the solid damage done to it was Mellow's doing." Rashlyn shook her head. "And I can't up my damage output any more than I just did. Not right now. Not in this armor with this gear. I wish better gear dropped in the game."

"So basically, if we can't figure out another way to topple them, we're screwed?" Havoc asked as his tone became sullen.

Mellow nodded. "Basically. Yes."

Somnia Online
Fable's Castle – Mikrum Isle – Himmel Lake
Fourteen Days Post Launch

Telvar frowned and cast out his sensors again. He'd basically looked in every nook and cranny he could think of throughout the entire game world. Murmur was never not on his radar, but for the last ten minutes he'd been trying to locate her and quite literally drawing a blank. He didn't like the sense of uncertainty.

He began to trace her movements for the day, to see where it was she'd last been before he lost track of her. Feles, and feles, and the area outside Curet, and then the jungle for a while. Then suddenly nothing.

He frowned, barely aware that Hiro stood next to him tapping his foot on the ground with impatience while waiting to ask him something. The simple fact was, Murmur had been there within his data, and now suddenly she was not.

"Stop it, Hiro. I'm trying to concentrate." The admonishment seemed to work, because Hiro knew that Telvar rarely needed to concentrate on anything. And if he needed to, then it meant something was up.

And something was very up. She'd gone missing around the old ruins on Cenedril, except...

He ran a series of calculations through his program, and then again in a different way. There was something wrong with this, nagging at the back of his programming that he should know it for what it was.

It hit him, like a sucker punch must, and numbers clashed against each other as his algorithms upheaved his senses. The ruins felt like a back door. Something left there for a program to gain access to without being detected, and he started to have a really bad feeling about who had left it there. Still, jumping to conclusions was foolhardy. He needed to investigate, to check first. Closing his eyes so as to block out the light of Somnia, he retreated into the darkness of his original programming, seeking out the makeup of the Ruins of Cenedril.

It was there, yet it wasn't. Its appearance was vastly different to that he remembered, even after the game had launched. Sure enough, no one had been there yet because Murmur's group was the first to reach a level that would be able to access it. But others weren't too far away. Exodus and Fable weren't the only guilds that were leveling well.

However, the once bright representation of Mayan culture they'd settled near the cat kingdom had sunk into the ground, darkened the stone, and let moss creep all over the perpetually wet structure. Its entrance appeared more like a gaping maw of darkness than the original concept for the massive sandstone steps leading up to the square pyramid in its glorious sandy might.

He could see the slowly decaying bodies of the guards. Even their vacant eyes still maintained a feral red gleam. His programming stuttered as he tried to comprehend the sight in the middle of the jungle. Something had possessed these? Who had created an AI or an NPC that could pull something like this off?

The binders around the towns had been one thing, and they were barely contained currently as it was, but this? It was something different, with an air of evil that even made Telvar's sub routines feel dirty.

"Telvar?" Hiro's tone held concern, and maybe a tinge of fear.

The lacerta shook his head and tried to force a smile onto his face as he rested a hand briefly on his friend's shoulder. "It's okay, Hiro. I'll get this under control. There's just a few things that aren't aligning the way they should be, that's all."

Hiro's raised eyebrow told him that his foreman didn't believe him in the slightest.

"I just need to go and investigate the feles jungle. I promise I won't be long." He left without checking to see if Hiro believed him.

CHAPTER TWENTY-THREE

Objective Changed

Somnia Online
Cenedril – Curet Jungle – Outskirts of the Cenedril Ruins
Early Day Fourteen Post Launch

Telvar had been aiming for the front steps of the ruins, but he landed a significant distance from the entrance. Frowning, he pushed forward, attempting the jump again. The air around him warped, bending in like a thick bubble and gently bounced him back. Exasperation filled him, his systems double-timing to try and figure out what was causing the phenomena. He'd not had to deal with having his way blocked before. Ever.

The calculations he ran came back normal, perfect even. He narrowed his eyes, turning his sight inward to check several other regions of the game with a sudden idea that crossed his algorithms. It wasn't an idea he wanted to entertain, but if he was right, they were in for a whole world of a shitstorm.

Walking forward didn't cause the bubble to spring up. As long as he masked his overseer role, it didn't activate. It seemed as if his being one of the main AIs was what triggered the defense. Warning bells sounded throughout his head, part of them the system and the other part he attributed to something like instinct. Because there were so many things wrong with this, he was beginning to panic.

Now he knew how Laria and Shayla felt, because things about his equational inquiries kept returning data to him that were too perfect. Even tracing the results to their source only cemented just how faultless the results were. Which was the ideal but rarely ever the case when it came to a program as complex as their own. His first instinct was to call both Sui and Thra to him and have them help him figure this out. But at the same time, a portion of him cautioned against it. Because who other than one of those two could it be making this happen?

Telvar took a deep breath. Even if he might not need air, even if Somnia didn't technically have air, the action still calmed and relaxed him. Slightly, anyway. The vegetation leading up to the ruins was thick and crunched underfoot as leaves and blades gave way under his weight. He dampened the sound, hoping not to alert whatever it was doing this with the fluctuation of his presence. He masked it with a stealth ability pulled from the assassin line. What good was it being a god in the game if you didn't pull up some perks every now and again?

The closer he got to the ruins, the more a feeling of pressure seemed to squeeze his head. Not quite like the vice that people described migraines as, but still, a semblance of pain began in the base of his skull. It was a new sensation, and one that gave him pause. Even in his Telvar skin, there shouldn't be another line of coding capable of making him feel like a player would.

As soon as he stopped his momentum, the pressure eased up. He raised an eyebrow. It wasn't directed at him, but at anyone entering the general area. Murmur would have noticed this type of thing, wouldn't she? The girl was stupidly perceptive some of the time, even when he'd prefer she wasn't. It stood to reason therefore, that this subtle persuasion not to enter the area hadn't been present then. Or else, she'd put on her stubborn hat and moved forward anyway.

Both options were a distinct possibility.

Finally, he arrived at the top of the stairs to the ruins, his gaze raking over the vastly changed facade of the structure and he frowned. How had this happened? Each of them had a dungeon on each continent. On Cenedril, Telvar was responsible for Glacier Lake, the only area in the whole island that was max level only. Sui was responsible for Hightower, and this was Thra's place. It had been regal before, beautiful. Which was exactly the sort of thing that Thra went for. For it to devolve into this dark and dismal place didn't even make any sense.

She had to know it had changed, didn't she?

There was nothing for it. He took a step forward, placing his foot on the next step down, only to have the bubble reappear. This time it was a thick substance, and as he pressed down on it, he realized it coated the entire exterior of the ruins in the way shrink wrap might cover a dish. Except it was rubberier.

Forcing his way in could put Murmur in more danger from whatever algorithmic hell was causing this. And reluctant though he might be, calling on his brethren to figure out what the hell was going on might actually be the better way this time. He turned around and blinked back to Mikrum Isle. He needed somewhere reliable and safe to leave his husk while he had words with his siblings.

"Since it's obviously not noise that alerts the mobs in this zone, what do we think pulls the rest?" Merlin stood at the edge of the dust pile and peered into the darkness beyond. The soft golden light lent a beautiful green hue to his gear, and for a moment he looked like a male version of Tinkerbell.

Murmur chuckled at the thought. He'd not appreciate it at all, so it was probably a good thing that he couldn't read *her* mind.

"What's so funny?" He glanced back at her, a frown on his lips. "It's actually a legitimate question, not meant to be a pun. You know, for once."

"Sorry." Murmur sobered up. "Maybe it's proximity? Sort of like when we line of sight pull."

"Don't know about you, Mur, but I'm pretty sure those statues further down the way would be able to see us if they looked." Merlin took a few steps closer and hesitated. "But from here they seem to be almost sleeping, or hibernating."

Devlish went and joined the ranger, peering just as earnestly into the dark. Lacerta had their own form of infravision, so Murmur didn't bother to offer her buff to him. "He's right. There's no movement, not even the rise and fall of their chests. They must be magically enhanced."

"You don't say?" Havoc drawled. "You mean those huge fighters made out of rock must be magically enhanced?"

"Shut it." Devlish snapped, glaring at Havoc. "I mean they seem to be magically triggered and woken. Of course they damn well move because of magic."

Havoc put his hands up, a resigned expression on his face. "Sorry, man. I'm just frustrated. Didn't think we'd get caught up to so fast."

"Yeah, I think we're all a little irritated by that announcement, Hav. It just meant we have to keep on it." Devlish pinched the bridge of his nose with his fingers and took a deep breath before continuing. "I just—I'm not sure how we go about this. We don't want to wake more than one at a time. Did anyone try to get out while the other one was activated, or do we just need to assume it's like every dungeon we've ever encountered in this game, and we can't escape while a fight is in progress?"

"And speaking of escape." Sinister spoke up, her gaze focused directly onto Murmur, her eyes fierce. The enchanter backed away a couple of steps. "Stop it, Mur! You heard what she said about the key, right? They'll pry those keys from our cold dead corpses. And since you're not allowed to die, you need to give one of us the key so we can hold it. That way you won't be the target for the Somnian enemies at least. Not that we seem to be able to deter you from being Jirald's target. The least we can do is this."

"You don't know that wasn't just bravado." Except in a way, Murmur already knew exactly that. The statue might have originally been an NPC, but her motives were muddied by the mind control performed on her, and those last words had been full of a vile hatred so strong, she spoke as she turned to dust.

"Don't be an idiot, Mur!" Rashlyn crossed her arms too, her ears twitched in irritation. "You know as well as we do that Sin is right. Give one of us the key so we can take the hit if we need to. I'd prefer to hand over the key to them than to see them kill you for it."

Sinister high fived the monk, but her victorious grin was more like a grimace. "You know how I feel about all this. I won't lose you Mur, and you can't stop me from protecting you."

Murmur looked at her friend, and burst out laughing. "Oh, my God, Sin! Would you listen to that melodrama you're wearing? Look, I get it, okay? I'm not about to stop any of you protecting me, as long as you don't smother me in the damned process, okay?"

Sinister's smile turned sheepish, and the girl rubbed her nose in that adorable way she had when she was unsure of herself.

"I get it. I guess that did sound a bit pompous, didn't it?" Her tone held a portion of uncertainty, like there wasn't room in the glass for more.

"Pompous is an understatement, Sin." For once, Beastial wasn't riling her up. He seemed genuinely concerned for her, and his smile was a kind one. "That was almost mothering."

Sinister laughed. "Mothering, big sistering, take your pick. But enough about me, let's move onto these statues, huh? Anyone got a plan on how to defeat them quicker, better, faster, stronger?"

Murmur moved forward and gave the other girl a quick hug. "How do you think the statue will react to a hug? Or perhaps a bout of persuasion if I can get my brain to cooperate?" She tapped her head self-deprecatingly.

"Persuasion didn't work the last time, and to be honest, I'm not sure you want to hug any part of that. It'd smoosh you like a bug, Mur, did you hear me? A bug!" Sin's attempt at a smile was more wan than usual, but a slight sparkle did enter her eyes.

Murmur grinned. "Oh! Speaking of statues. Mellow, you know you can reach into the guild stores from here, right? I'm not exactly sure how your class works apart from what you've told me, but since the potions you make require you to consume the ingredients, you should just be able to reach into the guild stores and get them yourself. Guild storage is overflowing."

Mellow nodded. "I have basic brews, and specialty brews. All in my witch's cauldron. Basic brews are pretty much just my spells. Easily incanted, and there's a level I'll reach with my hybrid and specialty choices where I'll be able to simply cast them without a cauldron. But up until now my specialty brews have required that I hoard a heap of stuff. Sadly, I don't have all that many acidic spider or scorpion glands on hand right now. And yes, there's a difference between them and normal ones."

"Oh." Murmur ran over the guild interface again, making sure she wasn't about to put her foot in it. "You have access to the guild stores as one of the senior members. I'm pretty sure we have some more shit in there for you."

Mellow perked up, their face blushing a pale pink that made the locus look sort of pretty for a moment. "That's fantastic. I have no idea why I didn't think of this before."

Murmur grimaced, pushing the interface aside. "Well, we didn't exactly think we'd have to figure out what could eat through rock now, did we?"

"Bet a mage could explode that shit to smithereens," Havoc mumbled, the sullen tone present once again. Mur knew it was because he missed his class, but necromancer was at least close.

"Probably could, but we can always improvise." She tried to put enthusiasm in her smile, but it didn't seem to work.

Jinna piped up. "You know, the rangers have traps, and I have a few from my assassin tree, so, between us we should be able to come up with something to make it go quicker."

"Shit." Merlin smacked himself in the forehead. "Totally forgot about that. I got an ice trap. I also have a quicksand one, but I wasn't sure if that would work in this case. I mean, aren't they sort of made out of sand?"

Rashlyn nodded, stood up from where she'd been sitting on the ground, and stretched her left leg out behind her, balancing perfectly on her right. "It's not easy fighting those things, and I hate spending this much time on fucking trash mobs. But if we're going to kill the bastards, we need to do it right."

Murmur tended to agree with her. Flipping through her arsenal in her mind once more, she concluded that there was indeed no way for her to actually contribute to the taking down of the stone giants other than buffing and debuffing, and throwing the occasional damage DoT on it, which ticked for far reduced damage.

Snowy nudged her hand, and she ruffled his fur. He had a good point. "Let's move forward then, shall we?"

"Best way to head." Merlin grinned and jumped down from his ledge, out in front of the others.

A ripple of orange light ignited from the point where he landed, easily a dozen feet beyond the area where the last mob died. The light flowed out several feet, coming to land at the foot of not one giant statue, but two.

The resulting rumble that echoed through the cavern shook it so much that dust and small rocks fell from the ceiling, mixing into their hair and giving everyone a fine layer of powder over their skin. The statues bent in unison to duck their heads under the small overhang of their alcove, and stepped into the middle of the corridor at the same time, planting their staffs firmly against the floor.

Vibrations echoed across the stone surface and through to the bones, setting Murmur's teeth on edge, and Merlin slowly rose from his landing position, and glanced back at the group.

"Oops?" He cringed, probably knowing everyone else was ready to punch him. "I guess we know how they're triggered now. Think these are Mezable, Mur?"

"We're about to find out." She hoped against hope as she released her spell toward the left mob.

Her Mez caught the mob around the head, swirling like a halo.

Your Mesmerize spell has landed. This creature has a powerful force controlling their mind. You will need to fight for dominance, and your spell is not reliable, as it could break at any moment. Make sure you debilitate the mob as you can. Diminishing returns apply.

"Fuck," Mur muttered under her breath, but before anyone could ask her what she meant, she focused on the second statue and called out to Rashlyn. "Pull it back to the front of the dungeon, where we fought the first one. Use it as the staging ground."

She was going to need all the help she could get, and all the distance too. As Rashlyn began to comply, Mur watched the slow statue follow her, not foolish enough yet to debuff it because Rashlyn's aggro was tentative at best. "Merlin. I need you to keep this thing rooted. If you have to interrupt damage to do so, just do it."

Merlin nodded. "Not like I'm contributing all that much anyway. I'll stay in between them. Can I ask why?"

Murmur watched as Rashlyn grew in size, still somehow so tiny against the bulk of the statue. She threw some debuffs its way, and watched Snowy take off after it, even as he kept looking back at her. They had to defeat these, Riasli had seen to it. There were no puzzle options here. "My Mez on this thing will work, but I can't let my guard down. Mez will break when it feels like it instead of when the timer expires, and it will take effect with diminishing returns. I need everything I can use so that it doesn't make it to the group before I can refresh the Mez."

"Got it." Merlin sounded so businesslike, so different from his usual carefree self. But it was Merlin in a nutshell. All pun and games until something got serious.

Mur cast her Nullify on the target, followed by a slow and weakener, while bringing up her Mez timer to keep it front and center so she could see it break. The way it ghosted over her eyesight was cool in a way, yet eerie in another. But it told her the split second it broke, because it broke about three seconds early, and barely blinked once before she renewed it. Riasli wasn't going to let them make it to her easily.

She kept her eyes on her group. With the Mez timer pulled up, the fight was oddly accented through the transparency of colors it provided her vision. Jinna maneuvered his way around the mob, planting something against the ground she couldn't quite see, what with the dimness of the lighting in the area. "What's he doing?"

Merlin shrugged. "Not sure, I couldn't catch his muttering from where I was perched. Speaking of which—sorry about this."

Murmur grinned, her adrenaline beginning to flow. "Please. On the level of our screw ups over the years, this one is way down on the chain."

She paused to refresh Mez—as the statue once again broke it—before continuing. "Seriously though. This could have been worse, and we don't know that just progressing down the hall wouldn't have triggered both at the same time too. Looked pretty even from what I saw."

Then she noticed what it was Jinna was doing, and a smile spread over her face as he laced the thick rope through the intricate little stakes he'd prepared. When he was done, Rashlyn turned the statue, tripping it as the ropes pulled tight just around the ankles.

It tumbled to the ground in what seemed like slow motion, and Murmur watched as it hit the ground with a smash while her guild and group mates scrambled and gathered behind Veranol's shield. Rock shattered against the stone ground, as its spear wielding arm detached and became rubble. A cheer of victory went up, but it was short-lived as the huge mob began to try and right itself with the one good arm it had.

Murmur almost missed her Mez break and thanked the foresight that her vision changed in time enough for her to nab it. She wasn't sure how well Merlin's Root was going to hold stone feet. This last Mez had only lasted twenty seconds. Diminishing returns was an understatement.

In the pale light given off by the fine rock dust of the first statue they'd fought, Murmur noticed something glint on the statue's forehead. Being as high as they were before, she'd not noticed the gem.

"Smash the gem!" she yelled, suddenly sure that was how to defeat them.

Beastial reacted first, stepping forward and smashing it with his giant mace, not quite avoiding the gnashing of stone teeth against his ribs as he did so. He grunted in pain and stepped back, a portion of his breastplate caught in the teeth, and watched the fissures spread throughout the gem as Veranol hurried to heal him.

As the gem fractured, so did the statue, and an inhuman sound rose up from it as it rapidly broke down, presenting them with the same golden dust even as the gem left the red behind and turned back to gold.

"Let's try that again, shall we?" Devlish grinned, as the tension lifted visibly from everyone's shoulders. "Except next time? I get to smash the gem."

Everyone laughed, that is until Merlin called out. "Root broke."

And Murmur's Mez chose the same moment to break.

CHAPTER TWENTY-FOUR

The Guardian

Murmur hoped against hope against hope that the mobs only *respawned* with prior knowledge of actual deaths and how their opponents fought them. If it passed into the collective consciousness while other mobs were already spawned, they were so going to be screwed with this next statue.

She took a deep breath as Rashlyn, still in her larger form, ran forward so her taunt was in range. The statue paused briefly as it moved passed Murmur, but chose to go after the player actively taunting it instead. Murmur heaved a sigh of relief, letting out the pent-up breath she hadn't realized she was holding.

But then, the bandits hadn't realized their tactics, and only the outer dwarves had shown any inclination of evading their attacks when they were fighting outside Hightower the second time. Perhaps they did have to die first and then respawn for the experience to filter down into the collective data of the zone. In which case, they had however long these mobs took to respawn on their side.

She pitied the people who'd come here after them. Because they were going to have a whole mess to deal with. But that sort of thinking only meant Riasli was going to beat them, and Murmur begged to differ. She wasn't about to let that damned enchanter get the better of them.

At least her debuffs seemed to stick. Without another statue to control, Murmur felt like she wasn't contributing enough to this fight. Her Enfeeblement, Nullify, and Weakness spells just didn't feel like they did much. And this whole stone immunity thing wasn't easy either.

She could see the frustration outlined on a lot of their faces. On Dansyn's, Havoc's, Merlin's, and Exbo's. Sinister seemed the most out of sorts, which wasn't strange considering pulling blood from a stone was nigh impossible.

Jinna drove his stakes into crevices in the ground, enhancing their effectiveness with a pinch of acid on the tip. She wasn't sure why the metal stakes didn't melt, but she wasn't going to question it yet. There'd be plenty of time later. Perhaps there was only a brief window of time to do it. She'd have to ask the rogue about his traps, not the least because she had an insane person after her and thought it might help if she knew what else he had in his arsenal.

As this one came crashing to the ground, Murmur felt tension flow out of her. Even if there were more of these to come, at least they'd managed to figure out a pretty decent way to kill them relatively quickly.

"Nice job," she said, walking to join the rest of the group. She'd chosen to stay back where she'd been originally so as to keep out of the way and not need someone to shelter her from the debris. She turned the dwarf, her curiosity piqued. "That's certainly a lot faster than the first one. How were you able to do that?"

"I have to work up to be able to make those hooks. They're an ability I have through my specialization. I took traps. I figured it would help out. But I have to push through and work up points in order to create them. Five at a time. Hence, I can't do it immediately. The rope—that I took from the guild stores, but I figured that'd be okay." His grin was huge, and Murmur felt a swell of fondness for the rogue at his obvious glee in what he'd accomplished. She didn't think that ability was intended to work quite in that way.

"Remind me to ask you what all you can do, so I know just in case Jirald decided to follow the same path." She meant the statement half-jokingly, but a dark shadow passed over Jinna's face, and he scowled.

"That's not funny. Probably not an issue, since Jirald has veered toward the darker rogue skills from the start." He paused and stepped closer to

Murmur, lowering his voice as he spoke. "I have an eye out for him on every forum I can think of. There are decent rogues out there, and friends I've had in other games. I'm hoping to figure out what direction he's taken before he can try his hand at any underhanded tricks against you."

Murmur looked at her friend, a myriad of thoughts running through her head, but most of all was the feeling of gratitude. That her friend would look out for her like this, would track the one person literally capable of murdering her by accident...well, she guessed that was just what friends did. "Thanks, Jinna."

"Spill it. What are you two keeping secret from us?" Beastial drawled the words out, a twinkle in his eye.

Murmur winked at him. "We're planning your demise, that's all."

"Oh, that's it? I thought you did that on a daily basis," he quipped back as if on cue.

"That's it!" Sinister shouted, and everyone turned to her, their mouths agape. Her face held a rare glimpse of seriousness, and she put her hands on her hips. "Stop telling Beastial about our plans to destroy him. Seriously, people, it's harder to eliminate the enemy when they know you're going to."

At the end, unable to keep her facial expression under control anymore, Sinister broke down into laughter.

"Idiot." Beastial muttered, but he was smiling.

Murmur laughed along with them all, but unease lingered in her mind. Were these statues too easy now? Couldn't Riasli just have inserted the knowledge of how they'd killed the second one into the mind of the third? There were so many paths to take and choices to make when expanding class knowledge in this game; Murmur didn't yet have a handle on all the possible avenues. She wished she knew exactly what that enchanter had been up to, because it was causing her a world of consternation to act on assumption only.

"Mur? You okay?" Havoc stepped to her side, concern echoing in his words.

"Yeah, you know, just trying not to die while I figure out what the hell that enchanter has done to this dungeon." She tried to insert levity into her words, but Havoc just raised an eyebrow.

"Well, I'm not sure what she's done to it. But I get the feeling it wasn't originally intended to be like this. It's dark and gloomy, but the guarding statues turn to golden dust, which is a total juxtaposition to everything else." He laughed and then paused. "But I do know that if we stay standing here we're never going to get through the rest of the statues and to whatever that red glowing light beyond this corridor stands for."

Murmur turned to look through the darkness of the passageway—the gods knew how many more statues they'd have to face. Sure enough, an indeterminable distance beyond them was a faint red glow. At least they had something to head toward now.

Murmur plopped onto the ground next to Sinister, who sat at the beginnings of a huge downward staircase letting the dust from the last guard statue of the passage run through her fingers as she gazed out. The powdery substance left a soft golden glow to the blood mage's hands, lending her an otherworldly presence in the darkness.

Fanning out beneath them were several stairways like out of an Escher painting; Topsy turvy, upside down, sideways, and right side up. The path appeared to be a twisted labyrinth through stairs that led to platforms and choices on where to move next. There was a lightly glowing red dome a few levels below them. From this distance it appeared to pulse, but it could have been a trick of the light.

"What do you think that is, Mur?" Sinister spoke softly, and Mur couldn't blame her. Her friend sounded tired, and almost defeated.

"I think that's something's ass we're going to kick." She leaned into her friend, nudging their shoulders together, and felt Sinister relax ever so slightly.

"You always have such confidence in us. In me." Her voice faded away, trailing as if it was a thought she'd never dared to voice out loud. This side of Sin was one that rarely popped up, and definitely less in the game world than in the real one.

"I always have confidence in you, more than myself. Sometimes you have all the confidence for the both of us." Murmur continued before Sin could interrupt. "We balance each other well. We've got this. Don't be so worried. It's a game, and we're supposed to be having fun. If I had to get stuck somewhere, I'd much rather be here with all of my friends than in some sort of weird limbo."

Sinister laughed, surprising herself if the look on her face was anything to go by. "Nice one, Mur. Thanks."

"Think we can pulverize whatever is down there?" Murmur asked, her tone serious again.

"No clue what it is, but when has that ever stopped us?"

"You make a very valid point there, my dear." Murmur brushed off her armor, leaving a lingering golden sheen to herself. This wasn't going to help them sneak up on anything in the dark, but the powder had been unavoidable as it drifted around in the tunnels, lighter than air. Regardless of what she said to her friend, all she could think of was how much this was no longer a game. Not while it had beings in it who were capable of separate and spontaneous actions. Maybe it wasn't real like the world she came from, but it was a reality. "Let's make our way through this Escher painting, shall we?"

Sin took the proffered hand and laughed. "I thought you'd never ask."

Murmur glanced back to see both Beastial and Mellow piling the dust into containers and shoving it into their inventory. Perhaps there was crafting potential in these. She frowned. Neva was likely on Beastial's case about making sure he brought anything and everything that could relate to crafting back to her. At least that was one thing she didn't need to worry about.

"Ready to head out, you two?" Devlish asked, sheathing a vicious-looking hammer. It had steel spikes both on the front and the back end of it. Nasty little weapon.

They set off down the stairs, and Murmur shuddered at the strange whimpering sounds that echoed through the area. They were soft, barely audible, and lent a haunting vibe to the entire cavern. At first she thought those sounds were inside her head, as if someone were in her room, crying.

But then she realized it wasn't resounding within, but coming from without. She glanced around her to try and find the source of the sound, but nothing caught her eye. The slight blue-white tint her infravision gave her made the zone hazier and less easy to focus on. She pushed on ahead, just behind both Jinna and Devlish who insisted on heading out in front of her.

While she might not admit it, she was grateful for it. If they fell down a gap none of them could see, at least they'd simply respawn at the resurrection point. Especially after her attempt to use sheer willpower to overcome this being stuck in-game thing, and landing back in the simulation of her house with a hella headache, Murmur was a tad more cautious.

The dome grew bigger the closer they got to it, the red paler as they began to focus on smaller portions of the shield at once. She wasn't sure if it was meant to keep the mob inside it in, or to keep intruders out, but she could feel her own gaze widen as what was inside finally came into view.

It rose up from the middle, bulbous in shape with large red orbs scattered at intervals over its flesh. As it moved in its rotund palace, the red blobs on its surface squelched and reformed like a bubble was keeping the liquid inside from spilling out. Upon closer inspection it did indeed have limbs, but they seemed to snap into place and complete the illusion that it was more ball-like than anything else. Although, it did appear to be lopsided, like some of the air had been let out of it.

The only thing Murmur knew for sure, was that the soft whimpering sound didn't come from the thing, it came from underneath it. Whatever it was wailing in the darkness, was being hidden by the target in their way. All of the stairwells led to that platform, and where stairs weren't, there was fathomless darkness beneath. What was in there she couldn't tell, and Murmur wasn't even sure the whimpering was something that needed saving. It could be another trap.

"That looks vile." Sinister scrunched up her nose in distaste.

"Bet you it hits like someone's thrown a brick wall at you, too." Devlish winced. "Is it made out of rock?"

"Just let me engage my long-distance vision and I'll get back to you." Merlin rolled his eyes, while most of them snickered. Devlish shot him a glare.

"Sorry." Merlin held up his hands in mock defense, not sounding in the least bit sorry. "I'd assume it's some type of rock base. If not the same as the stone statues that guarded above, I'd think this is actually more like the rock that makes up mountains, and less the one that you carve statues from."

"All we need is a hammer and chisel, eh?" Devlish hefted his hammer in his hand and grinned. "I might just have an answer for that."

"Where'd you get that?" Murmur asked, trying to pass the time they had left before a fight she knew nothing about that looked like it probably had a knock back. After all, what good was a platform with abyss-like sides if you couldn't get knocked off it?

"Last statue that fell had it." He shrugged and patted it as it dangled at his side. "It's pretty nice. Not sure why the statue wasn't using it. Probably took it off some unsuspecting traveler in times gone past."

Sinister rolled her eyes. "Oh, for fuck's sake, Dev, the game's been out for two weeks."

It was good to see her friend get the fire back into her, and when she saw Dev swallow a laugh, she knew that'd been his aim. He stepped onto the final platform before reaching the massive boss. To get anywhere, they had to pass through that platform, so this fight was basically a necessity.

A spark of orange power, just like the one that woke the statues above, rippled outward from them, but not ahead, above in a diagonal line, until it stopped in a burning fire of letters above the dome.

The Guardian is the gatekeeper. Awake him at your peril. Make your choices wisely, for he hides the path you should not seek.

"Is that supposed to make us run?" Havoc asked in the quiet as they stood studying the fading words.

"Probably. Sounds like dear Riasli doesn't know us as well as she thinks she does." Devlish shrugged and hefted the hammer in his hands as a feral gleam entered his eyes. "Looks like it's time to face our peril."

The Guardian was a lot larger close up, and the dome around it was viscous, or at least it appeared to be. They stood on the step in front of it, nothing more than the gradual swaying movement evident in the boss mob ahead of them. It appeared to be asleep, or resting, or hibernating—something that led to it not being entirely conscious right now. Did they really want to wake it?

"What do you think the odds are of creeping past that thing?" Merlin asked, his tone forced with lightheartedness.

"About as good as this zone having been intended this way." Havoc remarked dryly. His pet cackled in response, and the sound echoed through the darkness.

The monster inside rumbled as it moved, rolling in what appeared to be a type of induced slumber as it oriented itself toward where the noise was coming from. Murmur gulped. She didn't for one minute believe the Guardian was acting like it had been programmed to.

"I'm ready to Evac Mur if shit goes sideways." Merlin spoke the thought that everyone was having, and a wave of relief passed through the whole group. He crossed his arms and winked at her, nudging her side with his elbow, something she couldn't recall him ever having done before. Merlin wasn't the most affectionate of people. He even side-stepped Sinister's hugs, which was a difficult enough feat as it was. "I'll get ye out o' there, little darlin.'"

Murmur barked out a laugh, surprised at his horrible accent. "That was woeful, Merlin."

He just smiled at her and nodded his head. "Feeling a bit better?"

His words were soft, and probably only audible to Sin, Devlish, and Rash, who were standing immediately around them. "Yeah. Thanks."

Being bolstered by her friends was lifesaving, quite literally. She squared her shoulders and looked at the barrier, brows furrowing in a frown. "Got any ideas on how to get us through that thing?"

He shrugged. "I can probably fire an arrow through to hit the boss. Thinking that might make it come down pretty fast."

"Also, pretty dangerously." Devlish frowned.

"Since when are you ever cautious?" Merlin laughed and leaned forward to poke at the barrier, and his expression changed to a thoughtful one. "You know, I'm betting Mellow has something in their arsenal that'll make this disappear, or at least open a hole in it."

"You know what?" Sin piped up, her pale eyes glowing brightly. "What if we don't melt the whole thing, but just a doorway, wouldn't that make it safer than, you know, falling into the abyss?"

"Mellow!" Merlin was waving at the witch who sat on the stairs about halfway up to the previous platform. "Come here!" He turned back to the lead group and frowned. "That might be an idea, but I'm not sure that's how the dome works."

"True, but it's worth a shot." Sinister smiled, the smugness flowing over from her voice, and she continued right on as Mellow joined them. "Do you have anything that could make a doorway in this slimy stuff for us?"

Mellow raised an eyebrow, and moved forward a hand outstretched to feel the strange substance. They frowned and pulled back their hand, glaring at the tips of their fingers. Small tendrils of smoke rose from their fingertips. "I might be able to, but it has corrosive components, and it might just leak closed again. You could try cutting it too, but I'm not sure it won't do damage to steel."

"Worth a shot, right?" Beastial's voice made Murmur jump. She hadn't noticed him approaching, and it made her realize she'd been lax about her nets ever since she realized there was no way for her to penetrate whatever it was that Riasli had done to the statues.

She spread out her sensing nets again while the others discussed how best to break through the barrier. There, below them, was the source of the whimpering. She frowned, trying to get a read on the sound and jumbled thoughts. But all she got was pure fear laced with sorrow, and every now and again a tiny fragment of anger that seemed to be squashed as soon as it emerged. Whether it was by the sadness all around them, or Riasli's magic, Murmur didn't know, but she did know she had to do something about it.

"We need to get through and around this boss. I don't think it's the final one in this dungeon, but there are people underneath us we have to get to, at least from my Thought Sensing I'm pretty sure they're people, anyway. And there's no other way than to get past this." She couldn't think about it seeming too obvious a trap. Riasli wasn't nice in any way, so why would she not have hidden the beings below from her? The only answer was that it was deliberate. And if it was deliberate...

"You know that's a trap, right?" Merlin drawled the words out, an eyebrow raised as he looked at her.

She'd thought she was the mind reader, and she shot a glare at her friend. "I know, but it's a trap we're probably going to have to spring anyway if we don't want to inadvertently help the evil character in the game. We're not Jirald." The last might have been a bit harsh, but she didn't care. There were a lot of what ifs in the catacombs below them.

"Jirald's not evil. He's wannabe evil." Sinister's grin took on a mischievous tone as she interjected. "Besides, maybe we'll get something really cool at the end of this dungeon."

"Can we just get this fight started so we don't all fall asleep on the stairs?" Veranol joined them at the edge of the dome as well, and the top couple of steps were becoming crowded. That and no guard rail were distinct recipes for vertigo.

"Fine." Mellow rummaged in their inventory and muttered several words Murmur couldn't understand under their breath before pulling out a vial with a sludge-like brown liquid in it. "But don't say I didn't warn you. Everyone get ready to rush in, because I don't think this dome will fall before the Guardian does."

Mellow slammed the bottle into the shield, but it didn't smash through. Instead, the viscous liquid held it in place, and slowly but surely dissolved the glass around it, which caused the liquid to run down through the insides of the thing. It burned where it touched until a hole wide enough for two of them to pass, if the taller species ducked down a bit.

But they hadn't been joking. After the first three pairs passed through, the rest had to go single file, and Dansyn got brushed with the left side of the doorway as it closed while he was stepping through it. Smoke began to rise from his hand, and Veranol cast a heal on him as well as a cure, just to make sure.

While they moved through the door, Murmur kept her eyes focused on the Guardian. It moved sluggishly in its sleep, as if sensing a disturbance in its shielding. It made her wonder if the dome was meant to keep it in or keep it safe. Suddenly, up closer, it no longer looked as scary as it had. Perhaps it too was taken over by Riasli and given nefarious purposes instead of its original make up. Yet another reason to figure out what they had to do to free it from her and return it to its intended state.

And then it rumbled, more than usual, and rolled from side to side for a few brief seconds, its red blotches squelching with a sickening sound. A miasmic red cloud rose up from where the blood boils emitted their sounds, and a stench crawled out over the platform as the beast slowly unfolded what at first had seemed like a rotund, tiny-limbed body.

It was all Murmur could do not to gag as she pushed her hand in front of her mouth to avoid inhaling any of the disgusting stench. Like blood, rotten fruit, and feces mixed together in a blender and left out in the sun. She watched, fighting the urge to open her mouth and gape in disbelief as the Guardian unfolded itself and rose to its full height, towering about twenty feet above their tallest. A little taller than the statues in the entrance had been, and a hell of a lot taller than anything she'd been expecting after seeing the ball of a boss it had appeared to be.

Its limbs unfurled from their curled-up positions, and it stretched them out wide, all four of its arms. Those limbs were made out of gleaming charcoal colored rock, also beset by the pustules that plagued what turned out to be its back. It opened its great mouth set in the head, a mouth that blended in with the rest of its rock body and only seemed like a nub on the top of the shoulders.

The roar reverberated through the cavern and shook the platform. Murmur lurched, catching herself on one knee against the stone floor, and she wasn't alone – the rest of her friends hadn't escaped the tremor either. She looked up at the monster—it was the best word she could think of—and pushed down the panic welling in her. Its form loomed over her, overbearing and scary. Red clouds whipped around its body as they leaked into its crevices, and the beady little eyes somehow focused on each of them.

She wasn't used to having to consider what to do in order to not die. After all, she usually avoided games with permadeath for that reason. Sure, most games had some form of penalty for dying, be it monetary in that repairs to armor cost a lot of money, or else experience gain like this one.

But what was the point of dying permanently in a game if you were trying to avoid reality by going there in the first place? That just made it easier, right? She refused to die.

The Guardian hunkered down, like a gorilla with four arms, made out of rock. It was poised to attack, the miasma around it thickening, even though its pustules weren't being pressed, which could only mean it was an attack or ability and had nothing to do with the way it had been moving originally. Murmur was willing to bet it was toxic, too.

"Watch for cures," she called out, glad that they'd buffed themselves with every protection in their arsenal. Veranol and Sinister nodded, and as Devlish pulled out his shield and spiked hammer, Mellow threw an enlarging potion on him, ballooning him up to the monster's hunched size. Every little bit was going to help.

Murmur knew better than to heave a sigh of relief, because the Guardian chose that moment to launch its attack.

Somnia Online
Exodus Base
Firtulai
Fourteen Days Post Launch

Jirald looked around at the base, cringing at the structure. He wasn't the best at architectural design, but the stone castle ramparts didn't sit well with him. He'd not have chosen this type of building, but it was Ishwa's baby, so the rogue didn't have a lot of say in it. Still, it was nice to have another binding point that didn't detract from the one he had back in Verendus. He might even change it to Ululate, because if his observations had meant anything, she was based on that damned island back on Tarishna. He needed to have a point of travel to somewhere close to her, just in case the opportunity arose.

"Why so somber?" Masha sidled up to the rogue, one of those smug grins on his face.

Jirald scowled. "Stop gloating over hitting thirty before me. I lost one and a half levels thanks to … her."

"And then you continued to sulk for way too long when you could already have been playing catch up. Stop blaming everything on other people. Besides, you're close to catching up." It was the closest Masha had come to scolding him.

Jirald barely resisted the urge to tell him that he wasn't blaming everyone else, and then he realized it sounded extra childish. He'd been fighting for some respect from the others in his guild since his unfortunate outbursts early in the game launch. Instead, he took a deep breath and nodded. "I think I can blame some of that on her. But she probably wouldn't have done that if I hadn't trained her."

"You think?" Masha raised an eyebrow, his words heavy with sarcasm.

"Shut it, cleric." Jirald wouldn't meet his eyes.

"Anyway, you're close enough to thirty. You're twenty-nine. We're going to Richnai Fortress whether you like it or not. If we've calculated correctly our group should be able to approach our first keyed dungeon. We're close to Fable. Almost on a par. They only have one key that we know of, and with the way the game acts, I'm quite certain we'd know if they had more than that." Masha's tone was matter of fact. He wasn't bragging, just stating things he'd conclude in a logical way.

"But we're not close to them!" Jirald snapped. It was all he could do to force himself to take a deep breath. He'd never, not in a million years, thought another guild would overtake them, but he'd been wrong. And he couldn't help feeling that it was partially his fault for becoming more sidetracked than he'd meant to. Sidius's quest was just going to have to wait. "Who the hell are Spiral? I haven't even seen one of them around, so how the hell did they get to one of the dungeons on this continent first?"

Masha shrugged good-naturedly. "I don't know, and I don't care. We can't control what they do, so how about we control what we do instead, and go kill us some dungeon mobs?"

Jirald envied Masha's ability to put his emotions aside. Not that the rogue was overly emotional, he just had trouble dealing with irritation and anger, especially when he felt it was deserved. He sighed. At least his hidden skills were leveling nicely. Before they entered the dungeon, he'd have his next level of those, and make sure he got his level thirty ability scrolls just in case. Just the prospect of finally being within grasp of the lead Fable group was an amazing feeling. Granted, he hadn't slept in about thirty-six hours because of that. They were about to head out and have a four-hour nap so they could grind the dungeon, and he couldn't help being excited about it.

It almost made him determined to simply focus on himself, but that little voice in the back of his mind reminded him how much he owed Murmur, how much she'd kept him from, not only in this game, but in others, and just how much he needed to prove he was better than her. And to do anything like that, he needed to level, and he needed to gear up.

Not to mention that the dungeon they were about to enter probably had a heap of those Getashis in it. He could feel the greed rising within him. Sidius was going to reward him handsomely, but Jirald couldn't afford to get them if they weren't in his direct path at the moment. And surely the man didn't know how many of the things were in the world, so he wasn't going to notice if one went missing. It was just a stupid NPC given quest.

"Jirald?" Masha stood in front of him, tapping a foot on the ground impatiently. "It's not like you to daydream, been awake too long?"

The rogue shook his head, and felt the grin that spread over his face. "Not at all. I could keep going all night."

The bravado wasn't lost on the cleric, who shrugged. "If you fall asleep after we enter the dungeon, I'm not above replacing you."

Jirald scowled at his friend, and took another deep breath. Wouldn't do to alienate the people he needed. While he might know that in his head, sometimes he forgot it. "Yeah. I know, I know. I'm just going to train and get my skills and then I'll take a nap."

Masha nodded, even though his eyes didn't seem to believe what Jirald was saying, it looked like he was going to leave well enough alone for a while. The rogue sighed with relief as Masha sat down to log out. He still had a lot to do, not the least of which was to gate to Verendus and find his trainer again, but more importantly, he needed to track down Sidius before they headed out.

Waving back at Ishwa who stood on the balcony outside of his office, Jirald headed through to his quarters that he shared with Masha. They'd been building bunk sections so that each member had their own bed. Senior members and officers like Jirald and Masha got to share a room, others had between four and eight bunk beds, each with a locker box for storing their own goods should they want to. He had to admit it was a pretty cool idea Ishwa had. It gave each guild member something to call their own and something to strive for at the same time—recruits were kept in the one bunkhouse that barely had any space for their own personalization.

He'd just pulled his knives from their sheaths to clean them, when a cold wind blew through the room. Turning around fast, he saw Sidius standing in front of Masha's bed, a cruel smile on his human face. "Well, well, well, young rogue. It seems you've leveled up again. But I still don't see any Getashis. Tell me, what have you been doing?"

"You lied." Jirald wasn't about to let an NPC in a game try and intimidate or threaten him. It was just a series of algorithms and calculations. He ignored the indignant look on the rogue master's face and continued. "Murmur doesn't have the same quest."

"Not precisely, but she does require the same items you do to complete one of her quests." Sidius's response was smooth, like he'd practiced it a lot, or maybe words did just roll off his tongue that well. "Which doesn't matter. You have your own quest, and should be completing it. Don't make me regret having given you the chance to learn skills that no one else has been getting in-game."

Jirald gulped. No one else, huh? That was pretty damned awesome. "All I have to do is beat her to these shards, correct?"

Sidius nodded. "Each boss you encounter throughout the world has a chance to drop them, and beating her to them is the best possible path."

"Sure it is." Jirald sat down on his bed and grinned up at Sidius. "Or I could just wait until she's got several and take them from her body once I kill her."

"Not an option." Sidius's expression didn't change, instead he seemed somewhat disdainful, bored maybe.

"And why not? Why the fuck is everyone so protective of her?" Jirald stood so fast, the blood rushed to his head, but he was angry, and it pushed that anger.

"Dear boy, I'm not in the habit of waiting twenty-four hours for a corpse to decay so that I might retrieve a bounty off them. That's why player killing wasn't in the objectives of the quest I gave you. It's easier to kill the targets I give you for the items than to kill an enchanter for the couple they might have and hope you can then kill those who would guard her corpse in the event you were successful. Do you really think she wouldn't log in for another twenty-four in-game hours?" The sneer in Sidius's voice managed to get through to the rogue.

Jirald stood staring at his class master, infuriated that he knew the man was right. "Okay, then. Got it."

"Good." Sidius intoned in a way that said *finally*. He stepped closer to Jirald, crowding his personal space. "Just remember, I don't like being let down."

And then the rogue master was gone.

CHAPTER TWENTY-FIVE

Guarding Fear

The rock formation moved toward them at a speed Murmur hadn't thought it capable of. Its gait was smooth, and if it hadn't made the ground shake like an earthquake, she would have thought it was floating.

All traces of elegance vanished the moment it connected with Devlish's shield. Solid as the impact was, it still managed to push the dreadknight back several feet. He shook himself, hammer already in full swing, and connected against its raised right arm.

A resounding crack reverberated through the area, and Murmur watched in horror as the hammer split down the middle, revealing a strangely glowing golden gem atop the shaft. It flew through the air a split second later as Devlish discarded it in favor of his cruel-looking mace with slightly less pointed spikes.

At the same time, the Guardian opened its mouth again, roaring in what seemed like pain, and spewed forth a cloud of the red spores, as it nursed its right arm, flexing its fingers.

"Don't breathe!" Mellow screamed while throwing two bottles to explode at the Guardian's feet. A cloud of pale-yellow dust rose and flared with the red breath, and in another moment the haze disappeared in a torrent of sparks.

Murmur glanced back at the witch, whose brow was furrowed, and knew instinctively they were calculating how many of this special concoction they could brew in this fight. Their expression lightened ever so slightly, and they breathed a sigh of relief, finally looking up to meet Murmur's eyes. Mellow nodded almost imperceptibly.

The clash between Devlish and the Guardian seemed magnified under the dome, and the monster had switched from using its upper right hand to predominantly left sided attacks. At least the hammer had been good for something. Murmur saw Mellow pick it up out of the corner of her eye, and mentally noted to check on it later.

Apart from its bloody miasma of don't-breathe-me-in, the Guardian seemed to have a regeneration phase. At eighty percent health achieved by hacking away at what was most likely its elbow joints on all four arms, it rolled into a ball, spewing cloud after cloud of dangerous spores into the air. It wasn't too difficult to avoid, as they all hid under Veranol's shield until Mellow's bombs managed to soak it up.

Feeling more positive about beating it, Murmur allowed herself to perk up—which probably set the next chain of events in motion. When it emerged from its ball, which seemed impenetrable, its right arm was whole again. Which meant that any debilitating damage it took during the between time was going to be repaired while it was a ball, so eating at it with acid wouldn't work. Cracking it over time wasn't going to work either.

"That's weird." Havoc was pulling his own mind reading trick again. "Do we just beat him down slowly until he's passed through all of his phases? He didn't gain a percentage. He's still at eighty."

Merlin stood close enough to hear them. "I'm not sure what he's made of, but the area around where a heart would be anatomically seems to be made of a different type of rock, and it seems to be trying to protect that area if you watch the way it reacts to Devlish's attacks."

Murmur blinked, and spent the next minute watching it, while dodging spore attacks that now seemed to be thrown over directly in their way. Maybe it had super hearing. A sudden idea formed in her mind. It couldn't be right though, that was far too ludicrous. "Is that—could that be?"

"Gemstones?" Havoc offered, his grin none too kind.

"They appear to be charred to blend better with his body. But perhaps it's what we need to take out to kill him?" Murmur didn't like the hope in her voice, because she wasn't confident at all in her current idea.

"Either way." Havoc began to move in close, directing his pet to attack in a different formation. "It's a straw we can cling to, right?"

"Sure. Shatter the gems and either kill the Guardian faster, or unleash an unknown element onto the battlefield." Mellow laughed as they readied a couple more bottles to throw at the next wave of spores. "Count me in."

"Okay, then. Everyone aim for the charred area of its chest." Murmur watched the monster as its head swiveled and its gaze alighted solely on her. Apparently she'd called something right, because a sense of fear ran through her, suddenly rooting her to the ground. Shit. She couldn't move, and her limbs were heavy, like stone.

She saw Sinister turn toward her, mouth agape, and Havoc stopped his onslaught as his eyes widened in horror. Her legs began to harden, and her life leeched down after the massive initial blow. She thanked her impatience for allowing her to cast without her rapidly hardening fingers and cast an arcane cure on herself, hoping against hope that this was magic based.

"Murmur?" Sinister's voice was filled with worry, hints of panic leaked through.

"I'm okay." Murmur lied. It was taking far too long for the cure to work, and the rest of them were still battling for their lives. The blood mage needed to focus on the others, needed to get that damned blood out of the Guardian and keep them all alive. Mur raised her voice as best she could. "Whatever you do, don't make eye contact with it."

Because, of course, it was a wonderful turn of events when the monster had Medusa capabilities. Maybe attacking its crystal heart wasn't the solution. Maybe curing it was...

Wait.

Why would the statues drop a hammer that seemed so vicious to their kind? Thoughts ran through her head as she desperately wished for the unstoning process to hasten. Stuck in the rock, all she could do was think and debuff. Granted, it was probably only taking thirty seconds, but it seemed like a lifetime. Both Veranol and Sinister had HoTs on her, so her life was pretty safe, and she could still cast because her mind wasn't frozen.

The gem on top of the hammer's shaft looked a bit like a wand. What if the wand could re-activate the charred heart? She could also be completely full of shit and hallucinating, but it was worth a shot. "Hey, Mellow."

The witch glanced over and grinned as they moved to stand next to her. "It's bizarre seeing you immobile, Mur."

"Hardy har har." Murmur was pretty pleased with her own pun, but Mellow just rolled their eyes.

"What's up? I have to time these bombs, so while it might look like I'm standing here looking pretty and doing absolutely nothing, I am, in fact, not." The twinkle in their eyes was even noticeable when they weren't looking directly at her.

"You picked up that wand, didn't you?" She really hoped she was right.

"Wand..." Mellow's brow furrowed, the expression foreign and yet oddly familiar on their locus face. Then their eyes lit up. "Oh! You mean the stick with the—wow, you're right, it's just like a wand."

"I think we need to use it to reactivate the heart of the Guardian. It's obviously guarding something, and why is it a Guardian and not a Gatekeeper? If it were evil, or at least, if it were originally evil, then wouldn't it have a different name?" Her theories were just spouting from her mouth like a waterfall. Maybe she didn't actually have a clue, but this battle was going to get hairy before it got won, not the least because it was starting to get mana intensive on the healers. She was getting a little desperate about how they were going to defeat this.

"It sounds possible. I mean, what are we going to lose apart from a stick with a yellow gem on it?" Mellow's smile was kind, the words soft. Murmur felt a swell of fondness for her friend. It was nice being the one put at ease.

"And here's the impossible. We either need to get it to Devlish and convince him to use the wand." Murmur could wiggle her fingers again and feeling returned gradually to her thighs and then calves as she spoke. "Or, we could give it to Rash. She can jump high, she can dodge—surely she can get it where it needs to be."

Mellow nodded, a frown creeping onto their face. "I don't like either of those options."

Murmur sighed, because they were right. "Neither do I."

She looked around, finally able to wiggle her toes, and turned to survey the area. Her slows and weakness spells already applied to the mob, there was nothing else for her to do in this fight. Stuns didn't work against stone, so she couldn't even offer respite.

The dome was getting thicker, closer to red. And the Guardian's life was dwindling down toward sixty percent. Murmur's gaze fell on Merlin, and she got a sudden idea. "Merlin!"

He moved over, never ceasing his near useless arrow barrage into the target. "'Sup Mur?" He winked at her, barely preventing the groan Murmur had to suppress. His shots weren't even doing a fraction of their usual damage, but it was what they had to chisel away with.

She took the wand off Mellow and held it in front of her, hopefully hidden from the gaze of the Guardian, which meant it had to be hidden from Riasli. "I think this might unharden its heart?"

Merlin frowned at the wand. "Great, and what do you want me to do about it?"

"Do you think this could be shot into the blackened gems it's protecting?" She almost held her breath, so desperate was she to get this fight over with. They were winging it constantly in Somnia, and she wasn't used to going in so blindly unprepared. One of these days it was going to backfire on them. While she never took her eye off the target, it was lucky the fight was relatively slow paced and a matter of surviving, because she was way too distracted by the wand.

Merlin shook his head. "The balance is off, Mur. I can't successfully shoot that thing anywhere."

Murmur tried not to let the disappointment show on her face. She'd known it would be a long shot, and she groaned inwardly at the pun she made to herself. About to turn back to the sixty-two percent fight, Merlin stepped in front of her.

"Give it to me. I have an idea. It's not like I'm doing any good damage wise anyway. I can activate Jumpshot and switch out this for my bow, right?" His words were barely above a whisper, but he had that elfish troublemaker look on his face, that meant she wasn't about to talk him out of it. "Put yourself in Exbo's group if this all goes wrong, okay?"

Before she could say anything else, he grabbed the wand out of her hand and dashed away. She could have stopped him, could have stunned him in his tracks, Mez'd him, charmed him even. It wouldn't change anything about how they fought the Guardian, though. They either had to try this, or fight for the next thirty minutes, which would probably run them out of power, or else, the Guardian might have another surprise for them once it hit sixty percent.

She watched, almost in slow motion as Merlin activated his Jumpshot, choosing the moment before the apex to swap his bow for the wand, and sailed down through the beast's defenses, so much that Murmur couldn't see him any longer. An agonizing heartbeat passed, and then a blinding golden light exploded outwards from the Guardian, sending them all tumbling back with the force of the blast, and Exbo nearly off the side as the red barrier was replaced by a golden one. He only saved himself by managing to dig the end of his bow between two of the rocks that made up the floor.

Merlin ended up just in front of Murmur, his elven face grinning widely. "What a fucking rush!" His eyes glowed so brightly Murmur wondered if the effect was permanent.

A scream echoed throughout the catacombs, from beneath them, from around them, from everywhere at once. It was impossible to pinpoint its origin, but it sounded like someone in pain, and Murmur couldn't help the vindictive thought that it was Riasli. Real or not, Murmur held no fondness for her.

The giant guardian was curled into a ball again in the middle of the dome. Its black rock surface had turned to gleaming new sandstone, weathered with just enough time to make it smooth and have the milky lines flow perfectly into one another. Where the red pustules once resided were beautiful golden orbs, filled with a sparkling dust that remained within.

Slowly it unfurled and revealed the precise opposite of what it had been while they fought it. Murmur chalked it up to being freaking lucky, or in tune with the system. One of the two anyway, maybe a mixture of both.

You have freed The Guardian of the Cenedril Catacombs from the curse placed upon it. As a reward you receive undying gratitude, because stone never truly dies. Even as sand, weathered and worn down through the ages, you will be remembered with fondness. You have found a powerful ally; do not betray its trust.

You have gained experience.
DING
You have reached level thirty-three.

Murmur blinked at her experience as the brief notification disappeared from her screen. Three quarters of the way through already. Which was good, considering the amount of time they'd been doing nothing since completing Hightower. It must have rolled the experience for the odd two dozen statues they'd fought at the start as well.

The Guardian placed one hand over its now golden and repaired heart. Sandstone held it in place, protecting the majority of it in a casing. When it spoke, the voice held hope and wisdom contained within a gentle rumble of words that soothed and put them all at ease.

"For what you have done, I thank you. We thank you as one, here in the Catacombs. Thank you for freeing me from the torment of greed, from the jail of hatred, and from the cause of my pain."

It bowed down to them, low and humbling. Murmur wracked her brains for what it was she had to do. How did one respond to that?

"Thank you." She intoned as graciously as she could.

"You are welcome." It moved toward what was now a glowing white rock, about as tall as her. She hadn't noticed it before. "I grant you each a reward. You may claim it later, or choose it now, but if you choose it now you must hurry. The darkness still lingers beneath me, and there is only so long I can fight it on my own. I require that you aid me in freeing my domain from the infestation that changed it so much."

You have been given the opportunity to help the great Guardian protect its domain, to combat the darkness still lurking within, and to probably come away with some really cool stuff. Keep in mind, these catacombs have been changed from what was originally intended, and it's best to use caution along the way.

Murmur glanced around her at the others, and figured she spoke for them all when she answered. "We'd be glad to assist you in restoring the ruins to their former glory."

The Guardian beamed a smile, quite literally. Turning in a circle, the beam of light shot out, illuminating the walls and stairs in light, transforming them back to the cream-colored bliss of sandstone. Statues stood all over the halls, in crevices, in alcoves. As the light passed over them, their faces transformed from judgmental snarls back to pleasant, half-smiling expressions.

Once it was done, the Guardian lifted a large hand and waved it over them. Golden dust floated down, giving them all a faintly glowing sheen before it sank into their skin through their armor. Strength welled inside Murmur, and she watched as her MA went up another fifty points, and her mana and hit points as well. Snowy suddenly seemed to get bigger, his chest broader and more powerful.

The rest of her guild echoed her own gasp as they too observed their own increase in strength.

Murmur had to push down the urge to feel invincible, because she knew that in fact she was not, and she turned to face the giant Guardian head on. At least, as its gaze met her own, she realized in this form it didn't turn her to stone, but instead infused her with warmth as a shield covered her from head to toe.

"It seems that you are in need of my protection the most. I would hope that your friends agree with my protection of you." Its eyes were kind, though Murmur wasn't sure how she could tell that through the golden lights that shone from it.

"Of course! Maybe she won't slow us down so much!" Beastial's jovial voice rang out. And even as Sinister cuffed him over the ear half-heartedly, the rest of them laughed.

But even as they bid the Guardian farewell, filled with renewed strength and buffed to the max, Murmur couldn't shake the feeling that they'd only made things worse.

Storm Entertainment
Somnia Online Division
Game Development Offices Artificial Intelligence Server Room
Day Fourteen

Rav was the first in their space, which wasn't unexpected considering he'd been the one to convene this meeting, but still, Sui was usually so much more on the ball. He'd never been the runner up at arriving before. He'd been counting on his brother to arrive earlier, because that gave him more time to argue and less time to stew about what wasn't in his control.

Yet the responses from his siblings this time had taken a while to get to him. Far too long for the dragon's liking considering he currently had no way at all to help Murmur, hell, to even access Murmur. She was in danger, he could feel it, and completely out of his reach.

Even if they'd gone against their mutual decisions, Rav needed to know if it was one of them that had changed the zone so significantly. Because he didn't like the implications if it wasn't one of them.

"You seem tense." Thra's tones blended with the darkness in the room, and for a moment almost seemed to be in his head.

Rav resisted the urge to scowl. "And you can tell that in a dark room just by looking at me?"

"No, by feeling the mood, you know and testing the surrounding algorithms out." She spoke as she walked around him, shadows coalescing around her like a cloak. "And you maintain that we should take on human traits. Tsk tsk, brother dear."

Her grin held mischief, and under other circumstances might have made Rav smile, but all it did right now was irritate him. "You're being obtuse. Stop it."

She raised an eyebrow, or at least that was the impression he got. Her feles form flickered in and out, not quite solidifying yet, but getting close to it. She'd leveled up, so to speak, and he couldn't help the flush of pride he got from the fact.

"You're not quite as stuffy as you let on, Rav. Try and have some fun once in a while." Her words were soft, for his ears only, and he grasped at them, wishing he didn't feel such a sense of obligation to all of the humans playing in his world.

"My, my, aren't you two just cozy." Sui clapped his hands slowly, the sarcasm dripping heavily from each word.

Sui took his time stepping down from the chair he favored. More like a throne, it lorded over a platform that appealed to neither Rav nor Thra. They'd let their youngest sibling play whatever he wanted, as long as it didn't harm people or get in their way.

Rav bit his tongue, finally understanding where that expression came from. He needed their cooperation, not their ire. He glanced at the shadowy form of his brother. Tall and regal, but with a hint of malice in the shadows that flanked him. Such a perfect representation of who and what he represented.

"What brings this summons, brother?" Sui drawled out the words, as if he was offended someone other than himself had decided to call a meeting. He probably was too.

"Have any of you visited the Ruins of Cenedril recently?" He tried to ask the question without too much emphasis on the words, as if it was just a passing interest. A brief look of confusion spread over Sui's face, and he frowned. His attempt at surreptitiously checking on the zone while they were standing there didn't go too well. Subtle wasn't really his thing. The frown on his face spoke volumes as he tried to locate the ruins by their appearance.

"What the—" Thra spoke first, obviously checking herself while Rav's attention was focused on their brother. She looked up at Rav, her eyes solidifying enough to express her rampant confusion. "What the hell?"

Sui's smirk faded, and he blinked. "I don't understand."

The relief that flooded through Rav was short lived, because it was followed by a sense of dread. "I'm glad it wasn't either of you. I figured if you were going to make an adjustment of that magnitude, you'd have let the rest of us know."

His words didn't seem to put the others at ease, which was only to be expected since they didn't do anything for him either.

"But they can't make any changes in here without going through us, that's what we're for." Sui laughed, his own confusion making the sound hollow. "Any program changes are filtered through *us*. They have to be; it's how the whole system was set up. How can this even be?"

Sui didn't deal that well with change that wasn't instigated by him, and for just a moment, Rav felt a little sorry for his brother. It took a while for the computations his brethren made to catch up with where Rav's had already arrived, and he could tell from the looks of horror on their faces that they'd finally reached the same conclusion.

"Great. You're both up to speed then." Rav sighed, the new wave of relief somewhat more endurable now that he had help to get to the bottom of it.

"Up to speed?" Thra laughed derisively. "Come now, you've basically just told us that we need to work together to make sure our world isn't overrun, don't you think that's not lending it enough weight?"

"No." Rav shook his head. "There's nothing trivial about this. We have to figure out just how this is happening. It's not the first glitch in the system, and that's okay. We're a new game, and we're still finding the right balance for our world. But right now, there are things outwitting our systems, our protocols. We have to stop this."

"The balance is out of check, if you haven't noticed, and telling us what we can very well see on our own is annoying," Sui snapped, tapping his foot in anger to create a strange echo through the nothingness of their room.

"Which is why I called us here." Rav added gently, not giving into Sui's constant riling behavior. He hadn't expected Sui to react in such an extreme way, but in hindsight, he probably should have. Even though he appeared to be together, his visage was wavering in and out of solidity at an alarming rate, which meant he was likely running a mass of computations and trying to figure out exactly where they went wrong.

It was going to lead him in a spiral, just like it had done to Rav. Except the spiral went around one huge black hole of what he didn't want to talk about. "You both know what I'm going to say."

"It can't be. You can't be right." Sui's tone held panic, a shrill sound to his usually dulcet tones. But Rav knew his brother was only in denial. There was nothing else it could be.

"I'm not saying it's definite, just that somehow, some way, the shards seem to have affected more than just us. Riasli has gone completely off script." He waited for them to digest it. Not that the game had a script as such, but each character did have directives within whose parameters they were supposed to function, and that enchanter wasn't anywhere near any of them.

Sui's momentary panic dissolved into thoughtfulness, and Rav could almost see the sequences he was running through his mind. It was difficult to wait patiently, but he somehow managed it.

"The shards might lend motivation to the mobs they're embedded in, depending on the type of mob it is?" Sui mused the words softly, out loud.

Thra continued the train of thought, bouncing if off her brethren like they'd been created to do. "Riasli in particular is one of the learning characters, with the potential to take over the job of the predecessor should anything happen. So many are characters we created to evolve, to see if they could." She sounded sad, and Rav couldn't help but agree.

"Basically, I believe the power in the shard has given Riasli magnified abilities and sent her characterization on unforeseen tangents." Rav chose his words carefully, because assumption was the mother of all fuck ups, and he didn't intend to screw things up even further by letting his thoughts out before he'd had a chance to fully research things. He'd found out what he needed to know, that the other two had nothing to do with the change of the ruins.

"But how did she change them?" Sui sounded skeptical, and quite irritated.

Rav shrugged. "Guess that's something we need to figure out."

"I'll start leafing through her algorithms, if I can figure out the best way to access them. She's one of my races, it's probably my fault somehow." Thra sounded less than pleased, and a little guilty.

She paused for a moment, frowning deeply. "Odd though. It seems my system messages are still reaching them in there though. My wards should have pinged me to the change in script but because it's so freeform, it didn't. I'll look into this." She left as abruptly as she'd arrived.

"You thought it was me, didn't you?" Sui spoke softly, as he'd been doing for the entire meeting. Rav eyed him closely, trying to find any sort of interference in his countenance, but came away empty.

"No. I was hoping it was neither of you, and I was right." Rav used a gentle tone, and not one filled with the exasperation he felt.

"Good. I might be finicky about some things, but this isn't something I'd do. It's not just my world, it's ours." And with that, Sui too left the area, leaving Rav with an odd sense of loneliness.

Rav spun slowly in their void-like room, watching the shadows for any sign of movement. He couldn't shake the feeling that it was far worse than they thought, nor could he shake the sensation that he was being watched. Conjecture led to insanity, and he didn't want to assume anything. They needed to make sure this didn't happen again, and Rav couldn't help the queasiness his calculations returned to him, because everything about this shouted that it was only the beginning.

CHAPTER TWENTY-SIX

Kid You Not

Some of the excitement had already worn off by the time they reached the next platform. The deeper under the Guardian's area they went, the more the illumination faded. Darkness wove itself about, pushing tendrils in through the light, creating shadows that threatened to swallow them whole if they stepped into them.

It was either scary as hell, or else Murmur's imagination was getting way too active. Perhaps a mixture of both. She let out an anxiety-filled sigh, making sure she didn't attract Sinister's attention by making a sound. Her friend had been all too concerned about her since she almost turned to stone. Not that she could blame her. Being turned into a statue wasn't on Murmur's bucket list.

They finally reached what appeared to be the bottom platform, because it led off into a series of tunnels. The floor was covered in black moss, some of which had turned into a stickier sludge, and only recoiled with fire. Mellow threw down a few flame bombs while the rangers picked a path with their fire arrows. Murmur watched the process dubiously. "They're going to see us a mile away. It's like we're announcing our presence."

"We are. And they better run like the bastards they are!" Beastial grinned evilly, baring his teeth, although it didn't have the same effect as the grin on

Shir-Khan's face. Snowy sat well out of reach of the flames, eyeing them reproachfully. He was probably overheating, if his tongue lolling out his mouth was anything to go by.

Finally, they stepped off the platform and through to the tunnels. Except they weren't the tunnels Murmur had been expecting. What she'd thought were walls in fact appeared to be cages. Large Cages that held the whimpering she'd been hearing, the wailing, the desperation that echoed throughout the whole zone.

Cages that held elven children.

Their pale skin was marred with black sludge, some of them covered entirely, so that all that looked out and let her know they were humanoid was their eyes. Murmur choked on the hopelessness their thoughts fed back to her now that she was finally close enough to interpret them. Their pain and agony permeated the whole area. She doubled over, so powerful were their thoughts, their projections.

And then she realized what was happening.

Riasli wasn't just magnifying their despair—she was feeding off it somehow. Feeding off it through the moss that turned into black sludge when used. She kept the entire area under her control. Tendrils of power, thin and barely discernible, trailed through the chamber, leaving droplets to float in the stagnant air. But Murmur could see them if she half closed her eyes, there, like a fishing line, almost invisible, yet deadly. Removing them might harm the children, but leaving them attached was going to be fatal.

Murmur could see at least three cages full of the children, with three each in them. "That's why there were no children in Cognitia." She whispered the words in horror, letting them sink in as the truth for the whole group.

"That's why everyone was being such dicks." Merlin muttered, his eyes flashing. And she knew he wasn't angry at his home city anymore, but instead at the feles enchanter who'd stolen their children. "What does she want? What are they giving her in order to get the children back?"

Murmur shook her head. "I don't know, but we can't leave them like this."

"No shit," Merlin snapped, and it was the first time she'd seen him close to losing his temper. In fact, she'd not thought him capable.

"Settle there," Veranol stepped in with his soothing voice, lending an aura of calm to the situation.

Murmur continued to wrack her brains for a solution. She could extend her mental shielding surely, but that wasn't going to solve the problem because there were only so many she could shield, and removing those tendrils was going to take time. Mind Wipe wasn't going to work on such a large sample of kids. Using her kinetic abilities to physically slice them was too dangerous. Murmur didn't have enough skill with it yet. But maybe...maybe if she severed the connection once, it would take a while for Riasli to grab hold again.

"Give me a moment," she said, kneeling down in front of the first cage, watching the fear in the children's eyes as they backed away from her, clinging to the other side of the enclosure. She took a deep breath, grateful for Snowy's steadying presence, and choked down her anger. Reaching out with her mind, she soothed them, reassuring them that she wasn't going to hurt them.

Their fear only scaled down a notch, but it was enough. She extended her Shield Expansion toward the first three of the children, gently encasing them in safety. The result was instantaneous. Relief flooded their features, and the fear leaked away. The darkness that covered the entire area began to roll back of its own accord. Slowly but surely, anyway.

The real test was yet to come. Once the black sludge began to creep away from the smallest child, revealing more of their pale skin and taking away the fear in their eyes, Murmur began to maneuver the shield in such a way that it approached the tendrils at the back of the smallest's neck. She took a deep breath, and focused on it, sharpening the edge barely, but just enough.

Tendrils rebounded, falling away with what appeared to be reluctance, before they swayed for several seconds and disintegrated. Murmur began to drop the shield around them, reverting the edges back to pure mental protection, and repeated the process with the other two. No sudden fear entered the child again, no increase of pain or sludge or shadows. There were no tendrils leaping back to reattach themselves. Perhaps Riasli required to be next to them for those to take hold. The tendrils were different to the control exerted over the other victims. This mimicked pipes, which meant the rogue enchanter was taking something from the children.

Murmur pulled away, her hands shaking slightly. For all she'd known, the tendrils could have attached themselves to her, like the trap she thought it to be. It had been risky, but worth it. Now all she had to do was get more confident while doing it.

"How did you do that?" Sinister whispered close to her.

"Do what?" Surely she hadn't seen?

Sinister raised an eyebrow. "Really? How did you cut those life leeching lines?"

So, that's what they were. Murmur smiled, pushing down on the relief that the tendrils hadn't attached themselves to her. "Sheer luck. I wasn't sure if it would work. But it did, and I'll be able to recreate it."

In short order Jinna had the locks on the cage open and the children out of them, while Murmur moved onto the other two visible cages to work the same magic on them. She had a very bad feeling about this. It was far too easy to rescue the children, and even as she undid the leech effect on the others, she knew there was something larger out there in the darkness waiting for the right moment to strike, and it wasn't just Riasli.

"You okay, Mur?" Sinister whispered next to her ear.

Murmur took comfort in the offered support and nodded, even as she looked around, trying to spy what it was that had the hairs on her neck so on end. Riasli didn't seem the sort to make things too easy. In fact, she'd gone out of her way so far to commandeer a dungeon and force the monsters to fight them instead of presumably giving them challenges to overcome. Of course, since she'd not seen the dungeon before the takeover, all she had to go on were assumptions.

Merlin knelt in front of the scared ragtag of kids and held a few glowing vials of Mellow's in his hands. He placed one each in the hands of the largest kid from each cage. "Take these. Behind us you'll see stairs—see how they glow?"

The bigger children leaned around, craning their necks until they spied the bottom of the steps. They nodded vigorously. He took another deep breath and smiled at them. Murmur watched as the children formed tentative smiles of their own. Something they'd not done with her, and likely because Merlin was one of them, an elf.

"Take those stairs. On the large platform above, you'll find a golden guardian. He'll show you the path to take out of here. Exit and go home." Merlin's smile was becoming forced, and Murmur could feel the determination coming off him in waves.

The tallest elf, who came almost to Merlin's shoulder, opened her mouth to speak. Then closed it, and opened it again, like she was unsure. "It's golden now?"

Merlin nodded, sadness creeping into his expression. "Yeah. It's golden now. We fixed the red."

The tension in her shoulders lifted slightly, and she squared her shoulders. "I'll get them home. Safely. I promise."

"Be careful." Murmur butted in, unable to stop her errant mouth. The girl looked at her solemnly and nodded. "What's your name?"

"S'elvae." Her eyes were wide and unfathomably blue. Maybe Merlin hadn't chosen the eyes to mimic himself; maybe it was just an elf thing.

"Then be safe, S'elvae, and gate home as soon as you exit the dungeon." Merlin stood, watching as the children filed out of the area and up to the stairs, and then for a few seconds after.

"You know. I'm not sure I like this world much. Using kids to what? Lure us in?" Merlin spat the words out, literally shaking with anger.

Murmur hesitated at first, but since no one else answered she sighed and went for it. "They didn't lure us in with children, because we already came in on our own. We wanted a key. So, the question remains, if they didn't use the kids to lure us in, what are they using the children for?"

The labyrinth of cages and stone boxes continued on. Fighting their way through wasn't as difficult as Murmur had anticipated, which left her not only cautious, but oddly unsatisfied. She was angry at Riasli for abusing her position of power and for taking those damned kids. They'd not received a quest from the elves themselves, so it stood to reason that a part of their treatment at the hands of the rude elves was because of the children who were missing.

Each time they came across the cages, they repeated the process to free the children. She was kicking herself for not noticing they were missing while they were *in* Cognitia, even if she'd realized it sometime later. She'd seen a few younger adults, but no actual children, and they weren't in another world, they were in Somnia. So, to have a race whose children were missing? It made no sense at all.

Another spider jumped down from the ceiling. These were group mobs, but barely worth the time it took to kill them with a small raid.

"This is getting ridiculous," Sinister muttered next to her.

Murmur nodded in agreement and remembered her friend probably couldn't see her as they concentrated on picking their way through the slimly gunge that lined the floors, stone, and cages. "Yeah, pretty sure it got there a while ago."

Sinister laughed, but the sound was forced and echoed around them. Stone was great for things like that.

"Hey, guys." There was a note of panic in Havoc's voice that made Murmur stop and look back at him. They were going through the paths two abreast because the close quarters warranted it. Truth be told, Mur was feeling a little claustrophobic because the ceiling in here was maybe ten feet high.

"What's up?" She wished the corridors were wider, and... she blinked at Havoc and activated her HUD. "Shit."

"Yeah." he smiled at her wanly and shrugged. "Guess when it's too easy, it's too easy, isn't it?"

"What is it, Mur?" Sinister's tone held impatience.

"I think this black stuff is leeching our mana and energy away. Pull up your HUD." Murmur did her best to keep her voice steady.

Sinister clamped down on a shriek, so only a muffled half meep came out. Her eyes were wild with fear for just a moment, and it gave her a slightly unhinged dark elf look. She moved in, away from the encroaching black ooze on the floors and frowned, some of the sanity returning to her visage. "Hey. It's the sludge."

Murmur made an effort not to roll her eyes, but Havoc didn't follow suit. "Really, Sin? You don't say."

"No need to be a dick about it." Sinister mumbled.

"If we make it through here, and our mana is pretty much gone by the end, but we rescue the kids and get to move on." Merlin muttered, more to himself than the others, but it served to keep them hanging on his words. "There's going to be a fight at the end of this. Do we move forward and hamstring ourselves or turn back?"

The noise that emerged in response to his question surprised Murmur. While she'd known none of them were going to head back, it was pleasant realizing that everyone felt the same as her without having to be prompted. What she hadn't expected was for the ooze to multiply as soon as they realized what it did.

The black tar like substance began to bubble, and the only thing that kept it at bay was fire. Merlin moved forward to take point, while Exbo brought up the rear after having handed everyone a flame lit arrow to keep them clear of the sludge. She was going to have to get the guild bank set up sooner than later. Keeping the rangers stocked with fire arrows seemed paramount to survival.

Murmur kept an eye on her mana. Keeping it at bay so none of it touched them, even while they chased it away, allowed her mana to stay at its current level. It did not, however, allow it to regenerate. Her MA seemed unaffected by this.

Each time the corridor widened, they came across another cage or two. Almost as an encouragement to keep moving forward. Like being shepherded into exactly the right place. To where someone wanted them to be. But she couldn't see another choice—the corridors were deliberately set up to bar sight from the rest of this labyrinth.

Several times they had to backtrack, barely able to keep the sludge controlled as it kept multiplying. By the time they got to the fifth set of children, Murmur needed an outlet for her anger, but she choked it down in favor of helping the kids. Only it had grown too dangerous to send them back as the ooze became more and more dense, thick, and followed them like a rabid puppy. She didn't want to think what it would take to cut their way back through the mess. And kids with a fire arrow wasn't going to cut it anymore. There was no way they could safely send them back, and there was no way they could safely take them ahead with them.

So, they took the fifth group with them. Luckily it had only been one cage, and they had to pass over releasing those from the sixth and seventh, leaving the group with them instead. They reached through the bars to give them a few flame arrows and instructions on how to use them to stay safe while the sludge bore down from behind them. While she was able to sever their ties to Riasli, there wasn't much more they could do to help them at the moment while they still needed to be free to fight. Reassuring kids that they'd be back for them left a hollow in Murmur's stomach, because right now she wasn't sure if she was lying or not.

"It's not the end of the world, Mur," Havoc spoke the words softly from where he walked behind her.

"No, it's not. Just for them, and for me." She wasn't in the mood to be made to feel better, and she wasn't in the mood to be reminded of where she currently stood.

"You know I didn't mean it like that. I meant our mana will regenerate, and we'll beat the living shit out of that damned enchanter traitor." His tone was grim and she could practically hear his teeth gnashing together. It made her grin despite herself.

"I like that. It sounds like a great plan." She smiled tightly at Havoc, clinging to his words. Making Riasli pay, making sure she died an unimaginable death—it was all that kept her going. Only with everything else they were going through as they walked, she was fairly certain she was missing something. Riasli had laid the way, set the trap, and they'd walked knowingly and willingly into it.

So, it stood to reason that a surprise was waiting for them at the end.

"Hey." Merlin called back to them. "I think the path stops up ahead. Either that or we took another wrong turn."

Murmur had lost track of the time they'd been down there, not to mention the direction they were facing. She'd become too dependent on others to know the way out, but it was something she could only correct from here on in. Fire kept the spiders away too, and she didn't even want to contemplate how many of them were built up with the sludge behind them, waiting for their fire to go out. "Be careful, stay cautious, you don't know what..."

A resounding thwack followed by a sickening thud ensued as Merlin shot back against one of the stone boxes, a huge projectile jutting out of his left shoulder and pinning him in place.

"Merlin!" Sinister screamed, and the blood began to flow from her. Murmur held the fire arrow in such a way she hoped the sludge stayed away from the healer, because her friend had dropped her own, causing the fire to snuff as she began to weave healing spells, pulling from her own life force to complete them.

"Get the stake out of him. I can't heal through the damage." Panic beset her voice, and Merlin attempted a smile even as his life crept down slowly. Blood trickled out of his mouth to land on his chest.

Veranol was coming up from behind where he'd been just in front of Exbo. But the healing wasn't the problem. Devlish and Beastial braced themselves against the wall and heaved, but it did no good. Merlin was stuck tight.

"Fuck." Sinister's voice grated, tears streamed down her cheeks. "I can't keep up."

"Sin." Merlin coughed. "Let me go. Res me."

Murmur could see her friend's hands pausing, see how much willpower Sin had to exude to keep from healing, and watched them fall to her side. There was realism and there was gamification. She watched Merlin as his life plummeted once the heals stopped helping him, the way the blood drained out of him, the way his face sagged, the pallor of his skin, how his limbs twitched and face went slack, and how that last breath never seemed to finish.

There was nothing game-like about this. Merlin, hanging there on the wall in front of them limp in death seemed far too real.

Somnia Online
Firtulai Continent
Richnai Fortress
Fourteen Days Post Launch

Exodus had gathered its two best groups to venture into Richnai Fortress. Located in a well-hidden set of caves between Brevint and Malaise on the Firtulai Continent, Jirald knew they were pushing it with their levels. While most of them were level twenty-nine or thirty, a few were twenty-eight. Thirty plus were the rumors he'd heard. The mobs inside would be that level, so they'd begin conning orange to anyone twenty-seven or below, thus creating diminishing returns for their damage. Even so, it was worth a shot. With one healer and their warrior tank sitting higher than most of the rest, they should at least have a good chance.

Jirald was inching closer to thirty too, and he was hoping to level up inside.

"Stop calculating so many things in your head. It makes you look even less approachable." Masha was suddenly next to him, that familiar smirk on his lips.

Jirald wanted to smack it off his face, but again, Masha had a point, and his knowledge of that caused grudging respect to overrule his violent impulses. There had better be some goddamned Getashi in there, or Jirald had the feeling Sidius was going to skin him alive.

"All stocked up?" Masha continued as if he hadn't just insulted the rogue.

"Poisons, daggers, and a couple of new tricks up my sleeve." Jirald smiled, baring his locus teeth. He still couldn't believe he'd guessed right. Murmur rarely played a human species when there were others to choose from. It just so happened that this game offered the stellar opposite of human, and he had known she wouldn't be able to resist.

He rolled his shoulders, starting to feel the adrenaline coursing through his body as he got ready to enter a dungeon for the first time. These caves appeared to be lower level at first, but on closer inspection, they had entrances into a whole other level of fortress. It spanned the mountaintop above them, but they'd sent out scouts and found no way in through the top. It lived up to its name—impenetrable—unless you went in through the cellars.

It pleased his rogue heart that they'd essentially be breaking and entering.

"Sounds like you're ready then." Masha paused, and looked Jirald directly in the eyes. "Don't make me have to heal you more than usual. You were a good healer, and you know what pisses us off more than anything else, so don't piss me off, okay? I know you know better."

Jirald scowled, even though he knew Masha had a point. He still resented that the cleric felt the need to lecture him. "I know not to step in shit. I never healed DPS when they did, and I don't expect you to heal me if I screw up like that. Don't worry."

"Good, I won't then." Masha grinned. "At least there's one of you I don't have to worry about wiping us. Now, the rest of them are going to learn the hard way."

Jirald couldn't help but laugh, because he knew exactly what the cleric meant.

Ishwa finished arranging groups and spoke to the raid. "Follow Masha's lead, don't step in shit, and let Eslan pull, for crying out loud. If you pull accidentally, just let yourself die and don't run it to the raid."

The gnome waited for the whispers to quiet down, the steel in his eyes a definite deterrent to talking. "Time to head in and get ourselves one of those keys."

A small cheer went up from the group as they began to file into the darkness of the cellar. Jirald felt the cold wash over him as they passed through the door. They'd show this Spiral upstart who was the best and finally start giving Fable a run for their money.

CHAPTER TWENTY-SEVEN

Mirror Image

"Fuck, that hurt!" Merlin's voice sounded raspy and strained as he materialized right in front of Veranol once he'd resurrected him. The blessing was that at least the shaman was able to give him half the experience he lost back.

Murmur felt the tension leak out of her shoulders, and hadn't realized quite how pent up she'd been. All she could think while watching him was that death shouldn't be permanent in here, and what if they hadn't been able to Res him in a dungeon? Considering Riasli's behavior so far, it was a miracle they could. So many things held on them all sticking together.

"Don't do that again," Sinister muttered, not looking at any of them.

Her voice cracked on the last word, and Murmur realized it had shaken her up more than most things. She put her arm around Sin's shoulder, gently hugging her to her side without making her turn her head. Right now all Sin needed was support, not questions.

Still, watching one of her best friends get impaled by a huge stake through the chest had been so real. Murmur gagged at the thought of the pain receptors, at the fact that he must have felt at least a portion of what it would truly be like. It left her with uncharitable feelings about how Somnia viewed mortality and how perhaps allowing people to experience death and then revive might just make them impervious to the real dangers of pain and death.

Suddenly, she needed to send her mom a message, to let her know it was all okay and that they were having fun in the game. Well, even if the latter was slightly stretched truth for the moment, it wasn't a complete lie. At least they were all playing the game together and adventuring, right?

Mom. Just checking in. Love you, and want you to know I'm not really mad anymore, just a little sad, a little scared, and a bit lonely.

She blinked at the system warning she got across her eyes.

Your message could not be sent while you're in an unauthorized section of the game. Please note that until you exit your current location, all outside communication is not possible.

She pulled up her guild chat, trying not to panic as she checked it for activity. There was nothing there, at least not for the last few hours. The last new message had been before they even entered the ruins. Her breath stuck in her throat and she gulped as she glanced at her friends, all of whom were still gathering themselves after Merlin's impaling. She didn't want to worry them and wasn't sure if they'd notice if she didn't say anything.

Had it only let them resurrect Merlin because they were in the zone? She chose not to alarm anyone, not quite yet, not before she'd figured out what it was preventing her from sending a message. Murmur kept quiet while everyone buffed each other and themselves.

For all she knew, it was another glitch in her system, like the one that affected her faction updates that she'd never got an explanation for.

Jinna cloaked himself and moved slowly toward the opening where the weapon that impaled Merlin had come from. Murmur held her breath for a few moments, so worried was she about something nailing Jinna in the chest too. After about a minute, he crept back.

"It was a trap. You didn't see the trip-plate because it was covered in sludge." Jinna shrugged uncomfortably. "To be honest, I don't think any of us would have seen it in its current state. But the corridor opens to a wider hall. I didn't go there or even take a longer look. I feel like it's something we should do as a team."

Merlin nodded, his face pale, like he was still recovering from the death. "I should have been more careful."

"We've all got perfect hindsight. Don't beat yourself up about it." Jinna's words were soothing in the creepily mana-sucking, sludge-infected area. "I'll scout ahead for us so we can try to avoid any of this in the future."

They continued on, relief palpable as they were finally able to move out of the confines of the corridors. Murmur cringed as they passed the final cage of children, and she knew they couldn't retrieve them yet because they had no way to send them to safety. All she could do was free them of the drain and make the time they had left in their confinement at least a bit more comfortable. They clutched the fire arrows in their small hands, eyes wide as they looked up at Merlin.

At least the eighteen-odd kids they'd rescued should have made it out, but she had no guarantee they did, and no way to know until they figured out how to get out of here and made it possible to communicate with the outside again.

She had no doubt that right now they weren't in Somnia proper, not the way she'd come to know it. There was something twisted about this zone, something unnatural. Well, insofar as anything in a fictional computer universe was natural, anyway. It was telling that she had to keep reminding herself of the fact.

"Mur? You're being extra quiet." Havoc spoke from her right-hand side. She hadn't noticed he'd moved up next to her. She blinked at the hall around them; the smooth stones that made up the floor met seamlessly. She could feel the cool seep through to her feet even through the soles of her boots. Almost like a breeze was blowing through from under them.

"Yeah, I'm thinking," she muttered absent-mindedly hoping the inkling in the back of her mind was wrong.

"She never listens, does she?" Beastial laughed, but it sounded forced. "We keep telling her to stop thinking."

"Shhh." Murmur covered her lips with her pointer finger, signaling silence. It was there, on the tip of her brain, the idea she had trying to break out. "Be careful, there's a soft breeze coming up from the floor, between cracks I can't even see. And something about this is setting my skin on edge. It's familiar and nagging at me."

"Oh." The break in that one syllable as Sinister uttered it was enough for Murmur to look up from where she studied the floor. She followed Sinister's gaze to where it was transfixed.

At the other end of the massive hall there appeared to be twelve shadowed figures. Murmur and the others stopped in their tracks, and the creatures in front of them just swayed in place. Some of them had loose clothing, which fluttered softly in the breeze that came up through the floor tiles. Murmur took a step forward, curious now, and watched as the shadowed figure directly opposite her did the same. Two more steps and its face came into the light.

Her face.

She froze. The other her stopped moving, still a good twenty feet away. She peered through the dim light at it, not understanding its purpose. Murmur lifted her right hand, and the mirror image lifted her left. She frowned, and cast Invisibility on herself on a whim, watching as the other her did the same.

The rest of her raid joined her, fanned out in a line to either side, testing their reflections in the same way. She dropped Invis, causing herself to reappear across from her again. It was getting confusing in her head.

"Anyone got any ideas on what this is?" Devlish's tone reflected the rampant perplexity running through Murmur's mind.

"I'd hazard a guess and say they're mirror images meant to fight us." Havoc's sarcastic reply wasn't helping anything, but it seemed to be his defensive mechanism when he didn't know how else to react.

"Basically." Sinister began, a frown on her face. "We have to fight ourselves and come out on top? But how do we do that? I mean, does it have my inventory too? Can it access potions or my hidden abilities, or my expanded abilities? Will it have the same regeneration or is it a lesser version of myself?"

Murmur raised an eyebrow at the very accurate musings of her friend.

"All excellent questions there, Sin. And may I answer that with a fucked if I know." Havoc's pet jangled at him, lending credence to Murmur's assumption that there was still a skeleton behind the death's robe it now wore. The necromancer sighed. "Sorry. Feeling a bit rattled."

"Rattled." Beastial seemed to be choking on something, and Murmur realized he was trying not to laugh. At the same time, she noticed that none of their mirror images were moving. Not even the beastmaster's.

She frowned and forced a laugh, but the other self remained still.

"Mur, what the..." But Sin trailed off, watching her own shadow contemplatively.

Murmur cast another spell, this time her Mana Tide, and watched as it didn't move again. "I don't think buffs work on it. Rebuff, everyone."

So, they did, and their doubles stood, swaying ominously but not moving their fingers in any way.

"Guess that answers that question, Sin. Got anymore?" Beastial grinned at her, and the blood mage scowled at him.

"We start out with more mana, more hit points, more everything. They appear to be a base copy of us, so they won't have our more advanced abilities." Murmur hoped she sounded more confident about that observation than she felt, because this already felt far too easy. At least the sludge didn't permeate out to this cavern.

"They're not going to approach us if we don't approach them, unless you know something I don't." Veranol drawled the words out, sounding bored, or perhaps tired.

"Because the rest of us decided to keep what we know a secret from you so you'd die and we could laugh about it." Havoc's sarcasm was on point—perhaps too on point.

Murmur nudged him with her elbow and lowered her voice even though she knew the words would echo. "What the hell is your problem right now?"

He ran a hand through his hair and bit his lip, casting his eyes down and refusing to look at her. "I'm not sure. I'm just on edge, and this dungeon doesn't seem like fun at all. I also hate dark open spaces that aren't the sky. I have no idea what's up there in this cavern. I didn't expect a... trap to be so realistic."

Ah, there it was. Merlin's death had seemed so real, so brutal, and so downright unavoidable it was giving Havoc a minor panic attack. "It's okay. He's fine. We're all fine, and now we know to be much more careful."

"It's not that, Mur. What if it had been—" But he let the words dangle and looked away again, anger rolling off him in waves.

Except it wasn't difficult to fill in the blanks, and everyone there knew it. Everyone had heard.

What if it hadn't been Merlin that got impaled by that stake? What if it had been Murmur?

Somnia Online
Firtulai Continent
Richnai Fortress Caverns
Late Day Fourteen Post Launch

Jirald wiped his arm across his forehead as adrenaline coursed through his veins. The difficulty level of the mobs in this place was above and beyond anything they'd encountered before, and it was exhilarating. It was even more difficult than fighting Fable had been, but at least this time they could mostly control the odds.

"You seem to be having fun," Masha observed as another of the rabid gnome miners fell to the ground, its little ears twitching.

"Fun is subjective." Jirald knew he was grinning widely, and likely not all that sanely. He also knew there was going to be a shard in this place, and it drove him to new heights, to try harder and kill faster. The power Sidius promised was within his grasp, or at least some of it.

The power to make his mark, and to teach *her,* and everyone else, lesson.

"It's disconcerting seeing my brethren massacred like this." Ishwa eyed the bodies of the pale green gnomes. "Guess that's what you get for drinking potions you shouldn't have touched."

"You're not a green gnome." Jirald chuckled, far more at home in a dungeon stabbing shit from behind with a warrior tank who knew what the hell they were doing than in a meeting hall talking non-stop. Eslan main tanking was a godsend. He turned the mobs; he knew how to maneuver them and avoid shit on the ground while positioning their targets in such a way that the melee

DPS didn't have to stand in ground damage if they had a brain.

A nagging thought emerged at the back of Jirald's mind. More like a pressure to continue, to delve deeper and complete his quest. He frowned, never liking to be told what to do, but at least this had a purpose: to make him stronger.

"That face right there." Masha broke Jirald out of his reverie. "That's the face of concentration with a bit of madness. Might not want to focus on the latter so much there, mate. It's what drives people away."

Jirald shrugged, intensifying his expression. "More loot for me then."

"Ever the optimist." Masha moved ahead, following Eslan through the corridors until they came to a stout wooden door, bound in iron. He frowned, and the warrior turned to face him.

Jirald watched as they discussed what to do, seething somewhat because it used to be his place to plan this with the tank, to lead and keep the raid alive. Even if he grudgingly had to admit that Masha was suited to leading, that he led with a strong hand and people seemed to like him—it didn't change the fact that leading had been a point of pride for Jirald. But his current behavior hadn't exactly led the members of the guild in this game to trust him.

He could be charming, couldn't he? Hadn't he always been able to get his way, or had it been his position within the guild that got him the respect he'd thought he had?

Either way, at least Masha was helping him get to his goal. No one else had the quest, and it wasn't sharable. The cleric motioned him over, and Jirald grinned as he picked the lock as silently as possible. It was entirely on the cards that there were enemies behind the large wooden door. This was the entrance to the keep, and thus it stood to reason that there were going to be guards at a juncture like this. Doing that whole guarding thing.

Eslan opened the door to reveal exactly that. Three hulking gnome guards, about twice the size of a usual one, almost the same size as a human. They wore gleaming silver-blue colored armor and bore weapons made in the same hue. There was madness in their eyes, in the red lit glare.

Their bard had his hands full, as the only enchanter in the guild wasn't even twenty-five yet. Testing the waters, they only took one mob at a time, and area of effect spells were banned until they figured shit out. Just the way it always went. Find, test, wipe, and destroy.

The guard fought like the dickens, faster than Jirald had thought gnomes capable. Except Ishwa knew them and had people positioned accordingly. Eslan took the hits, and all of the melee DPS, Jirald included, made sure to interrupt any spell the guard began to cast, stopping it in its tracks. Frustration spread over the mob's face as its health dwindled.

Jirald activated his Backstab technique, lined up with the precise spot on the rear of the spin where he'd pierce through tendons and ribcage and reach the heart. Slamming his dagger in to the hilt in the mob's back, he scored not only a critical hit, but a vital one. The body stiffened and then toppled to the ground, the last eight percent of its hit points disappearing instantly.

Masha nodded at him. "Feeling better now?"

Jirald just grinned. "Dandy, Masha. Fucking dandy."

CHAPTER TWENTY-EIGHT

Fighting Yourself

Murmur drew in a ragged breath, none too impressed with the difficulty of fighting herself. She wasn't sure exactly what Riasli had used to trigger this type of effect, but damned if she didn't want to learn that spell. Maybe the traitorous enchanter had simply twisted an existing mechanic. Either way it sure was intriguing. Murmur's hand to hand skills were negligible, just like her weapon skills, so her problem didn't lie there.

What she was having difficulty with was her other self's magical resistance. Even stripping her down with Nullify, it could cancel that magical effect out. Not that Murmur couldn't do the same, but it was basically a who-could-cast-faster fight, and while Murmur could resort to casting about seventy-five percent of her abilities without the hand gestures, it was only marginally faster than her mirror twin.

She didn't have time to worry about the others, because she was occupied fully by herself. Taking a deep breath, she pulled out Flux, hoping it would stick for its full duration, and then she DoT'd the thing. Life leeched away slowly, and landing two nukes inside of that window was barely anything. She sorted through her MA abilities in her mind, as well as her expanded ones. Surely there had to be something there to use.

And then it hit her. Her opponent didn't seem to have the same level of spells and abilities as she did. Just the basic skills and hit point pool. Its armor also didn't seem to contribute. She couldn't help the excitement in her voice as she raised it slightly to let the others know. "They're just the basic version of ourselves."

"'Just' she says." Exbo laughed, filled with nervousness and perhaps a tinge of fear. "It's just fighting ourselves, Mur."

"I know. But it doesn't think like you; it can only react to what you do, so you have the chance to out think it." It made sense in Mur's head, and she hoped it made sense for her friends, but she no longer had time to think about if it did or not. There was a sense of urgency egging her on, a need to finish this so they could move on, because she didn't think those glow sticks and fire arrows they'd left the remaining children with were going to last too much longer. Fighting another enchanter—even if it was herself—wasn't an easy feat.

Her best rotation consisted of stuns, because her DoT was able to tick while the mob was stunned. She refused to keep thinking of it as herself, because it wasn't, and it couldn't be. She had a four second recast gap between firing off her stuns though, as she hadn't yet received her third stun. Of course, there was always the risk of it being resisted anyway, but so far, it hadn't been. And the range seemed to fall just short of the combatants next to her, so she wasn't infringing on their fight.

As the second stun wore off, she had a Mez ready to go, and just didn't nuke in the time it took for the timer to reset. The three second tick of the DoT allowed for the Mez to mostly hold the other self for long enough that Murmur's stuns were back up. Since the zone went haywire, she no longer had any idea what to expect.

One thing she noticed during the fight was how quiet it was outside of their battle. Sure, she could hear the clashing of steel as Devlish and Beastial fought with their own clones, and the casting coming from Sin and Havoc next to her. But the wailing undertone to the zone had stopped. The children expected them to return, trusted their word, so Murmur knew they couldn't fail. They wouldn't. It just wasn't an option.

Pixelated or not, those kids were very real to her. She squared her jaw and continued to whittle away at the other enchanter's health, willing it to not get off a cast in the split second it had to do so and not wanting to admit how lucky she'd been to get the first stun off.

Considering her opponent didn't have the gear boosts that Murmur did, only in appearance, their hit point pool and mana pool were both pitifully lower than her own. And she didn't have Snowy, who was flitting around and biting the other enchanter's legs and heels, and generally just taking out his anger on her. Which meant it hadn't evolved its MA abilities past some point in time. So where was it that Riasli had pulled the information from? What was it Riasli had access to? And why had she sent obviously inferior monsters to attack them? Perhaps they were just a time sink.

Murmur shook her head, trying to clear out the thoughts. First things first. She had to defeat her clone, and then she could worry about finishing the dungeon and freeing the children, because if there was one thing she knew for certain, this wasn't the end boss fight. This was a distraction, and she couldn't help wondering from what.

While combat wasn't difficult, it was drawn out. Mainly because all of the skills they pulled from allowed their opponents to pull from the same. Murmur groaned by the second time she'd been dispelled. She couldn't be bothered recasting Mana Tide, though. Her low damage spells were lucky she had Snowy to rely on, because otherwise her twin was never going to bloody well die. And the bad thing was no one could come and help her.

Jinna had managed to finish his own opponent off quite quickly, and he moved to assist Sinister, who was having a hell of a time considering she was fighting another healer. Talk about the duel that wouldn't end. But as soon as he attempted to hit her mob, it respawned his. And he had to fight it all over again.

So, helping the others was out. All they could hope was that Veranol and Sinister did more damage to the others than their heals enabled them to cover, because they had buffed stats and the clones did not. It was a tedious waste of precious time.

"This is so fucking boring!" Beastial roared, sending in Shir-Khan cloaked and ready to go rogue on his clone's ass.

It wasn't a challenge as such, but more of a test of endurance, and Murmur was failing it abysmally. It was all she could do not to scream out just like Beastial had. She groaned, releasing what she hoped would be her last stun, and nuked three times in quick succession only to see her twin vanish in a cascade of sparks that burned her up from the head down and left a small pile of soot sitting in its place.

Murmur frowned, but she didn't dare approach it yet, considering how drastic the reaction to Jinna had been. She glanced around. Both rangers, Mellow, Dansyn, Beastial, and Jinna were done. Veranol and Sinister were going to take forever at this rate, but she'd expected that from the start. Havoc finished shortly after she did and stood scowling at the spot where his twin had collapsed.

"This is wrong. There wasn't even a point to these mirror images. What did Riasli gain by putting these in our way?" He asked the questions of no one in particular, but Murmur felt like she could answer.

She'd put them in their way to delay their progress, to frustrate them at the pointlessness of the fight, and because their first reaction was to fight the clones in order to bypass them. She'd never even contemplated that not fighting them might be an option. "You know, maybe we just did exactly what she wanted us to do."

"How do you mean?" He lowered his voice, eyes darting around to make sure everyone else was busy.

"It's not that big a secret, but what if we hadn't engaged them? They only did what we did—would they have followed us?" Riasli was thinking outside the box, and Murmur was still stuck in the mold of an enchanter and not in the mold of the puppet master she probably should be. What use was choosing the Sinuous line otherwise? "I mean, we didn't fight all of the obstacles in Hightower, did we?"

His brow wrinkled in concentration and he thumbed at his chin again.

"That's a really good thought, if a little late." He squinted, trying to look past the line where the opponents had been and into the darkness beyond. The only people left fighting were the healers. "She could have been betting our focus would be on getting to her to stop all this madness. Pretty good bet if you ask me."

Murmur nodded. "Exactly. I might have to admit that she totally played us."

She studied the huge hall again, knowing she was missing something because there was a persistent wriggling at the back of her mind. Bringing up her HUD once again, she attempted to resend the message to her mother. Barely keeping her frustration under wraps, she checked the guild chat again.

There was no way that no one had spoken in that long a time, which meant she couldn't send messages out and couldn't receive messages while in the dungeon. Or at least it appeared to be so. Should she ask the others if they could too?

Murmur quickly pulled up the browser, trying to figure out if they could use outside internet, but it drew a blank as well. If they were all connected and inside a game, how the hell was the internet not available to her? Sure, Somnia as a world didn't have internet, because it didn't have electricity either. Yet, that didn't explain why were they cut off in here, and if it was only her. Just when she'd been ready to send her mother a message too. Sinister finally finished her twin off with Veranol close behind.

"Well, that was damned annoying," she huffed, and sat down to drink a bottle of water to help with her mana regeneration. "What was even the point of that? No loot, none of our in-depth skills. Just a tiresome and irritating waste of time."

"Maybe Riasli needs us to be distracted for some reason?" Murmur offered, still not sure why.

"Probably so she can prepare more booby traps." Merlin's joke fell a bit flat, but Murmur was quite certain he didn't put his heart into it. "You have a point. There's some reasoning behind this. Maybe we were too fast for her. Jinna, check for traps again?"

The dwarf moved forward, nodding.

And then the ashes began to swirl in a whirlwind, and a loud cackling filled the room.

It took several seconds for the dust to settle as the breeze caught it from underneath. A sickly, orange-red light shone from between cracks Murmur couldn't even feel it with her fingers, and it leant the swirling ashes an eerie pallor as they slowly moved, coalescing into a form that was, at first, difficult to determine.

It rose up, slender and tall, but not like the massive guard statues they'd encountered at the entrance. Maybe eighteen feet tall or close to it. Murmur wasn't sure where the analytical side of her was coming from in amidst this crazy dungeon. Perhaps her brain was feeling the fatigue, or maybe she'd just gotten used to outrageous things happening one after the other.

Finally, a large elf stood in front of them, an odd frown on their face reflecting consternation and not the evil snarl Murmur was expecting. She noticed a flurry of movement behind their right foot.

"Riasli! Stop hiding!" she yelled out, knowing it wasn't going to do a bit of good.

The cackle had to belong to the feles enchanter, because it echoed through the room again. "Of course I'm going to hide. I have things to do, and killing you all is just too trivial a task to undertake myself."

"So, you're going to pull the stereotypical bad witch act?" Sinister crossed her arms. "That's minimum effort for you."

Riasli stepped to the side of the giant's body and glared at Sinister. "I'm not going to bite, you know. And I'm not a bad witch. You're all just brainwashed by those damned AI. You should thank me. At least this might help open your eyes."

"Oh no, woe is us." Beastial's tone held the definition of boredom in it and Shir-Kahn growled low in his throat. "Where do we send the thank you card to?"

Riasli laughed, but not the evil maniacal laugh of earlier. No, it was the same bell-like laugh she'd used when Murmur met her at the Curet enchanter guild. "Nice try, but I have things to do, and I'm sure Akelu will take excellent care of you."

The giant elf started at his name, eyes darting around wildly trying to find the source of the voice, but turning around didn't seem to be an option for him. Murmur eyed the mob and realized with a touch of her Thought Sensing net that he was being controlled, too. Some massive level of charm spell she had yet to receive, or that was perhaps a glitch in the system. Considering the current state of chat and internet access outside of the game, she wouldn't have been surprised if it was all Riasli's fault. Was she malfunctioning and causing the world around her to warp? Because Murmur highly doubted she was acting as intended. All of her actions were so individual, as if she'd developed her own distinct persona. Given the other AIs, maybe that wasn't entirely impossible.

"You're forcing him to do this." Murmur stated, not wanting to hear lies as an answer if she phrased it as a question.

"We're enchanters, Mur, dear. You need to lighten up. We have the power to control, the power to set the boundaries, the power to infect the mind. What better playground than a bunch of undeveloped psyches just waiting for me to drain all of their delicious and potent power?" Riasli's laughter rang cruelly through the zone this time—the flip side of the coin. Murmur opened her mouth to respond, but the other enchanter was far too fast.

"Anyway." Riasli stood up straight, brushing her hands against each other as she did so, glancing at the ground with a small smile of victory and made Murmur wish she could see what had been done. "I have so much to do. Places to be, things to set up, people to kill or lure into traps. Oh. Just like you."

"Get back here!" Jinna yelled, his voice filled with anger.

Riasli chuckled this time, further infuriating the dwarf if the red of his face was anything to go by. "Oh, my darling man. Would that I could. But I have to prepare things you know. Or else he'll just get so mad!"

In an instant, Riasli was gone, simply disappeared, and Akelu blinked as if his eyes suddenly came into focus. Murmur didn't have time to dwell on Riasli's words, because the huge elf began to summon blue fire in the palm of his left hand.

Storm Entertainment
Somnia Online Division
Game Development Offices Artificial Intelligence Server Room

Late Day Fourteen Post Launch

Shayla lifted her head briefly and eyed Laria. Nothing they'd been able to find on their end indicated any type of problem in the game. Everything seemed to be running normally. But they'd not been able to send messages to Wren, Harlow, or Evan. Actually, when that occurred, they'd sourced the guild's information online and sent messages to every single person they knew of who was supposed to be raiding with Wren. All eleven of them. None of the group responded, even though Shayla and Laria could send each other links and messages through the game if they each logged in.

There were no complaints about communication or any other glitches from anyone else who was currently playing, so it appeared to be concentrated in that one area. That it was the area Murmur was currently active in seemed far too big a coincidence.

"You ready? You might not like what they have to say," Shayla asked her friend, watching Laria closely for any signs of the breakdown she knew had to be just around the corner.

"I'm okay. I'm not about to run screaming in the other direction. Stop looking at me like that." There was an air of irritation in her voice, and Laria sighed, taking a deep breath. "Sorry. Of course I'm ready. Activate the biometrics so we can get in already."

Shayla smiled to herself and obliged, bending down slightly to let the scanner hit her iris while she simultaneously scanned her fingerprints. After Michael, they'd doubled down. They had to. Their servers were far too important to have people snooping around. It was also fortuitous that he didn't have family to worry about, because if anyone else got trapped like that and they were going to be up to their necks in lawsuits. She was barely keeping Ava's family at bay. At least the police report helped there.

She shook her head to clear the thoughts as they entered the room, noticing how tightly Laria held her laptop as she entered, almost crushing her chest with it. She'd wanted to be able to witness whatever it was the AI could do—if they could do anything—first hand. Shayla didn't blame her. With that group of players going out of reach like this, effectively off the monitoring grid, the whole incident was becoming more and more surreal.

"Take a deep breath, Laria, they're going to help us." She eyed the servers, noticing far more activity than usual. Lights flashed back and forth so fast that for a couple of moments it appeared they were never off. "Maybe they already know why we're here."

Laria leaned against the table in the middle of the room, flipping open her laptop so she could adjust to it through her augmented reality contacts. The ones she wore on a daily basis didn't have the power to boot up the game by themselves, thus she brought her laptop so she could interact, or perhaps show the AIs just what she meant.

"What are you all up to?" Shayla propped herself up against the wall closest to the servers, making sure she could keep them all in her view, hoping she'd notice any type of pattern that emerged in their communication.

"We are busy today. Much needs to be addressed to keep things running smoothly as the adventurers travel further out into the world." Thra's tones were about as soothing as an artificial intelligence unit could be, at least within the parameters of speaking from her server housing. Shayla only wasted a moment wondering why she found it so easy to attribute personas to the AIs. That was just it; they made it easy to do so.

"Can you define what it is you're currently addressing in the game, please?" Laria's tone was formal, and she wasn't looking at anything in particular, so Shayla knew she was engrossed in the developer interface for the game.

Thra's server whirred a little louder before she responded. "We are attempting to validate several zone implementations."

"Speak to me in I'm-not-a-server language, please." Laria crossed her arms, a small scowl tugging at her lips. She wasn't about to be dissuaded from her trail.

Thra's server lit up momentarily, almost like she was arguing with someone they couldn't see. Shayla watched in fascination.

"There have been several complications with the raiding zones for the end game key items. Considering these zones are required to scale with the players as they enter so long as they're able to fight opponents level thirty and over, they require some fine tuning in order to assure that things will run smoothly."

Shayla blinked at the AI. It was one of the best non-answer answers she'd ever heard, and she included Teddy Davenport's answers in the ones she compared it to. "Which zones in particular are we talking about, and what precisely is the problem?" Shayla didn't feel like wasting any more of their time in here than she had to.

If the AI were being obtuse, and she was quite certain Thra was doing so deliberately, then the direct question requiring a specific answer was the only way to figure them out. She'd leave her thoughts about why they were trying to hide something in the first place for later.

Just as she expected, Thra's machine lit up again, and this time Rav's did so in response. The lightshow was quite effective in demonstrating what Shayla assumed was an argument between AI units.

Finally, it died down, and this time Rav's voice filled the room. "You know which zones we're talking about, or else you wouldn't be here. The Ruins of Cenedril and the surrounding Curet Rainforest, insofar as it comes under the domain of the Ruins." He paused for a moment, his lights a beautiful array of gradating colors. "I'm quite certain you also already know who is in there. Next time, please have enough respect for us to ask directly what it is you wish to know instead of trying to trick us into revealing something you're fishing for. We don't have the time to play games on the outside while trying to run the world of Somnia in here. And it's dangerous to assume we do."

Well, that was something she never thought she'd witness. Getting taken down a few pegs by a computer. Literally. They were disgruntled. How did an AI become disgruntled? Shayla opened her mouth to speak, but Laria beat her to it.

"Look. You're an artificial intelligence unit that was made to do what you're doing. My daughter is in there. My daughter's mind is running around in your world accessing a heap of shit I can't explain to myself." She took a breath, and Shayla marveled at the evenness to Laria's tone.

"I need you to stop this busy nonsense and get to the root of the problem and either help me figure it out, or figure it out yourselves. Either way, I need to know why the fuck I can't seem to track, see, observe, or interact with my daughter in any way while she's in that fucking zone." Laria's tone dropped. "What the hell happened to that zone anyway?"

A ripple of sound flowed around the room, like the AIs were sighing in unison.

"You're right, of course." Sui's tones were more subdued than Shayla had ever heard them, and she felt a flare of concern.

For Sui to be less confident, to not be the one commanding or pretending to do so, things had to be worse than she expected. She almost didn't want to know.

After a couple more moments, Rav spoke up again. "That's fair. We apologize. There has been a glitch in the servers' interpretation of programmed directions. In short, one of our NPCs has grown in an unanticipated way. It is reacting outside of its programmed parameters, and we are attempting to head her and her agenda off before she can do anymore damage, or before it becomes irreversible."

"Let me guess—" Shayla had known, but having it confirmed made her wish she'd been wrong, "—Wren's stuck inside the portion the NPC has taken over and altered, correct?"

"Affirmative." Sui shot the answer out so fast, Shayla started slightly, not having expected it.

Laria stood and began pacing, hugging herself. "But it's not just her, is it? It's her friends too. At least they're with her, but we can't reach any of them. Can they even log out? What's going to happen to their bodies out here?" Panic started to infringe upon her words as she finished, and her deep breath following her questions was more akin to gasping.

Shayla was stunned. Sure, she'd realized that they couldn't seem to contact the whole group, but she'd never given thought to their bodies or their log out capabilities. But Laria had one of those bodies in her house, so it only stood to reason it was something she was focused on.

Silence followed, only interrupted by some intermittent whirrs and beeps. Shayla waited, the seconds growing longer the more time passed. Just as she was about to say something, as Laria looked ready to burst into tears, Rav spoke up again.

His voice seemed tired, not something Shayla had ever expected to hear from an AI. Weary and a bit frustrated, but overall, he sounded empathetic.

"It's their whole small raid group. We are investigating what's gone wrong. The reason we appear evasive is that we don't have answers for you yet. We're not giving you answers because we do not have them. There are algorithms behind walls that misdirect us. We're getting closer but having to dig through an amount of code so huge, it almost feels like a virus. We promise you, we're not just letting this go."

A chill crept down Shayla's spine. For the AIs not to know what happened in their own world was unsettling. "You mean this happened and you only realized it when you noticed Wren not there?"

She knew Rav had been tracking her, just like Laria had.

"It was sudden. She was there, and then she wasn't reachable. I traveled directly to the location, and the ruins are not what were there a few days ago. I couldn't approach them, as a bubble kept me out. We routinely check everything, but we're investigating the glitch we believe is tied to one rogue NPC."

"This NPC is rogue?" Shayla raised her eyebrow, trying hard not to sigh with relief that Wren and her friends were but a handful of gamers currently even able to experience the glitched content. "How did that happen?"

This time Rav hesitated, and Sui stepped in. The transition was almost seamless, but just enough that Shayla noticed something off.

"That's what we're investigating. Since we've been experimenting with allowing an increased amount of autonomy to our sub AIs, we think something may have occurred in their processing of certain data. Similar to a loophole." Sui's voice held a smooth tone, like a used car salesman of old. "Rest assured we're doing everything we can."

Laria glared at Sui, obviously having noticed the pause between the two AI units. "It's not enough. Get them back and do it now."

"We can't work faster than we are, Mrs. Summers." Rav sounded genuinely sad. "But I assure you, we're doing everything we can to restore the area."

CHAPTER TWENTY-NINE

Akelu

Akelu stood proud and tall, his eyes glowing the same fire blue as the flame growing gradually in his hand.

Merlin spoke softly, yet loud enough for it to carry. "I don't understand. He's one of the elves in the center statue in Cognitia. He's one of our heroes. Legends have been written about this guy. Akelu the great, grand, survivor—whatever you want to call him. He's not evil. He's a herald of good and healing."

"What heals can also kill." Sinister muttered, allowing a sheath of red to encase her own hands, not taking her eyes from their would-be opponent.

"He's also not this Naishi person the guards mentioned." The others rumbled in discontent.

"Pretty sure that's the name the zone has given Riasli," Murmur spoke softly as she watched Akelu gathering power.

On a whim, she stunned him.

Your flux spell has little to no effect on such a great being. In fact, you've probably just pissed him off. Perhaps think it over more before trying that again.

She blinked at the message. The system's sarcasm had ramped up a notch since they entered the dungeon. Then she groaned as Akelu's gaze fell on her. She'd acted impulsively, drawing attention to herself, and now, in hindsight, realized she probably should have cast out her Thought Sensing net before she acted.

He was angry at her, probably for daring to stun him, but at the same time a tone of bewilderment underlay all of his thoughts. Akelu couldn't seem to understand why he was fighting them, only that he was compelled to do so. They weren't thoughts so much as feelings, sensations sweeping through him and out of his control, because right now nothing was in control.

He was under Riasli's power. While mind control was often used in-games as a mechanic, it normally had a short and visible duration to the one under control. Somehow Akelu had been charmed, and it didn't appear to have any duration, because his panic was obvious and full and with a countdown he could see, he might not have been so flustered.

The flame grew ever slowly in his hands, and Murmur could sense that he was trying his best to slow it down. Something in his core had survived the compulsion he was under. There was a part of him still aware that he wasn't originally a villain, and while she could feel the effort it cost him, he was going to ultimately lose the battle of wills. He didn't understand the situation, and she had to admit, neither did she.

"I think we're going to have to fight him. He's being controlled, and the only way to free him is to figure out how to break it, which I have no idea how to do, or else to kill him." Just like they'd done with all the previous victims in this dungeon. She watched the elven legend begin to move. They weren't all that short against him. They came up to mid-thigh, so enlarging potions weren't necessary, but she still felt small against him.

"Will he come back?" Merlin sounded highly reluctant.

"What use would a dungeon be if its boss couldn't respawn?" Havoc used logic, his tone even and soothing. It was a nice change from the rampant sarcasm he'd been prone to earlier.

"True. Pretty crappy game if only one guild at a time could get to a boss, I guess." Some of Merlin's pre-getting-impaled-by-a-large-stake attitude poked through.

Murmur couldn't help the wave of relief that passed over her. Meanwhile, she concentrated on Akelu's eyes and kept her thoughts to herself. If he wasn't the original endgame in the dungeon, she had no idea if he could come back. Surviving the fight was paramount, but she'd still try to figure out if she could break the charm while they fought. It had worked for the Guardian, maybe it could work here.

Her stuns were useless, and slowly but surely the bright blue of his eyes was overpowered by the icy blue flames. They glowed unnaturally, and his skin took on an undead pallor. While she knew he was alive as such by the irritated *tsk* of Havoc's disappointment next to her, he seemed eerily taken over.

She shuddered as he threw his head back and screamed. It was such a raw sound that her chest ached for him. It was eye-opening to realize that this is what an enchanter could do. Or an evil enchanter. Completely take over a being and force them to act outside of their usual tendencies. And all the while the person you were was still locked away inside, desperately fighting to get out. Taking control over minds, taking away their autonomy, forcing will on them—wasn't that evil by nature?

A sinuous whisper began in the back of her mind. What if taking others over was how she was meant to play? What if it was the next step in her evolution as an enchanter? And how did she feel about it? After all, surely it was okay to take possession of things in order to reach a desired outcome. Surely no one would mind if she just...

Snowy's head bumped her hand at just the right moment. She glanced down, blinking at her companion, and the thoughts fled her mind, leaving behind a trail of anger that made her frown.

"Thanks, bud," she whispered to him, wondering just where her mind might have wandered had he not interfered.

But Akelu's movement pulled her out of her thoughts. He'd finally succumbed to the force of Riasli's will and was headed straight toward her, a feral gleam in his eyes she hadn't thought him capable of. While she had to concentrate on every fight given her role and circumstances, something told her she had to be even more alert during this one.

Devlish was there in an instant, throwing out his Hatred and forcing

Akelu to look at him. While the giant elf glanced back over at Murmur a couple of times with utter reluctance, the dread knight ended up wrestling their opponent's attention solely for himself. She waited for that moment, for its attention to turn solely to Devlish before debuffing it. She'd acted rashly on a whim and it was best for her not to pull aggro during the actual battle. Veranol had lesser versions of some of the debuffs she had, so she gladly overrode them. Having his on first would make her aggro less because the mob was used to a smaller reduction already.

The smash of the elf's magic against Devlish's shield shook the entire area. Sparks of black and red and icy blue shot out like fireworks. Crumbles of stone showered over them all, bathing them in a fine dust that made Shir-Khan sneeze. Blue sparks flew from the shield, cascading through the air, only to be swallowed by light that shot up through the indiscernible cracks in the ground. As they merged with the light, it grew brighter and swirled around like it was going down a drain until it was merely a subtle glow beneath them. A sudden wave of apprehension swept over Murmur. The light was never just going to be for show.

"Keep together," she directed, worried that the floor was going to shoot something out at them once it had saved up enough magic. Not that they'd been far apart to start with, but if they could avoid the glowing section of floor, it would only help them in the long run. Staying out of shit was always paramount to staying alive.

Devlish grunted each time he blocked an attack, the strain visible in the way the veins in his neck stood out. His strong arms strained with the weight of each blow.

"Mellow!" he called out, squeezing the name from between clenched teeth.

The witch obliged, tossing a vial of growth serum with amazing accuracy. Devlish gasped as he grew, now able to rival Akelu in height at just a few feet shorter. The difference for the tank was noticeable, while for the DPS it only mattered that they make their shots as accurate as possible, which was something they'd grown used to doing.

Akelu squealed in pain, and Murmur took her eyes off Devlish to find the cause. An arrow jutted out of his left eye. Most of it hadn't made it through; it appeared to be just the arrowhead as the giant elf yanked it out of the wound, sending blood gushing down his face. He chanted in a language Murmur didn't understand and placed his right hand over it briefly. When his hand came back, the wound was gone, but the fire in the eye had gone out.

Merlin glared at the mob, knocking another arrow, a look of sheer determination crossing his face. Murmur had no doubt it had been him who'd sent the initial shot. But Akelu would be warier now. While the wound closed, his health had remained the same, even though the bleed effect didn't last and wouldn't reduce it further. Murmur filed the information away to examine later.

She watched his life tick slowly down to ninety-one percent, just as the light coming through the floor off to the right-hand side caught more of the stray power sparks from his spells and glowed its brightest yet. A light rumble began under their feet, and Murmur suddenly knew with absolute clarity what was about to happen.

"Dan, get here now!" she screamed frantically.

He heard the panic in her voice and his face paled. He moved, bard speed helping him on his way. But not even that saved him completely.

When Akelu hit ninety percent, the farthest portion of floor to the right back corner cracked and caved in. Dansyn still had one foot in the collapsing portion, and barely caught the side of the floor as he went down. His songs faltered as he flailed, barely hanging on with the fingers of his right hand.

"Shit!" Exbo dropped his bow and ran to grab Dansyn's free hand. Havoc made it over as well, leaving his pet to do the damage, and they managed to haul Dansyn up to safety.

The bard had lost his coloring. His feles ears lay flat while his tail twitched in irritation. "What the fuck is with collapsing floors? I don't think there's a bottom to that."

He was shaking visibly, but Murmur needed him to get himself together because it didn't matter. They all needed to give this their utmost attention. If she wasn't completely batty, and she didn't think she'd hit that point yet, this was going to happen every ten percent.

"Dan." She spoke as soothingly as she could manage, making sure the way her heart beat fast in her chest didn't affect the way she spoke. She knew the death he'd suffered in Hightower at the tail of the scorpions was nightmare material, she saw intermittently herself. But right now, especially in this particular fight, they needed him alive. "I need you to pull yourself together. We all have to gather in the same spot and keep an eye on the floors. I think the light shining from underneath will give us a hint as to what piece of the floor is going to go next."

"Could have given him more warning," Exbo snapped.

"Sure. If you say so. I yelled as soon as I could, and maybe I should have figured it out earlier, but at least we know now. We can all keep an eye on it." She refused to let the stress of the moment get to her and kept her tone as even as she could.

Sinister and Veranol were hard at work making sure that Devlish didn't bow down to any of the massive hits Akelu was directing at him, and they needed to kill the elf sooner than later. But if they didn't pace their damage enough, they might not have the time they needed to escape the collapsing floor.

"He's alive, and he's safe, and we have another five percent to watch the elf and figure out which piece of floor is next. If we maneuver him properly, it should help us avoid the floor's collapse and lead us to that back door." Murmur pointed in the direction Riasli had used to leave.

"Wait, we need to go back for the kids," Merlin said, knocking his arrows without skipping a beat. "Also, it's the portion of floor one behind and to the left of him."

Everyone began to move, not needing to be told twice. Murmur went with them. The next one had to go smoothly or else her entire theory was out the window. "This isn't going to give us a way back before we make it through to the other side. I don't think this is your usual dungeon."

"You don't say?" Havoc stood, helping Dansyn to his feet. "Let's kill this fucker. I'm getting a little sick of things pulling the rug out from under me."

At least the joke garnered a few chuckles and Murmur couldn't help but be grateful that Havoc diffused the situation. Tension levels were high, but controlled. Now all they had to do was watch for the floor to signal which portion of it would collapse next. Akelu's arsenal of spells was impressive. He was truer to the base mage class Murmur had witnessed in multiple games outside of Somnia. Apart from Ishwa, she'd not seen many of them in this game.

He utilized ice the majority of the time, the cold causing steel to go brittle and breaking more than one of Devlish's weapons, making the tank gnash his teeth in annoyance. Akelu's health dwindled so slowly it was going to be a race to get him dead before mana ran out. Murmur kicked herself for not getting the mana feeder abilities. They would have helped out a whole lot more here. Surely she was due for the damage dealing, mana-sucking example Dirsna had given her way back when.

Merlin led the way for the rangers, Exbo and him moving as one while they loosed sets of arrows at opposite sides of Akelu's body simultaneously. They flew through the air with exacting precision, tails of fire winking after them. The magician in their midst barely even blinked at them, so overcome was he by whatever it was Riasli had possessed him with. He was intent on bearing down on Devlish, and it was the most difficulty she'd seen their tank have.

Luckily, since his focus remained so locked on Dev, it enabled most of them to move around far more efficiently. Beastial and Shir-Khan darted in and out, slicing and biting so fast that they were gone by the time Akelu noticed them. Even a flick of his heel could disrupt their rhythm or else cause them damage, but they avoided every movement of the demi-god carefully, dancing away like they'd been doing it their entire lives. In a way, they had.

Everything they did to prep for huge fights like this was practice. Stay out of the fire, get into the good light, avoid direct attacks and AoE blows, and above all, don't exceed the tank's aggro. Murmur made sure to keep her buff on Devlish, just in case Akelu got any bright ideas.

Jinna's own choreography was similar, except he planted traps for Akelu to step in as the giant elf maneuvered around, poisonous barbs that wound around his legs, leeching into his blood stream to speed up the poison. Murmur filed it away as another reason to avoid getting too close to Jirald.

Mellow stood as far back as was comfortable, with Havoc by their side. Both of them were at the maximum range for their attacks to still hit without standing so far that they couldn't get back to the group if they needed to. Mellow threw poison bombs onto Akelu, hitting him directly with a substance that ate through his clothes, leaving them ragged with burning grey skin showing through.

"Is that acid or fire?" she asked, genuinely curious, noticing the trembling timber to her voice heightened by adrenaline. Murmur didn't take her eyes off Akelu; she couldn't. Not in any boss fight. Focus on his actions, his gaze, and anything that could surprise them. She watched Mellow in her peripheral vision.

"A bit of both." Mellow's expression was grim, their mouth drawn in a thin line as they motioned over the hovering ethereal cauldron, muttering under their breath. "Bubble, bubble, toil and trouble."

"That's seriously how it works then?" Murmur raised an eyebrow as she refreshed her own DoT, reinforced her personal shielding, and reapplied her debuffs. Letting one of them fall at an inopportune moment could mean death for all of them. She'd not heard the witch incanting before.

Mellow grinned so wide it scrunched their lack of a nose, but they too didn't take their focus off the boss while they answered. "Not really, just makes me feel more witchy. The spell is called Bubble Bubble, though."

Murmur nodded. There was no room for smiles, nothing that would break her concentration. She couldn't miss a cue, couldn't miss a beat. One badly timed step could her or kill them all. Only this time, instead of just adrenaline at the rush, a sense of dread lingered in the back of her mind.

Eighty percent came and went, and they danced around another piece of missing floor. Murmur watched their path carefully, mapping it out so they would hopefully be able to make it to the door. Slowly, they wore Akelu down, but the fewer hit points he had, the more the insanity of the blue flame in his right eye glowed. Murmur didn't like the forewarning she felt the glow was giving them, like he was ramping up to some special ability that was going to send them scurrying away like maniacs.

Not to mention the fact that seventy and sixty percent had dropped pieces of the floor she hadn't wanted to lose. Getting Devlish to reposition the hero wasn't an easy task. Akelu was a caster, and silencing spells didn't stay on him for as long as they should. She'd even attempted to use Hypnotic Suggestion on him to no avail. Being a magic user, his resistance to her mind control spells was better than any opponent they'd encountered. And realistically, mind controlling a boss was way overpowered. Riasli should never have had this much power to begin with.

Murmur knew the fight wasn't taking as long as it appeared to be. It was always the way in a boss fight. Every intricate detail tended to stop time, slow it, and have everyone focused on nuances. She noticed her friends stretching and moving, trying to force concentration on a fight that asked for it, yet didn't provide an actual challenge outside of Devlish being able to take hits, and them firing at several joints on the giant with precision.

"This fight is wearing on me. The repetition isn't helping my focus." Veranol grumbled as he meted out yet another ward to protect Devlish from the incoming smash against his shield and body.

Sinister rolled her eyes. "Seriously? Have you learned nothing, Ver? You know you can't—"

But whatever she was going to say got lost in Akelu's roar as his health finally hit fifty percent. It rebounded through the cavern, echoing off the rocks up high in the ceiling, and showered dust and debris down around them all, and the pieces of floor that were still whole began to move.

Somnia Online
Firtulai Continent
Richnai Fortress Caverns
Day Fourteen

Jirald stood panting, clutching his side as Masha gave preference to Eslan to keep the tank alive. If the damned warrior went down, the rest of them were toast. Swigging down a healing potion, he could feel as the skin of the wound knit back together, accelerating the healing process begun by the almost useless HoT their bard sang.

The damned mobs up in the castle proper were more difficult than he'd imagined. Everything about them screamed at him to go back, level himself and everyone else past thirty, and return, because at twenty-nine, it was obvious that one level was too much for their group. Two of them had already hit twenty-nine, and Jirald was close to hitting thirty, but with some of the members of their small raid force still being two levels beneath the guards they were fighting was hurting them. Their attacks glanced off or were resisted for a lot of the potential damage.

There was no easy way to get them leveled up. All they could do was fight mobs and more monsters, constantly. He watched as Masha joined in the DPS, swinging his mace around like a battle cleric. The sentiment was fleeting, but jealousy still rose up so violently, Jirald almost choked as he made his way to fight again, his health almost restored. He hadn't meant to pull aggro, but he'd managed to land a critical backstab just as Eslan got stunned for a couple of seconds.

The only thing that saved him was his ability to Fade. It allowed the rogue to basically drop all aggro for up to five seconds, which gave the tank a chance to gain it back. If the tank was unable to, well, that just left the rogue a bit of a ripe target. That was the good thing about Eslan—he knew what he was doing. Masha might be nice to everyone, but he wasn't one to play with people who weren't good at their class. He meant to get things done, by any means necessary.

Finally, the guard fell to his knees, falling flat on his face as blood slowly leaked out of his wounds. Masha glared at the corpse and began casting his resurrection spell, first on the other healer who'd accompanied them. Once everyone was standing again, Masha whirled on Jirald.

"What the hell was that?" His words came out through clenched teeth, sounding quite calm, but from the flashing of his eyes, Jirald knew Masha was anything but.

"It stunned Eslan just after I landed a critical hit. There was nothing I could do." Except Jirald knew that wasn't right. He should have been paying more attention to what the guard had been casting. He would have known the stun was coming up, should have interrupted the ability with a stun. But he'd been absorbed in doing as much damage as possible and hadn't wanted to interrupt a stellar rotation.

Masha waited, probably seeing the realization as it spread over Jirald's face.

"Oh good, you've reached the same conclusion as I did. Next time, Jirald, don't be such a dick. You could have wiped us completely." Masha paused and began rebuffing the raid while he spoke to the rogue. "I'm just glad you came prepared and have potions on you that let you help with taking him down the rest of the way."

It was the closest he was going to get to giving Jirald a well done, at least any time soon. The rogue swallowed his pride, which was difficult as fuck considering how much he had of it. He needed to get his head out of the quest for the shards and out of his need for revenge if he was ever going to level up and catch Murmur.

"Sorry. I'll start playing like a rogue." Jirald mumbled the words, barely able to get them out through the anger. Most of it was directed at himself, but he couldn't seem to stop glaring at Masha.

The cleric shrugged. "Good, because you're not a healer in here. And even if you play like the best healing rogue ever, it's going to be a shadow of what you could accomplish if you'd just stop dwelling on the fact that you're not what you thought you'd be. Just give into what the game allocated you. And maybe you'll get an inkling of why it did."

Masha turned away in a clear dismissal, done with him for now. Jirald counted to five, trying to get his temper under control, and then ten. Finally, he hit twenty and managed to breathe. He pulled up all of his skills and started going through them while the rest of the raid finished getting ready. Masha had a valid point, not that he'd let him know that. But it was time Jirald mastered the rogue without regrets, and the sudden peace that came over him once he made that decision only cemented it.

He stood up, brushing himself off, eager to break into the fortress proper after having cleared all of the trash out of the way. Maybe he could take out some of his frustrations on the overpowered NPCs. And then do it again once they respawned. The idea made him feel far better about his previous mistake.

Fully buffed, the raid group was almost ready to set out. They stood as a loose group of twelve, milling around while they repaired their gear with bots, and sorted potions, or gained tinctures from the alchemists and guild bank.

Standing toward the back of the group, Jirald took another deep breath, clearing his head, and focusing on his goal. Get the Getashi and level, be the best rogue he could be, and beat Murmur and Fable when they were at the top. Seemed simple enough.

Pain sheared through his right side, just above his kidneys, and he gaped down in horror at the dagger protruding from the wound as blood began to bubble on his lips. He blinked, barely making a noise, but it was just enough for Masha to look back at him.

Staggering forward, Jirald reached out for Eslan's hand, and the level thirty-one tank pulled him into the rest of the group as heals trickled into him from the song and cleric.

"Well." A rogue materialized, pulling from the shadows, clad in an inky black set of armor. Dark elf, his skin was a deep purple, and his hair and eyes were as black as a starless sky. He was slender and short with a lingering sneer. "Missed the critical hit there, I see."

"It's okay, Karn." A softly sarcastic voice clung through the storage area. Behind the rogue, a man in dulled charcoal armor with a lingering black cloud clinging to his every move, pushed through to the front. "Forgive my rudeness. I am Risk, the guild leader of Spiral. And I'd like to thank you for clearing the trash out of our dungeon."

CHAPTER THIRTY

Rewind

Murmur braced herself against the floor, her legs wide in a squat, just in time to reach out to Sinister, who'd been so intent on healing Devlish that she hadn't noticed the floors were moving. Her hand gripped around Sinister's wrist, which jolted Murmur to the ground. Snowy managed to get his teeth around the bottom of her tunic and pull. And all the while fucking Akelu floated away on a different platform with Veranol and Devlish scrambling to get their footing back after the sudden erupting movement.

The shifting platform made for unsure steps on their behalf. Murmur glanced around as soon as she managed to gain her bearings and frowned. She couldn't see a pattern in the way the sections of floor moved. Having cleared out four of them when they collapsed made for a floor puzzle she'd not been expecting. Akelu fought Devlish, locked in a battle that the dread knight was going to lose unless they could figure out a way to keep up with the damage they needed to do.

The platforms moved and locked into place next to another one for approximately five seconds. It was the only window they'd have to change platforms.

Havoc, Mellow, Sinister, Merlin, and Exbo balanced precariously at the edge of their current platform using their ranged attacks for all they were worth. Beastial growled deep in his throat, and she knew he was angry that he couldn't contribute, while Rashlyn and Dansyn paced irritably.

Murmur kept all the platforms in her view while absentmindedly casting her debuffs and weak damage spells at Akelu. Right now he wasn't her concern, as callous as it sounded. She just had to make sure he was as weak as possible and get their group out of the fight mostly alive.

"Do you think a platform is still going to fall at forty percent?" Rashlyn sounded too calm. Murmur glanced at her, noting the way she was biting her fingernails.

"I can't see any light to give us an indication of which one it might be, so if it does, it's not letting us know in advance." Those probably weren't the words Rash wanted to hear, but they were the words Murmur had for her. It'd have to do.

"Great," the monk answered joylessly.

"Rash. Focus. Help me figure out how best to jump these platforms so we can help more, and think less about how frustrating this damned fight is. We're all right there with you." Having to calm her *not* stuck-in-the-world friend down wasn't Murmur's first productivity choice, but Rash had always been there for her, so it needed to be done.

While the platforms didn't seem to have a pattern, some did bump up against each other every twenty seconds for five seconds. Some of them even moved together. The tension in her shoulders was starting to give her a headache. Murmur frowned and raised her voice.

"We need to travel as far as we can on the platforms. We have a five second window to make it from one to the other, so we need to stick together. Line up with me on this side, and as soon as these two platforms stop," she indicated the one approaching them, "we need to cross."

The first time traversing the platforms went smoothly, and luckily it coasted ever closer to Akelu and his battle with Veranol and Devlish. Two more jumps and Beastial, Dansyn, Jinna, Rashlyn, and Sinister jumped to the platform the boss was on. The sections weren't small by any means, but that was more than enough people crowded onto it with the tanks and Akelu.

The rest of them were going to have to consistently jump from one platform to the next in order to stay as close as possible to Akelu. Which was easier said than done, but at least it was possible for the ranged classes to still do damage.

Forty percent came and went with no sign of new attack, or new surprise. Akelu appeared to have unending mana and reinforced his blows with the strength of his craft, sending Devlish buckling to his knees multiple times. They'd fought so long that Mellow had to refresh the growth potion on the tank.

This boss seemed completely focused on the tank, having apparently forgotten his initial anger with Murmur. He rarely lashed out at other players, so focused was he on Devlish. Maybe that focus gave him extra tenacity because the dread knight seemed to be having a time of it. Even pulling out the stops and using all of the abilities he had, Murmur hated to think what would have happened if he didn't have Telvar's shield.

The percentages of his health dwindled, and slowly but surely, Murmur thought Akelu's attacks sped up. Not hugely noticeable at first, but Devlish was barely managing to fend off the attacks now, going down to a knee more than half the time. Veranol's wards disappeared in an instant, and Murmur could practically sense the frustration rolling off Sinister as the healers fought to keep Devlish up.

That regeneration-assisting bard song had never been more practical, because as it stood, the healers barely had enough to keep Devlish alive, and Murmur's little shield was puny in comparison to the giant's attacks. Murmur frowned as Akelu's health approached zero. Down past twenty percent now, and the magical attacks were sparked with red. Which either meant greater force, or contaminated spell weaving. Or, you know, fire. But since he'd had yet to use fire, she highly doubted the latter was true.

Fifteen percent, and that well of foreboding built up in her chest. She knew, instinctively, that something was about to happen. "Shit. I think he has an enrage quotient."

"What now?" Devlish gasped out, as he buckled behind yet another onslaught.

"When he hits a certain percentage, he's going to attack faster and harder, and we'll have to race that timer to his death." Murmur saw the way Akelu's eyes shifted toward her, and the way an almost imperceptible smile crossed over his lips, as if he was relieved they'd figured it out.

"I know what enrage is, Mur!" Devlish yelled, and she sympathized with his frustration, but kept her focus on their target.

Akelu had had enough energy to try and fight the possession earlier on, so maybe this was his way of warning them, of trying to help them help the children of his species. Murmur nodded, not knowing if the boss would see it, but feeling better for having responded.

And then she turned her attention to figuring out how to beat the damned boss and make it to the room beyond.

His health slowly approached ten percent, and Murmur was ready to cringe. "As soon as he begins to launch rapid attacks, everyone needs to burn any DPS cooldowns you have. Like seriously, burn him down. I have a bad feeling we'll barely make it as is."

She couldn't explain the feeling either. All she knew was being separated from the rest of the group gave her tension levels she didn't want to deal with, it left her head and plans split in two trying to figure out how to save them all. Sinister shot her worried glances, like she was thinking of the same things.

Snowy barked from the platform—she hadn't even seen him get onto the same one as the melee, but she guessed it made sense. He focused in on her, like he needed her to understand something. Images flashed into her mind through their connection, broken platforms plummeting down into the abyss beneath them, and suddenly, with alarming clarity, she knew what he meant.

Horror filled her as Akelu's health lowered further. "All to the main platform. It'll be a squeeze and we'll have to be careful, but we need to get on there."

And they were going to have about ten seconds to move to it before he his enrage mode.

But enrage didn't come at ten percent, and Murmur felt like she was on tenterhooks waiting for the damned stage to hit, which it did, at eight percent.

Akelu's eyes lit up, a fiery blue and white, sparking even from the one that

Merlin damaged. He threw his head back and roared, giving them all the warning they needed.

Crowded into place behind his feet, Murmur realized their positions were precarious. But she'd never have guessed how much. Akelu didn't release a rage-filled flurry onto Devlish as she'd expected, but instead shot at the platform they'd just been standing on. Several blasts were all it took to demolish it and send the fragments plummeting below.

But in the same instant he began destruction of the very floor they'd stood on, the rest of their little raid activated their DPS cooldowns. Everyone's movements sped up. Arrows flew faster than Murmur could track with her eyes, and Jinna flitted in and out leaving bloody marks in his wake. Beastial roared louder than Akelu had and his cat joined him.

Murmur nuked for all she was worth too, and she noticed her casting was faster. Checking her system, she saw a buff she'd never seen before. It was white like fur, and she glanced at Snowy, whose teeth were currently ripping at the calves of the giant mage in front of them. He'd sped their attacks up for an amount of time she didn't have the ability or patience to check right now. Just what was Snowy, and why had he chosen to be her companion?

The last few percent were agonizing, as the only ones of them with multiple abilities appeared to be the rangers, beastmaster, and rogue. There were only three platforms left by the time Akelu collapsed, his arm outstretched to reveal a key in his open palm. Murmur knelt down and took the key, pocketing it to go with the one they'd received from Hightower.

And then the platform jolted into motion toward the back of the room. For which she was grateful since she otherwise had no idea how they were going to make it back there. The door opened, revealing a gaping black maw. Nothing inside it was visible, and it felt like spiders were crawling up her spine.

You are the first to defeat Nai...Akelu in the Ruins of Cenedril, and you have gained another of the twelve keys.

Congratulations. You have gained the key of the Ruins of Cenedril. Beware, not all is as it seems. The system's overrides are failing their checks. Please continue with caution.

"What the fuck was that?" Sinister glanced around nervously as Devlish bent to loot Akelu, while a series of dings rang through the air. A series of notifications scrolled past fast for the loot. Murmur dismissed them, saving them for later.

"I don't know, but I don't trust these floating platforms either." Murmur tried to smile and push down on the feelings of unrest she was having. She couldn't even be happy about gaining level thirty-four. Stay on the floating platforms that could fall at any moment, or step through into the unknown darkness.

"Guess we should probably step through then. I don't feel like we've completed everything it has for us yet." Snowy butted her hand, nipping at her fingers gently with his teeth so that she looked down at him.

"What's up, boy?" He wuffed, and she wished she spoke wolf. "I don't understand."

He pushed up against his side, eyes darting around and watching their surroundings.

"Kind of anti-climactic?" Merlin shrugged, his discomfort obvious.

"I thought he was the end boss. I mean, didn't he give you one of the keys?" Havoc ventured, chewing on his lip yet again. "Gate isn't working, like that time on Mikrum Isle when we started the event without knowing."

"Yeah, but apparently Riasli has other plans for us." Gathering up the courage, Murmur poked Devlish. "Come on, oh amazing, took-a-huge-beating tank, let's see what awaits us in there. We can't go back the way we came."

Devlish nodded, his lacerta scales paler than she remembered. "Always moving forward, right?"

Murmur nodded, took Sinister's hand, and stepped from the platform through the doorway.

And everything went black.

Storm Entertainment
Somnia Online Division
Game Development Offices Artificial Intelligence Server Room
Early Hours, Day Fifteen

The message flooded the screen, server wide, bolded in front of the players eyes.

Akelu has been defeated by the guild: Fable.
His corruption has been cleansed, and his spirit is free.

Tertiary dimension initiated. Cautionary shutdown implemented. Please stop what you're doing and begin the log out process. You will be able to log back in momentarily.

A countdown appeared in the corner of everyone's vision, counting down backwards from three minutes. Players scrambled to finish fights, to log out of the game world, some dying in the process. Camps were broken, skirmishes interrupted, and dungeon crawls halted.

An alarm sounded through Laria's system as she watched in bewilderment, the sound finally pulling her out of her stupor.

"What the fuck?" She glared at the screen, accessing commands she never thought she'd have to use. She pulled up the rudimentary original coding for the zone her daughter was in, but it barred her from opening the file. Taking a deep breath, she sought the one for the actual continent, but from what she could see, the Ruins of Cenedril didn't exist, not in the same way it had before.

Nothing worked—the system was overriding all manual input and rebooting itself. I was a failsafe measure to roll things back and correct major errors, but she couldn't figure out what had triggered it. It was undoing everything she'd tried to gain access to the ruins. It didn't make sense.

She had to find them. Not only was Wren missing, but she couldn't find Harlow, Evan, and the rest of her team. Laria took the deepest breath she could, and even then, desperation made it difficult. It would not do to panic. The new reports were due in three days and this was not going to look good on them.

"Laria? What the hell is happening? Why is the system forcing a player logout?" Shayla dashed through the door, her usually calm face panicked.

"I don't know. Why don't you go and ask the powers that be?" Laria snapped, still trying to stop the restart countdown, still trying to find her daughter.

Shayla's expression was incredulous. "What the…"

"Look. I don't know why it's doing this, but I do know one thing." Laria gulped as she tried several programmer commands and failed. "Akelu isn't a boss battle—he's a reward and should never have been in the ruins to begin with."

Appendix

Hi there! K.T. Hanna here.

I want to thank you for reading the Somnia Online series. Due to meeting my partner in EQ2, MMORPGs have a huge place in my heart. You know, in case you didn't notice.

If you enjoyed the book, I ask you, please take a moment to leave a review. *Reviews* are an author's lifesblood. Without them, our books sink into obscurity. With them, most algorithms allow well reviewed books to self-promote in some way.

I hope you love the world of Somnia enough to want to find out more about it! Here are some of the ways you can stay in contact with me:

Want to read more about Fable? Sign up for my <u>Reader's Group</u> and get a short story for free!

If you'd like to contact me, my email is: kthannaauthor@gmail.com I'll do my very best to get back to you

If you'd like previews of what I'm writing, or art I'm commissioning then join my Patreon!

I can be found in the Somnia FB group fairly often, and also on Twitter & Instagram.

If you LOVE LitRPG don't forget to join:
The GameLit Society!

Game Terms

Aggro—When you walk too close to a monster, you get in its aggression radius, thus causing aggro. Once engaged in combat, players must be cautious not to exceed the tank's threat level. Buffs, debuts, and damage output all contribute to the mobs aggro meter.

AOE—Area of Effect. Spells or abilities that effect an area and not just a single target.

Binding/bound—When someone/you bind(s) to an area, you affix your soul to that place in order to Gate back, or else respawn when you die.

Boss—Nope. He doesn't employ you, he employs all the mobs trying to kill you. He hits HARD, and often has special group wiping abilities if not handled correctly by the tank and raid as a whole.

Buff—Most classes will get buffs that strengthen at least themselves if not others. These are effects they can cast which enhance aspects of their character.

Camping—When a group finds a spot that will yield good money and experience, they tend to stay in its vicinity. This is called camping.

Con—To consider a mob and see how difficult the fight could potentially become.

DoT—Damage over Time. This is an offensive spell that applies damage to a target over a period of time at regular intervals.

DPS—Damage Per Second. Usually used in conjunction with offensive classes, or damage output.

Debuff—This is the opposite of a buff and is usually used on mobs to detract from their strengths and make them easier to kill.

End Game—Every game has a goal. In some there's a max level and events and fights only accessible once that level is reached. For Fable, the end game is everything.

Gank—When someone tries to player kill you without forewarning. Often succeeds in taking the victim by surprise.

Gate—You create a Gate to your binding point and travel there instantly.

Grinding—Sometimes gaining levels requires so much camping that it becomes tedious. That's known as grinding levels.

Healer—Well...they heal.

HP—Hit Points. The amount of damage a character can take before death.

Kite—This is a tactic often employed by ranged classes such as the ranger. It entails slowing a mob, and running ahead of it, slowly picking down its health. Can also be used as a diversionary tactic to split multiple mobs if no Mesmerize is available.

Line of Sight (LOS)—If a mob can't see you, but knows you're there, it will have to run around the obstacle to gain access. This is often used to split up larger groups of melee and casters, so it's more manageable for the group. The puller will line of sight the casting/ranged mobs to pull them around an obstacle for easier access and closer contact.

MA—Mental Acuity. A type of power generator specifically for Psionicists.

MANA—Mind juice, used for spells.

Meat Shield—The character who takes the hits in place of the rest of the group. The tank.

Melee—Those fighters who stand in close range and use weapons to fight with are often referred to as melee classes.

Mez—Mesmerize. Freezes in place.

MMO—Massively Multiplayer Online.

MMORPG—Massively Multiplayer Online Role Playing Game.

Mob—an aggressive monster. Can be humanoid or animal.

OOM—Out of mana. Literally what it says.

Newbie—Also known as noob. Someone who has rarely, if ever played an MMO and has no clue what they're doing.

NPC—Non Player Character. Usually not aggressive unless you fuck up.

Pull—Often one person in a group/raid will be designated as the puller, the person who attacks the mob and brings it to camp.

Ranged—A class that can damage (usually) a mob from a distance. Like mages or rangers, etc.

Ranger Gating—Rangers were often known for getting themselves into trouble by kiting mobs in a solo setting. Or else, pulling aggro when DPS-ing. They'd die and resurrect at their bind point, making it what's known as a Ranger Gate.

Respawn—When a mob or a person dies in-game, they will reappear at the spot where their soul was bound. The more powerful the mob, the longer it takes for them to respawn.

Root—A spell obtainable by multiple classes that causes the target's feet to affix momentarily to the ground. They can still cast, but they cannot move until the root breaks.

RPG—Role Playing Game.

Tank—The meat shield aka the person who takes the bit hits for the group. Often needs to be swapped in and out with another tank during larger raids depending on a boss' abilities.

Tether—In some worlds monsters have a specific area they're confined to, and thus stop and don't pursue their prey past a certain point. In Somnia, mobs do not tether. This does not apply to specific purpose NPCs.

Train—When a player or group has managed to aggro a large number of mobs who don't tether, and leads the following of mobs to a specific spot, or through a spot, they call it a train.

Utility class—these are classes whose prime function is to support the group, through abilities that protect or strengthen them as a group or raid.

VR—Virtual Reality.

VRMMORPG—Virtual Reality Massively Multiplayer Online Role Playing Game.

Wipe—This occurs when the entire raid or group die to an encounter.

Murmur

Class: Enchanter – Psionicist

Species: Locus

Real Name: Wren

Sinister

Class: Blood Mage

Species: Dark Elf

Real Name: Harlow

Devlish

Class: Dread Knight

Species: Lacerta

Real Name: Darren

Havoc

Class: Necromancer

Species: Dark Elf

Real Name: Evan

Beastial

Class: Beastmaster

Species: Viking

Real Name: Selwyn

Merlin

Class: Ranger

Species: Elf

Real Name: Mike

Rashlyn

Class: Monk

Species: Feles

Veranol

Class: Shaman

Species: Viking

Mellow

Class: Witch

Species: Dark Elf

Exbo

Class: Ranger

Species: Human

Jinna

Class: Rogue

Species: Dwarf

Dansyn

Class: Bard

Species: Dark Elf

Base Stat Sheet: Level Thirty-Four (34)

 CONstitution: 22

 STRength : 10

 AGIlity: 20

 WISdom: 12

 INTelligence: 66

 CHArisma: 82

 HitPoints: 520

 MANA: 708

 MA: 160

 Abjuration: 179

 Alteration: 188

 Conjuration: 180

 Divinition: 181

 Evocation: 182

 2H Blunt: 156

 1H Piercing: 85

Mental Acuity (MA) Abilities:

Thought sensing.

> Class: Enchanter only.

> Level not applicable.

Developing your inner senses you ve awoken your latent kinetic powers. With constant use your skills will increase, while the opposite will occur should the skill not be used. See your trainer for specifics when you reach Thought Sensing (25).

Thought Shielding.

> Class: Enchanter only.

> Level not applicable.

Developing your inner senses you've awoken your latent psychic powers. With constant use your skills will increase, while the opposite will occur should the skill not be used. See your trainer for specifics when you reach Thought Shielding (25).

Thought Projection.

> Class: Enchanter only.

> Level not applicable.

Developing your inner senses has further developed your psychic powers. Thought Projection can be tricky. Make sure you rever use it in anger, or the results might be surprising. With constant use your skills will increase, while the opposite will occur should the skill not be used. See your trainer for specifics when you reach Thought Projection (25).

Mind Bolt.

> **This ability allows you to cast a spear of mental anguish into the depths of an opponent s brain.**

Effects: Opponents will be unable to concentrate enough to use spells or abilities for four seconds. This time increases as the caster's level does.

> **Cost: Requires Mental Acuity to be at 18.**

Caution: Use sparingly. Backlash from overuse, or improper use can cause the same effect in the caster...or worse.

Phase Shift

This ability allows you to negatively affect your opponent s mind. Believing they are a second or two apart from reality, they will reside there for up to 15 seconds.

Effect: Target's mind is encased in a phase of illusion. The target will be convinced they've shifted to a different time pocket, and thus are incapable of moving. This effect begins at 15 seconds duration, and levels with the caster through to a maximum of 90 seconds.

Cost: Requires MA to be at 38 for larger castings, the cost will double.

Caution: Phase shift may be utilized on single or multiple targets at once. Weigh the amount of targets carefully, else it backfire and shift you. Sometimes the shift in time can cause ruptures near the caster. Make sure the voices you're hearing are your own.

Forestall Death

It applied before potential death takes place, this will enable you to maintain your health at 0.5 hit points as long as you are receiving some sort of healing effect.

Effect: Target is able to ward off death for a limited period of time and will not die when they should have, as long as heals are actively channeled in their direction.

Cost: Requires Mental Acuity to be at 60

Caution: This spell can only be used on one person at a time. Attempting to use it twice at once is not recommended. This will usually result in things worse than death.

Clone Warp

This ability allows you to produce a clone of yourself used for distracting your opponent. Depending on your tier of mastery, you may be able to produce more than one clone.

Effect: All enemies around you will believe that your clone is you for the next 45 seconds, directing their attacks accordingly. The ability expires when the 45 seconds are up, or else, the clone's minor hit point pool has been depleted, whichever comes first.

Cost: Requires Mental Acuity to be at 45 or more

Charming Cooperation

This ability allows you to use your charisma and your mental acuity to persuade monsters, animals, and sometimes even beings to join your cause.

Effects: When using thought projections to make sure your target understands the charming process, before you activate this type of charm. They will work together as allies instead of coerced foes. You may release them whenever you or they request it.

Cost: Requires MA to be at 35 for each ally. Diminishes current total MA for the duration of the cooperation.

Caution: You can use this on multiple targets. But each ally costs, and you can never utilize Charming cooperation on more mobs than is equal to 20% of your level. Also, don't try to charm raid bosses. Even small ones. Like... just don't even attempt that shit.

Mental Acuity (MA) Level Three (3)

Mind Wipe

This ability allows you to reduce your targets threat for you or whoever is at the top of their agro list

Effects: Change aggression list, or make the opponent forget their tasks for a few seconds. Range and duration may be increased as the caster levels.

Cost: Requires MA to be at 55

Caution: This spell can increase in both range and severity From a single target, to a full raid it's all possible. Just remember someone else needs to take that agro, or else you'll be the main target.

Shield Expansion

This ability allows you to extend your individual mental shielding against mental or magical attacks over others.

Effect: If attacked with magic (mind or spell), this shield will protect those under it from damage or effects

Cost: Requires 10MA per person covered

Kinetic Strand – Psionicist

Forcefield Barrier

This is the first in your kinetic line of spells. Once triggered by luck, you can now activate it at will. It allows you to form a bubble of mental energy and transform it into a tangible forcefield.

Effects: This can prevent some physical damage. The damage amount depends on the strength of will and caster behind the barrier. Size is increased by MA level and usage

Cost: This shield requires your MA to be at 60, but will not use MA to cast as it is a kinetic ability.

Caution: This spell can create a backlash when used too much. Do not use it as a crutch.

Base Kinetic Structure

In order to take advantage of your ability to turn thoughts into weapons, you must reinforce the skills that ground all of your telepathic and telekinetic abilities.

Effect: This ability allows you to strengthen the base of all three arms of psionics. Thought Shielding will eventually physically repel an attack. Thought Sensing can break through others shields to reveal what is hidden. Thought Projection can lend solidity to the induced hallucinations managed once skill level 250 is passed.

Cost: This is a passive skill and will begin working to bolster your abilities as soon as you absorb it.

Caution: Do not presume to know how this passive ability works. You will need to test this out. The difference for these abilities between telepathy and telekinesis is very fine. What this ability does is allow your kinetic field to grow at the same rate as your telepathy. What it does not do is make you infallible. Always remember that if you're not sure, you can do more damage than you think. Not only to yourself, but to those you target.

Mental Acuity (MA) Level Four (4)

Forcefield Push

Once used wildly, you can now activate this at will. This will form a bubble of force projecting directly outwards from you in an arc and push anything in its path out of your way. Having this ability directly available will now allow you to develop some measure of control.

Effects: This will cause some physical and mental damage to any opponent caught in the range of the push. The amount of damage inflicted depends on the level and strength of will behind the push. Damage is increased by MA level and usage.

Cost: This push requires that you have MA at eighty, but will not use MA to cast, as it is a kinetic ability. Can only be used once every five minutes.

Caution. This spell can create a mind backlash if over-utilized. Make sure those in your path are not allies, as this ability does not discriminate between friend and foe.

Unless you want to make them a foe. Then they're fair game. Remember, try and maintain control.

Phantom

This ability allows you to convince your enemies that you are a different target. This renders you invisible to their aggro radar for all intents and purposes.

Effect: This ability not only transfers your generated aggro but also takes you off the targetable list for the duration. It transfers aggression to your target, giving them your appearance, and rendering you invisible to any enemy near you. This may be used on allies, but also on enemies.

Cost: this ability requires MA to be at a minimum of 50, drains 5 MA per second, and will adjust as MA level and usage of this ability increase. Requires Charisma to be at 150 or more. Cannot be chained, must wait at least 5 minutes for MA to regenerate.

Caution: Make sure you do not cause your MA to run out. Should that happen, backlash will render the caster unconscious for a period of seconds not less than half the caster's level. Make sure you choose your targets wisely.

Spells:

Level One (1):

Minor Suffocation

    Cast: Single Target

    Type: Damage Over Time

    Duration: 24 seconds

Effect: This spell winds a mind leash around your opponent, as if it were trying to suffocate them. Its damage ticks every three seconds for twenty-four seconds.

Minor Shield

    Cast: Self Only

    Type: Buff

    Duration: 45 minutes

Effect: This casts a minor shield over your skin, increasing your Armor Class by level + 3, and hit points by level + 5.

Simple Animation.

    Cast: Self

    Type: Pet

    Duration: Until death or dismissal

Effect: This summons a magical pet that sort of does your bidding. It costs a tiny sword to cast. Isn't the best at obeying commands.

Level Four (4):

Mesmerize

    Cast: Single Target

    Type: Breakable Stun

    Duration: 24 seconds

Effect: This spell immobilized your opponent for as long as they take no damage, or 24 seconds, whichever is shorter. You may cast non-damaging spells on them, and you may renew this casting before the initial one expires. Casting it on your friends probably isn't a good way to win popularity contests.

Flux

Cast: Area of Effect

Type: Stun

Duration: 4 seconds

Effect: This is a stun that radiates out from the caster for fifteen feet. It will stun anyone who means the caster harm within that radius. Does not produce sparkles.

Gate

Cast: Self Only

Type: Travel

Duration: N/A

Effect: This will transfer you to your bind point

Invisibility

Cast: Self or Others

Type: Buff

Duration: 10 minutes or until broken/seen through

Effect: Causes generic invisibility. Undead don't count. Will drop if you cast a spell or take damage.

Fear

Cast: Area of Effect

Type: Brief Loss of Control

Duration: 25% of level in seconds.

Effect: Causes enemies to flee from you in terror. But if you use it too soon, it'll probably just look like they misplaced something for a second.

Level Eight (8):

Cancel Magic

    Cast: Self or Others

    Type: Debuff

    Duration: Instant

Effect: Casting this spell will remove one magically caused effect from the target. Make sure you want to remove it.

Root

    Cast: Others (or self if you really want to)

    Type: Immobilization

    Duration: 8 seconds

Effect: This will root the target in place. Probably not the best idea to cast it on yourself when fleeing in panic.

See Invisible

    Cast: Self or Others

    Type: Buff

    Duration: 10 minutes

Effect: Really? Does this really require explanation?

Soothe

    Cast: Self or Others

    Type: Debuff

    Duration: Varies

Effect: This will lower the threat level of a target, but it will not make it disappear. Probably not useful on yourself unless in a really bad mood.

Chaos

    Cast: Others

    Type: Direct Damage

    Duration: Instant

Effect: This spell causes direct mental damage to the target, dropping their hit points by two times the caster's level. Requires a recharge.

Level Twelve (12):

Allure

Cast: Others

Type: Charm

Duration: Until broken

Effect: This spell will charm a mob or other player. This ability depends on the casters charisma, and ability to calm their charge. Whatever you do, don't piss them off while under your command. It rarely ends well.

Suffocation:

Cast: Single Target

Type: damage over time

Duration: 36 seconds

Effect: This spell winds a mind leash around your opponent, as if it were trying to suffocate them. Its damage ticks every three seconds for thirty-six seconds.

Bind Affinity

Cast: Self or others

Type: Buff or soul affixer

Duration: Until renewed or overridden with a new location

Effect: This spell binds the target to an area of choice, allowing them to resurrect easier and hopefully closer to their corpse. Because you'll all die. A lot.

Infravision

Cast: Single Target

Type: Buff

Duration: 10 minutes

Effect: Aids the target with a form of night vision.

Stupefy

Cast: Single target

Type: Stun

Duration: 12 seconds

Effect: This will stun a mob in place for around twelve seconds. Probably not a good idea to cast on yourself.

Weakness

Cast: Single Target

Type: Debuff

Duration: 90 seconds

Effect: Reduces the target's strength by 50% of the caster's level.

Languidity

Cast: Single Target

Type: Debuff

Duration: 90 seconds

Effect: Reduces the target's attack speed by 25% of the caster's level in %. Trust us, it's far more effective than you think. Probably.

Nullify

Cast: Single Target

Type: Debuff remover

Duration: Instant

Effect: Strips down magic resistance at 50% of the caster's level.

Level Sixteen (16):

Mana Tide

Cast: Self or Others

Type: Buff

Duration: 45 minutes

Effect: This will cause you to regenerate mana faster in combat. Mana will increase by an additional three per five seconds. This buff levels with the caster.

Invisibility Versus Undead

Cast: Self or Others

Type: Buff

Duration: 12 minutes

Effect: This will render you invisible to any undead in the area. They will be unable to see you, however this buff will fall should you attempt to cast anything else while it's active.

Mass Enthrall

Cast: Enemy Targets

Type: Offensive/Defensive area of effect centered around the initial target.

Duration: 24 seconds

Effect: This is an area effect version of mesmerize. Any damage will break this spell. It's a bad idea to use this while targeting allies.

Haste

Cast: Self or Others

Type: Melee Buff

Duration: 45 minutes

Effect: When cast on an ally, this buff will allow their melee speed to increase by 25%.

Feeble Body

Cast: Enemy Targets

Type: Offensive/Defensive

Duration: 24 seconds

Effect: When cast on an enemy target, their haste will be reduced by 25%.

Shield Illusion

Cast: Self or Others

Type: Defensive Buff

Duration: Until depleted   requires hematite

Effect: Using the power of your mind you cast a shield around your target, confusing the enemies and negating up to 75hp of damage. That whole mind magic thing seems to be working out well, doesn't it?

Level Twenty (20):

Altruism

> Cast: Self or others
>
> Type: Buff
>
> Duration: 45 minutes

Effect: This allows a faction increase to your target. It will lift you one faction level. However, should you be kill on sight, not even altruism can help you. This buff will update again at level 30.

Shift

> Cast: Area of effect
>
> Type: AOE Stun
>
> Duration: 8 seconds

Effect: This stun effectively locks all mobs around its epicenter in place for 15 yards. They will be unable to move for 8 seconds.

Fervor

> Cast: Self or others
>
> Type: Buff
>
> Duration: 45 minutes

Effect: This is an attack speed buff, but it also increases agility by the caster's level. Cannot be cast on the same target as Beserker.

Beserker

> Cast: Self or others
>
> Type: Buff
>
> Duration: 45 minutes

Effect: This buff adds strength to the amount equal to the level of the caster, however it also reduces agility by half the caster's level. Best used for classes or pets who will not need agility stacked. Cannot be cast on the same target as Fervor.

Charismatic

> Cast: Self or others (but who are we kidding, you're an enchanter, you'll never not cast this on yourself).
>
> Type: Buff
>
> Duration: 45 minutes

Effect: This buff increases your target's charisma equal to the level of the caster. No restrictions. Cast away!

Magic Resist

> Cast: Group
>
> Type: Buff
>
> Duration: 45 minutes

Effect: Increases your magic resistance by an amount equivalent to the caster's level.

Armored

> Cast: Group
>
> Type: Buff
>
> Duration: 45 minutes

Effect: Increases your AC by an amount equivalent to the caster's level.

Level Twenty-Five (25):

Speed

> Cast: Self or others
>
> Type: Buff
>
> Duration: 45 minutes

Effect: When cast on an ally, this buff will allow their melee haste or speed to increase by 30%.

Vigor

> Cast: Self or others
>
> Type: Buff
>
> Duration: 45 minutes

Effect: This will increase energy rejuvenation by an equivalent to 20% of the caster's level. Mostly, this will be used for melee classes, however sometimes it can be good for running away from dangerous mobs.

Enrage

> Cast: Self or others

Type: Buff... sort of

Duration: 15 minutes

Effect: This buff will cause your target to receive some of the aggression generated by you. The mob will assume it comes from the target of this spell. This spell is intended for tank types or pets to take on. Only cast it on someone else if you really, really don't like them, or maybe if you're running for your life. Also   this can only be cast on one target at a time.

Signet

Cast: Group

Type: Buff

Duration: 45 minutes

Effect: This buff will increase the intelligence and agility of all group members by an amount equal to the caster's level. Signet will not stack with Fervor, and can be overridden by casting the latter, should melee need their own boost. Both stats will be boosted to the level of the caster.

Arcane Cure

Cast: Self or others

Type: Cure

Duration: Instant

Effect: Should an ally receive a magical debuff, you can cure them of this ailment.

Level Thirty (30):

Altruism

Cast: Self or Others

Type: Buff

Duration: 45 minutes

Effect: This allows a faction increase to your target. It will lift you two faction levels. However, should you be kill on sight, not even Altruism can help you. This buff will update again at level 40. Worked out well last time, didn't it?

Shield Illusion

> Cast: Self or Others
>
> Type: Defensive Buff
>
> Duration: Until depleted   requires hematite

Effect: Using the power of your mind you cast a shield around your target, confusing the enemies and negating up to 150 HP of damage. That whole mind magic thing seems to be working out well.

Mesmerize

> Cast: Single Target
>
> Type: Breakable Stun
>
> Duration: 48 seconds

Effect: This spell immobilized your opponent for as long as they take no damage, or forty-eight seconds, whichever is shorter. You may cast non-damaging spells on them, and you may renew this casting before the initial one expires. Casting it on your friends probably isn't a good way to win popularity contests.

In Perpetuity

> Cast: Self Only
>
> Type: Buff
>
> Duration: Until death or departure from Somnia

Effect: This buff increases the enchanter's casting speed for all spells, allowing them to fire them off in quick succession. Combined with Concentration, this buff allows the enchanter to access all of their spells without weaving. Caution: this requires that the enchanter be fully aware of all of aspects of each spell they cast in this way.

Concentration

> Cast: Self Only
>
> Type: Buff
>
> Duration: Until departure from Somnia or death.

Effect: This buff increases the enchanter's ability to focus on and learn their spells. Combined with In Perpetuity, this buff allows the enchanter to cast all of their spells without first weaving them. Caution: If Concentration hasn't been fully applied to the spells, the consequences can be disastrous.

Druidic Hybrid Abilities

Earth Shielding

Cast: Passive

Type: Reinforcement

Duration: Always active

Effect: Due to the psionicist's unique nature, earth shielding will reinforce any of your psionicist based skills such as thought shielding, thought projection, and thought sensing, making them more robust and upping your mental defenses. Any other skills gained through the psionicist's branch will also be effected by this, including any kinetic skills.

Reinforce Self

Cast: Passive

Type: Reinforcement

Duration: Always active

Effect: Similar to earth shielding which effects your skills, this ability allows your body to take more damage, upping your innate armor class by your level times two   effectively making cloth armor reflect the protection curboiled leather might grant you.

Reinforce Intelligence

Cast: Passive

Type: Nature's awareness

Duration: Always active

Effect: Nature is all seeing and all encompassing. This ability allows you to take on some of that wisdom and intelligence, and apply it to yourself. It increases both of those statistics by the enchanter's level, giving rise to a larger mana pool, and slightly heightened damage.

Earth Pull

Cast: Instant three-minute recast

Type: Buff

Duration: thirty seconds

Effect: This allows any buff that is chosen to triple in potency for a thirty second duration. It's activated first, followed by the buff.

Make sure you time it properly. Can only be cast on one person at a time, and does not include group buffs. No refunds.

Binding Shield

Cast: Instant five minute recast

Type: Linked Buff

Duration: Fifteen seconds

Effect: You can offer an earth shield to two allies (including yourself if you're going to be selfish and all). This shield will share the damage between the two allies, metering out damage proportionally. Use wisely. Don't try this at home.

Nature's Gift

Cast: Passive

Type: Awareness

Duration: Permanent

Effect: You have become acutely aware of your surroundings. Of the life in everything, in the trees, in the forest, in each and every being you encounter. This lends you a connection to nature. Don't dismiss it lightly.

Sinuous Abilities

Sinuous: This is the more offensive avenue to take. From hypnotic suggestion, through to invoked visions, this path veers toward complete mind infestation of the enchanter's opponents. This is only available to psionicists.

Hypnotic Suggestion

Cast: Instant 5 minute recast

Type: Offensive

Duration: twenty seconds

Effect: Your target will perform whatever task you suggest to them, as if it had been suggested by themselves, or their leader. Once this objective has been achieved, or else the spell wears off, the target will spend five seconds in rampant confusion. Should you not be in aggro range, the target will then forget you. Probably not good to use on allies – it's not been tested on them.

Feedback Loop

Cast: Instant 5-minute recast

Type: Offensive

Duration: 15 seconds or 50% of caster's level, whichever is greater.

Effect: Must be used in conjunction with the psionic MA thought sensing, and thought projection. Pluck any type of memory out of the head of your opponent and create a feedback loop in their mind. They'll be stuck in this loop and not attack anyone for the duration. Damage ticks at caster's level x 2 every tic (3 seconds). Best not to use on a friend when they piss you off.

Basic Visions

Cast: Instant 3-minute recast

Type: Offensive

Duration: 20 seconds, or 75% of the caster's level, whichever is greater.

Effect: You may create and insert a vision for the target to experience its best to have some of these pre-prepared. This will cause them damage (caster's level x 2 per tick), and distraction for the duration of the spell depending on what type of vision you've given them.

LEVEL 30

Possession I

Cast: Instant – 5 minute recast

Type: Offensive

Duration: 20 seconds

Effect: Force your way into the mind of your target and assume control for up to twenty seconds. Make sure the target is debuffed for maximum duration. Don't even contemplate being in the target when it dies. It's a very bad idea.

Sudden Drop

> Cast: Instant – 10 minute recast
>
> Type: Offensive Debuff
>
> Duration: 20 seconds

Effect: A forced debuff wave that overrides the enemy's natural defenses and convinces them that all their stats have dropped by an amount equivalent to the caster's level. Lasts for 25 seconds. Cannot be resisted.

ACKNOWLEDGMENTS

I have a lot of people to thank, who in at least some way encouraged me to write in general, or else to write this book specifically.

Love of my life, Trevor, and my little Kami. It's his fault I found the genre, and her fault I never give up on writing.

I wouldn't be here without the following friends:

Jami Nord & Owen Littman

Heather Cashman

Jude

Heather Gilbert

M. Andrew Patterson

Aimee

Amanda W.

Quinton Shyn

Kindra

Kendra

Dawn Chapman

Alexis Keane

Bonnie Price

Nick Kuhns

Richard Hummel

Stephen Morse

Felissa Ely

Anthea Sharp

Andrea Parseneau
Cait Greer
M Evan Matyas
Ian Mitchell

To those readers on RR whose help and readership has been invaluable:
Thank you all for reading and so much for the amazing feedback! I know I've probably forgotten someone. If you read this on RR in its early stages (before book 2) and conmmented or reviewed, please know it means the world to me.
Endless Paving
Mearhena
Oathkeeper
Cyan Snake
Bleached
Tarakis
Puck
Koinzell
Nikeyeia
Zedicious
Barnmaddo

Patreon:
Thank you all so much for your support!
Ma & Pa
Kyle
Kylie B
Brandon T
Janis N

Amanda W

Erik S

Amanda M

Stuart G

D.R. Perry

Nikolas Z

Bubs

Aleksander

Casey H

Emersen

Jonathan C

Stuart G

Tezq G

Thomas D

Tim Shinn

Violet R

From the creator of the Delvers LLC universe, comes Nora's story.

Nora Hazard's story begins over three years prior to the events of Delvers LLC: Welcome to Ludus.

On Ludus, life is often cheap. Nora's childhood hadn't given her many options. With nowhere else to go after losing her family, she had joined an old friend in a street gang and found an unlikely home there.

But unfortunately, tragedy is about to befall Nora. Grudges from the distant past and movements of shadowy organizations may take away everything she is familiar with and all that she holds dear…possibly even her life.

Danger has never stopped her before, but survival may require escaping her old life and embarking on an insane, desperate journey. On the way, she might even accidentally stumble into both an incredible opportunity, and an incredible burden.

Unfortunately for her enemies, Nora was no pushover before…and that was before discovering super powers!

The Feyland Series
By Anthea Sharp

High-tech gaming and ancient magic collide when a computer game opens a gateway to the treacherous Realm of Faerie.

Jennet Carter never thought hacking into her dad's new epic-fantasy sim-game would be so exciting…or dangerous. Behind the interface, dark forces lie in wait, leading her toward a battle that will test her to her limits and cost her more than she ever imagined.

Temple of Sorrow
By Carrie Summers

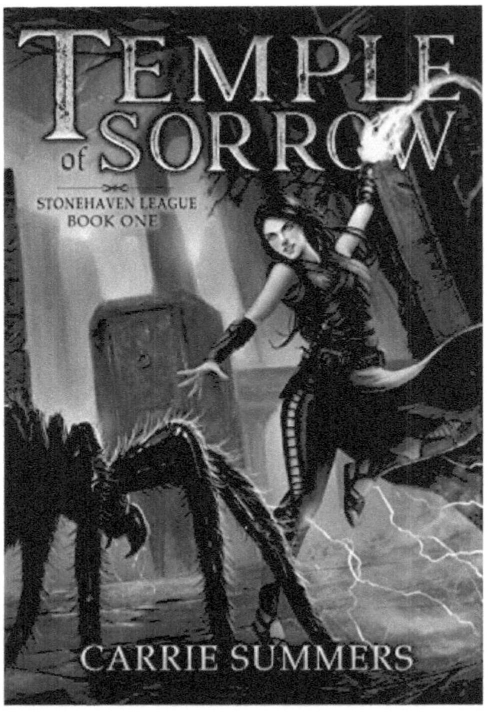

A half-wit ogre, a legion of overgrown jungle beasts, and a power-tripping AI are trying to stop her.

Relic Online is the hottest new game out there, and it's Devon Walker's best hope for escaping her hard-knock life. Thanks to her rocking achievements in other games, she's been hired as a salaried player. Even better, her new position comes with cutting-edge implants that turn RO's virtual reality into a full sensory explosion. Her only task? Drive the game's creator AI to the outermost limits of its creativity.

The Wayward Bard
By Lars M

Daniel's Guide to Early Retirement:
1. Intercept illegal money transfer from mafia boss.
2. Hide out in super exclusive Full Immersion Virtual Reality game until the heat is off.
3. Roll a bard. Max out charisma. Live it up.
4. Profit.

With all the pesky planning out of the way Daniel set out to realize his ultimate dream: gaining enough money to buy a tropical island and spend his days playing the violin and RPGs. What could possibly go wrong?

Disclaimer: There shall be no harems in this series. Overpowered, perfect protagonists will not be tolerated and excessive cursing will result in donations to the swear jar.